SET IN STONE

Book One of
The Petralist

Set in Stone

Book One of
The Petralist

Frank Morin

ISBN: 978-0-9899005-3-9

A Whipsaw Press Original

Book Design by RuneWright, LLC
www.RuneWright.com

Edited by Joshua Essoe
http://www.joshuaessoe.com

Cover art by Brad Fraunfelter
http://www.bfillustration.com

Illustrations by Jared Blando
http://www.theredepic.com

First Whipsaw printing, May 2015

ACKNOWLEDGEMENTS

As usual, there are more people to thank than I could hope to remember, but I'll make the attempt. First and foremost, my family. Kate and Kyle for helping generate the original idea and providing brutally honest feedback, Emily for her undying enthusiasm, and Jacob for comic relief. And my sweet Jenny for loving me, the biggest kid of them all.

Many people provided feedback across several versions as I tore apart the story and reassembled it like a Frenkenstein project. Special thanks to Michelle Wilber for asking the hard questions I sometimes wished she wouldn't. And for my very own team of Fast Rollers for feedback over ice cream: Jeffrey Steele, Adam Smith, Matt McLaughlin, and the Johnston clan. Remote members of the team included Truli Wright, Jesse Rudd, and Lee Ann Setzer. So much enthusiasm in such confined spaces can be dangerous.

Thanks to Joshua Essoe for a brilliant edit, Jared Blando for illustrations so much better than my hen-pecked, stick-figure drawings, and Brad Fraunfelter for a magnificent cover.

Many people influenced me for good and don't even know it. Or at least didn't openly mock me for my strange eccentricities. I count both as forms of support.

GRANADURE
GRANITE MINE
ALASDAIR
QUARTZ-ZINC GOLD MINE
THE WICK
PUMICE MINE
BASALT MINE
MARBLE MINE
MERKLAND
SLATE MINE
OBRION
CRANN
TRODAIRE
SAOL RIVER
DONLEAVY
MACANTACHT RIVER
GRANITE MINE
BASALT MINE
FREASTAL
GRANITE MINE
CASUR
MULRENNAN
CARRAIG
DEIFUR
LIMESTONE MINE
RAINEACH
LAIGE
SANDSTONE MINES
CHOSTALAN
SPEIRMOR
RADHARC
THE DESERT
BLANDO
THE LANDS OF
OBRION
N
W
E
S

Wick Tor
loch Sholto
Mount Alasdair
loch Ladhar
Upper Wick
Mount Ingram
A Alasdair
Powder house
River Barges
Lord Gavin's Manor house
Loch Wick
Lower Wick
The Valley
N
BLANDÖ
The LANDS OF ALASDAIR

PROLOGUE

The warm-faced midwife swaddled a screaming newborn baby boy, wrapped him in a homespun blanket, and handed the tiny soul to his eager new mother.

"You're lucky. He looks healthy despite the difficult labor."

Hendry, dressed in the worn, but clean clothing of a laborer, leaned over the birthing bed and wrapped his arms around Lilias, his wife, and their child. He blew out a relieved breath and his knotted muscles relaxed.

As they marveled at the baby's perfect, tiny hands and feet, Lilias whispered, "Welcome to our family, Connor."

The midwife crossed the whitewashed room to a small table next to a row of blocky stone cradles. She opened a thick ledger and thumbed to an empty page.

"With the rush to save the baby, I don't even have your names registered." Nodding toward the stone cradles she added, "We'll want to proceed with the testing straight away."

"Of course," Hendry said.

"You have the birth tax?"

"Of course," he said again and reached for the small leather purse at his belt.

"Good. You're a nice looking family. I hate seeing firstborn taken. Now, your formal names, please."

Before Hendry could respond, something crashed, like a door being slammed somewhere in the building. Shouting voices pounded past the birthing room, and another door slammed.

The midwife frowned and put down the quill. She headed for the paneled wood door that led into the rest of the birthing center, but it flew open before she reached it.

A young woman, barely more than a girl, stepped through, eyes wide and cheeks flushed. "It's High Lady Elspet! She's here, and the baby's coming early." She wrung her hands in her simple white linen dress and continued in a terrified voice, "There's problems."

The midwife's face paled and she rushed for the door. Pausing in the entrance, she called back to the new parents, "Wait here. I'll be back." She waved one hand toward the stone cradles. "Pick one and we'll test your son as soon as I return." She pushed past the young woman, who pulled the door closed behind them.

The parents shared a surprised look. "I hope the high lady and her child are safe," Lilias said as she cradled her baby tight and arranged him to try nursing.

"I'm sure she'll be fine." Hendry caressed her sweat-streaked face and gazed into her eyes. "I'm just glad you are."

An hour later they still waited. From the urgent footsteps that regularly passed their door, the situation with the high lady's birthing did not seem to be improving.

Finally Hendry stood. "Enough. Let's get this over with." He took the now-sleeping Connor and turned to face the row of stone cradles. After a deep breath, he marched across the room, his face determined.

The four cradles looked as different as the stones from which they were carved. Hendry approached the first, a crude thing made of a solid block of Alasdair White granite, the top chiseled down into a rough depression to hold a child. It was ugly and cold, perfectly suited to its onerous task. He frowned at the slipshod workmanship and his hands itched for his tools. He'd never seen a block of precious granite so ill-treated.

The next two cradles were little better. A much smaller cradle fashioned from dark basalt seemed to huddle beside the larger white granite block, while a shiny black obsidian cradle next to it glinted with reflected lantern light.

Hendry ignored the fourth cradle entirely and faced the blocky one of granite. No son of his would be first tested in anything but granite, no matter how rough the stone might be carved.

"Wait."

He turned at Lilias' voice. "It must be done, love."

"I know." She spoke calmly despite the worry lines wrinkling her forehead. "Put him in that one."

She pointed at the last cradle in the line, the one he had not even considered. Set apart from the others by workmanship more than space, it was fashioned into a beautifully sloped depression formed by six distinct stones, fitted together perfectly. The polished surfaces were lovingly carved, with colors merging so beautifully, it all but shouted aloud the blessed state of the highborn children who would be tested there, children like High Lady Elspet's imminent newborn.

"We can't, love."

"Why not?"

"You know why not." He glanced nervously at the door. "If anyone found out …"

"No one's coming any time soon." She cocked her head and added, "This way we only test him once. Do you really want to put our Connor, in those others?"

After another glance at the crude stone cradles, he sighed. "You're right."

He then moved to stand before the beautifully crafted one, slipped the swaddling blanket off the child and placed the infant onto the merciless stone. At the first shock of cold air, the baby began wailing. He shook his little arms and legs angrily and bellowed at the chill touch of the stone.

Then he stopped.

An ominous silence descended over the room. Hendry bent over the cradle, while Lilias sat up in the bed. The baby lay silent, his little hands and feet pressed down against the cold stone as if stuck there. His mouth opened, but he made no sound. His little body began to shake and every tiny muscle tensed until they all stood out clearly against his naked skin.

"Oh, no," Hendry whispered as his worst fears were realized in the tiny body of his son.

Connor began to swell. His body grew, as if he'd taken an impossibly huge breath of air, and the muscles of his limbs bulged to twice their normal size. He started to rock side to side, and the cradle began to rattle in time with his movements until it bounced against the wall. The movement spread to the other cradles and they thumped against the wall like caged beasts trying to escape.

Panic-stricken, Lilias stumbled up out of the bed. "Get him out of there!"

Hendry, who had stood rooted in place, reached for the baby, but flames exploded to life from the very stone of the cradle. He yelped and pulled back from the intense heat.

Lilias shouted with terror and tried to rush across the room. Her legs, still weak from the difficult labor, buckled, and she sprawled to the floor.

The flames disappeared as quickly as they had started, replaced by a fountain of water as thick around as Hendry's waist.

Now on hands and knees, Lilias gasped, "How can he make so much?"

He gave her an incredulous look. "That's not his water, love. It's the stone doing it."

A powerful gust of wind sprayed the water across the room over the parents, chilling them to the bone. Hendry pulled the baby into his arms as Lilias crawled toward them. For three heartbeats, silence reigned. Tiny Connor hung limp in his grasp, and the two of them shared a fearful look over his prostrate form.

Then he started to cry. They swaddled him quickly and Hendry helped Lilias return to the bed. She clutched Connor with shaking hands. Hendry hugged his family close, and for several minutes he stood tense, breathing fast, eyes clenched to hold back tears.

Lilias buried her face against his neck and whispered soft words until he slowly relaxed. "It's not your fault."

"It's my blood, love," he said, voice thick with emotion. "It's Cursed."

She sniffled and gave him a weak smile. "It's not all bad, dear one. If he's accepted, Guardians give important service."

"I won't risk it," he snarled. "They'll kill him at a whim." He released her and savagely wiped his eyes. "They won't have him, not yet. Not until he can face them as a man." He squeezed her shoulder, his face determined. "No one knows. We're leaving, right now."

Hours later, the midwife slowly entered the birthing room, her face drawn, shoulders slumped with exhaustion. Tears shone in her eyes. She stared at the empty room for a couple seconds before realizing the family was gone, although several small coins lay on the blank page of the register.

She grunted and took up the coins of the birthing fee. She shouldn't be surprised at the lack of names. Most commoners couldn't write. Out of habit she glanced in the three crude stone cradles, but saw nothing of interest.

A gasp turned her around. She hadn't noticed the young apprentice enter behind her. The slender young woman stood before the cradle intended for highborn children, one hand at her mouth. The midwife frowned and stepped over to see. The sight struck like a blow to her stomach.

Indented in the very stones was a perfect outline of a baby's body.

"Impossible," she whispered.

"Where are they?" the young woman asked.

"Gone."

"What are their names?"

"I don't know."

"Where are they from?"

She only shook her head. She'd never seen anything like this, and lacked the emotional strength to grapple with the situation so soon after losing Lady Elspet's son.

"We have to tell someone," the young woman said.

"Tell someone what?"

They spun at the deep, cultured voice that spoke from the door behind them. High Lord Dougal stood there, his face lined with grief, but his intense blue eyes bored into them.

Without a word, the midwife gestured at the cradle. He crossed the room and, although he remained calm but for a widening of the eyes, he grabbed the midwife's shoulder and forced her to meet his gaze.

"Tell me all you know about this family. I must find that child!"

CHAPTER 1

onnor leaped out of bed and yanked on his hunting leathers. The dim light of dawn glowing through the one small window of the attic he shared with three of his four siblings showed the other beds already empty.

How could he have slept in so late? He'd be grouted if he didn't take something today.

His mother's voice called from downstairs, "Connor, where are you? Are you sick?"

"Coming!"

Couldn't she think of a different question, just once?

It didn't matter that the itching had already begun, a constant irritation just under the skin that already tugged at his resolve. Tomorrow, two days max, the Curse would strike hard.

Not today, he vowed.

Today he felt strong, but the very thought it might strike tomorrow made him snarl into the shadows.

He almost landed on Lilias, his mother, as he slid down the ladder to the main floor. At almost sixteen, he stood tall enough to look down into her brilliant green eyes, but he couldn't avoid her warm hug.

"Mom, I'm late," he protested, but did not pull away. She gave the best hugs in the world. Still, he wasn't ten any more.

Unruffled, she pushed his sandy blond hair out of his face. "Eat before you leave."

His siblings clustered around the table, already eating the usual hot breakfast of porridge, eggs, and dried rabbit. Hendry, Connor's father, must have already left for the quarry.

As soon as Connor entered the room, four year-old Wallace shouted, "Connor, shoot me a pedra today!"

"You don't eat pedras," Roderick said, disgusted. At eight, he was an expert in everything.

"I want to fly it." Wallace sprayed porridge from his mouth as he talked, and Roderick gave him a dirty look.

Blair, his black hair already combed said, "Starting this late, I doubt Connor will shoot anything."

"Eat rocks," Connor punched his younger brother on the shoulder.

No way he'd come back empty handed. Not today.

He wolfed down a bowl of food, grabbed a chunk of yesterday's bread, and headed for the door. He belted on his hunting quiver and carefully checked his bow and string.

"Good luck, son." Although now holding baby Fiona on her hip, Lilias still managed to hug him again. She didn't have to voice the question he knew she was thinking.

"I'm fine, mom."

"Are you sure? It's been almost a week."

"I know. Hunting's been good."

Of course, that was all just build-up for today. Today's kill had to be something special.

She didn't need to know about the growing itch. If things worked out according to plan, he'd escape the next bout of crushing sickness. He'd know tomorrow.

Connor slipped out the door and jogged toward the town square of Alasdair. Their house stood at the southeast corner of town, at the end of a long, straight street of similar, if slightly smaller, homes set close to the river-facing wall. The houses here stood tall enough to enjoy the spectacular views of Alasdair valley.

The street was known as Wall Street, and was one of three main streets running parallel east to west through town. He passed a couple of smaller lanes to reach Merchant Street that ran through the center of town, straight between the two gates and the town square.

Men and women were already beginning preparations for the next day's festival. Several of them called to him and he waved but did not stop to field the inevitable questions about his health.

In the square, Cinaed, the foreman's wife, called out to him from where she monitored the setup of tables in what would be the cooking area for the feast. "Connor, what are you still doing in town?"

"Running late," he called cheerily and tried to hurry past.

She placed fists on hips and frowned. "This is no day for your sickness or laziness, young man."

"Yes, ma'am." It never paid to anger the red-haired, foul-tempered woman, so he ran faster. He'd show her. Today he'd settle for nothing less than a mountain deer from the far eastern slopes.

Tomorrow was the Sogail, the midsummer festival that would consume the entire. Thinking of it restored his grin, and his pace quickened.

"Hey, Connor!"

Hamish, his best friend, waved from across the square where he and four men were unloading heavy planks for assembly into long feasting tables. One day shy of sixteen, the lanky Hamish already stood a full head taller than the other workers, and he ate more than any two of them.

Connor jogged over. "I thought you were working with Neasa."

"Well, she ah …"

"How many sweetbreads did you eat before she threw you out?"

"Fifteen."

Connor laughed and glanced toward the bakery where the fat, jolly woman worked. He still couldn't figure out how Hamish had managed to talk his way into that apprenticeship the week before the Sogail, but it could never have ended any way but in disaster.

Hamish grinned, shook his unruly red hair out of his eyes, and pulled a crushed sweetbread from a pocket. Connor refused the offer, and Hamish popped it into his mouth. "You don't know what you're missing."

"I'll wait till tomorrow." Over the years, Connor had learned to refuse most of what Hamish offered from those pockets.

"Good luck with the tables."

"Good hunting."

He headed for the eastern gate, his mind turning to the hunt. Tomorrow they'd both turn sixteen, along with Jean and Stuart. A good kill today would hopefully impress Jean enough to secure the first dance. He wouldn't let her go until he finally won the coveted first kiss from her.

No way Stuart kisses her first.

The town of Alasdair huddled at the base of the towering bulk of Wick Tor that reared thousands of feet in near-vertical cliffs immediately to the north. The Upper Wick River cascaded down the rugged western flanks of the mountain and emptied into Loch Wick, situated just west of town. From there, the Lower Wick began its much more sedate journey south, past rolling hills of sparse forest, and wide expanses of tilled farmland, toward distant Merkland, the seat of High Lord Dougal's realm.

No good hunting there, so instead Connor jogged east up the long road that skirted the high cliffs and led to the plateau where Lord Gavin lived. On that flat expanse, lanterns glowed in the outbuildings while the downstairs windows of the manor house blazed with multi-colored light. The expensive stained glass windows usually struck him with wonder, but today he couldn't spare the time to gawk.

The plateau ran south, paralleling the river, while the slope of Alasdair Mountain rose farther to the east. Connor turned north to where a treacherous switchback road crawled up the steep face of Wick Tor. He paused halfway up to rest and glanced out over the panoramic view. Much of the valley still lay in shadow, although Alasdair Mountain and the lesser peaks lining the eastern side of Alasdair valley stood out sharply against the light of the rising sun.

The road crested the first cliff about a thousand feet above the plateau, although the summit of Wick Tor still reared another mile higher. Here the road flattened and ran straight back along a bluff for a quarter mile to a cut that led down into Alasdair Quarry, the lifeblood of the town. There the Cutters chiseled precious Alasdair White from the flanks of the mountain.

Perched right up against the edge of the cliff, the icy waters of Loch Sholto lay still as a mirror to his left, while Loch Ladhar, another flooded quarry of old, cut deep into the mountain not far beyond. Connor passed them and paused at the head of the game trail he'd follow into the mountains, and stared toward the distant quarry. Already occasional echoes of hammer blows reached his ears. Part of him longed to risk a visit, but he dare not.

Connor rushed up the trail. He couldn't risk the quarry today, couldn't afford to push the limits of the Curse so close to the Sogail. Thinking of the Curse awakened it, and Connor shivered as it skittered along his body, just under the skin, like a hundred tiny insects. The itching intensified and he fought the urge to scratch.

He wouldn't succumb today. Tomorrow at the Sogail he'd finally get to claim Patronage and take the first step toward gaining mastery over the Curse. Today he would hunt and celebrate the last day of the only life he'd ever known.

Tomorrow ... well, after tomorrow, nothing would ever be the same.

CHAPTER 2

omething heavy crashed through a dense stand of fir trees at the uppermost edge of the tree line. Connor paused fifty yards upslope of the trees, and drew an arrow from the hunting quiver at his hip.

It sounded like something had spooked the herd of large mountain deer he'd tracked from the south side of the ridge since earlier this morning.

He hadn't expected them to run back toward him. The slope where he stood above the tree line was mostly bare, rocky ground. Only a few large boulders offered partial cover. To his left, along the hillside, a long ridge of stone dropped five feet to a horizontal shelf that offered no cover at all. If the deer came back uphill, he'd have to take one down as soon as they broke into the open.

Connor half-drew his bow and grinned at the challenge, but the crashing sounds intensified and his smile faded. Unless the entire herd was bolting together in the same direction, there was no way deer could make that noise.

Maybe it was a bear. Connor had never taken a bear. Few Saor-Linn had. A kill like that was exactly what he was looking for. What a perfect way to celebrate the announcement of his Patronage and appointment as Guardian.

Although the intensity of the Curse's itch just under his skin had grown all morning, he still felt strong. He'd be fine today, but he'd be lucky to make it to the Sogail at that rate.

He'd concealed the existence of his Curse for so long, it seemed impossible tomorrow he'd finally get to reveal the secret and claim Patronage. He yearned for that moment of freedom. Never again would he have to choose debilitating sickness as punishment for reining in the destructive power of the Curse rather than granting it deadly release.

He'd finally get to talk about it with Jean, and with Hamish.

A huge form crashed through the last screen of underbrush into the open. It wasn't a bear. It was a torc.

Where, by Tallan, had a torc come from? Connor wondered.

The rare monster snorted and swung its thick, bony head from side to side, gouging furrows in the rocky soil with its wickedly curved tusks. No one in Alasdair had seen a torc in years. He'd heard they were big, scary creatures distantly related to the boars that roamed the slopes near town. The description utterly failed to capture this beast's magnificence.

Hard, bony plates, almost like slabs of stone under its gray hide gave it an angular, menacing appearance. It pawed the ground with one thick leg capped with a sharply cloven hoof and centered the single long horn in its forehead on Connor.

A real live torc! Connor knew the mountains around Alasdair better than anyone. He'd tracked or taken nearly every kind of game, and even located the nearest pedra's lair, although he hadn't yet built up the courage to actually spy on the monster. He'd never even glimpsed a torc.

The beast took a single step toward him and grunted, a low rumbling sound like thirty wolf-hounds growling together that chased away some of the wonder. Built low to the ground, it still stood a full six feet at the shoulder, and its torso, from its thick neck to its muscled haunches, stretched even longer.

Connor tried to breathe slowly. Torcs roamed unpopulated parts of the Maclachlan Mountains and, unless angered, generally ignored people. At least that's what the stories said.

The only problem was, this one looked furious.

The beast bellowed a single deep note that triggered a flutter of icy fear in Connor, and he took a single, involuntary step back.

The torc charged.

It surged forward surprisingly fast despite an ungainly gait, as if its legs couldn't quite bend far enough. Even so, its low-slung body raced up the slope with terrifying speed.

Connor raised his bow despite the growing urge to turn and flee. If Hamish were here, he'd have already soiled himself and tried to run. Unfortunately, there was nowhere to run, and fleeing would only encourage the beast. He had no illusion that he could outrun it, and he shivered at the thought of that long horn plunging into his back.

Too bad Stuart's not here.

Then he wouldn't have to worry about outrunning the torc. He'd only have to outrun Stuart.

Connor planted his feet and drew confidence from the bow's solid weight. He'd trained hard for the past two years and had taken deer, mountain goats, and even one of the huge, flightless eoin birds.

The constant dull itch of his Curse intensified and raced along his limbs. He pushed the distraction aside and took a deep breath as he drew the goose-feathered shaft to his cheek. The familiar strain of holding the weapon steady as he aimed at the torc, only thirty yards away, helped him regain his hunting calm.

The monster sounded like an avalanche as it galloped up the slope toward Connor, and he felt the vibrations rattle up through his boots. He refused to acknowledge the growing fear, and held his breath for a single heartbeat that thundered through his chest. His vision contracted to a point on the torc's head where the arrow would strike. In that second, he felt connected to the beast across the distance.

Connor released the string with a twang, and the arrow leaped away. It struck true but snapped against the heavily armored head.

Connor's calm vanished. He tried to swallow, but his mouth was dry. His tongue felt like a lead weight and his arms itched so bad he could barely think. The shaking of the ground grew more pronounced as the mighty beast bore down on him.

Connor snatched another arrow and, as he nocked it, he recognized it by the single black feather. He snarled at the torc as he took aim. His hand had somehow found his lucky arrow, the arrow that never missed, never broke, and always took down its target.

Fifteen yards.

With soaring confidence, he released.

The arrow slammed into the torc's thick gray hide in the center of its chest. The steel point snapped off at impact, and the shaft splintered under churning hooves.

"No fair," Connor shouted. There was no time to draw another arrow, no time to run.

Rage at the loss of his lucky arrow burned away some of the desperate fear, while the itch of his Curse blossomed all through his torso, magnifying the rage into a towering fury.

He charged.

Connor shouted a wordless bellow and lunged forward to meet the onrushing monster, swinging his bow like a club. It slammed into the torc's head, across one heavy-browed black eye and snapped.

The beast flinched and, instead of impaling him, the long horn scraped along his hunting jacket. The torc slammed into him like an avalanche and tossed its head, throwing Connor high over its shoulders.

The world spun as Connor tumbled through the air and landed hard on his back. Breath exploded from his lungs, gravel scraped his neck and hands as he rolled over, and he tasted blood.

The torc bellowed again, and Connor pushed dirt out of his face to look around for the monster. Upslope, still running full speed, the huge beast gouged furrows in the packed earth as it ran a tight circle to charge him again.

It seemed in an awful hurry to gore him. It wasn't like he was going to get away. The beast had to weigh over a hundred stone, and ran twice as fast as he did. Connor glanced at the distant trees fifty yards down slope, just to be sure.

No way I can make it.

Connor climbed to his feet and managed to draw a full breath. Surprisingly, his chest didn't hurt where the torc struck. He felt nothing but a dull throbbing, as if the skin had gone numb.

He'd been trying to convince Jean for months that the worst injuries were the ones a person barely felt. She hadn't believed him, but maybe he'd been right. If he outlived this crazed pig monster, he'd be sure to have her examine him closely to prove his theory.

Connor dropped his broken bow and looked around for cover or anything to use as an effective weapon, but found nothing. Then his eyes fell on the long ridge of stone he'd noticed earlier, and he scurried across the slope toward it. On the way, he picked up two fist-sized stones.

Skidding to a stop at the edge of the drop-off where the ridge fell away to the lower shelf, he threw the first stone. It struck the charging torc on the head, now barely a dozen strides away.

The best stone thrower in Alasdair, today Connor's aim was spot on. Too bad he didn't have something more useful to throw, like Stuart.

The torc bellowed and came on even faster. As it bore down on him, it started swinging its heavy head from side to side. Trampling him was apparently no longer enough. The monster now clearly planned to rip him open with its wicked tusks.

Connor took a step back until his heel hung over open space, and cocked his arm back to throw the last stone. He met the torc's black-eyed glare, and in that second he could clearly see the monster wanted to smash the life out of him.

Perfect.

Connor threw the stone and screamed a challenge at the top of his voice until the sound merged with the torc's bellowing reply. He dropped back off the edge of the ridge, and fell five feet to the stone shelf. He crouched as he landed, just before the torc's tusk ripped a deep furrow in the stone.

The torc plunged off the edge of the ridge and sailed over Connor before crashing to the ground with an impact that seemed to shake the very mountain. Its front legs buckled, its shoulders slammed into the ground, and its charge turned into a wild tumble. Its heavy, musky scent clung to Connor's nose and throat, and its pain-filled cries echoed across the slope.

Connor leaped to his feet and shouted with victory as the huge beast settled to a stop ten paces away. The monster shuddered, and its breath rattled in its chest, hopefully for the last time.

Before he could advance on the monster, it grunted and shook itself, staggered to its feet and swung its head around.

"Stones take it," Connor muttered as the beast took a shaky step toward him. He'd hoped the fall would at least break its front legs. If it had, the torc hadn't realized it yet.

Its head was bloody, and one tusk had broken off, but it looked mad enough that nothing but a fatal blow would stop it. Connor backed up and scratched at the raging itch of the Curse along one arm. His shoulders met the ridge of stone he'd just jumped off.

The torc took another step toward him, then another, stronger. With a deep grunt, it broke into a clumsy charge.

Only one option remained. The slope lay empty above him, and the thick pine forest so tantalizingly close below, blocked his view of anything beyond.

Good. No witnesses.

Three strides away, the torc bellowed again and aimed its long horn at his chest.

"Mother, forgive me," Connor murmured, and jumped straight up.

He vaulted in a single, convulsive movement and, as he cleared the lip of the ridge, drove his left arm down and twisted his legs over the top. The torc stood taller than the ridge and it lunged, trying to spear him before he could roll away.

Connor leaped again, straight up, and barely cleared the stabbing horn as the beast slammed into the stone ridge like an earthquake. It grunted as it bounced back a bit, and wobbled on unsteady feet.

As Connor reached the apex of his jump and started down toward the torc, he focused on his clenched fist ... and released his Curse. The itching sensation skittered across his torso and poured into his right arm, concentrating in his fist with such intensity that Connor screamed aloud.

His arm, all the way up to the shoulder, first burned like it was being scraped raw across the rocky ground, then went numb as all feeling drained away, leaving it a menacing dead weight. Connor drove that Curse-laden fist down between the torc's eyes with all his might.

The blow smashed the armored skull into the ground where it imploded like a loaf of crusty bread, spraying blood and flesh out its open mouth.

The impact jarred Connor all the way up his Curse-numbed arm and sent him tumbling over the torc's broad back. He fell hard and slid a few feet, protected by his hunting leathers.

The torc collapsed, and lay still but for one twitching hoof.

Connor examined his fist. He felt no pain. It looked undamaged, although covered in torc's blood. He slowly unclenched his fingers and shook them out. Feeling came back in a rush, an overpowering itch that made him groan with the need to tear at his own flesh. The itch subsided after a few seconds and radiated back across his body.

Before approaching the beast, Connor glanced around again to reassure himself that no one had seen what he did. He'd only ever released his Curse a couple of times. Both times he was alone, and the itch had nearly driven him mad.

The first time, he'd slammed his hand into a small tree, focusing all of his anger and despair into the blow, not caring that he'd probably break bones. His hand hadn't broken. The tree had.

He'd been so surprised the falling tree had nearly killed him. Never before had he understood the Curse's destructive power. All his life it had tormented him with crushing sickness. Now he knew the terrible truth. The Curse was trying to force him to kill.

Today it succeeded.

That itch was a harbinger of misery, a reminder of the danger he faced every day. Tomorrow could not come soon enough. He'd taken a terrible risk in waiting so long to petition for Patronage, and he was starting to wonder if he'd waited too long.

At the Sogail, those celebrating their sixteenth age-day, the Saorsa, would become near-adults. The Curse was not supposed to drive those afflicted with it beyond the bounds of their control before that age, but he was starting to wonder if perhaps the rule was not so hard and fast.

With an effort, he forced the worries aside. Tomorrow everything would be revealed, and he'd be on the path toward becoming a Guardian. Under the high lord's Patronage, somehow the terrible risk of the curse could transform to a force for good. Instead of becoming a danger to his family and perhaps his entire village, he would become their Guardian.

Connor grinned. To celebrate the announcement, he had bested the mighty torc. He could think of no better way to prove his worth to the Curse Finders, the high lord's men who would accept his petition in the name of their lord.

The itch of the Curse seemed weaker now, barely a distraction, as if appeased by the recent destruction. His best defense against it was normally to banish all thought of it, but a new thought occurred to him, one that disturbed him deeply. Without the Curse, he'd have died alone on this mountain today.

The torc twitched a final time. Connor cleared his mind through physical action. He drew his belt dagger and field-dressed the torc. Within minutes, it lay bled out, with its innards steaming in the clear morning air. Connor stayed upwind as he completed the work, and then sat back on his heels and laughed. He'd actually killed a torc.

Connor threw his head back and roared like a torc, and then grinned. That sounded pretty good. He could mimic nearly any animal after he'd heard it, and he planned to remember this one.

Alasdair lay six miles back beyond the far side of the saddle between mountains. After removing the long horn as proof of the kill, Connor started back. He needed to fetch a horse. Hopefully the carrion would be content to feast on its guts and leave the rest intact until he returned.

Tomorrow would be a day to remember.

CHAPTER 3

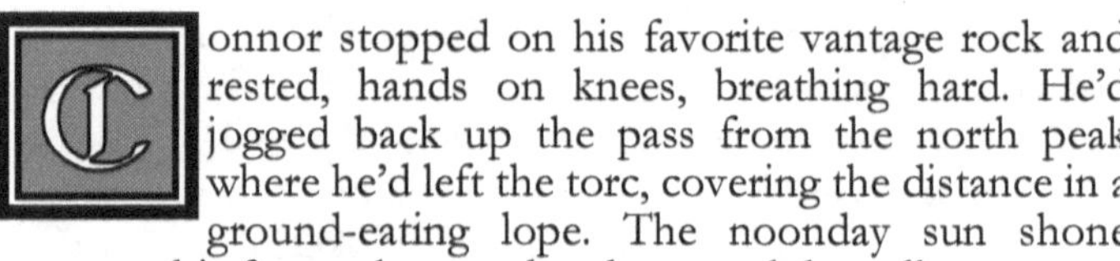

onnor stopped on his favorite vantage rock and rested, hands on knees, breathing hard. He'd jogged back up the pass from the north peak where he'd left the torc, covering the distance in a ground-eating lope. The noonday sun shone warm on his face as he stood and scanned the valley.

He loved the spot. To his right reared the majestic peak of Wick Tor, its high summit flanked by clouds, with the huge open pit of the quarry cut into its flanks about half a mile from where Connor rested. The pounding of hammers and chisels reached him dimly. The tempo was fast, constant, as everyone worked hard to finish early.

Those sounds taunted him, teasing him anew with the promise of the life he yearned to lead but never could. He fought down the urge to detour to the quarry, to prove he wasn't afraid. It wouldn't do any good. He didn't dare go again today and risk arousing the Curse. For some reason it hated the quarry and every time he spent any time there, its itch grew with terrifying speed.

Instead, Connor turned and forced himself to stare at the rest of the magnificent view. Beyond Quarry Road and the two deep lochs on the bluff, beyond Lord Gavin's plateau, the rest of the valley spread south, a patchwork of forest, green pastures, and square-tilled farmland with the river running through the middle of it all.

Connor knew every inch of it. He'd spent glorious summer days swimming with his friends in the Wick or hiding in the woods with Hamish as they spied on Jean and Moira. His recent hunting had honed his knowledge of the area even further.

He and Hamish had even discovered the girls' secret bathing pool recently. Protected by a dense grove of brush and hardwood, it was devilishly hard to approach quietly. They'd finally managed it, but instead of spying the girls, they'd seen Jean's grandmother preparing to bathe.

They had bolted immediately, chased by the fear of actually seeing grumpy old Mhairi disrobed. Connor shuddered anew. Some things were too scary to think about.

Connor pushed on, leaping down the trail to the road in a rush. He paused by the far edge of Loch Sholto, its solid stone bank barely a dozen feet thick along the outer lip of the ridge, close to the spot where the road began its steep switchback down to the valley below. He was tempted to stop for a swim, but didn't fancy returning to town blue-lipped and trembling with cold.

Halfway down the switchback road, he paused to drink at a small stream that cut the road there. It began higher up in a brush-choked cave that clung to the hill about three hundred feet below the upper rim. He'd made the difficult climb up to the cave once with Hamish, but he'd been the only one who dared enter the cave so he alone had discovered the iron gate blocking its upper end.

Connor moved quickly across the northern edge of Lord Gavin's plateau. Thankfully, he spied no one, even though the manor housed Lord Gavin, his family, and their slaves. A handful of soldiers and a dozen servants worked there, mostly in serving Lady Isobel. He broke into a run down the road that led along the base of the sheer cliff back to Alasdair.

He'd worried that Lady Isobel would spot him descending the road and send for him. He didn't want to waste hours in whatever nasty chore she might assign to him, like she'd been doing so often of late.

The road expanded as it skirted the flanks of Wick Tor and dropped toward Alasdair. Connor loved the tranquil town of modest homes. A high stone wall protected the downslope and downriver sides, giving it the appearance of a fortified town, even though there was never any reason for fortifications so far upriver. Connor had spent countless hours as a child in mock battles with Hamish and Stuart, fighting back and forth across the wall, seeing it as something far grander than one of the final vestiges of the original quarry that gave the town its name.

After passing through the wide upslope gate, Connor took Market Street toward the square. Built upon the site of the original quarry, abandoned fourteen generations ago for the purer stone higher up the mountain, the granite streets were perfectly level. The homes consisted mostly of wood, with some grout and field stone, particularly for the façades of some of the shops.

It was a shame they couldn't use the granite they quarried. Such a staggering expense would be unthinkable. Granite, especially the coveted Alasdair White, commanded premium prices and could never be wasted on the commoners who spent their lives cutting it from the mountain.

In just a few short days, Connor would finally get to see Merkland Tor, High Lord Dougal's castle, with its famous walls made entirely out of precious Alasdair White. Although only a full day's trip downriver, few villagers other than the bargemen ever made the journey to Merkland. As a soon-to-be Guardian, he would have to.

Alasdair was a beehive of activity as everyone worked to prepare for the Sogail, decorate the square, and clean every house. There were even a handful of children, led by Connor's brother Blair, washing down the granite streets. It seemed a silly chore, but it kept the Teagair-Linn, those children not yet twelve, occupied and out of the way.

People filled the square and bustled through the shops and businesses that commanded the center of town. They worked at the hundreds of tasks required to prepare for the celebration, including the hanging of banners with the red hammer and white stone of Lord Gavin's crest from every shop. The most successful merchants displayed carefully crafted small statues made of precious granite, draped in clover. Each had been a gift from the local lord to the town during Sogail celebrations dating back to the first decade of the town's existence. Each was a prized town possession, carefully guarded and brought out only during the Sogail.

Lord Gavin had never gifted one, although he'd hinted throughout the last year that if they met the increased quotas he might. Connor was as excited as anyone by the thought, but he didn't really expect Lord Gavin to do it. Not after the fiasco last year.

Hamish and the other workers, sweating in the noonday heat, labored to erect Lord Gavin's pavilion and assemble the long, heavy tables for the feasting. On the far side of the square a raised platform for musicians was already in place, and rope marked off areas for competitions.

The energy of the place washed away Connor's fatigue. To his right, a crowd of women bustled around tables where foodstuffs were already being prepared. Holding a place of honor in the center of the cooking area was the marvelous new Heatstone oven that had just arrived the day before on the upriver barge.

Connor's mother oversaw activity there with a contented smile on her round face. Connor grinned to see her so relaxed and obviously happy.

She caught sight of him and came to greet him. "Connor, you're back early. Are you sick?"

Connor sighed.

After tomorrow she'd have to come up with a new greeting.

"I'm fine." Lofting the horn, he added loudly for all to hear, "I killed a huge torc on the north slope."

An excited murmur ran through the crowd and spread across the square. People gathered around, talking over each other in their excitement, asking him about the torc and marveling over the thick horn.

Connor grinned under the onslaught of attention and happily related the story of the hunt. It was trickier than he'd thought to keep out references to the Curse, but he had lots of practice.

Lilias singled out a couple of workmen in the crowd and ordered them to get a horse from Lord Gavin and fetch the torc for Connor. They were so excited about the kill they didn't complain about the assignment, and Connor was happy to let them drag the monster back. It'd probably take all afternoon.

"Connor! You actually killed a torc?"

Hamish pushed his way through the crowd and spit out a small rock he'd been sucking on. "I can't believe it."

"Believe it. The monster broke my bow and my lucky arrow before I finished him off."

"Wow." Hamish looked dutifully impressed. "So how'd you kill him, with that thick skull of yours?"

"Very funny."

Stuart, the other boy in town who shared the same age-day with them, pushed through the crowd, frowning. As tall as Hamish, Stuart was built like a boulder. He already had a man's depth to his chest and his arms were thicker than Connor's and Hamish's combined. His dense, black hair was cropped close to his square head.

Jean followed, and Connor's heart skipped a beat and then raced to catch up. She stood almost as tall as Connor and had grown up with the boys, all inseparable friends.

A couple of years ago, she'd started to change. She'd developed a fascinatingly curved figure. When Connor looked at her, sometimes he found it hard to breathe. Her blond hair hung in an intricate braid stretching halfway down her back. Her eyes shone as clear and blue as the quarry lochs above town. Sometimes he struggled to figure out what to say to her, which annoyed him to no end.

Stuart stepped in front of Connor, blocking his view. The brawny youth lifted a long, stone chisel that he carried proudly. "Got my chisel today."

Connor swallowed a curse and smiled, trying to look pleased.

What terrible timing. Why couldn't Stuart get the blasted chisel tomorrow when he was supposed to?

It might not quite equal the feat of killing a torc, but getting their first diorite chisel was a major milestone in any Cutter's life.

"Congratulations," he managed. Stuart beamed.

Jean slipped around Stuart, placed one hand on his arm, and with the other slid a finger down the inner edge of the torc horn. "Is this really from the torc?"

Connor grinned. Her touch set his skin on fire right through his hunting leathers. "Aye."

"Baby one, huh?" Stuart asked.

"Not hardly. Must've weighed a hundred stone." He hefted the horn to emphasize the point. Even Stuart couldn't be that dumb.

Stuart laughed. "What'd you do, throw up on it?"

"You wish." He'd been teased about his sickness all his life. It no longer bothered him, although recently he'd started dreaming of using his Curse to put Stuart in his place, just once.

He buried the dangerous thought. He didn't want to kill Stuart, and after what he'd done today he doubted he could release the Curse without fatal consequences. Besides, after tomorrow, everyone would know. Stuart would have to show him some respect when he became a Guardian.

"So, are you ready for the Sogail Oran tomorrow?" he asked Jean.

She looked at her toes and blushed, then glanced up through her long lashes at him. His heart melted.

"I think so."

"You'll be great. You've got the best voice in town."

She beamed and lifted her chin happily. "For that, you get the first dance."

Really? For that? What about for killing the torc?

Stuart frowned and hefted his diorite chisel. "I thought I got the first one."

Jean rose up on her toes to kiss Stuart's cheek and said, "You get the second. It's always longer." Stuart smiled triumphantly at Connor.

Connor squashed the flutter of hot jealousy that burned in the pit of his stomach at the sight of Jean kissing Stuart. None of them had kissed her on the lips yet and he wasn't about to let Stuart kiss her first.

In the last year their friendship had faded behind the competition to win Jean's affection. She flirted with them all, seeming to change her affection constantly and never making it clear which of them she favored.

It was so frustrating!

"What about me?" Hamish asked.

Jean laughed, grabbed Hamish's hands, and spun him around in a circle. Several adults complained about nearly getting trampled, but that just set them both to laughing. Jean leaned in to kiss Hamish's cheek and said, "There. You've already had yours."

"Connor, you think Lord Gavin will appoint you the town cripple tomorrow?" Stuart asked.

"Eat rocks."

Despite his big plans, the question dug at a sensitive spot in his soul. At the Sogail they would celebrate the Saorsa and be recognized as near-adults. Lord Gavin would assign their vocations.

Well, he'd assign the others. Connor would claim his. Still, Stuart would clearly become a Cutter. For most of his life, Connor had wished for that too, but he could no longer pretend it was going to happen.

He knew little about Guardians. His father's brother had been taken as a newborn when the test revealed his Curse, and no one had seen him since. He'd have to be careful to conceal from the Curse Hunters how long he'd had his Curse. His parents risked being named Daor, enslaved to High Lord Dougal, if anyone ever learned they'd concealed his curse for so long.

The thought of leaving Alasdair filled Connor with powerful, mixed emotions, but usually excitement won out. In the past week he'd focused on hunting, so there would be more meat at the Sogail since before old Tam, the previous town hunter, had been killed in a pedra bloodlust three years ago.

Stuart hefted his long chisel again. "I'm a Cutter now."

"Not till tomorrow, you're not," Hamish said with a laugh. Stuart scowled at him.

"If you're lucky, you'll pay it off before your kids have kids," Connor said.

Stuart's frown deepened, but someone called for Connor to tell the tale of the torc again, so Stuart left with a final glare.

Jean leaned close to Connor and whispered in his ear, "Find me later at Granny's. I want to hear all about the torc." She gave him a dazzling smile that turned his knees to water, waved to Hamish, and slipped away through the crowd.

Connor watched her go, a smile on his lips and a song in his heart. If he could pry her away from her all-too watchful grandmother, he knew exactly what quiet spot they'd sneak off to. Alone and undisturbed, he'd tell her all about the desperate fight with the torc. She'd be so impressed. The Sogail was tomorrow, but who knew?

With such a great story, maybe she'd finally admit she liked him more.

CHAPTER 4

onnor eventually escaped the crowd and returned home to change out of his sweaty hunting leathers. Afternoons on the valley floor were hot, so he donned a pair of tan linen trousers and a white cotton shirt. Then he headed out through the wall gate on the western side of town, even though there had never actually been a gate to block the opening. Outside the wall, he took the road toward Loch Wick and the Powder House to see his father, the Ashlar.

Two long, stone piers jutted into the cold waters of the small loch where men busy loaded a heavy-beamed river barge with large sacks of granite powder. Situated next to the loch, near where the Upper Wick finished its wild tumble down the western flanks of the mountain, sat the Powder House. It was a heavy-beamed wooden building with a high, peaked roof and double doors that opened wide enough to drive a wagon through.

To the right of the Powder House, men worked in the blocking yard, a solid mixed-grade granite pad right at the base of the cliff where large blocks of granite were lowered from the quarry high above. As Connor approached, the reinforced lift platform that moved those huge blocks descended with a new load. Suspended by a rope as thick around as his waist, it made the five-hundred foot vertical journey in just under half an hour.

As soon as it touched down, men wrapped heavy ropes around the freshly quarried granite block and, using a block and tackle, hauled the two-ton stone into the center of the blocking yard. More men with chisels and hammers began pounding away at it, quartering it prior to final processing by the Ashlar, while others carefully swept up every particle of granite and ensured the area remained clean. A shipment would be leaving tonight, so all of the prepared blocks had already been moved into the Powder House for final processing.

Connor waved a greeting to the workers and headed for the Powder House. Inside, sturdy work tables flanked a wide loading area just inside the doors and filled most of the cavernous interior. The air lay thick with dust and smelled like broken stone. Low shelves ran the lengths of the far walls, although most of the tables and shelves stood empty since most of the shipment was already loaded on the barge.

Connor's father, Hendry the Ashlar, stood alone at his work table upon which rested a nearly processed granite block. Deep cracks marred its misshapen surface that had been beaten down to barely the size of Connor's head. It lay in a pile of what looked like white sand piled almost to the top of a three-inch wooden collar that ringed the edges of the special table.

Unlike the others, this table was made of polished steel, upon which sat the collar, making it look like a huge pan. A six-foot screen of fine mesh rose above that collar around the entire table.

The Ashlar, with hands driven through two leather-lined holes in the mesh, barely big enough for his arms, was beating the block to dust.

Hendry, a muscular man with thick, gray-streaked dark hair, concentrated on his heavy, double-headed stone hammer already raised for another blow. Made of diorite, like Stuart's chisel, the hammer played a critical role in the processing of granite blocks. It was Connor's family's most treasured possession, passed down through four generations after his ancestors had worked for five decades to pay its staggering cost.

Steadying the block with his left hand, Hendry slammed the heavy diorite hammer down onto the granite block in a slow, steady, rhythm. The blow struck true and precious stone dust and small stone chips flew in every direction, only to be caught by the mesh ringing the table.

The sound reverberated through the room like thunder, and faded to a low buzzing as the hammer, still seated on the block, blurred for a second. Sheets of granite dust broke off and slid away.

Connor grabbed tufts of loose cotton from a bin near the door, twisted them into his ears, then pulled a thick woolen band over them. The ear protection reduced the thunder to a muffled thump.

Connor watched his father process the stone with conflicting emotions. He'd spent countless hours as a boy dreaming of the day he'd take up the hammer and become the next Ashlar. Now that dream lay shattered like a block of processed granite, and he fought to fill the void left behind with thoughts of becoming Guardian. The mystery surrounding Guardians enhanced the excitement, but made it hard to sustain.

Hendry raised the hammer again, but paused to greet Connor with a smile, then nod toward a pile of large empty canvas sacks on a nearby table. Connor fetched one while Hendry continued pounding at the stone block. Within minutes he ground it to powder, then carefully brushed stone dust from his shaved arms and rattled the mesh screen to ensure no particles were lost.

Connor helped him detach the screen from the table and, while his father went for a drink of water, he scooped stone dust into the sack with a short handled steel shovel. When he'd cleared most of the dust, he used a fine-bristled brush to carefully gather every last grain.

When all was gathered, he ran his hands over the smooth steel surface. Some grit remained, so he brushed a thick, orange eoin feather across the table. After shaking the feather out over the open sack, he tied it securely.

Two workmen appeared and carried the sack to a scale near the door. They weighed it and marked the number on a tally sheet next to the weight of the original stone. Hendry joined them, confirmed the weight, and all three made their marks at the edge of the sheet. The workers then hefted the full sack and carried it out toward the barge.

Connor fetched another heavy granite block for his father and placed it on the scale. It weighed in at almost thirteen stone, almost exactly his weight. He marked the number in the ledger and Hendry confirmed the weight. Then Connor carried the stone to his father's worktable.

He picked up the diorite hammer and hefted its familiar weight. His family had held the prestigious vocation of Ashlar for four generations.

Until now.

Even as he longed to find a way to take his place as a Cutter and future Ashlar, the itching of the Curse intensified. He hid his frustration and placed the hammer on the table next to the block. He would never live the simple, honorable life of his father.

Isolated in silence by his situation as much as by the ear protection, he wordlessly helped his father replace the mesh screen around the table. Then he stood back as his father pushed his arms through the holes and took up the hammer that Connor would never wield. His father began pounding the new block in the same slow rhythm.

Between blows, Hendry glanced over at Connor and shouted, "Good hunt?" His voice sounded through the ear protection like he was talking underwater.

"I killed a torc!"

Hendry grinned as wide as Connor. "Congratulations, son. Those monsters are dangerous."

Not as dangerous as me.

A worker stepped into the wide central doors of the Powder House and shouted, "Ashlar, the foreman wants that block finished double-quick. This shipment can't be late."

Hendry nodded, and after the man left, he said to Connor, "Keith is riding everyone hard today, stones take the man."

He slammed the hammer on the block of granite. It struck off-center and shattered the entire left side where he held it steady with his free hand. He grimaced, put down the hammer, wiped his arms free of granite dust, and withdrew them.

"What's wrong?" Connor asked.

"Sprained my hand." Hendry carefully massaged his left hand. "Never strike in anger, son. It'll mar your work every time. I've just given myself a painful afternoon."

His father was always trying to give him counsel like that, but Connor's mind turned back to when he Curse-punched the torc.

Had he struck in anger, or out of a need for self-preservation?

As Hendry grimaced again and turned back toward the table, Connor placed a hand on his arm. "Wait. Let me do it for you."

"Connor, you know you can't."

"Why not?" The question was so ridiculous he expected his father to laugh it away even while he desperately wanted him to say yes.

Hendry gave him one of his long-suffering looks and said, "Son, now's not a good time to start this. I didn't touch this hammer until I'd been a Cutter for years."

"I don't have that much time. After tomorrow ..." He glanced around to ensure they were still alone. After tomorrow, the entire town would know he'd never be a Cutter.

Hendry frowned. "I know, son."

"Please, just once, let me try it. I'll never get another chance."

Hendry glanced around as well, then nodded. "Just one try, then I have to get back to work."

Connor tried to hide his surprise. The Sogail was a time of gifts, but he'd never imagined he'd get such an amazing one.

Before his father could change his mind, he rolled up his sleeves and stepped up to the table. His arms did not fill the openings in the mesh screen the way his father's did, nor were they shaved, but none of that mattered.

Connor reverently took up the hammer and hefted it. Hendry moved close to his side. "Start easy."

Connor grinned, raised the hammer and slammed it down onto the granite block. It struck solid, and the vibration rattled all the way up his arm. Even though he'd swung hard, it sounded weak compared to his father's. A few flakes of dust drifted off the stone, but nothing more. The hammer did not vibrate the way it did when his father used it.

"Strength isn't everything, son. The hammer does the work."

Connor frowned. "I don't understand."

"It's hard to explain. It's something you feel here." Hendry tapped his chest. "Like a fire in your chest. That connection somehow unlocks the hammer's strength and breaks down the stone a hundred times faster."

Connor stared down at the ancient hammer. His father had never spoken so openly about his work as Ashlar. Only proven apprentices learned such secrets. He ran his left hand over the worn double head of the hammer and could not help but think about his Curse.

It had grown since he'd entered the Powder House and begun working with his father, as if intent on thwarting him, preventing him from tasting the life of Ashlar.

Well, he wouldn't let it win, not today, no matter the cost. Connor raised the hammer and struck the stone again. Again the blow felt weak, so he tried to mimic his father's regular, measured cadence.

Hendry gave him an encouraging smile but said, "Don't feel bad, son, it can take a long time to find the connection, and not everyone can do it."

Connor struck the block again, and poured everything he had into the blow. The block rang from the impact, and a burning energy suddenly raced up into his arm from the hammer, like lightning in his veins.

"I feel it, dad!" he exclaimed.

"I know you want to, son, but I really need to get back to work."

"No, I really feel it!"

Connor embraced that lightning-like feeling and slammed the hammer down onto the block again, willing the hammer to respond. That energy flared through him, and the hammer seemed to blur in his hands just before it hit the stone.

Then it struck, and the stone exploded.

Dust and stone chips rattled the fine mesh screen, and the sound pounded at Connor's ears, despite his ear protection. Hendry shouted in surprise and covered his own ears, while Connor stared at the cloud of dust that filled the area inside the mesh and obscured the tabletop.

He exchanged a startled look with his father and laughed. He did it! He'd proven once and for all that he could be Ashlar. If not for the Curse, he could have done it. He wanted to shout with exultant joy.

Connor raised the hammer high, but as it emerged from the dust cloud, he gaped. One end of the double-headed diorite hammer ended in a jagged stump.

Hendry gasped, and Connor met his father's horrified gaze. He dropped the hammer and stepped away from the table. Hendry ripped the mesh screen away, and granite dust billowed out into the room.

Connor gasped, "Dad, what are you doing?"

"It's riprap to me, son."

Connor winced at his father's words. For him to say the precious block meant nothing to him right now drove home the severity of the situation.

Hendry retrieved the hammer, and the two of them stood together as he slowly turned it in his hand.

Connor finally found his voice and said, "Dad, I'm so sorry. I didn't mean to."

Hendry shook his head. "It's not your fault, son. You weren't ready. I knew better. It's my fault."

"But I felt it," Connor protested. "I don't understand."

"Nor do I."

The dust cleared enough for Connor to see the table top. No trace of the granite block remained. Tiny chips of granite lay piled against the collar where they'd been flung up against the screen, and white granite dust lay piled almost to the top of the collar.

In the center of the granite powder rested half a dozen ragged diorite chunks, all that remained of the hammer head. Connor picked up one that looked blackened, as if burned. It felt somehow lighter than it should. The sight of the diorite pieces seemed unreal.

In one blow, he'd processed an entire block of granite.

In one blow, he'd broken the Ashlar's hammer.

Should he shout with the joy of having connected with the hammer, or hide in shame for what he'd done?

The hammer should have lasted for many more years. He could scarce comprehend its loss.

"What in Tallan's name?"

The same worker who had called to them a few minutes ago stood in the door. He stared at the granite dust scattered around the table, and then at the broken hammer, and then spun and raced away.

Hendry grimaced. "Let me do the talking, son."

In half a minute Keith, the foreman, charged into the Powder House, followed by every worker from the blocking yard.

"What happened," Keith demanded.

"You're not blind. You see as well as any what happened."

"How?"

Hendry shrugged. "Probably a lot like how a chisel breaks."

Keith glared. He was a giant of a man, a full head taller than Hendry, and half again as thick. He was a legend among the Cutters, and had held every cutting record for the past decade. At least, he had until he broke his diorite chisel two years ago in a competition against Hendry.

Keith pursed his lips. "So you broke your hammer. How does that justify this mess?" He gestured at the screen tossed aside with granite particles still clinging to it, and to the dust and flakes of precious granite scattered around the table.

"I'll clean it up."

"You bet you will. Any discrepancy in the weight will come out of your pay."

"I said I'll deal with it."

Keith grunted, and started to turn away. Then he paused and stepped closer to Connor. "How'd you get granite on your arms, boy?"

Connor glanced down, and for the first time noticed the particles of granite covering his arms up to his shoulders. Before he could think of a reply, Hendry said, "Leave off, Keith. I'll clean it up."

Keith rounded on Hendry. "You let this sick, useless whelp of yours try your hammer, didn't you?" The accusation triggered a round of murmured oaths from the other workers.

"You'll not talk about my son like that."

"Answer me."

"I broke my hammer. That's more than enough."

Keith barked a hard laugh. "You did, didn't you? You couldn't bear that tomorrow Lord Gavin will assign him a vocation, and it won't be Cutter. And the unworthy sickling broke it."

"Insult my son again, and I'll call you out tomorrow."

Murmurs ran through the crowd again, and Keith laughed aloud. "You wouldn't last half a minute."

He was probably right. Hendry was a powerful man, but no one had ever held their own against Keith.

Hendry looked unfazed. "Perhaps."

Keith snorted. "Too bad council members are barred from duels."

"You always find an excuse."

"You boulder-brained son of a pedra," Keith cursed and grabbed Hendry's collar, his other meaty fist cocked back to deliver a blow.

Hendry raised the hammer in turn, unafraid.

Instead of striking, Keith pushed Hendry back. "Clean up this mess. We have eight blocks to process today. You better hope that broken hammer holds up."

Hendry took a couple of experimental swings with the hammer, and frowned. "The weight's all wrong."

"Your problem."

"I'll get it done," Hendry said.

Keith spun and pushed through the crowd. Several of the workers gave Hendry their condolences, but none dared ask if he would take on the enormous debt of a new hammer.

It was a difficult question. Connor could not become Ashlar, but one of his younger brothers might. If they did, a new hammer would be required, but if none of them showed talent, the debt would cripple the family.

Two of the other workers helped them fill a bag with the powdered granite, clean off the mesh screen, and carefully sweep the floor. The final weight looked good, and Connor breathed a sigh of relief.

"Come on, son," Hendry said. "I want to talk with your mother."

"What about the other blocks?"

"It'll wait. I'll finish up this afternoon."

Thankfully, Keith didn't notice them leaving, although Connor didn't breathe easy until they passed through the wall gate.

"Mom's going to be really mad."

Hendry nodded. "Timing is pretty bad. I'm just glad nothing worse happened."

Connor could not imagine anything worse.

CHAPTER 5

s they walked toward the central square, Connor noticed his father still massaging his sprained hand. "Maybe we should stop by the healer's."

"No. It's just a sprain. Not worth risking one of Mhairi's potions."

"They're not all bad."

Hendry laughed and ruffled Connor's hair. "The first time you drank one, you threw up four times."

"I wasn't used to it then."

"How many have you drunk now?"

Connor mumbled something vague. He was not sure of the number, but it was a lot. Ever since Jean took over initial treatment of new patients in the healer's house about eighteen months ago, most of the men of the village suddenly began suffering a flood of aches and vague ailments. She'd been inundated with eager patients, much to the growing resentment of the rest of the women in the village.

Old Healer Mhairi, her grandmother, dealt with the epidemic by producing what she called a basic cure-all tonic that she forced on every new patient that could not produce a specific ailment. The vile brew worked, and restored stability to the town.

Unfortunately, Mhairi seemed content to let the treatment stand, so Connor and Stuart and Hamish, who still visited Jean at every opportunity, were doused with the nasty potion several times a week. Connor had built up a resistance to it through sheer stubbornness. He was not about to allow one of the others win Jean's affection over something as simple as nasty-tasting medicine.

Hendry said, "After we speak with your mother, you can go visit your sweetheart."

His father spoke as if it was a foregone conclusion that Jean would choose him, even though they both knew that tomorrow everything would change forever. His father's simple confidence boosted his spirits immensely.

His smile faded as they entered the central market square. Several angry female voices shouted from the cooking area. In the center of the brewing conflict, Connor's mother stood facing Cinaed, her normally happy face red with anger, while Cinaed stood with hands on hips, grinning back at Lilias.

Between the two, arms raised placatingly, stood Jean.

Although groaning internally, Jean forced an expression of calm on her face as she sought a way to head off the brewing confrontation between Lilias and Cinaed. Seeing them now, she could scarce believe they had once been dear friends.

Lilias exclaimed, "You can't take it."

Cinaed smirked. "By order of Lady Isobel, the Heatstone oven is to be confiscated in keeping with the King's edict on the removal of all contraband Grandurian merchandise."

"You can't," one woman called from the crowd. "Not before the Sogail!"

The thought of a scandal like this the day before the midsummer festival made Jean want to shriek with anger and tear at Cinaed's horrid red hair. Tomorrow she turned sixteen, and if the escalating fiasco ruined her day, the Tallan himself would cower from her wrath.

"We have to keep the law," Cinaed said, "especially during the Sogail." To Lilias she added, "Surely as the head of the women's circle, you agree."

"I am wondering how Lady Isobel heard about the oven so quickly, let alone how she would come to the conclusion that it's in any way contraband."

"She moves quickly when the safety of the town is concerned."

"Or when she sees a chance to steal," someone called from the crowd.

"Who dared say that?" Cinaed demanded.

Jean needed to bring the conversation back from the verge of impending violence, even though Cinaed seemed not to notice the signs. Jean had been trained as a healer, with her grandmother's mantra ingrained in her heart.

Look deep, see clear.

Healers couldn't afford hasty or ill-formed diagnoses that would lead to treatments that might kill. The same skill she honed in treating patients proved effective now as she picked out the angry glares and clenched fists of the crowd packing in closer toward the arguing ladies.

She could not allow her feelings to cloud her judgment, although she wished they could all just take turns slapping Cinaed for a while. It might not change things, but it would be very satisfying. Blinded by jealousy, and impelled by ambition, the woman probably considered this a spectacular coup, without realizing how it only undermined her influence.

"Surely there is some mistake," Jean said. "The oven arrived on the barge only yesterday with clear ownership."

"You're not on the circle yet," Cinaed snapped, not breaking eye contact with Lilias. "Stay out of it."

That generated a new round of angry muttering from the crowd. Jean couldn't understand how the flame-haired woman failed to see.

She made a little curtsy to appease Cinaed's need to feel superior, as she sought a way to avert this disaster and still allow the woman to retain a pretense of honor. There had to be a way to make this work.

"Of course," she said. "It's just, I know you must have done everything in your power to persuade Lady Isobel to wait until after the Sogail. After all, the oven was gifted to the town by Lilias and Hendry just this morning."

Cinaed scowled at her, but finally seemed to recognize the universal anger directed toward her, and her irritation melted away. "Yes," she stammered, "yes, I tried to make her see reason, but she was adamant the oven be taken today."

Lilias, her expression neutral, said, "Perhaps if a united circle were to petition her again, she might relent."

"Perhaps, if only for one day."

Jean harbored no illusion that Lady Isobel would allow such a marvelous item to remain in possession of the common Linn of Alasdair, but there was a chance she might relent until after the Sogail. Before she could congratulate herself on finding at least a partial solution, Hendry and Connor pushed through the crowd. Hendry held one hand awkwardly, and they were both covered with an unusual amount of granite dust.

"What trouble are you causing now, Cinaed?" Hendry demanded. His words shattered all Jean's hope of salvaging the situation.

It never ceased to amaze her how leaders from both the town council and the women's circle so often spoke before they bothered to understand. Her grandmother's other creed, repeated endlessly to her, should be taught to them.

Act only after understanding.

Cinaed snarled, "Lady Isobel gave an order, Lilias. I'm sure your vaunted honor won't allow you to refuse."

"At least she has honor," Hendry said.

"My husband will call you out for that."

Hendry shrugged. "Perhaps. He missed his chance earlier."

"You lie."

"Of all of us here, Hendry is not the liar," Lilias said.

Cinaed's angry expression gave way to one of condescending superiority. "I know you're under a lot of stress, Lilias. You must be beside yourself with worry. I don't know what I'd do if my son faced the Saorsa with no chance of gaining a useful vocation."

Jean winced at the barb that surely stung deep, but Lilias betrayed no anger. She only said, "Your ignorance is all the more startling for how you flaunt it."

Cinaed's façade of compassion cracked and she pointed at Connor. "Wastrel, Lady Isobel ordered you to deliver the oven to the manor at once."

"You lie." Connor didn't bother to hide his anger.

"Watch your tongue," Lilias reprimanded her son. "Cinaed may be many things, but she is still your elder."

"If it arrives damaged in any way, it will be charged to you," Cinaed added to Connor. "You're old enough to pay your own debts."

Hendry said, "I think you've damaged your reputation quite enough for one day, Cinaed."

She glared and stomped away.

Connor slapped the top of the oven, a large ornate cube of polished pink marble that sat on a sturdy wooden table. A full span across, it somehow burned with constant heat without needing any fuel.

The oven was a princely gift from Lilias' sister, Ailsa, who lived far to the south, and its heat was supposed to last for decades. Their gifting it to the town had seemed a brilliant plan. Instead of fostering jealousy, the oven garnered tremendous good-will.

Jean wanted to go to Connor, to comfort him, but did not dare, not with the Sogail so close. He might make dangerous assumptions she could not yet allow. As she watched him, he idly rubbed a carved bear pendant he wore around his neck. She knew only that it was a gift from his Aunt Ailsa, arrived on the barge yesterday with the oven.

She cared deeply for Connor, despite his terrible sickness that regularly left him bedridden, sometimes for days at a time. She might just give her heart to him, but did not dare do so yet. She had to stay strong, until after the Sogail.

So many things would be decided then.

CHAPTER 6

amish welcomed the chance to escape the boring, heavy labor of assembling tables to instead help Connor transport the Heatstone oven to the manor house. Tall and gangly, Hamish had grown so fast in the past couple years, his muscles hadn't really caught up. Even so, he still managed to help maneuver the oven onto a cart they commandeered for the project.

Connor looked furious, and Hamish tried his best to cheer up his friend. People saw Hamish as a goofy, clumsy kid, and he used that appearance to his advantage. Connor's anger faded as they ascended the road up to the plateau and the manor house.

Hamish couldn't stop thinking about the Sogail. There would be so much food! His appetite had blossomed in recent months, and he never felt full. Besides, he loved to taste new things.

He expected to be assigned the same vocation as his father, working in the quarry at the lift that lowered the rough-cut stones down to the blocking yard. He couldn't wait for the official announcement.

"Connor, what vocation do you think you'll be assigned tomorrow?"

They used to dream about the Saorsa and talk about different vocations all the time. However, as the day drew near, Connor had shown less enthusiasm for the topic.

Now Connor glared, and Hamish realized his stupidity. Connor would never be named Cutter, would never apprentice to become the next Ashlar. Hamish had assumed his friend was reconciled to that fact. Connor certainly seemed to enjoy hunting, and the town would feast on more fresh meat during the Sogail than they had in years.

Then again, maybe Connor wasn't entirely ready to leave the dream of Cutter behind. Maybe bringing it up today, on top of the theft of the oven, wasn't such a good idea.

Then Connor surprised him. "Listen, Hamish. Tomorrow at the Sogail something big is going to happen."

"Like what?"

Connor paused, but then finished lamely, "Well, something you've never seen before."

Hamish chuckled. "Like maybe you'll finish a dance without stepping on Jean's toes."

"Eat rocks."

They crossed the wide expanse of the plateau, covered with thick grass, kept cropped short by a herd of goats and cows tended by some of the slave children. The manor house sat two-thirds of the way across the plateau, its main entrance facing north toward the quarry, the source of the lord's wealth.

The manor house stood only fifty yards from, and parallel to, the steep western edge of the plateau that dropped sharply to the Lower Wick. Stables, barns and sheds clustered around the eastern and southern sides of the manor, with fenced pastures and gardens set farther out. A few mature trees dotted the plateau, with a thin strip of forest clinging to the slope on the eastern side.

To the untrained eye, the lowest level of the manor might look to be made of precious Alasdair White, although Hamish could see the inferior grade of the stone. This was grout, cast-off waste deemed unworthy, generally due to veins of quartz or other mixed stone content. Above the grout, the manor rose in three stories of field stone and wood, capped with a crenellated parapet, as if it had dreams of one day becoming a fortified keep.

Long beds of flowers flanked the road. Lady Isobel loved her flowers, every conceivable variety that could be coaxed into growing in the harsh climate. A small garden with a stone fountain carved in the likeness of a man holding aloft a great hammer stood facing the main entrance. The road ended there, circling the garden where the fountain splashed loud in the otherwise quiet air.

As they skirted the self-important main entrance with its twelve-foot doors and flanking columns, Hamish pointed at the fountain.

"Remember last summer when you dared me to bathe in that?"

Connor laughed. "Should've remembered the women's circle was meeting that night."

"I think you did it on purpose."

Connor grinned. "You should have seen your face when they found you sitting up on that hammer in your smallclothes!"

Hamish shivered. "I still have nightmares."

The boys rounded the tower at the eastern corner and headed along the side of the manor. High above, the wooden central tower reared thirty feet above the manor's roof. The long east side of the building was far plainer, despite the three half-towers that bulged from the wall at regular intervals.

Lady Isobel met them at the kitchen entrance, a simple but wide wooden door positioned halfway down the eastern wall. The sight of her snuffed out their good humor.

Not young anymore, Lady Isobel dyed her graying hair an unnatural shade of black that bore no resemblance to her natural color. The dye tasted like vinegar mixed with mud, and tended to bleed onto the collars of the frilly dresses she wore, staining them with streaks of dark green. Hamish never understood how the dye could turn her hair black and her clothes green.

Today she abandoned her normal veneer of superior calm and clapped her hands together with delight when she saw the Heatstone oven. "Very good. Bring it right into the kitchen."

Instead of leaving them to the work, she hovered, giving useless instructions and nearly tripping them with the long hem of her dark blue silk dress as they labored to unload the oven without dropping it. It was like she didn't realize she was gleefully stealing from Connor's family. Or, more likely, she just didn't care. She was nobility, they were Linn, commoners with no recourse.

Hamish stumbled and nearly dumped the oven on her. She yelped, snapped at him to watch his feet, and shifted around behind Connor. As they staggered through the door and into the manor's expansive kitchen, he wished he hadn't caught the load. Breaking her legs would surely land him in lots of trouble, but people were used to him dropping things.

It would've been worth the risk.

Lady Isobel turned a slow circle in the center of the room, tapping her lips with the small wand she liked to pretend was a grand scepter when she gave orders. "This will never do. Wherever are we going to put it?"

"We could just bring it back to town," Hamish suggested.

She glared, and Hamish decided not to face her on an empty stomach again. He glanced around for Aileen, the cook. She always radiated a happy contentment, and made the kitchen a haven from the rest of the manor. She treated the boys like sons, sneaking fruit and sweetbreads to them. At least she would be the one using the oven, not Lady Isobel.

As if his thoughts summoned her, Aileen emerged from the large pantry carrying a sack of flour. She grinned when she saw them and brushed a lock of her brown hair out of her chubby face. Her blue eyes sparkled when she smiled, and Hamish found himself grinning back at her.

"Place that over here, boys," Aileen said, and moved to a sturdy table standing to one side of the deep hearth.

While they rested, Lady Isobel inspected the oven. She ran greedy hands over the carved pink exterior and exclaimed at its gentle warmth. She opened the matching marble door and held her hand there, savoring the steady heat that flowed over her fingers.

Hamish could not tear his eyes away. There was no marble like that anywhere near Alasdair. He wondered how it tasted.

He had always loved tasting things, and preferred to have something in his mouth all the time. Connor and Stuart teased him about it, but he didn't understand why they spent so much time with their mouths not occupied. He loved new tastes, and last year made a startling discovery.

Stones tasted great.

Not all of them, but every once in a while he'd suck on a stone that burst with flavor. He hadn't figured out why yet, but the mystery of it drove him to constant research. Connor thought him daft and refused to believe any stone tasted like anything but dirty rocks. Then again, he often refused the breadsticks or other snacks Hamish carried in his pockets.

Hamish couldn't figure out why.

"This is magnificent," Lady Isobel said. She closed the oven door and beamed at Connor, "I might even send a letter thanking your Aunt for such a wondrous gift. I bet I'm the first lady anywhere in High Lord Dougal's realm to obtain one of these."

Connor balled his hands into fists and stared at the floor, and Hamish considered tripping and falling onto Lady Isobel. He'd practiced the move often enough that no one acted surprised any more. He could strategically fall down just about anywhere.

Aileen said, "My lady, your afternoon tea is ready in your sitting room."

"Very well." Lady Isobel swept toward one of four doors that led from the kitchen, the one that would take her through the formal dining room. She paused in the doorway and said, "Aileen, I expect something grand for dinner tonight to celebrate."

Aileen curtsied, and Lady Isobel left without a backward glance. Aileen frowned after her, and then pulled Connor into her arms.

"Oh my boy, I am so sorry."

Connor let her hug him for a moment, but made a valiant effort to conceal his anger. She finally released him and fetched a couple of sweetbread pastries from a cupboard. Hamish popped the entire thing in his mouth and savored the explosion of taste. Connor ate with better manners, but Hamish couldn't help it. Aileen's pastries rivaled even those of Neasa, the town baker, and Hamish had sampled enough of her pastries to know.

While they ate, Aileen said, "I need a few things from the basement. I'll return in a moment."

"Do you need any help?" Hamish asked. They would do anything for her.

"No, dear. I'll only be a moment." After she left, Connor sat on one of the long tables in the middle of the room and stared glumly at the oven.

Hamish suppressed the urge to sneak another pastry. Aileen would know, and he would never risk her wrath. He would have snitched something lying on the counter, but Aileen kept her kitchen immaculate.

Rows of counters crowded the edges of the room while three long tables faced the wide fireplace with its built-in oven that took up half of the far wall. Shelves and cupboards clung to every vertical surface, filled with bottles, boxes, and cans containing the myriad ingredients Aileen used to craft her delicious feasts. Rows of pots and pans hung from hooks in the ceiling, and gleamed in the early afternoon sunlight that streamed through the large window.

Hamish approached the oven and started tracing one of the carvings. "Hey, Connor, tomorrow at the Sogail, I bet I'm going to win …"

He stared down at the oven in wonder, and forgot to finish the sentence. This stone felt different. More than smooth, more than warm from its inner heat, it thrummed against his fingers.

"Can't think of one thing you can beat me at, eh?" Connor joked.

Hamish no longer listened, but pressed both hands against the warm surface of the oven. The feel of the stone against his hands triggered a thrill of recognition. He'd caught flickers of this feeling from some of the rocks he tasted, but nothing so clear. He leaned close and put his ear against the oven. Then he licked it.

The explosion of taste, like spices dancing across his tongue, shamed everything he'd ever tasted in his life, and he gasped. "Wow. It's amazing."

"What is?"

"This." Hamish licked the oven again and pressed his forehead against the stone. As his skin made contact, he sensed something beyond the spectacular taste.

"What are you doing?"

"I can feel it … feel the heat."

Connor snorted. "Stick your tongue through the door. You'll feel it a lot better."

"Not that heat. I can feel, I don't know, it's like … come taste it."

"You're the only one who thinks rocks taste like anything but rocks."

"This one's different. It's spicy."

"Really?" Connor loved spicy food more than anyone Hamish knew, and would eat fire roots raw. No one else in town could, but he loved them. He'd love this.

Connor approached the far side of the oven and placed a hand on its warm side.

"Go on," Hamish urged. "Try it."

Connor licked the oven and then groaned. "I can't believe you talked me into this. It tastes like warm rock."

Hamish frowned in turn. "I'm telling the truth. I've never tasted anything like it." He licked it again and savored the explosive zest of it.

He'd never felt anything like this. Other rocks paled in comparison. Beyond the taste, behind the thrumming, something deep inside the stone had been fundamentally altered.

"What are you doing?"

"It's … like the heat is trapped in the stone and somehow they've opened it a crack to let some of it out."

"It's an oven. The heat has to stay inside, or it doesn't work."

"Don't be a pebble-brain." Hamish licked the oven again.

"Do you have to do that?"

"It helps me think."

"I think you've thought enough. I want to get out of here."

"Just a second. I can taste it."

Hamish gasped as the truth struck. Somehow he could feel deep inside the stone, all the way to the source of that crack that the heat was bubbling out through.

"What is it?"

"I'll show you." He barely contained his growing excitement as he felt awkwardly for that fissure inside the stone.

"I don't think you should …"

Then he found it, and pulled against it. He didn't really understand what he was doing, could barely comprehend the non-physical nature of it. In the quarry, they hit things with hammers, but this was more a reaching out with the mind, a tugging of the consciousness against this ethereal lid that held the crack shut.

It released.

The oven began to vibrate and something rumbled inside of it. Hamish laughed. "You won't believe it. I really …"

The door blew off the oven, flew across the room, and smashed into the far wall, knocking pots from their hooks. They fell to the stone floor in a cascading din.

Flames burst out the open door of the oven in a solid tongue of fire that stretched six feet into the room. The force of the flames drove the oven back against the wall, while the roar shook the room.

"What did you do?" Connor shouted above the din.

Hamish laughed, unable to fully express the joy that swept through him. "I really did it!"

CHAPTER 7

amish broke it. Connor's initial shock turned to satisfaction as he realized what that meant. There was no way Lady Isobel could use the oven after this. Well, not for anything other than char-broiling things.

Aileen's voice called up from the basement. "What are you lads doing?"

Connor's smile faded. They had to put out the fire before anyone saw.

"Help me," Connor shouted and raced to the water barrel next to the huge wash basin. Between the two of them, they slid the heavy barrel across the room. The overwhelming heat from the flames had already turned the kitchen uncomfortably warm, while the air smelled like a hot iron chisel.

The boys grabbed large pots and threw water into the open oven door where the flames still roared out into the room. The water flashed to steam and forced them to retreat to keep from being overwhelmed by the super-hot cloud. Aileen's footsteps echoed on the stairs. She was coming up fast.

"This isn't working," Hamish said.

"Turn it off."

"I don't know how."

"You turned it on."

Hamish shrugged. "But I didn't know I was turning it on. I just opened the crack."

"How far?"

"I don't know, a lot."

Connor didn't pretend to understand how the oven worked, but Aunt Ailsa had said it would produce constant heat for decades. This inferno would surely burn out much faster, but he could not guess how soon.

"We have to put it out!"

"How?"

"Grab your side."

Connor ran around the billowing flames, and had to shield his face from the incredible heat. He grabbed one side of the oven while Hamish approached the other. Where the stone had been warm to the touch before, now it burned his fingers.

"Try turning it off," Connor said.

Hamish grimaced and placed his hands on the oven. He concentrated for a moment, and absently licked the top of the oven. Then he recoiled and rubbed his mouth.

"Hurry."

"Burned my tongue."

Hamish focused again, and after a couple long seconds, he laughed. "Got it."

The oven seemed to groan, and the tongue of fire leaped out until it stretched across the entire room to the cupboards on the far side. They blackened and started to smoke.

"What did you do?" Connor shouted.

Hamish stared, mouth agape. "Wow."

Aileen appeared from the lower levels, and stopped in the doorway to stare. "What in the name of my lady's impure soul is going on here?"

Connor shouted, "Hamish, help me."

The two of them leveraged the oven forward to the front end of the table. It fought them, as if the flames were driving it back. It took all of their strength to slide it forward those six inches.

"Oh, my boys, be careful," Aileen cried.

"Stay there," Connor called. "We need to put this out."

"What happened?"

"The oven … just broke," Connor said between labored breaths.

With a final heave, Connor shoved the oven off the front of the table. The tongue of flame roared louder as it tilted down and scorched stones of the floor. With a thunderous bang, the heavy oven fell to the floor, with the flames facing down.

Hamish said, "Good thinking, Connor."

Aileen dabbed her face. "Oh, my."

Connor frowned and leaned over the oven. Now that it was face-down on the stone floor, there would be less air for the fire and it should smother, but the oven was starting to shake and rattle. It was as if it was trying to right itself.

Could it do that?

He had no idea. He knew almost nothing about it. It's not like Aunt Ailsa sent them detailed instructions. The itching in his arms intensified and spread all through his torso.

Connor grimaced against the urge to scratch, and leaned over the top of the oven to brace it. "Hamish, I think …"

Before he could finish, the oven shot up off the floor and drove into his chest. Flames poured out the open door, and Hamish dove back to avoid the inferno. Aileen screamed and retreated a step down toward the basement, ready to bolt.

Connor shouted as the oven pushed him into the air.

He was flying!

How could such a heavy oven do that? It didn't matter. He started to laugh, even though the oven was now hot enough to blister his skin right through his shirt.

His weight was not centered over the oven, and as it rose, it tilted, shooting flames toward Hamish while the entire oven started floating across the room in the opposite direction. Hamish yelped, retreated, and jumped into the huge wash basin.

Connor yanked on the oven and shifted his weight to try to bring the flames vertical and drive the cursed oven back to the floor. For a second, he held it level, but instead of sinking to the floor, the oven climbed higher.

Then the balance shifted again and it started tilting the other way. Connor heaved against it again, but over compensated, and it started to spin, with the flames scorching a wide circle in the floor. He gritted his teeth and tried again, but only managed to set it spinning faster.

Flames sprayed across the room, and the tables, cupboards and counters all started to smoke and blacken. The itch of Connor's curse intensified throughout his body, and he groaned against the maddening urge to tear at his skin. He'd never felt it so strong.

The roar of the fire seemed like a living thing, and the heat in the kitchen was quickly growing unbearable. The oven smelled like sulfur and fire root.

"Oh spirits, preserve us," Aileen cried as Connor spun wildly around the room toward where she crouched in the doorway.

"Look out," Connor shouted.

As flames sprayed toward her, Aileen jumped back out of the way. She disappeared through the door, and from the shrieks and loud clatter that echoed back into the room, she must have tumbled down the long flight of stairs to the first sub-basement level.

"Sorry," Connor whispered as he held on to the spinning oven. The thrill of flying had already faded, and he just hoped he wouldn't be sick. Although, if he threw up while spinning so fast, he'd get some great distance. He'd probably beat Hamish's record.

The oven carried him into the wall near the outer door. For a second, Connor was tempted to try to push it that way. If he could get the door open, he could get it out of the kitchen before it set everything on fire.

Then again, it was still climbing, pushing him up the wall. If he managed to get it outside, there would be nothing to prevent it from lifting him into the sky.

No, better to shove it into the hearth.

If he could wedge it into the huge fireplace, it couldn't do any harm until it burned itself out.

Connor pushed off from the wall and tried to twist the oven at the same time to point it toward the hearth. He misjudged the required force and instead sent himself spinning out into the room.

"Stones take it," he muttered. Flying was a lot more complicated than the birds made it seem.

Flames spewed around the room, and the already-blackened cupboards burst into open flame under the new fiery onslaught.

At the sight, Hamish leaped out of the wash basin and shouted, "Save the food!"

"Save yourself, grout-for-brains," Connor shouted. Smoke was filling the room, and he started to cough.

Hamish ignored him and raced to the sweetbread cupboard. He managed to pry open the burning door and started yanking the pastries out and throwing them at the window.

It was closed. Pastries bounced off and littered the floor. Hamish did not seem to notice, but moved to the next cupboard and started throwing fruit. One apple broke the window, and fresh air rushed into the kitchen. Connor breathed deep the cool breeze, but so did the flames, and the fire roared higher.

Hamish yelped, and ran for the washbasin again. He slipped on a burning muffin, lost his footing, and skidded across the floor on his stomach. He ended up under a burning counter.

The spinning oven collided with the wall not far from Hamish, and Connor pushed off again before the flames consumed his friend. This time, he set himself better and shot away from the wall in a straight line. He looked up to find he wasn't headed for the hearth, but for the closed door leading to the formal dining room.

Connor grimaced at the thought of what the flames would do to that door, but there was nothing he could do about it. He focused instead on figuring out how to bounce the floating oven across the room from one wall to another to reach the hearth, hopefully before the oven drove him into the ceiling. He should be able to make it in three bounces.

As he neared the door, Connor braced himself for the impact even though he started coughing so hard he felt like he might spit out a lung. Just before he reached the door, it opened and Lady Isobel stepped into the opening.

Their eyes met, and her look of shocked surprise was priceless. Then Connor realized the oven was about to kill her. He threw his weight against the oven to try to avoid the collision.

He forgot that the flames always moved in the opposite direction.

The roaring tongue of fire tilted forward and completely enveloped Lady Isobel and the door. She screamed and tumbled out of view. He caught a brief glimpse of her before the oven collided with the wall above the door, and the sight made him wince.

He'd never considered that the hair dye she used might be flammable.

"Sorry," Connor shouted as the oven floated in the opposite direction, straight back toward Hamish.

Hamish saw him coming, and crawled deeper under the burning table.

"Move!" Connor shouted, but Hamish just pulled his feet under.

The oven smashed into the cupboard above Hamish so hard, it knocked the entire cupboard off the wall. The oven twisted under the impact, and Connor's foot caught in the top shelf of the cupboard.

It started dragging him off the oven. Connor yelped and scrambled to hold on, but only managed to tilt the oven, which resulted in him slipping off faster.

Time seemed to slow as Connor's hand slipped and he started to fall free. The cupboard would drag him down to the table, and the oven would consume him with its flames.

As that terrible truth flashed into Connor's mind, the Curse raged through him, itching through his entire body, stronger than he'd ever imagined it could. Connor did the only thing he could.

He Curse-punched the oven.

His entire body went numb with the power of the Curse, and then his Curse-laden fist struck the oven and punched right through.

The oven exploded.

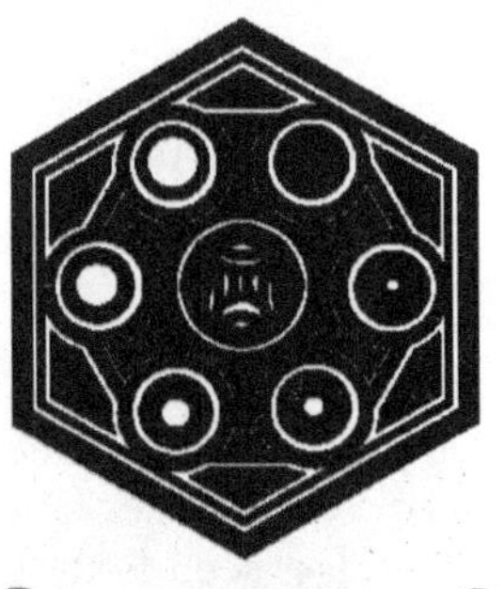

CHAPTER 8

he kitchen burned.

Connor blinked a few times as his eyes slowly focused on the floor as it slid past. His body felt numb, but he was pretty sure he wasn't trying to move.

Shattered boxes and crates lay strewn across the floor with pots and pans, while entire cabinets lay in splintered, burning piles. Chunks of pink marble, many of them still burning, glinted through the heavy smoke from where they were wedged into every possible nook and crevice.

Everything burned. Spices from broken jars filled the room with a wild aroma, mingled with the smoke and overpowering stench of charred wood. His ears did not seem to be working, so an eerie quiet cloaked everything.

Connor twitched, and only then realized why the floor was moving. Hamish had been dragging him by the wrists. As soon as he moved, Hamish dropped him onto his back and crouched beside him.

Through a fit of coughing, Hamish said, "I thought you were dead." His voice sounded like he was talking underwater.

"I am."

"You're heavy. Can you walk?"

Connor nodded. Feeling began to return, and he felt weak, but amazingly intact. "What happened?"

"The oven exploded."

Hamish pulled Connor to his feet and started dragging him toward the outer door that burned like a torch.

"Wait. Aileen."

Hamish glanced across the room. The door leading to the basements was just gone. "I forgot."

"Go help her. I can make it."

Hamish nodded, sprinted across the room, and disappeared down the stairs. Hopefully Aileen was all right.

A fall like that really hurt. Connor knew from experience.

He paused for a second and looked toward the formal dining room where he'd last seen Lady Isobel. She might be badly burned, but that entire wall was engulfed in flame, and he could not make himself risk it. Not for her. Not today.

He kicked the burning outer door, leaped the debris, and staggered outside, coughing.

Connor looked up to find Lord Gavin and his bodyguard, Bruce, running toward him past the stables. Well, Lord Gavin tried to run, more than Connor had ever seen. Never a tall man, the lord of Alasdair already stooped far over when he walked, looking even older than his fifty-odd years. His gray hair and heavily-lined face added to the impression that he was far older than his wife.

"What in Tallan's name is going on in there?" Lord Gavin shouted.

Bruce reached Connor first and asked worriedly, "Where's Aileen?"

"She fell down the basement stairs." As Bruce moved toward the kitchen door, Connor held him back. "The kitchen's burning. Hamish is with her. He'll bring her out the other end."

Bruce's tension eased. Aileen was his wife, and he doted on her almost as much as he did their young daughter.

"We've already ordered a fire team, and people will come from town to help. We'll get it out soon."

Connor breathed his own sigh of relief. If the fire weren't contained soon, it could easily threaten the rest of the manor. He and Hamish were in enough trouble already.

Lord Gavin reached them, panting from the unaccustomed exertion. "What happened in there, lad?"

"The Heatstone oven sort of broke," Connor said cautiously. One did not lie to the lord, but if he handled this carefully, perhaps Lord Gavin would not question them too closely, and assume things were not their fault.

That thin hope died a gruesome death as Lady Isobel staggered around the corner of the manor, leaning heavily on her daughter, Moira.

Lady Isobel looked like some wraith from one of Bruce's stories. Her frilly dress was charred and ragged. Her eyebrows had burned completely away, along with most of her hair. Her eyes stood out against her blackened, furious face.

Lord Gavin followed Connor's gaze and, at the sight of her obvious rage, he slipped a pace behind Bruce.

"Seize that miscreant," Lady Isobel shouted from twenty paces away, pointing one claw-like hand at Connor.

Bruce took Connor's arm and whispered, "Stones boy, what have you done?"

Connor only shook his head. He had to think his way out of this. There had to be a way to explain it. Lady Isobel hadn't really seen what happened.

"Murderer," Lady Isobel shrieked as she drew closer.

"Mother, no one is dead. He can't be a murderer," said Moira.

Connor willed a silent thank you to her. As much as he hated Lady Isobel, he felt the opposite for Moira. She might not possess the same heart-pounding beauty as Jean, but she was a good friend.

Where Jean was slender and supple, with a long, graceful neck and heart-shaped face, Moira's figure was fuller, with an honest, oval-shaped face. Her dark hair and hazel eyes attracted Connor as powerfully as her quick mind and adventurous spirit.

Lady Isobel waved a dismissive hand toward her daughter, "Don't interrupt. That boy tried to kill me."

"I did not," Connor blurted out as Lord Gavin turned a steely glare on him.

"Don't you lie to me, you worthless Linn," Lady Isobel shouted. She advanced on him, and only Bruce's strong grip on his shoulder kept him from bolting.

For a second, he thought she meant to strike him, but instead she only thrust an angry finger under his nose. "You spiteful, deceitful boy. You destroyed my beautiful oven and burned my kitchen after all I've done for you."

Connor blinked a couple of times at her audacity. The rage he'd felt for the past hour at the theft of the oven had largely dissipated, but now ignited afresh. He wished he could shout back at her, but that would just seal his fate.

"Now Isobel," Lord Gavin said placatingly. "Let's learn the details …"

"Don't you 'now Isobel' me," she snapped. "I will see justice done here today."

She spun back to Connor and said in a ringing tone, "For your crimes, I name you Connor Daor-Linn Gavin."

Moira gasped, Lord Gavin blanched, and Bruce's hand shook on Connor's shoulder. For Connor, the words drove into him like daggers and he staggered back a step. She named him slave, Daor to Lord Gavin or, more precisely, to her.

No, it wasn't impossible. Tomorrow he would reveal his Curse, gain Patronage. Tomorrow his life would change.

He could not help but blurt out, "But, tomorrow is the Sogail."

She snorted. "Not for you. Tomorrow my husband rescinds Teagair for you, and you will serve me to pay for your crimes."

The world seemed to tilt under Connor's feet, and he swayed. Would they really break him away from his family and make him slave? This could not be happening. He glanced to Lord Gavin for help, but the weak-willed man looked completely cowed by his wife and ready to lay blame on Connor.

Lord Gavin waved a hand. "Bruce, lock him in the turnip room until after the Sogail."

As Bruce started pulling Connor toward the far corner of the manor, he couldn't help crying out, "Please, don't do this! It was an accident."

Lady Isobel snorted in reply.

"You don't understand," he begged and dragged against Bruce's arm. "I have to go to the Sogail tomorrow."

"You should have thought of that before you tried to kill me," Lady Isobel said. "Away with you."

"No, wait!" Connor protested, fighting against Bruce. "You know this is wrong! Isn't stealing the oven enough?"

"I didn't steal it," Lady Isobel shrieked. "I confiscated it."

Lord Gavin said, "My dear, the boy does have a point."

Lady Isobel rounded on her husband and screamed, "Don't meddle, Gavin! He broke my precious oven! I will own him!"

Connor tried to protest again, but Bruce whispered, "Stop it, lad. She's in one of her moods, and you'll only make it worse."

"You can't do this to me," Connor begged as Bruce towed him back to the southeast corner of the manor.

"Who said I was?"

He looked up to meet Bruce's blue-eyed gaze for the first time. Bruce looked sad, as well he might. He knew all too well the hardships of slavery. He'd been a free Linn once, a great soldier if one could believe the stories.

Bruce winked. "All right, lad, now's the time."

"I don't understand."

Bruce rolled his eyes. "Struggle."

Connor frowned at the cryptic answers, but tugged at Bruce's arm anyway. He was unprepared when Bruce gave a great cry and staggered back three paces before collapsing to the ground.

As Connor moved to help him, Bruce glared and said, "Don't be daft, boy, run!"

Connor glanced back toward Lord Gavin just as Bruce gave a great moan and shouted, "Oy, the boy's gone and broke my leg."

Lord Gavin shouted, "Now hold on there," but Connor was already running.

As he rounded the end of the building and bolted for the road down toward town, Lady Isobel's voice rang out loudly, "Guards! After him. Bring me that slave!"

None of the guards were even outside yet. They were probably helping the servants fight the fire. Connor ran hard, but as he passed the manor's main entrance, Hamish stepped into the door.

"What's going on?"

Not slowing, Connor shouted, "Get back. Go take care of Aileen."

"She's fine."

"Just go. And if anyone asks you, just tell them it was all my fault."

He did not wait for an answer, but poured on the speed and sprinted down the long road toward Alasdair. He had to get home. His parents would know what to do.

In the distance, he could see a crowd of people pouring out through the upper gate and running toward him. The sight slowed him for a second.

How could they know he was a fugitive? And worse, why would they be so eager to help Lady Isobel?

Then the truth dawned on him and he glanced back. A dense column of smoke rose from the manor house. The townsfolk were responding to the threat of fire.

As Connor neared, people started calling out questions. Connor shouted, "The kitchen's on fire. They need help."

He pushed past the first ranks of villagers without slowing, and then caught sight of his parents in the press. A wave of relief washed through him and he ran to them.

"Connor, you're a mess, what happened?" Lilias asked.

"Is the fire bad?" Hendry asked at the same time.

"Never mind the fire," Connor said and drew them aside. A few people glanced their way, but no one stopped to listen.

"What's happened, son?" Hendry asked.

"Hamish and I sort of broke the oven."

When he paused, his father said, "That's not everything is it?"

Connor shook his head, took a deep breath, and added in a rush: "We kind of set fire to the kitchen and burned Lady Isobel."

"You didn't!" Lilias exclaimed.

"We didn't mean to, it just sort of all happened."

"I bet she's angrier than a grounded pedra," Hendry said.

"Worse. She named me Daor."

His parents paled at the news, and Lilias snarled, "That black-hearted pedra spawn."

"Watch your language, love," Hendry said out of habit as he glanced back toward the manor. "This is serious."

"She wants to lock me up," Connor continued. "What am I going to do?"

"For now, find a place to hide," Hendry said. "Soldiers coming."

Connor followed his gaze and noticed two of Lord Gavin's soldiers rushing down the hill toward them. A third appeared behind, mounted on a draft horse.

He turned to run, and his mother said, "Not at the house. They'll be sure to check there first."

"Don't worry," he shouted over his shoulder as he bolted for the gate. "They'll never find me."

"Wait until dark," Hendry called after him.

Connor did not bother to reply. He raced through the gate and darted to the right so the wall concealed him from the guards' view.

He threaded his way through Alasdair fast. The streets were all but empty, with every able-bodied hand already running to help fight the fire. Everyone else was still up at the quarry or down at the Powder House.

Laid out in a grid pattern, the streets of Alasdair would make it all too easy for the guards to sweep the town looking for him. Connor moved two streets to the right and then turned left down a main cross street.

As he ran, he considered his options. Several possible hiding places came to mind. As children, he and his friends had played find-the-devil and many other games that forced them to find all the best hiding spots. He doubted the guards knew the town half as well.

His best bet was the flood-under passage, but it lay on the downriver side of town, and the clatter of hooves on granite roads declared that the mounted soldier had reached Alasdair. So he bolted down a narrow alley between two shops, shimmied over an aged woodshed that would collapse if it were ever fully emptied, and climbed through a dust-covered window in the back wall of a maintenance barn behind the town council offices. The window was supposed to be locked, but the lock had broken years ago.

Inside, Connor moved slowly, clambering along one of the shelves, breathing shallow. This building was used only sparingly, and housed among other things, the town's store of pumice dust, which was used in the quarrying process. A fine layer of the light but gritty powder coated everything. A quick step and a deep breath almost guaranteed a coughing fit, while a careless step would leave telltale footprints.

Protected in this safe haven, he relaxed. He'd hidden here with great success many times. On the other hand, Hamish had only tried it once. He'd ended up sucking on a rock coated with pumice and coughed for ten minutes straight.

The interior was one long, open room lined with sturdy shelves that held tools, boxes of spare parts, and heavy barrels of pumice. Connor wedged himself into an open space on one shelf next to a moldy roll of burlap.

Men's voices sounded outside a moment later, and Connor silently shifted along the shelves to the front wall, where he peeked through the tiny, grime-crusted window set above the door. He could just make out the dim forms of two of the guards, but could not hear what they said. He crouched lower even though he knew they could not see him.

Connor stepped to the left, and his foot slipped on a box of hammer handles. He lurched to one side and barely caught himself, while the box tumbled off the shelf and struck the floor with a loud crash. Flying hammer handles made a thunderous din.

Connor's heart nearly stopped at the sound. The guards would have to be raging drunk and sitting on each other's heads to not hear that. Thinking fast, he stomped hard on the shelf, and it splintered under the blow, tumbling Connor to the floor with a crash.

For a second he lay amid the scattered handles. The guards' voices drew closer, as he had expected. Hopefully the sound of the shelf crashing blended in with the echoes of the fallen box.

The outer door rattled, and Connor quietly crawled along the lowest shelf toward the far window where he'd entered.

The door was always padlocked, and he doubted the guards had a key. While they fiddled with it, he could escape out the back.

Just as he was about to climb up onto a barrel of pumice dust under the window, one of the guards spoke just outside. "Aye, there's a window over here. I'll check."

Connor pried open the lid of the barrel that was only about a third full. Outside, the guard grunted loudly as he tried to climb up to the window. Connor prayed that the rickety woodshed would finally collapse, but it held.

He slipped into the barrel and squatted down. It was a tight fit, and he wiggled his feet deep into the pumice to gain the extra two inches he needed to squeeze his head in.

Before he eased the lid back into place, he scanned the room. He'd left some tracks near the hammers, but those would be easy to miss without close inspection. The smudges he'd made crawling on the shelves would be all but impossible to see from the window.

He tried to hold his breath as he eased the lid back into place. Not that he could breathe much, rolled into a ball like one of fat Neasa's Sogail pastries. If he coughed, the guards would have him.

"Empty," a voice called out. "Looks like a shelf gave way."

A low grumbling that sounded a lot like a curse was the only answer. Connor focused on breathing just enough to stay conscious. His face was pressed down onto his knees, and it felt like he'd picked up a splinter in his backside during the squirm into the barrel.

Connor closed his eyes and prayed the soldiers would leave soon, but he didn't dare climb out of the box for half an hour.

CHAPTER 9

onnor stopped in the shadows near his home to wait and watch, invisible in the deep shadows of twilight. He'd beaten most of the pumice out of his clothing, which of course set off a five minute coughing fit, but he'd had no choice. The light gray powder glowed in the dim light.

Then again, maybe it didn't matter. The streets were unusually empty as most townsfolk were gathered in the town square enjoying the pre-Sogail celebration that had become as much a part of the festivities as the holiday itself.

He waited for ten long minutes before sneaking up to the back door of the house. He slipped inside and crossed the storage room where spare tools, boots, and outer clothing were stored neatly on shelves or pegs. He listened for another minute, but heard no voices he did not recognize.

His mother, who stood kneading bread dough, caught sight of him as soon as he stepped into the kitchen. She handed baby Fiona to Blair, who nearly rivaled Connor's size at ten. He would rival their father's stature, and carried on his still-too-narrow shoulders the weight of the family's hopes for a son to take up the Ashlar hammer.

"Oh, Connor," Lilias said and enveloped him in her arms. Connor leaned into her embrace, and the tension that had knotted his insides all afternoon eased.

"Glad you're back, Connor," said Blair before leaving the kitchen. His voice drifted back to them from the family room. "Dad, Connor's home."

Connor expected his mother to release him so they could join the rest of the family, but instead, his father came into the kitchen and spoke over his shoulder, "Blair, see the other children upstairs."

His father then turned to Connor and, with hands on hips, said, "You've struck a fault line, sure as daylight, son."

"I know, dad. It's terrible."

Lilias held him at arm's length. "You didn't really try to kill Lady Isobel, did you?"

"No," he assured them. "Though she deserved it."

Hendry shook his head slowly, and chuckled, "I've never seen her in such a state. Serves her right."

Lilias covered her mouth with her hand to hide her own smile, and then said sternly, "Hendry, this is serious."

"Did you get the fire out?" Connor asked.

Hendry grunted. "Kitchen's destroyed, but we kept it from spreading. Lady Isobel swore you tried to kill her, but Aileen and Hendry both said they saw the oven break."

Connor nodded. "That's the truth."

"How did it happen?"

He shrugged. "I can't explain it."

"Did the oven really fly?" Lilias asked.

Connor couldn't suppress a grin. "Aye, it flew, with me lying on top." He told them about the experience, although he left out the part where Hamish tampered with the oven. He did not understand what Hamish did, and refused to tell it wrong.

When he told them how he Curse-punched the oven, they shared a worried glance. "Oh, Connor, why couldn't you have waited just one more day?" Lilias said sadly.

"That blasted oven would've killed us both."

"You did the right thing," Hendry said. "But how does it work, that Curse-punch?"

"Hendry," Lilias warned.

"I just …"

"No. Not until he's got Patronage."

Connor had yearned for years to talk with someone about his Curse, but his parents were so focused on keeping it secret, they never wanted to explore it. For once, he was relieved.

The Curse had grown in strength while he crouched in the pumice barrel, but something was wrong. Usually it itched along his arms and, as it grew in strength, up into his torso, but now it felt more like little bubbles flitting around under his skin.

He'd never used the Curse twice in one day before, and worried he might have broken it somehow. As much as he hated the Curse, despite how it prevented him from living a normal life, despite how it dragged him down to misery, it had always been a part of his life. He understood how to live with it.

Now, if he'd broken it, who knew what might happen?

"Lady Isobel won't let me go to the Sogail. I'll have to petition the Curse Finders tonight."

Hendry said, "That's the problem son, they're late."

"They can't be late, not this year."

This can't be happening.

They had to come, had to take him down to Merkland after the Sogail, take him to High Lord Dougal so he could receive patronage and begin the life of a Guardian.

"It might be for the best," Hendry said.

"What?" He couldn't believe his ears. If he failed to obtain Patronage before his sixteenth age-day, he'd be condemned. Executed before the Curse could rage out of control and hurt someone.

Could his father really think it best that he die?

"Think about it, son," Lilias said. "We've been talking while we waited for you. Lady Isobel wants you taken Daor. She will try to interfere with Patronage."

"But she's lying!"

"It doesn't matter. Lord Gavin won't overrule her, so there is nothing anyone can do."

"We don't know what would happen," Hendry added. "The Curse Finders might not be allowed to take a Daor for Patronage."

"That's why I have to find them tonight."

Hendry shook his head. "No, that's why you have to leave for Merkland and petition High Lord Dougal in person."

The words rang through Connor like an icy wind.

Leave Alasdair tonight, before the Sogail?

Suddenly the world felt immense. He'd always known he'd be taken to Merkland once he revealed his Curse, but that was supposed to be after the Sogail, after another night with his family.

Lilias slipped an arm around his waist. "Oh, my boy, I wish it could be different, but your father's right."

Connor had never traveled all the way to Merkland, although he'd often dreamed of it. Merkland was a full day's hike down River Road, and then only if one moved fast. He'd have to travel the unfamiliar road at night.

"Run along upstairs and change into your hunting leathers," Hendry said. "And say goodbye to your siblings. We have a few things packed for you."

The next ten minutes passed in a blur for Connor. None of his siblings knew anything about his Curse, so all he could tell them was that he was leaving on a journey.

Blair took the news stolidly, like he did most things. He was a calm, level-headed kid, slow to anger. Connor loved to tease him, to test the limits of his patience.

When would he get a chance to tease his brother again?

His younger siblings didn't really understand what was happening, so he forced a smile and promised to bring them something when he returned. Wallace, the four year-old, clapped his hands and said, "Bring me a baby pedra."

Down in the kitchen, his mother handed him a pack with spare clothing and food, while his father held out his spare bow and a small pouch of coins.

"Spend them carefully, and they should last until you are in the high lord's service."

Connor thanked them and hugged them, fighting back tears.

"Please be careful, son," Lilias said.

"Hurry now," Hendry said, "or you'll miss your ride."

Connor paused. "What ride?"

Hendry winked. "We finished the high lord's order late today, although we still had to send a few unfinished blocks to make the quota. The bargeman is having some trouble with the rudder. I expect he'll have it fixed soon. Hurry, and make sure no one sees you."

Connor hugged them again and headed out into the night, telling himself that his family was safe and he was embarking on a great adventure. It sounded better when he thought of it that way.

He silently thanked his father. He'd been more than a little worried about following the long road to Merkland alone through the night. This way, he'd arrive in Merkland by morning for sure.

As he slipped through town, careful to stay in the deepest shadows to remain unseen, a surge of excitement replaced the lingering sadness. He was really doing it, really leaving for Merkland. He'd explored the mountains for many miles, but hadn't ventured far downriver. The farmlands to the south weren't all that interesting, although he and Hamish often visited the hidden cave they had discovered three miles downriver. They'd often pretended to be bandits, with the cave their secret hideout. Tonight he'd journey far beyond everything familiar.

He reached the blocking yard unseen, and paused when he caught sight of the loch and the barge still tied to the pier.

Keith, the foreman, appeared out of the Powder House and shouted, "Stones take it, man, aren't you gone yet?"

The bargeman, who had been crouched over the rudder under a hanging lantern, stood and stretched his back. "Just about finished."

"Good. Sign the shipping statement and then be off with you."

The two men disappeared into the Powder House. With his heart in his throat, Connor raced for the stone pier and leaped aboard the barge. He slipped to the bow, past stacks of precious powdered granite in canvas sacks. There he pushed aside a couple bags from the last stack to make a little nest for himself. He slipped down into the hole and arranged the sacks so that no one would see him without close inspection.

A moment later, the bargeman stepped aboard, and the boat began to move. It rocked softly, with water slapping against the bow, as the bargeman plied the long oar at the stern and slowly propelled the boat across the loch and into the current of Lower Wick.

Connor huddled down in his dark hiding place that smelled of old canvas and granite dust, and couldn't help but think about the Sogail.

Why couldn't he have just controlled the Curse one more day? If he hadn't used it …

He'd be dead. As bad as things were, that was worse. Probably.

As the boat floated downriver, Connor focused on the Sogail, trying to bring it to life in his mind since he wouldn't see it in person.

The entire day would be dedicated to the festivities. Lord Gavin would provide mountains of food, and this year they'd have plenty of fresh meat thanks to Connor's hunting. He smiled to think of everyone gawking at the torc's head, which would hopefully be displayed in a place of honor.

All morning there would be contests and games to showcase the townsfolk's devotion to Lord Gavin, who would then grant the Teagair. Connor doubted anyone else would be denied possession of their children and made Daor.

It was Age-Day. Everyone born in the same year celebrated the same age day. Connor, Hamish, Stuart, Jean, and even Moira were all turning sixteen. They'd celebrate the Saorsa, their transition to near-adults. Lord Gavin would assign the others their vocations.

Connor's friends' formal names would change from Saor-Linn to Leigeil-Linn. When they eventually married, they'd be able to drop the Leigeil and be full adult Linn.

He would miss all that, but he tried to imagine the wonders of the Sogail in Merkland. He'd never been anywhere beside Alasdair, so it was hard. Surely Merkland would be wondrous, although he doubted anyone could sing as well as Jean.

Just before the feast tomorrow, Jean and Moira would sing the Sogail Oran and be recognized as eligible maids. Jean sang like an angel. Connor could listen all day.

After the feasting and whatever gift Lord Gavin announced would come the dancing, which would last through the night. Jean would be free to be courted. Moira too, although not by any of the locals.

Connor snuggled down lower into his tight hiding spot as the evening chill deepened, and imagined himself dancing with Jean, holding her as she twirled, her hair flying around her head while she laughed. He imagined really kissing her for the first time.

For long minutes, Connor forgot where he was, a little smile on his lips. He made a point not to think about Jean dancing with Stuart. Hopefully she'd slap him if he tried to steal a kiss.

Connor's Sogail would be so different. He knew little about the life of a Guardian, but he decided that it would be a life of adventure.

As he tried to imagine all the great things he'd do as a Guardian of the Realm, the gentle rocking of the barge, coupled with his own exhaustion, dragged him down to sleep.

CHAPTER 10

he barge lurched to a sudden, jarring stop. Connor pitched forward and three heavy sacks of granite powder rolled onto his back, nearly suffocating him. He struggled against the heavy sacks, but was so badly tangled he could not get enough leverage to escape.

What could have happened? Did the bargeman fall asleep and run the boat aground? If he had, he'd be grouted for sure.

Somewhere behind him, the bargeman started cursing.

A deep voice with a harsh, guttural accent called out from somewhere nearby, "Wait, boat man. We ask question."

Connor stopped struggling. The voice came from somewhere to the front, beyond the bow. Maybe the bargeman really did run the boat aground.

In the rear of the boat, the bargeman exclaimed, "Grandurians!"

Two quick footsteps sounded on the heavy wooden planks of the boat followed by a big splash in the river. Little splashes sounded in quick succession, growing farther away.

"Wait! We no harm to you," shouted the deep voice.

More footsteps on the boat, close beside where Connor lay pinned.

"That could have gone better," said a girl's voice. It sounded pleasant, with only a trace of accent.

The bargeman dove into the river to get away.

No matter how pleasant that girl sounded, he decided to lie still and wait until they left. Almost as soon as the thought formed, someone stepped on one of the sacks pinning Connor down, forcing an unwilling groan from his lips.

"Hey, someone's in here," the girl called out.

Someone pulled the heavy sacks aside and hauled Connor to his feet. Deep night covered the land, but a full moon hung in the sky, bathing the scene in a pale glow. The smooth waters of the Lower Wick reflected that glow from both sides of the barge.

Both sides? The boat floated far out into the river, unmoving, so how had the intruders gotten on board?

The man who held Connor's arms wore black armor that covered him like a dark shadow. Only his pale face topped with close-cropped blond hair was clearly visible. Worse, he wore a sword belted to his waist.

That could not be good. Only Lord Gavin's guards wore swords in Alasdair, although Connor had never seen them actually draw the weapons in anger. His big captor radiated power and danger in a way Lord Gavin's guards never could.

He must be some kind of soldier from downriver.

Beside the big soldier stood the girl. She looked young, close to Connor's age, and stood half a head shorter. She regarded him with big blue eyes that seemed to glow in the moonlight. She wasn't beautiful like Jean, but still cute. Her tiny button nose, shoulder length hair, and the inquisitive tilt to her head triggered a smile.

She returned the smile. "Why were you hiding down there?"

Connor tried to come up with a plausible explanation, but the single word the bargeman shouted before jumping from the boat rang through his mind and blanked out all thought.

Grandurians. Even in the remote town of Alasdair he'd heard horror stories of Grandurians. Once part of Obrion, Granadure had split away hundreds of years ago and, ever since, had fought to destroy Obrion. Those captured by Grandurians were never seen again.

The town of Alasdair actually lay close to the border with Granadure, but was protected by the impassable Maclachlan Mountains. The little Connor knew of their neighbors to the north was enough to set him shaking all the way down to his toes.

His mind whirled. He would have sworn by the Tallan's Eye that things could not have gotten worse. Good thing he hadn't. He didn't need that extra curse on his head. He instinctively feared the big soldier, but could the girl really be all that dangerous?

Better not to find out. Connor lunged for the edge of the barge in an attempt to leap into the river like the bargeman had, but the soldier held his arms securely.

"Calm down," the girl said. "We won't hurt you."

"No hurt yet," the big soldier said. He propelled Connor to the bow of the boat and pushed him off the edge.

Instead of falling into the river, he stumbled onto a solid earthen wall a full span across that stretched to the bank. That explained how they had reached the barge, but he'd never heard of an earthen wall blocking the river. The bargeman would have known about it.

As Connor traversed the wall toward shore, he glanced around. In the dim light of the moon, he didn't recognize any landmarks, and the mountains looked wrong. They must have drifted far south, beyond the lands he knew. That only made the situation more terrifying.

The night was cool, with a light breeze that smelled of river and nearby wheat fields. Frogs croaked along the bank, and an owl hooted nearby.

When they reached the shore, Connor again tried to bolt, but the soldier held him fast. The girl came up beside him and put a gentle hand on his arm. "I said we won't hurt you."

Her little accent was so cute, he found it hard to doubt her. "Then why are you holding me prisoner?"

She gestured at the soldier, and he released Connor and stepped back a pace. Connor had to fight the urge to flee.

The girl pushed her dark blond hair out of her face and said a little sheepishly, "We need directions."

"Directions where?"

She looked at her feet for a second, and said softly, "Home. We're lost. We need to return to Granadure."

"Seriously?" Connor looked from her to the big soldier and tried to relate this situation to all the stories Bruce had told of Grandurians. None of them ever mentioned these terrifying killers had a bad sense of direction.

How could a pair of Grandurians end up here anyway?

The girl met his gaze again. She looked so earnest, Connor squashed the urge to laugh. Instead he pointed downriver and said, "Go that way to Merkland. I've heard there's a pass near there to Granadure."

"We can't go that way."

"That's the only way I've ever heard about. There aren't any passes upriver. There's nothing there but mountains and Alasdair."

"Alasdair?"

Connor shrugged. "A small town. Nothing there but the quarry."

The two Grandurians shared a look and the girl's eyes lit up with interest. "What kind of quarry?"

Idiot.

He shouldn't have said anything about it. Lord Gavin had several guards, but this one soldier could probably kill them all. Connor looked around for a way to escape, but the girl stood in front of him, and the only open avenue was back to the river and that strange earth wall.

"What's your name, boy?"

Boy? He was celebrating the Saorsa tomorrow. He wasn't a boy. She didn't look any older.

"Connor. What's yours, girl?"

She smiled at the challenge in his tone and made a little curtsy. "I'm Verena."

Only then did Connor realize she wasn't wearing a dress like every girl he knew. She dressed in dark pants with a black leather vest over a dark blouse. He lacked sufficient light to see the details, but just knowing she dressed more like a soldier than a normal girl drove home the fact that they were Grandurians, not locals. He was surprised to find the knowledge fascinated him as much as it scared him.

"Look, Connor," the soldier said in his thick accent that made his name sound foreign and frightening, "We want only back our home." With a rueful grin, he added, "We no should be here. Be much trouble if we find."

Verena gave a little laugh and said, "You sound like a little kid, Erich. Your Obrioner is terrible."

Erich scowled. "No much have time practice."

She laughed again. "Just stop. No one's going to take us seriously with you talking like that."

Erich's hand dropped to the hilt of his sword. "Take serious when … spank with big knife."

Verena giggled and Connor asked, "You spank people with your swords?"

Erich frowned. "Word no right." He mimicked a stabbing motion.

"You meant stabbing with your sword."

Erich nodded. "Yes. Stab. Much kill. Take serious."

Verena wiped her eyes. "Just stand guard and look tough. Let me do the talking."

She drew Connor aside a pace and leaned close. She smelled like the mountains. "Connor, I really need your help. There has to be a way across the mountains. If you can show us, we'll leave and no one has to get hurt."

"What makes you think I'd know another way?"

She glanced meaningfully down at his hunting leathers. "You hunt. You know."

Connor frowned and looked away.

How could she know?

No one, not even his family, knew of the game trail he'd found around the supposedly impassable face of Mount Ingram not a month ago. He'd followed the tiny track across the steep slope where a single miss-step would have plunged him three thousand feet to his death. He'd turned back after reaching a wide plateau that offered ready access down to the lower slopes on the Grandurian side.

He could show Verena the way. Would she leave? Erich scared him, but surely she wasn't any kind of a threat.

Then again, once they knew the way, would they kill him and bring more raiders back across the border to attack the town? Every story he'd ever heard about the Grandurians made him suspect the worst.

He looked into her huge blue eyes, and found that he could not believe the stories applied to her. He could show her, but he needed to race for Merkland. His life would be forfeit if he failed to secure Patronage by the end of the Sogail. But how could he leave two Grandurians wandering around alone? They might kill someone.

As he struggled to decide, he turned and looked out over the river. His eyes fell on the odd earthen wall that the barge had crashed into. Realization struck and he couldn't help but ask, "You made that wall, didn't you?"

Verena nodded.

"How?"

"I show you," she said excitedly, her eyes glowing brighter. She said to Erich, "Secure the boat first."

He crossed to the barge and grabbed a towline. With some effort, he turned the heavy boat and towed it back to shore. Verena stooped and picked up a small rock at the point where the wall met the shore.

The earthen wall collapsed. Water splashed high as the river flooded into the space where the wall had stood. It was simply gone. Connor retreated a step from the river and stared in amazement.

At the edge of the water, Erich stooped and grabbed hold of the heavy crossbeam set across the bow of the boat. He blew out a breath and with a grunt, heaved. The muscles of his neck stood out in sharp detail, and his arms and shoulders swelled with the effort.

He lifted the boat. The entire front end of the barge, which was still stacked with heavy sacks of granite powder, came clear of the water. Erich's legs sank in the mud of the bank, but he did not seem hindered by that or by the incredible weight. With short, careful steps, he dragged the barge high up the bank. There he sagged against the bow as if completely exhausted.

Connor gaped. Erich looked tough, but Connor had grown up surrounded by men as tough as the granite they quarried. Not even the three strongest men in Alasdair together could have lifted that barge.

The stories of the Grandurians hadn't said anything about their incredible strength. As Erich pushed himself away from the barge, a fresh shiver of fear rolled down Connor's spine. This man could crush him if he chose.

Beside him, Verena stood bouncing the rock on her palm. "I love watching him do stuff like that."

"How is it possible?"

"I am Rumbler, that how," Erich said.

Before Connor could ask another question, Verena held up the stone and said, "Slate, touched by a Builder. I call it a Wallstone."

"A Wallstone?" Connor repeated softly, eyes glued to the little rock. He couldn't comprehend how it worked, but the wonder of it pushed aside some of his fear.

"Lady," Erich hissed. "No talk about this."

Verena huffed, "It's my rock. I'll talk about it with whomever I choose." She held it to her ear and shook it, as if she could hear some sound it made. "This has power for one, maybe two more walls." She extended it to Connor. "You show us how to cross the mountain, and I'll give it to you."

Connor took the rounded rock and ran his hands across the smooth, dark green slate. It looked completely unremarkable, barely filling his palm. He stared from it to the grounded barge. These people were foreign in so much more than their nationality.

"How did you get here?" he dared ask.

"It's a long story."

"I love stories."

"Later," Erich growled. "Need go home."

"He's right," Verena said. "All that matters is getting home before something bad happens."

Was that a threat? What would they do if he refused? Would they kill him and look for another victim? Would they attack Alasdair and kill his family?

He couldn't risk it.

"I'm heading for Merkland," he offered. "I could take you there and help you find the pass to Granadure."

Erich hissed when he mentioned Merkland, and Verena shook her head. "I told you, we can't go that way."

"Much fight there," Erich said, gripping the hilt of his sword. "Much kill."

"We don't want any trouble," Verena added.

Connor retreated a step from the hulking soldier and mental images of the powerful man wreaking terrible destruction in Merkland. High Lord Dougal's fighting men lived there, but could they stand against so powerful a foe?

The Curse Hunters had to arrive in Alasdair for the Sogail. He'd have to risk the attempt to petition them when Lady Isobel wasn't around. He could get these Grandurians out of Obrion, and still secure Patronage.

It's what a Guardian would do.

Connor made his decision. "I know a way around Mount Ingram. I'll show you."

"Done." Verena gave a little clap of excitement. "I knew you could help us." Then she added, "Be careful with that stone. When you drop it, it'll make a wall."

Connor tucked it into his belt pouch. "Thanks."

"Come." Verena took his arm and led the way into the pine trees lining the west bank of the river, and turned downriver. Erich trailed close behind Connor.

"Hold on, the path is upriver."

"I know, silly. We have to fetch the others first."

"Others?"

Of course there would be others. It made no sense for just two Grandurians to wander all this way. But how many others? How'd they get lost in the first place? What were they doing way out here?

They followed a narrow trail a couple hundred yards downriver while Connor's doubts grew. He liked walking so close to Verena, but she was Grandurian, so maybe she wasn't as nice as she pretended. Firelight shone in the darkness through the trees, and a moment later, Verena led them into a clearing with a modest campfire around which sat more than a dozen men, and a couple of women.

Most of the men were soldiers wearing chainmail coats painted black over black leather jerkins, with swords or axes swinging from their belts.

It's a war party, Connor realized. *What have I gotten myself into?*

He stopped in his tracks, but Erich propelled him forward with one hand in the center of his back. There was no going back, so Connor strode into the firelight beside Verena with feigned confidence.

Everyone turned to stare. The soldiers could have all passed for brothers. They were tall, broad-shouldered, with wide, rugged faces, close-cropped blond hair and blue eyes. They watched Connor with unreadable expressions.

On one side of the fire, a woman wearing a brown linen dress sat beside a whip-thin fellow with a pinched face. He bounced slightly up and down as he sat. Another woman, wearing a long, blue dress, stood off to one side of the group in the deeper shadows farther from the fir. She wore her black hair pulled back, and her eyes glittered with an inner fire as she looked at him.

Erich moved up beside Connor and said something loudly in a harsh, guttural tongue. A tall, shapely woman rose and called out something in reply and laughed. Her voice was rich and smooth. She wore her thick, blond hair tied in a braid that fell to her waist, and she dressed in black leathers like Erich. They looked a lot alike, and had to be siblings.

Another woman rose from where she sat at the far side of the fire and drew Connor's gaze as she approached. Slender, with raven-black hair, she shared the same bright blue eyes as most of the men, and dressed in the same black leathers as Erich and his sister.

She had to be a full Linn or noble-born Meur, although Connor had no idea if the Grandurian classes were equivalent to those in Obrion. Her face was strong and she walked with confidence. Connor couldn't guess at her age. She wasn't old, but wasn't young either.

Erich saluted smartly. She nodded a reply, looked to Verena, who grinned and made a little bobbing motion that might have been some kind of curtsy, and finally turned her piercing gaze on Connor.

"What have you brought us, Verena?"

Verena, still holding Connor's arm, gave it a squeeze. "This boy is going to show us the way across the mountain."

The soldiers around the fire did not outwardly react, but tension seemed to drain from them. The thin, nervous fellow jumped to his feet, but slowly sat again at a gesture from the woman seated beside him.

The woman facing Connor smiled and extended a hand and shook with a firm grip. "Very good. What is your name, boy?"

Again with the boy?

It had to be a problem with translating from Grandurian. "Connor."

"I am Ilse, captain of this company."

Captain? She looked tiny compared to the warriors. How was it possible? Granadure must be a strange place.

"Where is this trail?" Ilse asked without preamble.

Before he could reply, the flap of a nearby tent he hadn't noticed before whipped aside and a young woman marched out, past a pair of soldiers stationed to either side. She strode into the firelight and made straight for Connor.

He stared, transfixed.

Her figure was trim, but fuller than Jean's or Verena's. Her features were delicate, with high cheekbones, finely arched brows, a small nose, and a long, graceful neck. She wore her long blond hair braided. She was clearly noble-born, and looked to be close to his age, probably Leigeil-Meur. She wore an indigo silk blouse that clung to her figure, a black skirt that extended to mid-calf, and sturdy hiking boots. She looked nothing like the other Grandurians.

She stopped barely a pace away, her eyes never leaving his face. His heart began to beat faster and his palms to sweat.

"You are a local?"

He could have listened to her rich voice all night.

"Yes, ma'am," Connor said, eager to please this lady.

"And you have promised to show these invaders how to escape our lands?"

Connor nodded slowly, but realized then how foolish he'd been to agree to anything the Grandurians wanted.

"Why would you betray me?"

CHAPTER 11

onnor couldn't imagine what to say as the young woman's hazel eyes filled with tears on the verge of flowing freely down her smooth cheeks. In that moment, she looked completely vulnerable, and he felt like he could see right into her soul. The hurt he saw there nearly broke his heart.

How could he have done such a terrible thing?

He'd had no idea agreeing to show the Grandurians a way through the mountains would hurt her so, but he cursed himself for it anyway.

Connor fell to his knees before this lady and shook his head. "No. I didn't mean it."

Verena, who had stood forgotten close beside him, snorted and said, "Oh, please."

The other woman ignored Verena, leaned forward and placed a hand on his head, as if in blessing. She slid her finger tips down along his cheek, almost in a caress. "I believe you. It was unfair of them to do this to you."

Connor could barely breathe. He wanted to nod in agreement, but didn't dare move his face with her fingers still touching his skin. His cheek seemed to burn at her touch and his heart beat so fast it was a wonder she could not hear it from where she stood over him.

"I am Shona." She glanced at Ilse and said. "I am their captive."

"Enough," Ilse said. "Very nice performance, Shona, but it changes nothing."

"We shall see." Shona gave Connor a reassuring smile and said, "Remember your allegiance."

Ilse called out in a loud voice, "Break camp. We march in five."

Everyone seemed to move at once and the camp filled with bustling soldiers. Verena gave Connor a long, thoughtful look that made him distinctly uncomfortable before she moved off.

Exactly three minutes later, the group headed upriver with Connor walking in the lead beside the captain and Verena. Shona, who walked in the middle of the group, surrounded by four watchful soldiers, filled Connor's thoughts.

He was such an idiot!

What better reason for Grandurian soldiers to be here in Obrion than to kidnap a noblewoman? He'd heard rumors of skirmishes between High Lord Dougal's soldiers and Grandurian forces, but that all seemed so far away.

What else could he have done, though? No one in these peaceful lands could stop a war party like this. If the other soldiers were half as tough as Eric, they could slaughter the entire population of Alasdair. Getting them away would be the safest course for his home town, but what of Shona?

He was still pondering the situation, trying to determine what to do, when they reached the barge that Erich had drawn up onto the bank. The group paused and Ilse asked, "What is the barge carrying?"

Connor shrugged. "Bags of powdered granite, and a few unfinished blocks."

She gaped at him for a second before shouting, "Erich! Anika! The barge."

Erich and his sister leaped aboard, and a moment later Erich called out, "Is right, Captain. Many bags. Powder much good." The soldiers of the company, who had remained stoically silent ever since Connor met them, broke into excited murmurs.

Why would a war party lost and trying to get home get so excited about granite? Sure, it was valuable, but it wasn't like they could do anything with it here.

Grandurians were weird.

"How many bags?" Ilse called.

"Twelve!"

The excited whispering grew and Ilse grinned. She placed a hand on Connor's shoulder. "This is wonderful news." She raised a hand. "Secure the powder."

Men raced to obey. In less than a minute, the dozen sacks of granite powder were carefully stacked nearby.

Erich raised one of the unfinished blocks. "What do these with?"

"Throw them overboard."

"Wait!" Connor cried. He'd watched with growing concern as they pillaged the powdered granite from the barge. He couldn't imagine what they intended to do with it, but couldn't just watch as they threw the precious stones into the river.

Ilse said, "Do not interfere."

"But why?"

"Such resources cannot be left in the hands of the enemy."

"You're the enemy," Shona snarled as she approached. Even though the two women stood almost the same height, somehow Shona made it appear as if she were looking down at Ilse. "Enjoy your ill-gotten gains. It won't matter. Your venture is doomed to failure, and you know it."

"I celebrate each victory."

"My father will eat your heart," Shona said with such calm assurance that Connor did not doubt it would happen.

Ilse shrugged. "You already promised he'd skin me alive and boil my flesh. If he gets that far, he's welcome to eat whatever he likes."

Confused, Connor looked from one to the other. It almost seemed as if they considered the capture of the granite as important as holding Shona herself. Connor's family had been cutting granite from the mountain for fourteen generations, so he knew its value better than anyone.

On the barge, Erich and Anika lifted the heavy, unprocessed granite blocks and threw them impossibly far out into the center of the river. Connor watched, awed by their strength, and devastated by the loss. As each block splashed into the murky waters, the sound struck him like a blow from his father's broken hammer.

He had to turn away, and found Shona regarding him with an unreadable expression. He gestured at the boat and managed weakly, "They're ..."

"I know," Shona said in a disgusted tone. "Those two are Petralists."

"Petralists?" he repeated, his voice cracking.

On the boat, Anika lifted a block that easily weighed more than Connor high over her head, threw her head back and laughed. Her body looked hard, perfectly sculpted, and her skin seemed to glow in the moonlight like the granite block she carried. With an almost negligent flip, she threw the block far out over the water.

Bruce's countless stories of the superhuman warriors flitted through Connor's mind. If they really were Petralists, they wouldn't need him to guide them over the mountains. They'd just fly. Connor couldn't help but grin as he thought of the wonders Bruce had shared with them.

Lady Shona had to be wrong. He was about to tell her, but her disapproving frown silenced his words. Instead, he glanced around at the soldiers, and at Ilse, who regarded him with one raised eyebrow, as if daring him to ask a question.

He couldn't resist. "Petralists? All of you?"

Shona rolled her eyes. "Of course they're not all Petralists. Even they wouldn't risk so many."

"I don't understand," Connor stammered. "Why are you here? How did you get here? What are you--"

Shona's cut him off. "They are here for only one reason: to kidnap me and drag me back to Granadure."

Connor cringed back from Shona's displeasure, berating himself for disappointing her again. Ilse was watching him with an unreadable expression on her face. "Why?" was all he could ask again.

It didn't make any sense. Why kidnap Shona? Why take such a risk?

Shona stood to her full height which was just a little shorter than his and said in a ringing voice, "I am High Lord

Dougal's eldest daughter and heir to his domain."

Verena, who had stood silent until now grunted, as if unimpressed and Shona rounded on her. "Have you realized yet your fatal mistake?"

"I hardly think you're that dangerous."

"You took the wrong branch of the river," Shona said in a conversational tone. "You're stuck out here in the mountains and my father's forces are closing in." Shona stood tall, shoulders back, the image of composed, self-assurance. "You will fail."

Captain Ilse shrugged and said, "Don't celebrate your victory before it is won, Lady Shona."

Shona smiled as if humoring a child. "You've placed your futures in the hands of a simple common Linn who's terrified out of his mind. Do you really believe he knows a way through these mountains that have stood impassable for generations?"

"I'm not that scared," Connor offered, but Shona only glared. He wanted to protest that he wasn't so common, that he was to be a Guardian, that he'd only agreed to help the Grandurians in order to spare the helpless people all around from their depredations.

He said none of that, however. Too many thoughts, too many emotions, whirled through his heart. He couldn't see clearly the best solution. Every choice he considered presented too many terrible consequences to be the right one.

"That's enough," Ilse said with a tinge of annoyance in her voice.

Shona said softly, "You and your men will all die out here."

"Time will tell." Ilse dismissed her and ordered, "Take ten bags of powder. Destroy the rest."

Shona glared. "You will regret that choice, woman."

Erich and Anika vaulted from the barge, lifted the extra bags of granite powder and carried them back to the boat. They slit the tops and dumped the powder out onto the river.

Ilse frowned as the powder spread like a white stain across the dark water and shook her head. "What a waste."

Connor fell to his knees and barely kept from being physically sick. It was worse than a waste. They were destroying weeks of hard work. They might as well be spilling the lifeblood of Alasdair onto the river.

The consequences would be dire. One shipment of granite blocks was lost twenty years ago, and the town had suffered for months. Wages were withheld, food rationed, and work quotas increased. People still whispered of those dark days when the curse of the Tallan hung over the valley.

The casual barbarity of these invaders reminded him why people feared them. He yearned for Shona's prediction to prove true, for High Lord Dougal's forces to kill them all.

Then he realized, with icy dread, they'd kill him too for agreeing to help the invaders. He wanted to beat himself with a stick. How could he be so stupid as to believe a bunch of Grandurians? He'd agreed to help the nation's enemies kidnap his own High Lord's daughter. He glanced at Verena, who stood a little to one side, watching the Petralists work. She'd lied to him.

Then it all made sense. Of course they couldn't go south back down to Merkland to find the pass to Granadure. They'd just come from there, bearing Shona away prisoner with High Lord Dougal's forces in pursuit. Downriver meant death.

Soldiers hoisted the heavy bags of granite powder onto their shoulders, apparently planning to carry them the long miles to the border. That casual acceptance of such a heavy load revealed much about them. The troop resumed their march upriver with Connor plodding along with leaden feet.

How could I have messed things up so badly?

CHAPTER 12

They marched on through the night, pausing only briefly to rest. Connor did not speak with anyone as he wrestled with what to do. If High Lord Dougal caught them, would he kill Connor outright or just withhold Patronage, which would result in the same thing? If he didn't catch them, Shona would be taken to Granadure to suffer … something, and Connor would never secure Patronage.

Either way, his life was forfeit.

The unfairness of it enraged him. He would not accept that fate. He'd worked too hard, suffered too long with the Curse for everything to end this way.

He had to find a solution.

After a time, Captain Ilse stopped in an open stretch of shoreline and looked out over the river. Connor followed her gaze, and gasped.

A man was walking on the water.

The moon had nearly set so very little light remained, but even after Connor blinked a couple of times to make sure he wasn't dreaming, there could be no mistake. A man rounded the last bend downriver, approaching upriver with fluid movements, as if skating on the surface of the gently flowing river.

Ilse watched the man approach with a hint of a smile. The man skated upriver to the shore and stepped onto dry land. His hair was dark and he wore loose-fitting trousers and tunic over his lanky frame. A sword and long dagger swung at his side.

He stopped before Captain Ilse with a smile and made an extravagant bow that ended in a salute. Her voice held a hint of humor in it as she said, "Report."

"No sign of pursuit, Captain. They have gained no ground."

The tiniest of frowns crossed Shona's face, but quickly disappeared.

"Very well."

The man turned to Connor, who still stared open-mouthed, and laughed. "What's the matter, kid? Never seen a Water Moccasin before?" He spoke with only a hint of an accent.

Connor shook his head, not trusting his voice. His world had been shaken too much tonight already. Bruce had shared many wondrous stories about Petralists, but none included walking on water.

"Want to try?" the man asked, holding up a small flask. He gave it an absent flick, the exact same gesture some of the old timers used on their home-made ales to ensure the chunks didn't settle to the bottom.

Connor shook his head. "Why don't you just turn into a fish? Wouldn't that be faster?"

The man laughed. "Better yet, why don't we just fly over the mountains?"

Connor nodded eagerly. "You really can do that?"

"No, son. Where did you get such ideas?" The rest of the company laughed along with him.

Connor looked around, embarrassed. Only Shona and Verena didn't laugh, although Verena was grinning. Shona regarded him with a thoughtful, almost compassionate look. To have such a great lady see everyone laughing at him was too much.

"Bruce told me all about you Petralists!"

"And who is this wise mentor of yours?" The Water Moccasin asked.

"Lord Gavin's … guard," Connor said, realizing even as he said it how ridiculous he sounded. A fresh wave of laughter erupted from the group.

The Water Moccasin laughed the loudest. Finally he wiped his eyes and clapped Connor on the shoulder. "I needed that. I like you, boy. It is refreshing to meet someone so unconcerned with reality."

"Stop teasing our guide, Kilian," Ilse said through her own smile. "He's had a rough night."

Kilian shrugged. "Well, I can't tease you. None of you Rumblers will go near the water."

"You'll sink as fast as the rest of us when the time comes," Ilse said.

"But not tonight."

Connor studied the man. Such an ability must be amazing, but why laugh at his suggestion? Either they were lying to protect their abilities, or Bruce's stories were wrong. The thought was disturbing. If he couldn't trust what he'd learned from Bruce, he knew even less than he'd thought.

They thought him a fool, a simpleton. What did they know? They had no idea what he'd suffered.

Before he could formulate an angry reply, Shona spoke. "You do this lad a disservice. You should be laughing at yourselves."

"Why so?" Ilse asked.

"You call him fool and yet you follow him into the mountains, trusting your lives to his word. Who then is the fool?"

"Don't be too eager for us to fail," Ilse said. "You forget that should we find ourselves trapped, your usefulness might well run out."

Shona tossed her long braid over one shoulder. "You can't kill me. I am the only shield left to you against my father's wrath."

Kilian stalked forward, his face a mask of rage. "Pray, girl, that your father remains far from us, or I will boil his heart in his own blood for his crimes."

Shona met his angry glare with calm assurance. "We shall see who does what, lord water spider."

Kilian spat a curse in Grandurian and stalked back to the water. Without slowing, he strode out onto the surface, his steps changing to long, graceful slides as if he moved on a sheet of ice. In a moment the gloom swallowed him.

"Move out," Ilse said, and a now-somber group marched upriver again.

As they walked, Connor wondered, was he a fool for leading them out of Obrion, or for trusting them to let him go afterward?

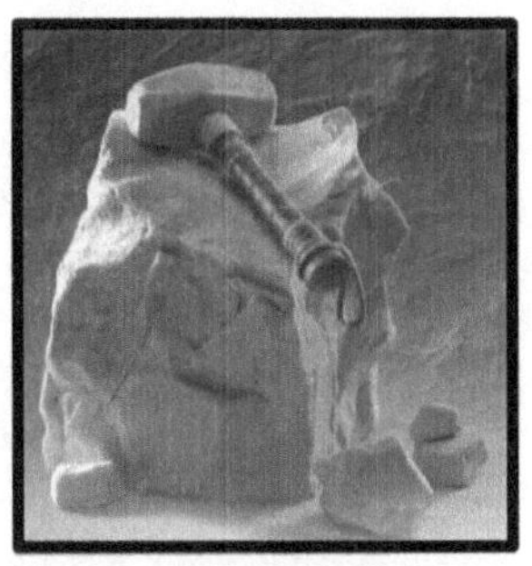

CHAPTER 13

ear dawn, Verena trailed Captain Ilse into a small clearing dotted with young trees, and sank gratefully onto a fallen log when the captain signaled the group to halt.

They started a small fire and set up Lady Shona's tent. As the group ate, Verena approached Connor and offered to share her rations of dried meat and biscuits.

As he chomped angrily on the food, she studied him. This boy intrigued her. He appeared earnest, if surprisingly ignorant of Petralists. In Granadure, everyone knew about Petralists, at least about the powers manifest in the lowest threshold, but it seemed here that knowledge had all but disappeared. Or perhaps it had been snuffed out?

After all, they cursed the Tallan. What else might be true of the barbarians?

Lady Shona fit the mental image of selfish, evil Obrioners Verena had carried with her across the border. Surely High Lord Dougal would be an uncultured brute, considering the crimes he'd committed.

But Connor challenged the stereotype, and the honest goodness she sensed in him drew her to speak.

"Connor, please try to understand. We don't want to hurt anyone."

Connor nearly choked, and spat out the food he'd been trying to swallow. "How can you say that?"

"It's true," she insisted, startled to feel herself growing defensive.

Connor barked a laugh. "You kidnap Lady Shona, and then me. You stole all that granite from the barge. Do you have any idea how long it's going to take us to replace it?"

She hadn't really considered the impact to the locals, but then the rest of his meaning registered. "So, the Alasdair quarry you mentioned is the source of the granite?"

"Forget about the quarry. You've done enough damage. If you didn't want to hurt anyone, why'd you come here?"

"Because High Lord Dougal hurt us first," she snarled. Just thinking about it set her fingers itching to dip into her satchel for one of her stones.

She had pushed the far limits of the possible through her Builder experiments, and several possible tortures immediately came to mind. She'd love nothing better than to try them all on the high lord.

"What did he do?"

Verena wasn't sure where to start, nor how much he would believe, nor how much she could trust him. It surprised her how much she wanted to think well of Connor, but how could an Obrioner, one of the high lord's own subjects, prove trustworthy?

Before she could formulate a response, Captain Ilse called her to the fire. She couldn't just drop the conversation, so she whispered, "We just want to make things right. I'll tell you more later."

As most of them settled to the ground to get some sleep, the captain called out, "Purge powers. We can't afford to get sloppy."

Erich and Anika groaned where they sat close together near the fire. Each of them closed their eyes as if concentrating, and cupped their hands over their hearts. After a few seconds, they opened their eyes, brushed their hands on their leather trousers, and settled back down to sleep.

Verena found the ritual fascinating. As Captain Ilse and the other Petralists completed their own purging, Verena decided when they returned to Granadure, she'd ask one of them for a sample of the lamacal, the powder they brushed away that was the result of their purging. What might it taste like?

The Longseer, with her lovely, glittering eyes spoke in Grandurian, "Shall I keep watch?"

After a moment's consideration, Ilse replied, "No. Get some sleep. We may need you tomorrow."

Connor approached the fire. "What are they doing?"

Verena smiled warmly to help put him at ease. She wanted to continue their conversation, explore what it meant to be a commoner in this barbaric country. "Purging."

"Looked to me like you were praying to the Tallan," Shona said.

Captain Ilse said, "The Tallan is not one we pray to, only one we strive to emulate."

"You admit following the devil?" Connor looked horrified.

"He's no devil," Verena snapped, amazed to find the rumors true. These people really had altered history almost beyond recognition.

"Right, and you don't want to hurt anyone," he snapped before moving away from the fire to lay down in the soft loam.

Verena watched him. Part of her still despised this nation and all who lived here, but now pity mixed with her anger.

If the high lord hurt Nicklaus, she'd use every trick, every bit of power she could muster to destroy him and everything he held dear. Hopefully Shona would prove an effective bargaining chip and all could be resolved peacefully.

If not, if the high lord stooped to hurting children, there would be war. She shuddered to think how the high lord's subjects would suffer for his crimes. She genuinely liked Connor, but as she stared into the glowing heart of the dying fire, she faced the hard truth.

If she had to, she would destroy him.

CHAPTER 14

onnor rolled to his side and studied Verena's profile. Part of him wanted to return to the fire and talk with her. Even though she was an enemy, he felt a deep curiosity about her and Granadure. Of all the company, he felt most comfortable around Verena, despite the lies.

Would he ever get another chance to learn about them?

Would they tell him the truth?

He was surprised to realize he didn't hate her. He should, though. They'd snuck across the border, invaded his country, and kidnapped Lady Shona. They worshipped the Tallan.

In the end, it didn't matter what he felt for Verena or her company. They were apparently too gifted in the arts of deceit for him to see through their lies. He was an inexperienced Saor-Linn who should be celebrating the Saorsa this very day. He didn't know enough to understand this situation.

He owed Shona his allegiance, but how could he help? He had to do … something.

But what?

As he lay pondering the question, Shona announced loudly, "I need to wash my face."

Ilse called from where she lay near the fire, "Someone bring Shona a canteen."

"I will not wash in your spit water. I will go to the river."

Ilse groaned and gestured to Anika, who had already sat up. "Escort her to the river."

Anika moved toward Shona, and once again Connor was impressed. She towered more than a head taller than Shona, and radiated raw power in her battle leathers. One of the soldiers stationed nearby proffered a leather pouch. "Need strength?"

Shona snatched the pouch and shoved her hand inside. She shouted with triumph and threw back her head, a look of ecstasy on her face.

Anika yanked the pouch away, and when Shona glared, she leaned closer and said in a soft, mocking voice, "Try make work. Maybe strong." She grinned and flexed her broad shoulders. "We fight."

Shona hesitated, clearly wrestling with a decision. Connor watched the exchange with interest.

What were they talking about?

After a moment Shona sighed, pushed past the bigger woman, and stomped down through the trees toward the river. Anika tucked the bag into her belt and strode out of camp after Shona. The other soldiers settled back again.

Connor looked around. No one was watching him.

He rolled silently to his feet and in three quick strides reached the deep shadows of a nearby bush. His heart began to pound as he slipped through the sparse underbrush toward the river. This might be his only chance to try to help Shona. He considered several ideas for dealing with Anika, but discarded them all. The problem was, she terrified him. Still, he had to try something.

Using every bit of woodcraft he'd mastered while stalking wily mountain goats through the Maclachlan Mountains, Connor ghosted toward the river. It was nearly dawn, and a hint of gray colored the eastern sky.

His hands started to sweat and he wiped them on his hunting leathers. His heart beat so fast he wanted to pant.

Just like stalking a nuall, he told himself. Of course, he'd only tried to stalk one of the giant, ferocious mountain cats once. It hadn't gone well.

Connor eased each foot forward, feeling for rocks or sticks while straining his ears for signs of his quarry above the constant gurgle of the river. Deep shadow cloaked everything, and the area smelled of pine trees and fresh water. He rounded a large boulder, and the river came into view, a gray ribbon that flowed through the impenetrable night.

Water splashed nearby and Shona said, "Didn't you bring a light?"

Anika chuckled. "Have light, yes. Have towel. Have hair brushing."

"You mock me?" Shona hissed.

Anika chuckled again. "You mock you. Very funny."

Connor followed their voices. As he drew within ten paces and crouched down beside a large rock, their forms became distinguishable. Shona knelt by the water, splashing water on her face. Anika stood nearby, her face and long blond braid shining in the darkness as she watched.

Connor felt around by his feet and located a fist-sized rock. He hefted it, getting a feel for its balance. Yesterday his aim had been perfect. Hopefully it still was.

Shona splashed again and then coughed, drawing Anika's full attention. Connor rose up, but paused with his arm cocked to throw.

He'd never hit a woman before. Anika scared him as much as her brother Erich. Worse, Connor wasn't even sure a rock would hurt a Petralist.

It had to be done. He tried to create a mental image of Stuart's face over Anika's. It wasn't too hard in the darkness.

Connor threw the rock with all his strength. It struck Anika in the side of the head and she toppled to the ground with a groan. Shona spun from the water and crouched in some sort of fighting stance, but remained silent.

Connor raced forward and was amazed to see Anika struggling to her hands and knees. He tackled her and drove her back down to the rocky shore.

She grunted with pain and then muttered something in Grandurian and pawed weakly at him. The blow to the head had clearly stunned her, but it should have knocked her senseless. Connor tried to hold her down, but couldn't bring himself to hit her again.

Already her struggles strengthened and she clawed at him and shouted something loudly in Grandurian. Connor slammed his knees hard into her back to drive the breath out of her, and ripped off his hunting jacket. He wedged one sleeve into Anika's mouth and tied it off behind her head. It wasn't the most effective gag, but it was better than nothing.

Anika surged upward and almost dislodged him. Soon she would recover enough to throw him, and then she'd kill him.

Connor drove her back to the ground again, but she clawed at his legs with her arms and thrashed side to side to throw him. He grabbed one of her arms and whipped the loose end of his hunting jacket around it, drawing it tight so that when she tried to pull free she yanked her own head back painfully. Connor grabbed her other hand and tied it up in the other arm of the jacket like the first.

Even as he congratulated himself on the clever move, Anika heaved upward so hard she sent him tumbling. He leaped to his feet just as she staggered upright despite lacking use of her arms. She turned toward him and, even gagged and bound as she was, Connor quailed with fear.

She took one angry step toward him, but Shona lunged out of the darkness carrying a heavy branch. She cocked it back to clobber Anika, and for a second, her body seemed to glow white in the darkness.

Then she gave a little moan and collapsed unmoving to the ground.

Anika kicked the branch out of her hands. Connor could not imagine how she could have knocked Shona senseless, but he wasn't about to wait for her to do the same thing to him.

He dodged around her and tried to tackle her back to the ground. Anika grunted under the impact and staggered a few steps, but did not fall. Instead she spun wildly as he clung to her neck with all his strength. Her battle leathers were made of a series of thick, overlapping plates and myriad straps that gave excellent purchase.

Together they staggered down the beach, Anika trying to dislodge Connor so she could kill him, and Connor struggling to choke her or knock her back to the ground. He did not dare let go lest she pounce on him.

I'm all seven kinds of idiot!

He should have known better than to try to take down a Petralist. Even the non-Petralist soldiers would be more than tough enough to beat him. He could not imagine how this was going to end well.

She tried to angle back toward the trail to camp, but Connor yanked on her braid and they crashed into a thick stand of hardwoods. Branches tore at Connor and threatened to rip him from his perch. The darkness grew deeper under the trees until they staggered completely blind through the grove.

Anika lunged through the close-packed trees, trying to scrape Connor off her back. He wedged his feet tight against a couple of her battle straps to secure his hold, but it was only a matter of time. One branch scraped along Connor's face and he could feel the tree looming ahead of them in the darkness.

He yanked Anika's long braid again. Her head twisted hard, and she stumbled sideways and collided face first with the tree she had been planning to run past. Connor reached up and found a thick branch where it connected to the tree trunk.

As Anika paused, stunned by the impact, Connor whipped her long braid around the heavy branch and drew it tight and tied it off.

Anika struggled, but the knots held. Connor slid from her back and pushed through the thick timber, back to the clear shoreline. Behind him, Anika fought to free herself, but her braid kept her from moving far. With her hands still tied up in his jacket, she could not break free. She shouted into the gag, the muffled sounds more like animal growls than human words.

Connor doubted she'd remain bound for long, but he could not bring himself to draw near to the raging woman and try to subdue her further. When he reached Shona's unmoving form, he paused for a second, bent over his knees, as a wave of shaking swept through his limbs. Sweat covered him and his heart pounded in his chest so hard it felt like it might knock its way through his ribs. His legs felt suddenly weak, and he wobbled and nearly fell.

After a few deep breaths, Connor forced himself to move. He crouched over Shona's limp form. She was breathing at least. He'd feared she'd somehow died. He shook her shoulder, but she only muttered something too soft to hear, and did not stir.

The night was silent but for the constant gurgle of the Wick. No wind stirred the cool night air. Everything seemed to be asleep, hushed and waiting for the approaching dawn. How could they not have heard the one shout Anika made?

He wasn't about to wait to find out. So he lifted Shona into his arms and cradled her against his chest. She was heavier than he'd expected. He'd found an excuse to lift Jean a couple weeks ago, and she'd been wonderfully light. He'd felt like he could carry her all day without tiring.

Maybe high ladies ate heavier food?

Holding her close the way he was, he couldn't help but notice her figure. Her silk blouse and soft skirt were smooth under his hands and his heart started beating faster for an entirely new reason.

She hung limp in his arms, her head resting at the base of his neck and her hair tickling his nose. She smelled good, like fresh water and roses. He took a deep breath and smiled despite the dangerous situation.

Turning downriver, Connor began picking his way along the shore. It was slow going with no trail, and rocks hidden in the deep shadows tried to trip him at every step. He fell once, and only just managed to not drop Shona and fall on top of her.

After ten minutes of hard going he hadn't made it more than a hundred yards. If Ilse and her men weren't out hunting them yet, they would be soon. He paused to rest and glanced to the right where the trees farther up the bank concealed the game trail they'd been following. He could move up there and make better time, but surely the soldiers would send runners that way.

The only other option was the river. Connor glanced left where the Wick ran gently by. The water would be chilly, but this part had been cleared of obstructions generations ago to protect the barges and their valuable cargo. Floating would be a lot faster than walking.

Shona still didn't stir, but maybe the water would revive her. Connor stepped to the edge of the river.

Upriver, Anika's voice rang out, loud and clear. She'd escaped her makeshift bonds.

Connor plunged into the river. The bottom dropped away sharply and he fell in over his head. He kicked back to the surface, spitting water and making sure Shona's head stayed clear of the water. She coughed and shook her head.

"What are you doing?" she asked loudly.

Connor covered her mouth with his hand. "Shhh. They'll hear."

She shook her head violently and he removed his hand. "It is forbidden to touch me."

Connor grimaced and whispered, "What did you want me to do? I had to get you out of there."

Taking her hand, Connor stroked farther from shore and towed her after. She struggled weakly but did not break free of his grasp. She lay back in the water and whispered, "How'd you escape Anika?"

"I hit her with a rock and tied her up."

"I wish I'd seen that."

He waited for her to thank him, but instead she asked, "Why are we in the river?"

"It was the only way to escape."

She tried to say something else, but her words turned into garbled whispers and her head fell back. She started to sink.

"Lady Shona?" Her hand hung limp in his, so he pulled her closer. "Shona, are you all right?"

She did not respond, so he pulled her close. He could feel the gentle warmth of her breath, but she'd passed out again. Connor sighed. He'd expected her to be stronger.

With a little support, she floated all right, so he drew her close, and together they floated downriver. Connor used his free hand to stroke, and pulled them farther from the bank.

Upriver, torches started bobbing around as the soldiers searched the shore. Even though the current ran gently, it moved them away. Only by running would the soldiers outpace them.

Connor was a very good swimmer, and he'd towed people before. Still, it surprised him how easily he stayed afloat with Shona resting against him. He looked for a branch or other floating debris to help buoy them, but found nothing. So he focused on his breathing and tried to make every movement count. If he was careful, they could float a long way before returning to shore. The river was chilly but not icy cold. They could survive in it for quite a while.

Connor allowed himself a smile and glanced down at Shona's face. Her beauty tugged at his heart and he wanted to shout with victory for having saved her from the evil Grandurians. To think he'd done this great service for her warmed him.

When he presented before High Lord Dougal, he'd be granted Patronage for sure. Of course, the high lord's men would still have to deal with Ilse's band. He prayed they'd be swift, and end the threat before innocents suffered. He lacked the power to stop them, but he'd certainly helped.

When he looked back upriver, the smile fell from his face. Skating downriver came the Water Moccasin, Kilian, drawn sword glinting with reflected torchlight.

CHAPTER 15

he Water Moccasin moved like a wraith as he skated across the surface of the water in long, fluid strides a hundred feet away. Connor fought a wave of panic and glanced at the shore. They'd drifted out into the center of the current and could never make it back in time.

Could he fight? Not a chance.

He was mostly submerged, forced to hold Shona afloat, and all he had for a weapon was his hunting dagger. The thought of being impaled by that sword while floating helpless in the chill river terrified him.

Would his body be left to float downriver to Merkland? Would the people there bother to pull him out and bury him, or would they leave him to the fish?

Connor pulled Shona closer, trying to draw comfort from the contact. It didn't help much. He looked upriver again and a trickle of hope eased the icy grip of fear around his heart. Here the river spanned fifty paces, and although Kilian was still approaching, he remained close to shore, his eyes locked on the deeper shadows there, searching the riverbank. It made sense. If not for Shona's dead weight, that's where Connor would have been.

Kilian would pass within twenty feet of the pair of them. If he didn't look around, he'd skate right past. Connor barely breathed. With such little light and being almost submerged, Kilian would have trouble spotting them.

Shona coughed. Kilian spun toward them instantly, his face alert. Connor placed a hand over Shona's mouth and, hoping she could understand, whispered, "Hold your breath."

Not waiting for a reply, he pulled them both under the surface. The chill water closed over their heads, impenetrable and mysterious. Shona's weight helped drag Connor down, as if eager to help him sink. He tried to peer through the murk, but could see nothing, hear nothing. He hung in the dark limbo of the river with Shona for several seconds.

His arms started to itch, but again the sensation flitted around under his skin like tiny bubbles that felt like they were trying to burst free.

Then suddenly he could *feel* the Water Moccasin. Like whispers across his skin, he *knew* Kilian was skating across the surface not far away. The itching of the Curse concentrated along his arm and torso closest to Kilian.

How was that possible?

He couldn't explain it but couldn't disbelieve it either.

Shona started struggling toward the surface. Connor couldn't see her face so he pulled her closer until their noses nearly touched. She pushed against him and tried to rise.

If they surfaced, Kilian could not miss seeing them. Connor held Shona down, wishing he could tell her what he felt. She had to be out of breath. He should be too, but he wasn't.

The Curse intensified and a memory flashed into his mind. He stood at the edge of the high cliff above Loch Ladhar on the bluff overlooking the manor house. The sun burned hot on his bare shoulders and nervous excitement filled him. Hamish shouted encouragement, but his eyes never left Jean, who sat on the edge of the loch far below. When he was sure she was looking, he charged forward and leaped far out over the long drop. He hung in the air, untethered to anything for an endless second, his stomach tight with breathless anticipation before plunging deep into the icy waters.

Shona struggled harder, yanking him from the memory. If he held her down much longer, she would drown. If he let her surface, they'd be caught and possibly killed.

Connor did the only thing he could think of. Pressing his lips tight against Shona's, he blew air into her mouth to try to fill her lungs. At first she tried to pull away, but he held her head firmly and blew harder. After a second, she seemed to realize what he was trying to do, and she pulled him tight, her lips pressed hard against his to draw in a deep breath.

Her lips tasted of river and salt, and the feeling of them against his triggered a warm thrill through his entire body. In that second, he became intensely aware of her arms wrapped around him, her body pressed to his.

He'd never kissed a girl on the lips before. He'd hoped to kiss Jean today at the Sogail, and he'd fantasized of kissing Moira. Despite the danger, despite the chill of the river, despite knowing he was forbidden to even touch Lady Shona, he didn't want this moment to end.

If he could have grinned, he would have. His lips tingled as he blew the life-giving breath into her. Finally Shona sealed her lips closed and eased her hold, but she didn't break free entirely and he made no move to take his hands from her face.

He'd given her a full breath of air, exhausting lungs that should have been empty like her own. Now they screamed for air and his sense of comfort fled. Had he just sacrificed his own life for hers? He fought to stay submerged against the almost overpowering urge to scramble for the surface. His lungs convulsed as his body tried to force him to take a breath.

The bubbling itch of the Curse drove deep into his torso, and suddenly the burning in his lungs eased just a little, as if he'd somehow managed to take a tiny breath. It was enough to keep him underwater a few seconds longer.

The whispers across his skin changed, and he focused on the strange sensation. Somehow he could feel Kilian turn away and begin skating back upriver. The sensation faded quickly and the bubbling itch dissipated.

Connor held them under for another ten seconds before pushing Shona toward the surface. She kicked upward and he followed. They breached the surface together and Connor filled his lungs. Breathing had never felt so good.

Beside him, Shona gasped and coughed softly. He could see her better. The approaching dawn was starting to lighten the sky above the eastern mountains.

"What do you think you were doing?" Shona demanded.

"Shhh." Connor placed a hand across her mouth and glanced upriver to see if Kilian had heard.

For the first time, Shona's control slipped and she slapped his hand away, giving him such a furious look he feared she might bite him.

"That Water Moccasin nearly found us after you coughed. We had to hide. Keep your voice down or he'll come back."

Shona regained her calm almost instantly and regarded him for a long moment as they floated close together. Finally she whispered, "You realize it is forbidden to touch me?"

"Would you rather I let them kidnap you again?"

"Of course not." After another uncomfortably long pause, she gave him a hint of a smile. "You are an interesting boy."

What was it with everyone calling him a boy?

He decided not to mention it. She had every right to be angry with him. She was high born after all. His place was only to serve and to obey.

He'd kissed High Lady Shona. Hamish, if he ever found out, would probably argue it wasn't a real kiss, but Connor didn't care. The memory of that kiss with her clinging to him for life was far too fresh, far too powerful.

Shona lay back in the water and said, "I think I'll ..." Her voice trailed off into a little snore.

Connor stared, incredulous as she started to sink again.

How could anyone sleep so much?

He grabbed her and pulled her close to keep her head above the water. He found it more difficult than earlier, forced to swim harder to keep her from dragging him down.

She might be a noblewoman, but this was ridiculous. He prided himself on his ability to sleep, but Shona had mastered the art to a level he'd never dreamed of. How could she just drift off while floating in a river with a score of angry Grandurians hunting them?

She'd probably get angry with him again for touching her after she awoke. He was tempted to leave her there, but he'd risked too much to save her to let her drown.

As dawn broke upon the eastern mountains, he studied her pretty face in the growing light and tried not to think too much about her body pressing against his in the water. He was not very successful.

The river ran wide and steady as it carried them south. He couldn't see much beyond the low bank to the east. The land must be very flat, probably farmland. To the west, the forest still ran thick along the bank, blocking his view of anything else.

As they drifted, he wondered where he'd gotten that last breath. Nothing like that had ever happened to him before, and that memory, although unusually sharp, didn't make sense. He'd often jumped into the lochs from the high cliffs, but had never been able to stay under for exceptionally long times. He couldn't explain it. Then again, he couldn't explain most of what had happened since he left home.

It had to do with the odd feeling of his Curse. Since he'd broken it, who knew what it would do to torment him. That meant he'd used it without really meaning to.

Or maybe he hadn't broken it. Today was the Sogail, his sixteenth age-day. Maybe it was already beginning to transform into a deadly power he couldn't hope to control.

I need to reach Merkland. Today.

They drifted downriver as dawn spilled beyond the mountains and light crept across the valley. The sun would not be visible over the eastern mountains until mid-morning, but the air began to warm. As the morning passed, Connor found it increasingly difficult to keep them afloat. What had been effortless at first became a constant struggle. His sodden clothes dragged at him and the chill of the water sapped his strength.

Just as he was about to give up and head for shore, the river pulled them around a bend and there ahead of them, drawn up on the bank, rested the river barge. The sight gave Connor a burst of energy and he swam for the bank.

After staggering out of the water and dragging Shona's limp form up the muddy bank, he collapsed and lay panting.

He glanced around and let out a tired laugh. So much work just to get back to where they'd started the night before.

How long before the Grandurians caught up?

CHAPTER 16

onnor allowed himself a delicious moment of relaxation before climbing onto wobbly legs. He'd worked too hard getting them this far to quit. He staggered to the barge, his muscles sluggish and weary, and pulled himself aboard. His soaked hunting leathers dragged against his skin and he shivered from the lingering cold.

Most of all, he was ravenous. He searched the empty barge for the food his mother had given him. He found a linen sack shoved under the bargeman's plank bench and eagerly shoved his hand inside.

Granite powder. He pulled out a handful and stared at it in disgust. He was hungry enough that he almost tasted it even though he knew better. He'd tasted enough granite chips growing up. Instead, he let the powder slip between his fingers and fall back into the sack. Then he took another handful and again let it slide away while he studied it.

It was just finely ground granite. He'd worked in and around the quarry all his life, and his father was the Ashlar who ground the blocks to powder, but even his father didn't know why they shattered the stone. Granite made excellent building material, but what else did they use it for? Connor couldn't imagine what that might be. No one ever bothered to tell the common Linn who cut it from the mountain.

After a moment spent idly running the powder through his fingers, Connor pushed the sack back under the bench and headed up to the bow. On the far side of the boat, under an empty sack, he found his hunting bow and quiver, and the food.

He wolfed down half of the provisions, swallowing chunks of meat big enough to choke a torc. When he'd sated his hunger, he leaned back against the gunwale and sighed. The situation seemed so much more promising.

Shona still slept, so he deposited the bag of food beside her. Maybe if she ate something when she woke up she'd stay awake a little longer. Or at least, it might help put her in a good mood.

Mhairi, Jean's grandmother, the healer in Alasdair, was normally a sweet lady, but she could be downright vicious when she got hungry. Everyone knew to bring food when they went to her for help, just to be safe.

Connor and Hamish made a special point of bringing her sweet bread every chance they could, in hopes she'd allow them to visit Jean without having to down the horrid universal cure. It hadn't worked yet, and Connor blamed Hamish. Half the time, the bread he produced from his pockets didn't look terribly fresh or very clean.

Back at the barge, he laid hands on the bow beam. The boat would be the best option, but it was well grounded. Erich had lifted the bow high above the waterline.

Connor dug his feet into the hard gravel of the bank and tried an experimental push. It was like trying to push over a tree. He didn't have the strength to move it, even though it now lacked the heavy granite cargo.

He looked around for anything to use as a lever. There were saplings along the bank, but he lacked an axe. If he didn't do something soon, the Grandurians would surely catch them.

Shona still slept soundly, her mouth slightly open, a trickle of drool running down her cheek. He could curse-punch one of the trees, but even Shona would probably wake up at the sound of a tree crashing to the ground.

Then again, maybe he didn't have to. The bow of the barge was heavily reinforced. With how weird the Curse had been acting, and given that today he needed patronage to avoid becoming Curse-condemned, did he dare release it again?

He could not think of any other way, so with a final glance at the sleeping Shona, Connor focused on his Curse and cautiously willed it to life. He was relieved when it rolled through his torso and down his arms with vibrant strength, setting his fingers twitching with the need to scratch at the buried itch. It no longer bubbled around under his skin, but locked onto his right hand and skittered up through his arm and shoulder like it should.

Connor cocked back his fist and the Curse pulsed as if it could sense impending violence. It deadened his hand and filled him with the need to crush something.

He punched the boat.

His curse-laden fist smashed into the heavy cross-beam with terrific force and a loud crack. The beam buckled a little, but did not snap. The entire front of the barge rocked up and back, and the boat started to slide down the muddy bank.

Connor grinned and pushed all his weight against the boat to keep it sliding. His right hand tingled and then itched like a thousand mosquito bites for a few seconds before returning to normal. The barge slid back down the bank until it floated free in the river.

Finally, I did something good with it.

He couldn't explain how it had replenished or how it felt right again. He'd never tried to understand it much in the past, but that ignorance could prove a very real danger. He'd have to pay more attention to its ebb and flow in the future instead of just trying to banish it from his thoughts.

After grabbing the bowline before the barge floated out of reach, he tied it to a nearby fallen tree, and returned to Shona. He lifted her into his arms and her eyes snapped open.

"What are you doing? Where are we?"

"Good morning," he said cheerfully as he carried her to the waiting barge. "Glad you decided to wake up today."

She frowned. "Put me down."

He dumped her onto the barge. She squawked and flailed her arms and legs but couldn't keep from plopping down hard on her back side. With her sodden clothing clinging to her, the effect was tantalizing.

Shona surged to her feet, but Connor was ready. When she opened her mouth to shout, he shoved a large chunk of his mother's bread into it. She gagged, retreated, and yanked the bread out. She started to speak again, but paused, looked down at the bread, and took a huge bite. While she chewed, Connor untied the bowline, pushed the barge out into the river, and leaped aboard.

He handed her the sack of food and she didn't bother to speak for several minutes. While she devoured everything, he set the long barge oar and maneuvered them out into the center of the current. He'd poled unwieldy barges across Loch Wick a few times and knew enough to avoid running it aground.

Shona finished her meal and sat back against one gunwale on a plank bench, her face tilted up to the sun, and for several minutes she remained silent, just basking in the mid-morning warmth. Sitting like that, profile to him, she looked younger somehow, and less intimidating.

Connor tore his eyes away to check their position in the river and make a minor correction. When he glanced back she was watching him. He thanked the spirits she hadn't caught him staring.

"I'm very tired," she said. "I'm going to rest. Watch for my father's soldiers."

Connor barely held his tongue. *She* was tired?

If sleeping exhausted her so much, she should try staying awake a little more often. But she was High Lord Dougal's daughter, and she could sleep all she wanted. It was her right.

"How can I tell if anyone I see isn't a Grandurian?"

Shona slid down to the deck and pillowed her head in her hands. She said softly, "They'll be wearing my father's colors, of course."

"Blue and green, right?"

Her only response was a soft snore.

They floated south through the morning and when the sun cleared the eastern mountains, the air turned hot. Connor's hunting leathers dried and he started wishing for a canteen of water. He dipped his hand into the river a few times and slurped some, but it wasn't enough, and river water didn't taste great.

Just past noon, as they rounded a long, slow bend, Connor spotted a man standing on the bank who looked a lot like the nervous, skinny fellow in Ilse's troop. For a second Connor thought the Grandurians had caught them, but even as his heart sank, he realized it was a different man. He wore similar baggy pants, although green, and he carried a pair of long-knives at his hips. His close-cropped hair was black, not blond.

Connor held his course in the center of the river. The man waved hard, and two soldiers dressed in chainmail much like the Grandurians joined him on the bank. Movement under the trees beyond the bank suggested more soldiers lurking there. One of the soldiers carried a bow.

The men wore black leathers under their armor, so they didn't look like High Lord Dougal's men. Their helms covered their heads, so he couldn't see if they were blond-haired Grandurians or not.

No normal soldiers could have outrun them downriver, but who knew what Petralists could really do?

As he drew even with the men on the bank, the first one cupped his hands over his mouth and shouted, "Pull in!"

Connor shouted back, "Who are you?"

The archer knocked an arrow and drew, but did not release. The first soldier shouted, "By order of High Lord Dougal, pull in and be boarded."

Connor frowned and held his course. Could he trust them? "No, thank you."

The archer let fly the arrow. It struck the barge several feet in front of Connor. Not a terribly good shot. The barge was wide and the gunwales low, but he could easily lie down on the deck and they'd have a hard time hurting him.

"Pull in," Shona said. She'd awakened finally and sat up to study the soldiers on the bank. "Those are my father's men."

"Your father's colors are black?"

"Of course not, but these aren't regulars."

That made no kind of sense, and he gritted his teeth in frustration. The archer drew another arrow, so Connor shouted, "I'm pulling in."

He aimed the barge for a rocky beach and as they approached, dozens of soldiers appeared from the trees and moved to meet them.

"I hope you're right," Connor said softly to Shona.

She tossed her bedraggled hair back from her face and smiled. "I'm always right."

Connor decided not to answer.

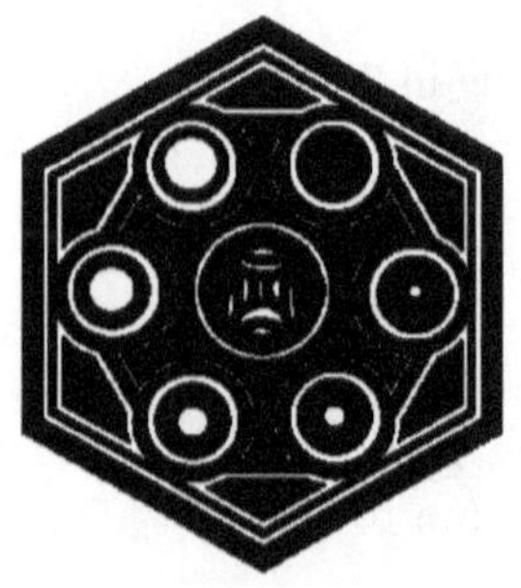

CHAPTER 17

thick-chested man, his face all hard lines and sharp angles, stepped to the front of the assembled soldiers. He looked as tough and unyielding as the north face of Mount Ingram, and watched Connor with one hand resting on the hilt of a wide-bladed sword. He wore black battle leathers like Erich and Anika, which made Connor even more nervous.

As they approached the shore, Shona climbed to her feet. The big soldier took a step forward and his face split with a smile. "Lady Shona!" He had a deep voice, rough like gravel shaken in a wooden box.

She waved to him. "Captain Rory, it is very good to see you."

The barge plowed into a submerged tree and lurched hard to port. Shona pitched to the side and would have fallen overboard, but Connor lunged forward and caught her around the waist. The two fell back into the bottom of the barge, arms and legs tangled.

Shona passed out again. Connor rolled clear, and turned back to check on her. The shining steel tip of a sword appeared in front of his face and rested against his throat. He froze then slowly looked up. The big captain stood over him, frowning.

"What are your intentions with the Lady Shona, boy?"

Connor held very still. "Nothing, sir. I mean, well, she almost fell out of the boat and I just pulled her back in. Didn't you see?"

Captain Rory grunted and glanced down at Shona's unmoving form. "Then why is she unconscious?"

Connor started to shrug, but decided against it with that sword pressed so close to his throat. "She's been doing that a lot."

Rory withdrew the sword and sheathed it in a single, fluid motion. He waved, and soldiers swarmed over the side of the barge. Two of them flanked Connor while the captain directed the others to transfer Shona to shore. The soldiers beside Connor pushed him along after.

On shore, more soldiers appeared until nearly a hundred of the hard-faced men clustered around the newcomers. Most of them wore chainmail coats, but five were dressed in black battle leathers like Rory. Despite the lack of steel on their bodies, the burly soldiers radiated power. Connor instinctively feared them more.

At the edge of the clearing, one fellow stood apart from the others. He dressed in simple leathers much like Connor's hunting clothes. He wore a wide-brimmed hat, and his eyes seemed to glow from within the shadow covering his face.

An elderly fellow with graying hair wearing a long, tan healer's coat, trotted over to Shona, followed by a brawny lad who looked a little younger than Connor. The lad carried a large wooden box and wore a sleeveless tan tunic. He set the box down and folded open the top, revealing several levels of shelves holding a variety of brown glass bottles, wicker baskets full of herbs, and fat rolls of bandages.

While the healer began examining Shona, Captain Rory called Connor to one side. "What's your name, lad?"

"Connor, sir."

"Well then, Connor, tell me how came you to be floating this river alone with Lady Shona?"

Connor explained about his capture and their long march upriver. Thankfully the big soldier did not ask about why he was on the river in the first place, and Connor left out his deal with the Grandurians. When he mentioned the theft of the granite powder, Rory cursed and his powerful hands clenched into fists.

"I'd hoped to re-supply from that barge."

Connor really didn't want Rory angry anywhere near him so he added quickly, "You wouldn't have gotten anything. There was nothing on board but the granite."

Rory stared at him as if he'd gone mad. Then he blinked a couple of times and said, "Right. I forgot."

Forgot what?

"Go on," Rory ordered.

Connor was about to relate the fight with Anika by the river when Shona joined them. She looked more alert than he'd seen her all day.

"Nice story. You just left out the part where you were conspiring with them to escape across the border."

The captain frowned at Connor and growled, "You lying to me, boy?"

"No, sir. I'm not lying."

"So you're calling Lady Shona a liar, then?"

"No. Of course not."

"Then in what way were you conspiring to help the enemy?"

Connor had to fight to keep his voice calm and not start shaking with fear. "I did promise to show them how to get through the mountains, but that was before I knew who they were and what they were doing."

"These mountains are impassable."

"Usually," Connor corrected in a small voice.

"They can escape?"

"No. We didn't get upriver far enough to show them the trail. They'll never find it alone."

Rory frowned. "How could a bargeman know about a secret pass across the mountains that no one else has ever heard of?"

"I'm not a bargeman. The last couple of months, I've apprenticed as a hunter. I know these mountains better than anyone."

Rory frowned again, "Stones take it, lad, what were you doing on a barge the night before the Sogail?"

That question triggered all of Connor's fear and frustration and he blurted, "Because the Curse Finders were late!"

Rory's frown deepened on his craggy face and the five burly, leather-armored soldiers standing nearby drew closer.

"You're Cursed?" Shona asked. She looked at him as if really seeing him for the first time.

Oh, I'm so grouted.

He'd kept the Curse secret so long, how could he now blurt it out in front of a group of strangers? Then again, they weren't recoiling in horror like the villagers of Alasdair likely would.

Connor swallowed a lump of dread and said softly into the silence, "That's why I was on the barge. I have to reach Merkland today."

Rory shook his head slowly. "You're in a fine pickle, lad. High Lord Dougal's not in Merkland."

Oh, no.

Connor had never considered the possibility.

How could the high lord not attend the Sogail? How could he grant Teagair to the families of Merkland?

Connor looked from Rory to Shona, close to panic. "Where is he?"

"He is expected from Donleavy soon on the Speedcaravan. Probably will arrive today, but he won't tarry in Merkland, not with this Grandurian threat. After you've answered the rest of my questions, you'd best head downriver fast, lad. Maybe you can catch him."

Shona turned away. "My father spends too much time with the king."

"It's not my place to say, miss, but sure as our lives, when he arrives, he'll be wanting a victory here."

"He'll get one. They can't escape."

"Do they know about the quarry?" Rory asked.

"They do," Connor said.

Rory frowned. "That complicates things. Time to move out. Maybe we can intercept them before they reach Alasdair."

"Unlikely," Shona said. "They have a big head start."

Rory nodded grimly. "Then we drive them out before they can settle in for a siege."

"Why would they want Alasdair?" Connor asked nervously.

"Leverage. Now that Lady Shona's escaped and they're trapped against the mountains, they'll be desperate for bargaining power."

"They said they just want to leave. Can't we just let them go?"

"Nay, lad. They should've thought of that before they invaded and took Lady Shona."

"What casualty count are you prepared to absorb?" Shona asked calmly, as if they were discussing supply logistics.

Rory considered for a few seconds and said, "We need to protect Lord Gavin and his family, and the Cutters of course."

Connor stared from one to the other as he faced the reality of his worst fears. They intended to fight Ilse and her soldiers in Alasdair, and people were going to die.

The truth left him feeling sick. It was his fault. His careless comment had given Ilse the information she needed. They would invade the town because of him.

He had to get to Merkland, had to petition for patronage.

He had to help his family.

Connor stood rooted in place, as his mind whirled and he struggled to decide what to do.

"Did you bring my leathers?" Shona asked Rory.

"Aye." Rory pointed to a pack lying nearby. Shona took it up and started moving away toward the trees.

"I want to help," Connor said, desperate to keep their attention. "I know these mountains."

Shona paused and looked back, but it was Rory who spoke. "You need to get to Merkland, lad. If you miss High Lord Dougal, your life's as good as over."

"I know. It's just, you said he'll be coming this way as soon as he returns to Merkland, right? Can't I see him then?

"He might not arrive in time."

"My family is in Alasdair. I want to help."

One of the other burly soldiers, who had all remained silent until now, spoke up. "Run along, boy. We're going to battle. This is a job for Guardians."

Everyone began turning away, but desperation drove Connor on.

These were Guardians? No wonder his Curse did not scare them. They knew all about it. Didn't they care if he lived? He had to show them he was worth helping.

"How many of you have beaten a Grandurian Petralist single-handedly?"

That got their attention.

"And you have, boy?" The same soldier said mockingly.

"Aye! How do you think Lady Shona escaped?"

Rory turned to Shona, who returned to the group. "How *did* you escape, lass?"

"Stop calling me that," Shona said irritably. "You're not that much older than me."

Rory gave the barest hint of a smile. "It's not the age, miss, it's the experience."

Shona frowned, "You assume much, Captain."

"Perhaps. How did you escape the Grandurians?"

Shona glared at Connor and his heart sank. She said quickly, as if the words were unpleasant, "He's right. He saved me."

The one soldier gave Connor an incredulous look. "Pardon, miss, but what could this boy do that you couldn't?"

Shona shrugged. "I don't remember much. When I tried to tap my strength, I fell. I've been weak all day."

"The effects lasted that long?" Rory asked.

"No. Whatever they used in Merkland wore off in about twelve hours, but they must have given me more."

"You have no idea how they administer it?"

She shook her head. "None, but it's completely debilitating."

So that's why Shona had been such a burden. She'd been poisoned, or something.

Rory turned to Connor. "So how did you rescue Lady Shona from the Petralists?"

"I hit the one guarding her with a rock, and tied her up with my jacket."

"You beat up a girl?" the one soldier laughed.

"She was the scariest woman I've ever seen," Connor said, thinking of the towering Anika. "She'd pound you to dust before you could laugh at her, I promise you that."

Rory barked a laugh, "Well done, lad."

The other soldier asked, "So how'd you get away? You telling us you carried Lady Shona all the way downriver and outran their Wingrunner? You got affinity to basalt?"

What was he talking about?

It didn't matter. They were talking with him, curious and maybe with just a bit of grudging respect. "We floated the river. I even saved her from the Water Moccasin, Kilian."

At the mention of the Water Moccasin, Connor couldn't help but remember Shona clinging to him, their lips pressed hard together in the chill, dark waters of the river. Shona flushed, and he wondered if she was remembering too.

Rory clapped Connor on the shoulder hard enough to make him stagger. "Good job, lad. I've heard of Kilian. Nasty fellow, that one. On behalf of High Lord Dougal, I thank you for saving Lady Shona."

"So, you'll let me come help save my family?"

Rory shook his head slowly. "Can't take the risk, lad. If High Lord Dougal is late, you're dead."

Shona, who now regarded Connor with a thoughtful expression that made him more than a little nervous, spoke up. "There may be another way, Captain. I represent my father until he arrives. I'll grant Connor Patronage."

Could she do that? Would she?

Shona gave him a little smile, and her eyes seemed to weigh him in a way that made him even more nervous.

"I appreciate what you're doing, Lady Shona," Rory said with a frown, "but can you really do that?"

Shona tilted her chin up a little and gave Rory a cool look. "I am a High Lady, and heir to my father's throne."

"Aye, but there's usually more involved in the process."

Shona hesitated. "You're right." Even as the fear rose to choke Connor again, she added, "I will grant conditional patronage until we resolve this conflict. Then we'll bring the matter before my father."

After a moment, Rory shrugged. "That should work."

Connor looked from one to the other. "What does that mean?"

"Prove yourself, lad, and you'll become a Guardian like us," Rory said.

"I will!"

He wanted to shout with triumph! One great weight eased its burden, and he felt giddy with the sense of security that flooded through him. He'd obtained Patronage, at least conditionally, and he'd do whatever it took to prove himself to Rory, and to Shona.

"Prepare your men, Captain," Shona said. "We march when I'm changed."

She disappeared into the trees, and Rory began barking orders. Men assembled into four-man squads and then grouped into twenty-man units.

Within minutes, the company was ready to move. Rory shouted, "Strider, take point."

The slender fellow with the loose-fitting trousers saluted and sprinted for the trees, faster than any man Connor had ever seen. Connor doubted even one of Lord Gavin's mounted guards could have caught him.

Rory noted Connor's surprised look. "Never seen a Strider before?"

Connor only shook his head.

The burly soldier who had teased Connor earlier said, "Well, what's your affinity, lad?"

"I don't know what that means."

"What stone, boy?"

"I don't …"

"How long have you known you were Cursed?" Rory asked.

Connor nearly said forever, but caught himself at the last moment. Newborns exhibiting any signs of being Cursed were supposed to be discovered at birth. Teagair would be rescinded, and they'd be taken by the High Lord. Those not showing signs of the Curse as babies generally didn't discover their curse until age ten or twelve. Hence the need for Curse

Finders to scour the villages annually.

So he mumbled, "A while."

Thankfully the soldier didn't seem bothered by the vague answer. "So what can you do with this Curse?"

The other leather-armored Guardians drew near. The attention made Connor extremely nervous.

Gathering up his courage, he said, "I hit things."

"That's it?"

"I've only done it a couple of times. I never tried anything else."

"We can explore it tonight when we make camp."

The matter-of-fact way he said it made Connor both excited and nervous. He'd never explored the extent of his Curse before.

"Sir, I know you're Guardians, but some of those Grandurians are Petralists."

"So am I," Shona said from behind him.

Connor turned and gaped. Instead of a silk blouse and skirt, Shona now wore black battle gear like Rory and the other Guardians, but she definitely didn't look like the others. On them, the leather tunic and breeches looked fearsome with their overlapping leather plates linked with myriad straps and buckles whose purposes Connor couldn't fathom.

On Shona, the form-fitting black outfit highlighted her shapely figure in ways that made Connor want to stare despite having been in such close contact all day. She'd re-braided her hair, and wore a determined expression. She looked like she was ready to kill someone.

Connor dropped his gaze as she joined them. Only then did her words register and he looked up again. "You're a Petralist?"

"Aye, she is," Rory said. He gestured toward the five other leather-clad soldiers nearby. "We can handle those Grandurians, don't you worry, lad."

All the amazing tales Bruce had related for years raced through Connor's mind. He looked from Rory to Shona and wanted to laugh with the wonder of it. He couldn't trust Bruce's stories, but here were a couple of the legends in the flesh.

He would have felt more comfortable if Shona wasn't watching him with that unreadable expression of hers, but still blurted out, "Sir, I don't know a lot about Petralists or Guardians. Can you tell me something about what you can really do?"

"Strength, lad. Power to thews and skin."

"That's it?"

Rory laughed. "Wait till you see what we can do."

Connor thought back to Erich and Anika and their amazing strength. Could a Guardian really stand against a Petralist? How were they different? Bruce hadn't spoken much about the Guardians.

Rory added, "You've seen the Strider, and we've got a Pathfinder, of course. Some of the men have secondary gifts with light or healing, but mostly we're all Fast Rollers."

The Healer, who had approached, trailed by his brawny assistant, snorted. "Healing he says. None of you lot could heal a hangnail."

"That's why we have you," Rory said.

Connor wanted to ask more questions, but Rory shouted, "Move out."

As the soldiers began marching upriver, Rory turned to Connor. "You know these lands. I want you to take point and scout ahead."

"Are you sure that's wise?" Shona asked.

Connor was already running for the trail. He didn't move half so fast as the Strider had, but any other man would have been hard pressed to keep up. As Connor raced up the trail, his relief at having obtained Patronage was tempered by growing fear.

What destruction might the Grandurians wreak before Rory's force caught up?

CHAPTER 18

ean stepped onto the musicians' platform at the southern end of the square in Alasdair, intensely aware that she held everyone's attention. She allowed a warm smile, but suppressed the foolish grin that threatened to erupt onto her lips and ruin the moment.

The morning had passed in a blur, and her stomach had clenched ever tighter as the moment neared when she and Moira would stand before the entire assembly and sing the Sogail-Oran.

Brightly dressed townsfolk filled the square and gathered around tables that groaned under the weight of mountains of food. Lord Gavin and Lady Isobel oversaw the festival from their raised pavilion, joined by the Curse Finders in their long russet coats over gleaming chainmail shirts.

The brown tunic Lord Gavin wore might be in his house color, but it made him look small and unhealthy. Beside him, Lady Isobel wore a red and gold gown with so many frills and layers of lace it was a wonder she could find her seat. Her face was heavily powdered to cover the burns, she'd drawn fake eyebrows, and she wore a bonnet to hide her hair.

At least Moira had the sense to dress elegantly. She stood beside Jean, resplendent in a red and gold gown far simpler than her mother's. She wore her dark hair braided, with a silver circlet set with carved stones on her brow.

Jean wore her thick, blond hair loose but for a complex braid ringing her head that supported a garland of flowers and holly. She wore a fine blue cotton dress Mhairi gifted to her that very morning. She felt more than a little self-conscious in the flattering dress, but standing before the entire town, she forced herself to accept the fact that they now looked on her as an eligible maid.

Once the dancing began, Stuart and Hamish would court far more aggressively. She wondered where Connor might be. Lady Isobel's assertion that he had tried to murder her shocked everyone, and generated many muttered opinions that the town would be far better off if he'd succeeded.

Jean wished he could be here, although it would prove easier to handle just Stuart and Hamish, plus several older men who had made it clear in recent months they fancied a dalliance with her despite already being married with families.

All she had to do was follow the pattern she'd painstakingly established over the past two years. She hated all the flirting, but it proved far more effective than any other method she had tried. She wished they would leave her alone until she was prepared to make a decision. Then she could make a simple choice and that would be the end of it.

It would have been so much better if the Carpenter twins were a couple years older so she wouldn't be the only girl for the boys to focus on. She enjoyed the attention, but hated how they constantly pressured her into choosing. She wasn't ready, and she refused to be ready until all the pieces fell into place. As Granny Mhairi always said, act only after understanding.

It regularly amazed her that no one saw through the act. In no other facet of her life did she act so capricious. Still, the boys were all well trained to jump to her will.

Jean shared a glance with Moira and took a single step forward. Their moment had arrived. Her knotted stomach loosened under a flood of excitement. She was ready.

Before the two could begin the hauntingly beautiful song, a stranger stepped out of the alley beside the stage. Slender, with raven-black hair, she wore some kind of black leather armor made up of myriad straps and overlapping plates. Two other soldiers, dressed in similar outfits, flanked her. One was a hugely muscled man, while the other was a tall, shapely woman. They shared blond hair and blue eyes much like Jean's.

Without preamble, they strode into the square and faced Lord Gavin's platform, and the lead woman spoke.

"I am Ilse. This town is now under my control."

CHAPTER 19

ord Gavin squinted down at Ilse. "Your timing is inconvenient, woman. A sign of flawed parentage, no doubt."

Jean wanted to scream at them both for interrupting her big moment. The timing wasn't inconvenient, it was disastrous!

The Curse Finder seated closest to Lord Gavin surged to his feet and his voice carried easily across the silent crowd. "Grandurians!"

Every voice gasped in unison while the other Curse Finders snatched for weapons. Lord Gavin paled and Lady Isobel glared at Ilse as if she'd personally offended her.

Jean shared a shocked look with Moira, but wanted to beat these intruders with a stick. Couldn't they at least have waited until after the song?

"Remove these intruders," Lord Gavin commanded.

"To arms," Bruce shouted and stepped in front of his master, while Lord Gavin's soldiers and the Curse Finders' attendants all rose from their seats scattered across the square.

The three newcomers all drained of color until their skin shone like ash in moonlight. At first Jean thought they paled with fear, but the change came too rapidly, spread too universally.

The leader of the Curse Finder shouted, "For Obrion!" And vaulted from the raised platform, slashing a mighty blow down at Ilse's head.

She caught his sword.

There was no blood, no shriek of pain. Ilse's expression of calm confidence never wavered. The Curse Finder grunted in surprise, and Ilse twisted the sword out of his hands. He stumbled forward and she caught him by the front of his mail shirt and easily lifted him off the ground. Her fingers dug through the mail and little rings popped out in all directions with loud pings.

The Curse Finder beat at her arm with no effect, and Ilse threw him over her shoulder with a flip of her arm. He soared across the square and crashed down on one of the feasting tables, splintering it and scattering food and villagers.

Even through her shock at the incredible feat of strength, Jean catalogued the likely injuries.

The other two Curse Finders charged Ilse, but the man and woman team flanking her intercepted them. One of the Curse Finders slashed the man across the face and the sword made a rasping sound as it slid across his skin, as if it were scraping stone.

The black-armored Grandurian snatched the sword away, and with his bare hands twisted it into a knot. The Curse Finder tried to run, but the soldier grabbed him from behind and threw him across the square. He tumbled like a rag doll and slammed through the front door of the bakery, scattering bread and pastries in all directions.

Jean added several more items to her rapidly growing list.

The last Curse Finder paused before the towering woman, and she punched him in the center of the chest. The blow drove him back against the pavilion with crushing force.

Lord Gavin's soldiers and the Curse Finders' attendants looked to each other for reassurance. The villagers stared in open-mouthed awe. No one ever interfered with the Curse Finders, and yet these strangers had overcome them with terrifying ease.

Ilse spoke. "Stand down. We have no interest in hurting you, but we will if we must."

One of Lord Gavin's guards pointed a sword at her and shouted, "No fear, lads!"

Ilse raised an eyebrow, "You really think you can fight a company of Grandurian Petralists?"

The man's face paled and he dropped his sword.

Ilse swept an arm across the square, and more blond-haired soldiers stepped out of places of concealment, blocking every road and alley into the square. "Last chance."

As one, the rest of the locals dropped their weapons.

"Wise choice."

To the villagers cowering in fear, Ilse added, "Behave yourselves and you will not be harmed. You may continue your feast, but no one is to leave town."

"High Lord Dougal will hear about this," Lord Gavin said. "His forces will be coming."

"I'm counting on it."

CHAPTER 20

ean forced herself to move. Her day lay in shambles, but she could not allow fear or fury to rule her. Questions buzzed like hornets through her mind, but she lacked enough information to answer any of them. How could Grandurians have invaded Alasdair? Had they already sacked Merkland? What did they want in this remote location?

As villagers scattered for their homes, and soldiers surrounded Lord Gavin and his family, she descended from the platform and dropped to one knee beside the Curse Finder who had been punched in the chest. A brief examination revealed he would live, but probably suffered several cracked ribs. That Grandurian hit like a rock hammer to do so much damage with one punch.

She urged the man to lay still until she could fetch bandages to wrap his torso, and then she turned to the other wounded men, who had been dragged across the square by Grandurian soldiers and dropped nearby. One of them was conscious, badly bruised, but did not appear seriously hurt. The other, who had tumbled all the way into Neasa's shop, smelled of sweetbreads where he lay unconscious with one arm clearly broken.

A Grandurian soldier roughly began tying the man's wrists together. The sight pushed Jean's simmering fury beyond the boiling point.

"Leave that man alone," she snapped and pushed the soldier hard. Surprised, he stumbled and fell.

Other soldiers advanced on her, but Jean stood her ground. "I will not allow you to harm these men. You may take them into custody after I treat them, but I warn you, do not mistreat them."

One soldier laughed and reached for his sword, but a sharp command in Grandurian from the raven-haired leader stopped him.

Ilse faced Jean with a little smile on her lips. "You show much courage, girl, to command my men."

"And you show a disgusting lack of civility."

That drew a chuckle from the woman. "Your town is invaded, and that is your chief concern?"

"As a healer, my concern is the well-being of the people of this town."

"You are Petralist?"

"Of course not. I told you, I'm a healer."

Ilse gestured at the unconscious Curse Finder. "How would you heal this man?"

Jean suspected the woman was mocking her, but the question seemed genuine. "I'll determine the extent of the injuries, set and bind the broken arm, and offer him a drink to dull the pain."

"So you are an herb healer."

"If that's what you want to call it."

"Very well, see to your patient. My men will not disturb you."

Jean examined the fallen man and then worked to set his broken arm. Hamish appeared, looking a little shaken, but still munching on a handful of sweetbreads, and she sent him to fetch more supplies.

As she began wrapping the arm with a clean bandage, a girl about her own age dropped to her knees nearby. She didn't look like the other invaders. Her huge blue eyes looked more innocent than threatening, and she concealed her barbaric heritage behind shoulder-length hair and little button nose. No doubt the blockheaded boys in town would tell her anything she wanted without considering the ramifications. She dressed not in battle leathers, but in dark brown pants and black leather vest over a forest green blouse.

The newcomer spoke cheerily, as if the festival was still under way. "Hello. Is that a broken arm?"

Jean nodded. "I'm about to wrap it."

"Oh, good." The girl dipped one hand into a leather satchel she wore over her shoulder and extracted a hand of dirt. She held it for a moment, as if to warm it, and then began sprinkling it onto the bandage.

"Stop!" Jean pushed her hand away. "You'll contaminate the wound."

"It's not dirt, it's Builded sandstone."

"It looks crushed to me."

The girl giggled. "No, I … made it stronger. It'll help."

Jean gave her an incredulous look. Granadure must be a more backward country than they'd been taught. It was a wonder any of them survived to adulthood if they put dirt in their wounds.

She reminded herself to look deep, see clear. Something was going on here she didn't yet understand, so she forced herself to withhold judgment.

"How could it possibly help?"

"You're not a sandstone healer, are you?"

"No, I heal people."

The girl shook her head. "I don't have time to explain. Just trust me."

She wanted to laugh aloud. "What's your name?"

"Verena."

"Listen, Verena. You invade our town, you wreck the Sogail, and you interrupt my song!" By the time she finished, she was shouting. "And you want me to trust you?"

Verena shrugged. "Maybe not." Then she dumped more dirt on the bandage. "But leave this on. You'll see."

Jean backed away and held her hands up. "I refuse. If you want to infect his wound, you do it."

"All right." Verena surprised Jean by efficiently wrapping the wound and tying off the bandage.

After the Grandurians led the injured men away, Jean headed for home and began preparing a list of supplies she would need to assemble.

She expected to treat many more wounds before this crisis
ended.

CHAPTER 21

onnor crouched behind the Powder House and peered around the corner toward the wall gate where a Grandurian soldier stood in plain view. He wanted to howl curses at the invaders. He'd hoped to arrive before they consolidated their hold on the town. He shuddered to think what suffering his family and friends might have already experienced at their hands.

Captain Ilse had not seemed bloodthirsty, but she might be seeking to wreak vengeance on the town, to punish them for Connor having spirited Shona out of her hands.

Part of him wanted to turn and sprint back to Captain Rory, but the burly captain would need specific information in order to best overthrow the Grandurians. Connor could provide that information, had to provide it. He couldn't think of a better way to prove his worth and secure permanent Patronage.

So when the guard stationed at the wall gate turned away to look at something in the town, Connor sprinted across the blocking yard toward the mighty cliff of Wick Tor that reared high above town. At the junction of the cliff and the wall of Alasdair, he climbed up a series of handholds he'd used hundreds of times.

At the top, he paused to peek over. From this angle, he remained invisible to the guard at the gate, and he saw no other soldiers. He would have been surprised if he had. Ilse's company was very small to maintain control of so large an area. He was a little surprised he hadn't encountered any villagers fleeing the invaders as he approached town.

After another visual sweep of the area, Connor slipped over the wall and stealthily moved deeper into town. Most windows were shuttered, but he caught glimpses of townsfolk. They looked frightened, but not hurt. He longed to rush home to check on his family, but his house lay on the far side of town. Instead, he headed for the one place where he could be sure to find accurate information.

Jean's home. The Healer's house.

Situated close to the base of the cliff, not far from where he slipped into town, it was a large two-story structure. The first floor held treatment rooms plus a large kitchen and huge storeroom for all of Mhairi's healing supplies. Jean and her grandmother lived upstairs.

Connor slipped through the kitchen door in the rear of the building and came up short when old Mhairi turned from a counter where she was kneading dough.

She squinted at him, "Town's in an uproar, Lady Isobel wants your hide, and all you can think of is to come a-courting?"

As she reached for the ever-present jug of cure-all potion she inflicted on everyone who came calling without a visible injury, Connor said, "Wait, I'm not here to see Jean." At her incredulous look, he added, "Well, I am, but I'm not."

"Hmm. Incoherent, but otherwise not damaged. Take a blow to the head, did you son?"

"No, it's not like that."

"Here to kill old Mhairi like you tried to kill Lady Isobel?"

"I did not try to kill her," Connor said angrily.

"Wouldn't blame you if you had," Mhairi said with a wink. "Now, what brings you here to see Jean but not to see her?"

Connor relaxed just a little, although he watched her hand carefully where it rested on the counter next to the jug.

"I have information about the Grandurians."

"Well, why didn't you say so?"

"I just did."

"Listen, youngling," she said sternly. "The town's been invaded. We don't have time to waste jabbering."

Connor just stared.

"Jean," Mhairi called loudly.

Jean came in from the other room, still dressed in her Sogail finery, and Connor drank in the sight of her. She stopped at seeing him, and her bright blue eyes sparkled with joy.

Hamish walked right into her back. They stumbled forward, and Jean almost fell. Hamish caught her, and then he almost fell and she caught him in turn. They ended up holding each other tight, faces close as they laughed. Connor had to fight down a wave of jealousy.

Hamish caught sight of him. "Connor!"

Connor shushed him. "No one's supposed to know I'm here."

"Where have you been hiding all day?" Jean asked. She was wearing some kind of perfume, and smelled like sunshine and green fields. It proved very distracting.

Hamish added, "How did you know about the Grandurians?"

"It's a long story."

"You could have warned us."

"I'm trying to."

"No you weren't." Hamish looked angry. "All you said was 'tomorrow something big is going to happen.'"

"What?" Connor and Jean said at the same time.

Jean frowned. "You knew they were invading?"

"No."

"That's not what you said yesterday," Hamish insisted.

Then Connor remembered the conversation in the manor. "That's not what I was talking about."

"Then what?"

"Never mind. Listen, I'm here with High Lord Dougal's men. They're going to fight Ilse."

"How do you know her name?"

"I was her prisoner."

"Connor, we're all her prisoners," Hamish said with a frown. "Are you all right?"

Connor blew out a frustrated breath. "Will you just listen to me?"

"I don't see any soldiers," Jean said. "Are they hiding too?"

"No, they're not here."

"Connor, you're not making any sense," Hamish said. "You said you're with the soldiers, but they're not here. So are you not here either? Are we imagining you?"

"No."

"I'm confused. Is there anything to eat?"

Mhairi silently handed Hamish a large mug.

He took a long pull and then gagged and spat. "I didn't need the tonic!"

She shrugged. "It usually works. Helps control the appetite."

Connor held up his hands. "Quiet! Just listen to me. I'm Cursed."

Jean gasped and Hamish dropped a stick of hard bread he was about to pop into his mouth. Mhairi only grunted and nodded.

"The Grandurians are here because of me."

Jean frowned. "Connor, how could they know you were Cursed?"

"And why would they invade Obrion just to come find you?" Hamish added.

Connor took a long, steadying breath. "Just listen and I'll explain." Then he realized they'd never believe everything he'd been through in the past day. "Never mind. There's too much. Here are the important parts."

"I've been granted Patronage by High Lady Shona, who I rescued from the Grandurians last night. She is leading an army to fight off the Grandurians. They should be here tonight."

"Wow. Why didn't you just say so?" Hamish said.

"I need to know what they're doing."

Jean said, "It's been crazy here, Connor." She related how Ilse interrupted her song, and although she tried to hide her still-simmering anger over the timing of the invasion, Connor picked up on it. She related in great detail the short fight in the square and concluded with, "Now they've dragged Lord Gavin, his family, the Curse Finders, and every Cutter up to the manor. They've posted a few guards at the village gates and told everyone to stay in their homes and no one will get hurt."

Connor grinned, pulled her close, and kissed her square on the lips. "You're amazing."

Jean blushed, and Connor barely suppressed a gasp of surprise at his own audacity.

I just kissed Jean!

Hamish gaped, "Hey, no fair."

Mhairi produced a long thin switch and whacked Connor across the shoulders. He winced, but couldn't stop grinning. Jean hadn't really kissed him back, but she hadn't pulled away either. His entire body tingled with the memory of her warm, soft lips against his.

I kissed Jean first!

Mhairi pushed him back, "None of that, boy."

"Sorry. I got carried away."

"I have a tonic that'll help with that."

Still smiling, Connor said, "That was worth drinking any tonic you can come up with."

Jean's blush deepened and Mhairi grunted and surprised him with a smile. "I bet it was, lad." She pointed a threatening finger at him. "Now, no more of that malarchy."

Amazingly, she did not force her tonic on him.

Jean said, "Connor, did you make all this up just to kiss me?"

"No, but I wish I had."

Hamish, still frowning said, "Connor, Lord Gavin ordered everyone to stay in town and obey the Grandurians on penalty of Daor."

Connor gaped. "Why would he do that?"

"Ilse said that anyone found trying to leave will be taken prisoner. If the town does not obey, she'll start executing Lord Gavin's family and the Cutters."

"She wouldn't."

"No one's willing to take the chance. The Cutters are all prisoner, but the women's circle met already and reiterated the order. No one is to leave."

Mhairi said, "If only we could be sure they'd execute Isobel first. That would make it a lot easier to decide."

Connor forced aside his anger at Lord Gavin's short-sightedness. The entire town was now effectively locked down under Ilse's control, hundreds of hostages for her to use against Rory and Shona.

He gripped Jean and Hamish by the shoulders, "It won't matter. The army is coming and they'll defeat Ilse. Keep an eye out. Watch if anything changes. I'll contact you when I return with the army."

"Can I come?" Hamish asked.

"No. You stay and take care of Jean." He regretted the words immediately as Hamish grinned, and Jean scowled.

"Better take the flood under," Jean said.

"Good idea."

Jean kissed him on the cheek, "Be careful."

Hamish punched him in the shoulder, a little harder than normal. "Hit a Grandurian for me."

"Already did that."

Hamish's eyes widened. "Really?"

"I'll tell you about it later."

Mhairi insisted on gifting him a satchel of food before he left. It took ten minutes to cross the village without being seen.

After carefully scouting the outer wall for any patrolling Grandurians, Connor crawled into a hole at the base where the granite had collapsed. Several years ago, during an unusually hard rain, the Wick had flooded its banks and washed away the ground under this section of wall.

Connor wormed his way through the narrow opening, happy he didn't encounter any of the large spiders that often made their homes there. The village children must have been playing in the passage recently. Killing the spiders was one of their favorite games.

A few minutes later, after crossing the Wick and returning to the wooded trail on the far side, Connor broke into a run. In his mind, he heard Shona and Rory discussing acceptable casualties, and fear for his father's safety drove him on all the faster.

He had to find a way to protect his family.

CHAPTER 22

onnor ran to exhaustion. His feet tangled and he fell hard. After a moment's rest, he stood and groaned as his over-worked muscles protested, and he tasted bile at the back of his throat.

Despite the need to rush back to Rory, he walked for ten minutes before breaking back into a loping run. Four miles south of Alasdair, he rounded a bend and nearly ran into a chainmail-clad soldier, and for a second he thought it might be one of the Grandurians.

This man was dark-haired, not blonde. "What's got you so spooked, boy?"

"Grandurians."

The soldier grunted and pointed down the trail. "Captain is back about a quarter mile."

Connor thanked him and continued his jog south. He felt a little better being back among the soldiers. Here he would find help. Rory and his band of Guardians could handle the Grandurians. And Shona, she was a Petralist. Surely together they could overwhelm Ilse's band and drive them away.

How many people would die in the process?

He passed two more scouts before meeting up with Rory and Shona who were leading the main force. "You made good time," Rory said. "Report your findings."

After Connor related how Ilse's force took the town, Rory surprised him by grinning. "Perfect."

"But they took Lord Gavin and the Cutters to the manor."

"We know where they are, lad. They've bottled themselves up there. When we surround them, they'll surrender, or we'll destroy them."

"I get Ilse," Shona said.

"Remember, she lives until she talks."

"What if they fight?" Connor asked. "I was told she caught a sword with her bare hand and Erich twisted another like a ribbon."

"Those poor fools never had a chance," Rory snorted. "But if Ilse fights, we'll destroy them." He spoke with absolute confidence. "The enemy is trapped. The chase ends tonight."

"But won't they start hurting people when they see you coming?"

"They might. It's a risk, but there aren't many of them, and if we hit them hard and fast, they won't have time to bother with the prisoners."

Connor started to protest more, but Rory said, "Enough, lad. This is our job. We know what we're doing."

"I don't doubt it, sir, but she knows you're coming, and she doesn't sound worried."

"Then she's a bigger fool than I thought," Shona said.

Connor fell into step behind her, new fears churning in his already upset stomach. He had to believe Rory. The big soldier and his army would sweep Ilse from Alasdair.

He couldn't help but wonder what would happen if they didn't.

CHAPTER 23

he troop hiked upriver for a mile while Connor fumed at the pace. These were supposed to be great warriors. Couldn't they walk faster?

Even the return of his bow, collected from the barge by the Healer's burly assistant, helped but little. He agonized over what Ilse might be doing to the villagers, to his family. He offered to run ahead again but Rory refused to allow it.

As they began crossing a wide field that ran down to the river, the unmistakable sound of a pedra hunting cry broke the afternoon stillness. Connor forgot his other worries and scanned the sky for the beast as nearby soldiers gave each other questioning looks.

Connor doubted any of them had ever heard a pedra scream, which was rare even in Alasdair. The last time Connor heard one, he'd been out hunting high in the mountains and the sound had left him shaken all day. Luckily, they didn't usually bother humans.

Then again, neither did torcs.

Surrounded by a hundred soldiers, he wasn't worried. The pedra would stay far away, but he'd like to catch a glimpse of the monster. The cry came again from the west, much closer this time. The beast swooped out of the late afternoon sun, impossible to see until the last moment.

The man with the wide-brimmed hat pointed to where the huge pedra was diving to attack. "Ware, Captain. Conjured pedra."

Rory cursed and shouted, "At the ready."

As men shifted into tighter formations and the steely rasp of scores of swords being drawn rippled through the air, Connor frowned. A pedra would never attack a company this size.

The beast shot over head, barely a hundred feet up, and screamed again. This close, the sound set the hairs on Connor's arms standing on end. As it passed directly over him, Connor caught his first good look at its magnificent, terrifying form.

Its long, sinuous neck looked more like a waist-thick snake, while its torso was similar to the nuall's, and it moved like the giant mountain cats when on the ground. Connor had once seen one of the beasts run down a huge, flightless eoin, mighty wings wrapped back over its body.

The wings of this beast stretched a full twenty feet, covered with thick plumes worth a fortune if anyone could get their hands on them. Unlike most dark-colored pedras, this one was a uniform light gray, so its feathers would be worth even more. While flying, pedras kept their legs tucked up under their body with their claws retracted.

Beside him, Shona's face faded to ash gray, and Connor realized with a start she must be using some kind of Petralist power. Surprisingly, Rory and the Fast Rollers all faded to ashen skin too. Connor peered at the Guardian standing closest to him whose gray skin looked like stone. He wanted to touch it, but didn't dare.

The pedra screamed again and banked to the left in a tight turn that would bring it back over the group. It kept its long, snakelike neck twisted to watch them the entire time. The head capping that neck ended in a blocky, elongated snout. Thick and ugly, that head held wide-set eyes and a scarred-looking jaw. As it swooped toward them, it folded open its overlapping outer jaws to scream again.

Connor shuddered at the sight. The outer jaws were flaps of muscle capped with hook-like teeth that folded open both vertically and horizontally to reveal the rows of sharp teeth set into the inner jaw. He'd never seen the jaws up close, and at the sight the months of practicing with the bow took over. Almost before willing it, he pulled his bow around and nocked an arrow.

Connor didn't have time to wonder at the beast's inexplicable behavior as dropped lower. His world contracted until nothing existed but his arrow and the monster hurtling toward them. He drew the arrow back, held it for a second, and released.

The arrow sped upward and intercepted the pedra in its steep dive barely fifty feet from the company. He aimed for the face, but it twisted its sinuous head to dodge the blow, and the arrow struck it in the center of the chest.

The arrow splintered. The monster drove straight for Shona, who threw herself to the side, barely dodging the grasping claws. Soldiers swung at the pedra with swords, but their blades slashed nothing but the wind of its wake.

One of the monster's wings brushed Connor's face as it passed. The blow struck like a sledgehammer and threw him from his feet. He moaned with pain and clutched his cheek.

How had that monster survived his arrow? His bow wasn't as strong as the one he'd broken fighting the torc, but it was strong enough to drive an arrow through a pedra's hide at a hundred feet.

Strong hands hauled him to his feet. "Are you all right, lad?" one of the soldiers asked.

"I think so," he muttered through swollen lips, but when he dropped his hands away from his face, he found them covered with blood.

Something dripped down the back of his neck. Connor frowned and reached back to see if he'd hit something when he struck the ground. His hair was soaked and his hand came away dripping with water.

Water?

The soldier standing beside him grimaced. "By the spirits, lad, dodge next time."

The pedra screamed again. As one, they all ducked. One soldier shouted, "Three points west of north, Captain."

It was coming around again.

Connor had another arrow nocked before he even caught sight of the monster. Anger, fueled by pain, was replacing fear.

I'm going to kill this beast. I killed a torc. I can kill a pedra.

The monster dove straight for Shona again.

"Ward the lass," Rory called. The big soldier stepped in front of Shona and hefted a rock as big as Connor's head in one hand. His arm swelled, the leather plates sliding over each other to accommodate expanding muscles.

He threw the rock. It flew faster than Connor's arrow, and just as true.

Just like the arrow, it shattered.

Rock fragments exploded over the group, mixed with thick droplets of water like a spurt of rain. Unlike the arrow though, the impact rocked the monster. It wobbled in its flight and nearly crashed to the earth. Two mighty beats of its great wings steadied it and lifted it into the air again.

"That was my kill," Shona protested.

"Nay, lass," the big soldier said, his eyes never leaving the huge monster. "Didn't you hear the Pathfinder? That be no regular beast. It's conjured."

"Impossible."

"No, just very, very difficult."

As he spoke, Rory's arm returned to its normal size with a scraping of leather plates.

A nearby Guardian said, "Captain, no doubt it's conjured, but even if they have the strength to call such a beast, where'd they get the powder for it?"

"They have it," Shona said. "They stole it from the barge."

What were they talking about?

Even his Aunt Ailsa couldn't have sculpted a Pedra from the granite powder the Grandurians stole, nor could a sculpture fly like a living thing.

One of the soldiers cried out, "It means to strike again, sir."

"All right, lads," Captain Rory called. "Missile barrage."

Soldiers scattered, hunting around on the ground for stones. They piled them near the five leather-clad Guardians

Rory had called Fast Rollers, and then assembled in units all around, swords at the ready. One unit prepared a weighted net.

The Fast Rollers hefted rocks and, as they readied to throw, their torsos and arms swelled with power, although not at the same rate. The biggest soldiers, already hugely muscled men, swelled only a little, while the rest expanded impossibly until they strained the limits of even their expandable armor. Connor finally understood the overlapping plates and straps. Regular armor would have hindered their powers, or split and been useless.

The pedra screamed and dove once more. Connor drew back the arrow.

"Throw!" Rory called.

Half a dozen rocks hurled into the air trying to knock the beast from the sky. Instead of trying to plow through the barrage as it had in the past, the pedra furled its wings, twisted in the air, and fell like a stone to the earth.

Most of the missiles missed it. One shattered against its heavy flanks. This time Connor clearly saw water spurting from its hide where the stone struck.

The pedra landed on its feet, already running. It covered thirty feet with each leaping stride and descended on the company in a blur of fangs and claws. It plowed through the first ranks, its dead gray eyes fixed on Shona the entire time.

Then the net-wielding unit moved forward and threw.

It leaped fifty feet straight up.

The net passed harmlessly just below its hind legs. The pedra hung in the air at the apex of its leap for a second, then its wings snapped open and it sailed down toward Shona.

One of the Fast Rollers, howling like a berserker, charged it, his skin as gray as the pedra's. The two collided with a resounding crash, and the man dug in his legs to halt the monster's advance with raw Guardian strength.

His ankles shattered.

He screamed and tumbled to the ground, the jagged stumps of his legs looking like a half-processed granite block in the Powder House. As he hit the ground, his body shrank to its normal size and the broken edges of the stumps of his legs softened and began to bleed. A lot.

The impact catapulted the pedra up into the air amid a watery spray. Cracks spider-webbed across its chest, and it screamed so loud Connor had to cover his ears. The monster glided over twenty men, just out of reach of their swords and hammers, still focused on Shona.

Shona stood defiant in some kind of battle stance with sword raised. She shouted, "By the fates and furies, I'll kill you!"

The pedra screamed again.

Standing behind Shona, Connor had a clear line of sight straight through both sets of jaws, so he took the shot. The arrow disappeared down the monster's throat and for a second it wobbled. Shona leaped forward and struck one of its grasping paws. Her sword glanced off, dripping water, and she rolled away.

With a battle cry that shook the valley, Rory vaulted high into the air, thrown upward by four of his men. He caught one of the beast's wings, dragging the monster down with his weight.

The pedra lashed at Rory with its horrible fangs, but the impact sounded like stones cracking together. They hit the ground fifty feet beyond the line of soldiers. Men charged, intending to swarm the monster and destroy it with brute force.

The pedra was just as deadly on the ground as it was in the air. While Rory landed on his back, his entire focus on holding the wing down, the pedra landed on its catlike feet. It turned on Rory and attacked with terrible fury.

The two rolled over each other as the beast raked at him with its sickle-like claws and, opening its outer jaws wide, engulfed half of Rory's head in its maw. It began shaking him violently, the corded muscles of its neck standing out in sharp relief.

Rory let go of the wing and grabbed the monster's outer jaw. There was no blood, but as Connor watched the fight, he wondered how the Captain could possibly still live.

As soon as Rory's grip relaxed, the pedra threw him aside. The soldiers were almost upon it, but it bounded away, and within seconds returned to the air.

It rose high above the valley while the soldiers re-grouped. To Connor's absolute amazement, Rory sprang to his feet, wiped water from his face, and started shouting orders. His face bore several white scratches, like the marks of chisels on granite. He growled at the men to make ready. Several of them prepared ropes while others gathered more rocks.

The pedra did not return. It flew high, crossed the river and disappeared beyond the thick forest on the far side.

"Coward demon spawn," Shona spat after it.

Rory ordered the men to remain vigilant while the Healer treated the man whose legs had shattered. Connor drew near, curiosity overruling revulsion. He circled wide around the Healer until he could get a look at the wounds.

The man's feet ended in jagged stumps, although it looked like the Healer had already stemmed the bleeding. The old man was bandaging them while soldiers prepared a litter to carry the injured man. Connor sidled over to where the man had fallen. The shattered remains of his feet were still lying there.

Connor frowned and bent down to inspect them. They didn't look right. There was no blood and they were shattered in a way he'd never seen in living flesh. He cautiously reached out to touch one, but hesitated.

The fragments looked more like ...

He touched it, and recoiled.

Stone.

He dared pick up a piece of stone that looked like it had been a toe. He turned it over in his hands, fascinated and horrified at the same time. If he hadn't known that only moments ago this had been part of the soldier's body, he would have thought it was broken from some sculpture.

He glanced over at the injured soldier who slept after having taken some draught from the Healer, then shivered and dropped the stone toe. The other Guardians had already returned to their normal size, but Connor had glimpsed their incredible powers.

What have I gotten myself into?

CHAPTER 24

I t's coming back."

Connor easily picked out the dark shape of the huge pedra against the blue sky to the east.

This monster was clearly not made of flesh and bone. Why then would it bleed water? What did they mean it was conjured? Did a Petralist turn into this great stone bird? What magic allowed such a vast weight to pull itself off the ground like a living animal?

Not knowing made it all the more terrifying.

The soldiers formed tight battle lines with Shona in the center. Connor stood close to her, an arrow nocked even though he knew it wouldn't do any good. He couldn't face this threat with no weapon. At least with the bow in hand he didn't feel completely helpless. The lie helped a little.

The pedra crossed the river with a large mountain deer dangling from its claws. The beast stayed about a hundred feet up in the air, out of effective range of their missiles.

"What's it doing?" Shona asked.

Maybe it wants to trade.

The stone monster seemed focused only on Shona. For whatever reason, it wanted her and her alone.

The pedra hovered directly over the company. Everyone tensed, waiting to see what it would do.

It screamed. Instead of the catlike hunting cry, this scream pierced their brains like needles. The high-pitched sound vibrated deep into Connor's chest and set his teeth aching. He stared in horror, comprehension giving wings to his fear.

"We have to get out of here," he shouted to Rory and pointing at the distant trees a couple hundred yards upriver. "We've got to get to cover."

Before Rory could reply, the pedra began tearing at the carcass in its claws. In a matter of seconds, it ripped the dead animal to pieces. Blood and chunks of flesh and bone rained down all over the company. The soldiers muttered angrily but the gore didn't bother them.

"Listen, Captain," Connor insisted. "That sound. It's calling more pedras."

That got Rory's attention. "What are you talking about?"

"That's a bloodlust scream. They don't do it often, only when they're in a blood frenzy, just before they mate. Other pedras can hear it for miles around. They answer the call. They come to kill."

"There can't be more stone beasts like that," Shona said. "Flesh and blood pedras won't bother a hundred armed men."

Connor raised one gore-splattered arm and said, "In a blood frenzy, they will. We're marked. They won't be able to resist."

In his mind's eye, Connor again saw the bloody remains of Tam, Alasdair's previous hunter. He'd been caught in a bloodlust and been ripped to pieces. They'd only been able to identify him by the shredded remains of his hat.

Rory began barking orders. A third of the troop sprinted upriver ahead of the main company, making for a large rock that lay halfway to the promised shelter of the trees and rose ten feet above the field. The rest of the company followed at a quick trot. The stone pedra hovered, watching.

Before they reached the sentinel rock, the cry of a hunting pedra floated down from the north, followed a few seconds later by another, and then a third.

The company paused and took up battle positions. Pedras appeared in the distance, coming fast. Six, ten, fifteen. Connor wouldn't have believed so many pedras lived within the range of the call.

He'd actually witnessed a pedra bloodlust slaughter once from a vantage high on a mountain with views down into the next valley. The pedras had been hunting there, miles from him, but their screams of blood rage had terrified him. Five pedras had answered the call that day and together they'd slaughtered an entire herd of mountain goats.

Connor had run all the way back to Alasdair.

The pedras gathered above the company, swirling overhead like a living, black tornado with a dead gray heart. Their cries merged into a continuous scream.

"I don't think they're going to attack," Shona said. "Not a company this size."

Almost as if in response to her words, the stone pedra folded its wings and plummeted straight toward her.

The other pedras followed.

"Brace! Brace! Brace!" Rory shouted.

Guardians swelled with strength and their skin shifted to gray as their powers transformed them into living stone. As the conjured pedra plummeted toward them, every Fast Roller launched heavy stones up at it. The monster snapped open its wings and veered away, dodging the missiles and banking hard around the company, skimming the ground so low one of its wing tips scraped a watery furrow in the soil.

The other pedras attacked the company, screaming in blood lust, lashing out at the soldiers. These beasts were smaller than the great stone pedra, but also far more agile. They spun and twisted, dodging sword thrusts and snatching at soldiers.

One man on the outer edge of the battle line staggered from a blow to the head and fell two paces from his comrades. Instantly two pedras pounced, grabbed him with their clawed forelegs, and lifted him into the air.

Connor shot one of them. The arrow took the beast in the hind quarter. It screamed and lost its hold on the soldier. The other beast, overburdened, lost altitude. The soldier twisted in the beast's grasp and slashed with his sword.

The pedra fell dead to the ground, its severed head still biting at the empty air. Half a dozen men broke from the main battle formation and raced to cover their comrade. Several pedras converged on the smaller group just as they would on animals fleeing a herd, but the men held them off with wild swings of their swords while, step by step, they fought back toward the main line.

The stone pedra completed its tight, banking turn and swooped through the melee on its single-minded pursuit of Shona.

Rory struck first.

The captain swung a heavy war hammer he'd borrowed from another soldier and slammed it into one of the beast's front legs. The leg shattered, exploding into a cloud of muddy chunks. The impact rocked the beast and knocked Rory to the ground.

As it passed, Shona and several other soldiers all struck at it with their swords, scraping across the monster's torso and wings. One great gray feather broke free and landed next to Connor. With a sweep of its giant wings, the huge pedra pulled itself airborne again.

Connor knocked a fresh arrow and looked for a target. Behind him, a soldier shouted, "Look out!"

He spun just as a pedra struck him in the chest. The impact sent him flying back off his feet and knocked the bow from his hands.

He didn't hit the ground.

Vice-like claws clamped over his biceps and punched through his thin shirt, sinking deep into the muscles beneath.

Connor screamed as the monster hauled him into the air and away from the soldiers. Its hind legs scraped against his sides, trying to gain purchase on his body. Connor hung close under its black hide, nearly overwhelmed by its heavy, oily scent despite the wind of their passage. Its torso rippled with corded muscle as it carried him away to slaughter him.

In a panic, Connor beat at the monster's underbelly with his free hand. His Curse roared to life as his normal control slipped and its maddening itch rolled through his torso, completely unrestrained. Even his head itched.

He tried to focus the Curse to punch the beast out of the air, but the monster screamed its ear-piercing shriek of blood lust. The sound scattered his concentration. The monster struck with its hideous head, outer jaws flapped open and inner jaws gaped wide.

Connor couldn't dodge. The itching of the Curse spiked to such intensity all through his body, it felt like his skin was cracking. He twisted his head away from the beast in a desperate but futile gesture.

The pedra's outer jaws enveloped Connor's head while its inner jaws bit down on the back of his skull with stunning force.

Pain exploded in his head. Connor's scream became muffled as the wide flaps of the outer jaw wrapped around his head and over his face, the curved teeth digging at his neck.

Connor thrashed wildly in the creature's grasp. The intense itching of his skin faded and all feeling drained from his body. The pedra bit at his head again.

He couldn't imagine how he was still alive, but something wasn't right.

Of course not. A pedra was trying to eat him alive. Maybe panic had addled his brain because the pain seemed to fade even as the monster's inner jaws scraped against his skull.

He'd heard that the most severe injuries were sometimes like that. People felt fine just before they drew their last breath.

The outer jaws dug at his face and neck, but they didn't puncture into his flesh. He couldn't breathe with it meaty jaws over his mouth and nose. When he tried, he got only a mouthful of pedra saliva that burned his skin and nearly made him vomit.

He couldn't die like this, eaten by a pedra.

He focused on the Curse roaring through his body and released it into his fist.

This pedra might kill him, but he wouldn't go quietly.

With a mighty wrenching twist of his entire body, he yanked an arm free. The muscle screamed in agony as the monster's claws ripped loose, but Connor didn't relent. Nothing mattered but getting one final breath of fresh air before he died.

Blindly, Connor punched at the pedra's torso, driving his Curse-laden fist with every ounce of strength he could muster. It was a clumsy blow, but he connected with something solid.

The pedra grunted and its jaws loosened their hold. Connor clawed at the outer jaws and wrenched them open. He gasped as the meaty jaw came free of his face and drew in a lungful of the creature's fetid breath.

His stomach heaved and spewed everything he'd eaten in the past day. Vomit coated the creature's jaw, making it slick, and splashed back across Connor's face as he yanked at the creature's jaw again.

The pedra screamed full in his face and released its hold. Connor swung hard in the wind, tethered to the monster by his other arm, while his ears rang painfully. The movement wrenched his shoulder and a fresh wave of agony lanced through his torso. The world spun below him and it took a second for him to realize where they were.

They'd crossed the clearing and soared over the first row of trees, although the pedra seemed to be dropping. The monster screamed again and raked at Connor with its clawed legs. He drew his dagger and slashed wildly at it. He scored a deep hit on the pedra's other foreleg and it screamed again.

Together, they crashed through the branches of a tall oak, and plummeted to the ground. They hit hard and Connor rolled away from the beast. It leaped upon him, striking at his throat with its horrible double jaws.

Connor drove his dagger up through its mouth and into the soft tissue at the back of its throat. Its jaws clamped down hard on his arm but he wrenched the dagger around with all his might.

The pedra convulsed and staggered away, blood pouring from its open mouth. Its wings flapped weakly and it fell over, heaving for breath and clawing at the soil.

Connor backed away, unaware of the tears streaming down his face. Every limb trembled from the shock of what he'd just experienced as he watched the monster die. His hand shook so badly he could barely keep his dagger pointed in the beast's general direction. When it was clear the pedra was no longer a threat, Connor collapsed.

All he could think was, *How can I still be alive?*

CHAPTER 25

onnor wanted nothing more than to curl up in a ball, but he couldn't stay there. He had to move.

He staggered to his feet and inspected his wounds as best he could. His head hurt, and when he touched the back of his skull, his hand came away smeared with blood. It felt like his scalp was still in place though, so he decided he'd live.

His arms had been punctured deeply by the pedra's claws, but when he cut open the sleeves of his hunting tunic, the bleeding had already stopped and the wounds did not look as serious as he expected. His skin felt raw as if it had been scraped with pumice stone, but it didn't hurt as much as it had just moments ago.

How could he possibly have survived that mauling with only minor injuries?

Connor stared at his fist thoughtfully. He'd Curse-punched the pedra and surely that saved his life, but the memory of his entire body going dead like his fist did just before releasing the Curse rattled him. The Curse had never done that before.

Maybe it also granted protection like Rory's Guardian powers had? How else could he explain it? The monster had him by the head. Those jaws should have ripped his face off.

If they survived until evening, he planned to hold Rory to the promise to explore his Curse further. He needed to know what it really meant. Perhaps Patronage had begun somehow altering his Curse already? He'd thought there would be more to it than that.

The distant screaming of pedras broke his train of thought. Connor headed back toward the clearing where the fight was still under way. He pushed through some trees and nearly stumbled upon a small herd of mountain goats cowering in some thick brush at the edge of a small glade. The goats huddled together, the entire mass of small bodies shaking with fear.

Connor got an idea. Lifting his face to the sky, he screamed a pedra hunting cry. He could mimic most of the animals that roamed the Maclachlan Mountains and had practiced the pedra cry in the days after he'd witnessed the pedra blood hunt.

The goats huddling nearby bolted from their concealment, bleating with terror. Overhead, a pedra plummeted out of the air onto one of the fleeing goats. The impact knocked the little animal from its feet and the pedra killed it with a single powerful snap of its double jaws.

Connor swallowed at the memory of those horrible jaws clamping down over his own head. The pedra easily crunched through the goat's bones. It should have done the same to him. He shivered.

The pedra launched itself into the air and screamed again. Other pedras answered, and soon half a dozen of the flying monsters circled overhead, diving into the forest and emerging moments later with dead goats dangling from their clawed legs. The successful hunters flapped north to feast, and later to mate.

Connor returned to the edge of the field just in time to witness the soldiers down the last of the living pedras with a barrage of thrown spears. Dead pedras littered the field. Connor looked for the great stone pedra, but didn't see it.

As he watched, the soldiers gathered into one body about thirty paces from the sentinel rock. Shona left the group and jogged to the rock, where she crouched, as if taking cover.

Was she insane?

A triumphant scream from overhead sent a ripple of new fear through Connor's overtaxed nerves. The stone pedra plummeted out of the sky.

Connor expected to see the soldiers sprint toward her in a desperate attempt to save her life. They did not.

Shona stood with a battle hammer in one hand, and screamed her own battle cry, a wordless shout of defiance.

The pedra struck. It bore down on Shona, grasping at her with its three unbroken legs. Shona shouted again and swung a mighty blow at one leg. The beast caught her hammer and pulled it from her hand. Then it dropped over her and grasped her with its wicked claws.

"No!" Connor shouted and although he had nothing but his dagger as a weapon, he ran from cover toward the rock. It was a useless gesture but he refused to admit it and ran as hard as he could. On the far side of the sentinel rock, Rory and his men finally began a belated charge to help.

The pedra flapped its wings hard to launch itself back into the air with its prize. It rose twenty feet with Shona dangling from its claws, its speed growing with each span.

Then unexpectedly it seemed to bounce in mid-air and veered hard to the side, arcing down as if tethered. It slammed into the ground hard. Shona rolled free and ran to where her hammer had fallen. The pedra leaped high, flapping hard to escape the approaching soldiers.

Again its headlong flight ended abruptly about twenty feet in the air. This time Connor was close enough to see the stout rope tied around one of its rear legs and anchored to the sentinel rock. Bound to the earth by the rope, the pedra rebounded and slammed into the ground. Even as it rolled back to its feet, Rory and his men swarmed over it.

Led by the five Guardians, soldiers bore it to the ground with their weight. Men wielding heavy war hammers pounded at its wings and then its torso. Captain Rory charged straight at its head and shattered part of its outer jaw with the first blow of his hammer.

Shona joined the fray by jumping onto the monster's back and slamming her own hammer down onto the base of its neck. Something broke, and the creature collapsed. The soldiers continued beating on it until nothing remained but a pile of muddy rubble. By the time Connor reached the fight, it was all but over.

Shona tossed her war hammer to a nearby soldier and swept hair that had come out of her tight braid away from her face. She stood panting, more beautiful and regal in that moment than Connor had ever seen.

Then she reached down and ripped off the leather plate over her stomach. The entire section of her armor came free, revealing her midriff.

Connor gaped. Her gray skin was perfectly sculpted, every muscle defined with exquisite detail. It shone like polished granite. She looked like, well, a perfectly formed living statue.

Shona tossed the leather plate to a nearby Guardian and said, "Replenish this for me." Her skin faded back to its normal tone, and her stomach rippled with living muscles again.

Connor approached while the Guardians gathered around Shona and removed plates from their stomachs and thighs. A couple of them produced small leather pouches, and the men knelt and sprinkled the contents onto the insides of the armor they'd removed.

The Guardian who had received Shona's armor divided the contents of the little pouch he was given between his armor and hers. Connor stepped closer as the man worked.

Granite. Connor recognized it instantly. He'd worked with granite powder all his life.

Why would they coat their armor with it?

As they moved and fought, it would surely chafe and irritate their skin. The powder stuck to the armor as if the inside edge were sticky.

"What are you doing?" Connor asked.

The man stood and handed Shona her armor. She regarded it critically. "This isn't full."

"That's all there is, miss."

Shona turned to Rory who was working on his own leather plate. "Are we so low on supplies, captain?"

Rory straightened and buckled his leather plate back into position. Connor felt he understood a little about their myriad straps and buckles, but the ritual with precious granite powder still didn't make much sense.

Rory said, "We brought enough for only one re-arming. We'd expected to resupply from the shipment from Alasdair."

Understanding finally hit Connor. That's why everyone was so concerned about the theft of the granite powder. Somehow they used it to fight.

"Why didn't you bring more?" Shona asked.

"By orders of your father. Stores in Merkland could not be depleted in case the Grandurians launched a full attack."

"That was stupid."

"Nay, lass. It was sound thinking. If the barge had arrived as planned, it would have been the right choice."

"We don't have enough," Shona said. "Ilse and her men will destroy us if our powers run out too soon."

Connor blinked with new realization. Somehow the granite powder actually triggered their powers. The magnitude of the realization rocked him to the core. He sat on the ground and stared, unseeing. His family had quarried granite for fourteen generations, powdering it to dust and shipping it down to Merkland, and they'd never realized why.

They'd been supplying the power to fuel the Petralists.

How could it also fuel Guardians?

No wonder everyone treated it like gold. It was unbelievably valuable.

Around him, soldiers were preparing to move out while the handful of men injured in the fight with the pedras gathered around the Healer.

One soldier caught sight of Connor and clapped him on the shoulder. "How'd you escape that pedra, lad? By the Tallan, I thought you were dead for sure."

"I got lucky."

Behind him, Rory said, "We proceed as planned. There is granite to be had at Alasdair. We outnumber the Grandurians five to one. We'll take them by surprise. They won't last long enough for the powder shortage to matter."

"Connor, come here," Shona called.

He rose painfully to his feet, suddenly more exhausted than he ever imagined he could be.

She grimaced, "You're a mess. Go wash yourself."

He washed off the blood and vomit with cold water soldiers hauled up from the river.

The Healer inspected his wounds, mumbling to himself. Tilting Connor's face toward the light he asked, "How old are these abrasions?"

"Maybe fifteen minutes."

The Healer frowned. "You're the Cursed boy, yes?"

"Yes."

"What's your affinity?"

"I don't know."

"Well, I can guess. Rare to show a secondary affinity without prior training." The Healer continued to mutter to himself, but Connor's mind was too preoccupied by what he'd just learned about granite powder. He needed to understand why, or how it worked.

The Healer gasped and drew Connor's attention. The old man was staring at Connor's chest, one shaking hand reaching out toward him. Connor looked down as the Healer hesitantly touched the carved sandstone pendant he wore around his neck.

As the Healer's fingers touched the pendant, a wave of warmth exploded through Connor and he rocked backward.

The Healer grinned like a little boy. "Astounding. Where did you get that, boy?"

Connor clutched the pendant. He felt suddenly wonderful. All the exhaustion and pain had washed out of him. He'd heard wonderful things about Healers, but had never imagined such a thing.

"That pendant, boy," the Healer repeated. "Where'd you get it?"

"It was a gift from my aunt."

"Such a gift," the Healer said in an awed voice.

Connor shrugged. "She's a sculptor. It's what she does."

The Healer grinned. "You have no idea, do you?"

"Probably not. Why don't you explain it?"

"In time, lad." The old man moved away to the next patient.

Connor headed back to where Rory and Shona were talking with Rory's sergeants. The cryptic answer kind of killed the moment. He gingerly touched his face, probing the well-formed scabs.

Impressive. He had so much to learn.

"Glad to see you're alive, lad," Captain Rory said with a smile when he joined them. "I saw that beast haul you away and thought you were a dead man."

"I got lucky," he said again.

Rory laughed, "Good lad." Then his expression turned serious. "Tell me about your town. Where do they store the powder?"

"In the Powder House down by the loch." Connor told him about it, the wall gate, the layout of the town, and the plateau with Lord Gavin's manor house looking out over the valley.

Rory glanced at the sun, "We can work with that. We attack after dark."

He issued orders to his men, and the company moved out.

CHAPTER 26

erena opened the door to Lord Gavin's study, which now served as Ilse's command center, to allow Erich to enter. He saluted to Ilse and spared a glance at Kilian, who snored softly in a plush couch against one wall.

"Captain, we have located the trail."

"That was fast."

"Without the pigeon I conjured with Kilian's help, I never would have found it. One of the locals pointed out Mount Ingram, but the boy must be part mountain goat to have discovered the trail."

"Very well."

As Erich provided a detailed description of the trail's location, Verena thought of the boy Connor. He had surprised them all with his daring rescue of Shona. Verena had never seen Anika so angry, and she shuddered to think what the powerful woman would do to Connor if she ever got her hands on him again.

Verena found it hard to hate Connor. He did not have all the facts, so of course his loyalty to Shona would trump the rightness of their cause. Still, he had made things very complicated. Verena trusted Ilse completely, but the company was now caught in a perilous trap. The location of the trail provided the one small chance they might survive the coming confrontation.

Ilse wrote a short note, rolled it tight, and slipped it into a tiny carrier tube and prepared for another summoning.

Verena watched with interest. The summoning of the spectacular pedra had proved fascinating, and she could still scarce believe they managed it.

Kilian had played the critical role in that summoning, wrapping Ilse's granite strength with his water powers that gave the summoned creature life. The account he'd shared of the battle with the Obrioners just before he passed out was incredible.

Ilse dipped her hand into a pouch of granite powder to restore her Petralist strength by absorbing it through her skin. Verena sometimes wished she could touch the power of stones like the Petralists, but only rarely. She loved her connection. Stones spoke to her through their taste, through the flickering of their powers against her fingers.

As a Builder, she could somehow reach into the power stones and unlock their power to the world. Petralists could only use that power within themselves, or drive it out, wrapped in elemental life, to form their conjured creations, but for Verena there were no limits.

Builders had existed in times of old, ancient days before the Tallan Wars, before Granadure broke free of the rule of the old queen. Every Builder died in those dark days, slaughtered to protect dark secrets no one could even guess at any more, although shadows of their previous accomplishments still dotted the land. Speedcaravans, and even the legendary Builded wall of Merkland were some of the ancient relics.

Verena stood at the vanguard of re-kindled Builder powers. They had made such progress in the last three years, but those baby steps only highlighted how much still remained to be learned. Verena planned to learn it all.

Ilse drove her hand into a bucket of clay that sat on her desk and bowed her head in concentration. The conjuring process still mystified Verena, although she hoped to one day replicate it with her Builded stones. Ilse had explained that she focused her granite strength into a tight ball before wrapping it with the steady, solid earth power of slate. She would direct the combined force out through the hand driven into the bucket of clay, using its mass to form the conjuring based on the image she held in her mind.

Verena yearned to dip her own finger into the bucket, or to taste the clay that began to bubble as Ilse's power infused it. The air above the bucket shimmered and split into rainbows of multi-colored light. The scent of recently turned earth filled the room while the brilliant colors reflected off the expensive leather-bound books and darkly polished furniture of the study. The light flared, and the bucket rattled where it sat on the desk.

With a tiny thunderclap, it was over. The empty bucket fell to the floor with a clang. Perched on the desk stood a perfectly sculpted stone pigeon. It cooed and nuzzled Ilse's still-extended hand.

Verena approached and stroked the stone pigeon's smooth feathers. This particular conjuring was Ilse's specialty, and this one looked exceptional. The heavy local clay mixed well with the local granite.

Calling forth that stone pedra earlier had taxed Ilse, and Verena had summoned the healer to check on her before she attempted the second, far simpler summoning. Kilian, who had remained lying in the wagon that had held the clay they used in that summoning, did not move until after the conjured beast died in battle. He had barely held on long enough to relate the story before drifting off to sleep again.

Verena glanced at the man. He looked barely forty years old, but he had to be far older than that. The rumors she'd heard of him suggested deep secrets and a wealth of lore knowledge she yearned to explore after they completed the mission.

Although the great stone pedra had been destroyed, the delay Kilian gained was well worth the price. Ilse was playing a dangerous game, walking a tightrope over a deadly gulf. One misstep would prove fatal.

Ilse attached the messenger tube to the stone pigeon's leg, pushed open the study's window, and tossed the little bird skyward. It shot up into the late afternoon sky and flapped northward.

Although part of her mind flew with the bird, she did not appear very distracted by the effort. "I expect the attack after dark."

Verena placed a new wafer of slate on the desk for Ilse and then rubbed her hand absently over her satchel. "That's plenty of time."

"Much depends on you tonight," Ilse said.

"I know," Verena said excitedly as she considered the myriad combinations she could deploy, most of which she had never tried before.

"I almost feel sorry for them. They have no idea what's about to happen."

CHAPTER 27

onnor led Rory's strike force upriver for two miles before the captain called a halt and they settled behind a thick screen of pine trees near the trail to wait for nightfall. Connor gratefully accepted some food, but as much as he longed to lie down under a tree and sleep, he instead moved to where the captain and Shona were speaking near the center of the company.

"Get some sleep, lad," Rory said when Connor joined them.

"Thank you, sir. I plan to." Connor hesitated and then continued in a rush. "Can you tell me what just happened? That thing was no pedra."

"No, lad, it was conjured, and by a mighty powerful Petralist too."

"I don't understand."

"Conjuring is a delicate business," Rory said. "Even a small creature, like a messenger bird, takes a great deal of power and control."

"And a metamorphic gift," the old Healer piped in from where he sat nearby.

"A what?" Connor asked.

Shona sighed. "You won't understand for a while, Connor. We don't even know your affinity yet."

"No better time than the present," Rory said. "We don't have all the stones here, but we know where to start."

Connor licked suddenly dry lips as he realized they meant to test him.

The Guardians drew near, and the one who had teased Connor when they first met said, "You said you hit things?"

"Aye."

The burly soldier nodded. "I started that way too."

"Really?"

He nodded. "Name's Tomas." He extended to Connor a small leather pouch.

Shona frowned. "We don't have powder to waste."

"It's not a waste," Rory said. "You wish to grant Patronage, you need to know his affinity."

Connor took the leather pouch cautiously, not sure what would happen. He sat on a nearby log, pried open the drawstring and peeked inside.

Granite powder, of course. So familiar, and yet in that moment, somehow alien.

Tomas said, "Granite's an igneous stone, lad. Absorbs through the skin." He made a dipping motion with one hand. "Go on, now."

Connor forced aside gnawing fear. This is what he wanted. These were Guardians teaching him, so now he could finally begin answering all the questions. He drove his hand into the granite powder, and its familiar grit eased a little of his nervousness.

Tomas leaned forward a little, his face eager. "Concentrate, lad."

"On what?"

"On the granite, of course."

That didn't entirely make sense, but Connor tried. With everyone watching him, he felt incredibly self-conscious, and felt nothing but granite between his fingers. He didn't know what they wanted him to do, but nothing was happening.

Shona sat beside him and Connor was intensely aware of her leather-clad form so close. She placed one hand over his eyes and leaned close to whisper softly in his ear.

"Relax, Connor. Nothing exists but the granite."

Was she crazy? How could he relax with her sitting so close, her warm breath tickling his ear?

She smelled like leather and roses, and her rich voice tugged at his heart. It was easier to fight the pedra today than to sit beside her and try to relax.

"Relax," she whispered again in his ear. "Focus on the granite. Feel every grain against your skin."

He tried to do what she asked. He rolled the granite powder through his fingers and thought back to that very morning when he'd done the same on the barge.

His hand started to itch.

Connor's eyes popped open and he met Shona's gaze. "It's working. I feel it."

She grinned and touched his hand. "Like an itch just under the skin?"

"Yes." The feeling intensified and rolled up his arm to his chest. He gripped the granite powder and willed its power into him.

With a rush, strength blossomed in every muscle, like nothing he'd ever felt before. He staggered to his feet, unable to remain seated with so much power roaring through his body.

The muscles of his chest and arms swelled impossibly, and his shirt ripped up the back. He stared in wonder at his bulging muscles, threw his head back and laughed with the pure joy of the moment.

The Guardians all leaped to their feet and shouted, as if he'd won a great victory.

Rory, grinning like the others, said, "Well done, lad."

Shona stood close beside Connor and traced a hand down his arm. She smiled, "Oh, Connor, I am very impressed."

Tomas stepped in front of Connor and said, "Your Curse-punch was just the beginning. You absorbed just enough power to focus it in your fist. Now you've taken a full measure of granite, confirmed your affinity. Now you're strong!"

He turned to a nearby tree as thick around as Connor's waist, and grasped it by the trunk. His body swelled with power and the leather plates on his shoulders and back shifted with his expanded size.

He ripped the tree out of the ground.

Roots snapped and earth flung in all directions as Tomas lifted the tree high, turned, and heaved it. It sailed over the camp, past soldiers who dove out of the way, and crashed down into the forest on the far side. The entire clearing shook, wood splintered as branches snapped off against other trees, and the air filled with the smell of earth and wood.

Tomas turned and thumped his chest as his body shrank back to his normal burly size. "That's the power of a granite Guardian lad, strength of the mountains."

Shona sniffed. "Show-off."

Tomas grinned. "Your turn."

Connor returned the grin. The feeling of overwhelming strength was heady, and in that moment, he felt like he could lift the entire manor house off its foundation. He selected a tree almost as big around as the one Tomas ripped from the ground, grabbed it by the trunk, and heaved.

Nothing happened.

Connor frowned, set his feet, and pulled harder. The hugely expanded muscles of his back strained, and the tattered remains of his shirt slid off his shoulders. The tree shook and groaned, but stayed fast in the ground.

Shona drew near and placed one hand on the center of his back. "Focus, Connor. One of the important things to learn is to regulate your power."

He paused. "What do you mean?"

"You absorb strength from the granite, but you control how much of it to use. It's called the tap rate."

She stepped to one side, to a rock half as tall as she and covered with moss. She gripped it and lifted it easily over her head. "I can lift this rock by applying just enough power. I don't need a full measure of granite."

She dropped the rock and returned to him. Her skin faded to gray and her body hardened to the perfectly sculpted lines he'd seen when she fought the pedra. She gave him a little wink, "Sometimes, we need to max-tap. It burns through the granite much faster, but can increase our power ten-fold."

She grabbed the tree he'd been struggling to lift, and with a single heave of her shoulders, ripped it from the ground.

Connor stumbled back as earth cascaded up from snapping roots. Shona tossed the tree aside, and her skin returned to its normal, softer lines.

She raised a single eyebrow at him. "Think you can keep up?"

Rory said, "Good show, lass, but ware the powder stores."

Shona tossed her hair back and said, "You insisted we do this, so we do it right. I have enough left for Ilse."

Connor rushed to another tree, this one even thicker around than the last. He grabbed it and focused on the granite strength burning through his body. He willed it to life.

At first it tried pooling in his fist, and he stared in wonder as the skin of his hand faded to gray. He fought the Curse, fought the granite power, and drove it out to the rest of his body. His muscles swelled with renewed strength, and the itch of the curse expanded through all his limbs.

He groaned with the need to scratch, but the feeling passed quickly, and his skin faded to gray all over. His feeling deadened until his entire body felt like living granite. He turned to the tree and this time easily pulled it out of the ground.

Connor laughed as he hefted the mighty tree. He turned to look at Shona, but as he did so, the tree shifted in his hands and started to fall toward the camp.

Connor grunted and tried to catch it, but the momentum built so quickly that despite his incredible strength, he could not stop it.

"Look out," Connor shouted. Soldiers scattered as the tree fell toward them.

Captain Rory and Tomas leaped forward and planted themselves directly underneath the falling tree. The image of the one Fast Roller's ankles shattering under the impact with the stone pedra flashed into Connor's mind. He could not allow that to happen to Rory.

Connor roared with the effort and drew deep upon the power of the granite. His body swelled further, and power burned up his arms. Connor leaned against the weight of the falling tree with all his strength.

"Thank you, sir. I knew the quarry triggered my Curse somehow, but never thought it was the granite. How does it grant us strength?"

Shona said, "We don't have time to explain it all."

Rory nodded. "For now, accept that it is so. Granite is the most common power stone in Obrion. More Petralists and more Guardians show gifts in granite than any other."

"There are other stones?"

"Of course," Shona said. "Did you think every Guardian used the same stone and had the same powers?"

"Well, yes." He should have realized there were different types of Petralists after his time with the Grandurians. Kilian was no Boulder. Then there was the fast-running Strider, and the Healer. Of course they used different stones.

"You need to pay more attention," Shona said.

"I didn't know." Now that she mentioned them, it made sense, but how could he have figured that out?

"Nine are the stones that grant their power," Rory said, his voice slipping into a cadence. "Three for the masses, two for the many, and four for the privileged few."

"Oh now he's gone and cracked," the Healer said with a wheezing chuckle. "The boy won't be able to keep up."

Rory smiled ruefully. "I don't know any other way to say it."

Shona groaned, "It's a wonder you can count high enough to lead these men."

"What did you mean?" Connor asked before they could get distracted.

"He means that even though there are nine power sources, most of us develop affinities with one of three."

"Igneous stones," the Healer piped in. "Most common. All manifest first through these." He gave Connor a thoughtful look and muttered under his breath. "Almost always."

Shona added, "Maybe half of all Petralists and Guardians can develop at least a basic affinity with a secondary stone."

"Sedimentary," the Healer added. "Light and healing." He said healing with pride and tapped his chest. "But at best half of those gain enough power to make it worth the effort."

"What's important to us today," Shona said, "is that only a few Petralists can ever develop an affinity with one of the four metamorphic stones."

"Why is that important?" Connor asked.

"Because," Rory piped in, "conjuring can only be done by someone with a granite affinity combining their strength with a metamorphic elemental power. To conjure that stone pedra, one of Ilse's band must have a powerful affinity to a metamorphic stone, and lots of experience."

"Kilian, the Water Moccasin." Shona looked to Connor, as if expecting him to understand. He felt like a dolt when he didn't.

"Aye, that would do it," Rory said. "Mighty tricky merging that much granite with enough soapstone to hold it all together."

"It has to be," Shona said. "Didn't you notice the water?"

Finally Connor understood. They were talking about the water spurting from the pedra like blood every time it got hit. Somehow Ilse and Kilian had worked together to summon that monster.

He shivered. This foreign world of Guardians was so different from his own it was like standing on the edge of a precipice. The little he understood about it only served to highlight its danger, but he still lacked so much knowledge. Any one thing he didn't yet know could be the stone that could roll under his foot and throw him over the edge.

"We'll know soon enough," Rory said. "I've heard of this Kilian, but even he'll be exhausted after that beast."

Connor started to ask another question, but Rory shook his head. "You can't learn everything in one day, lad. Right now, everyone get some sleep. We march in one hour. It'll be a busy night."

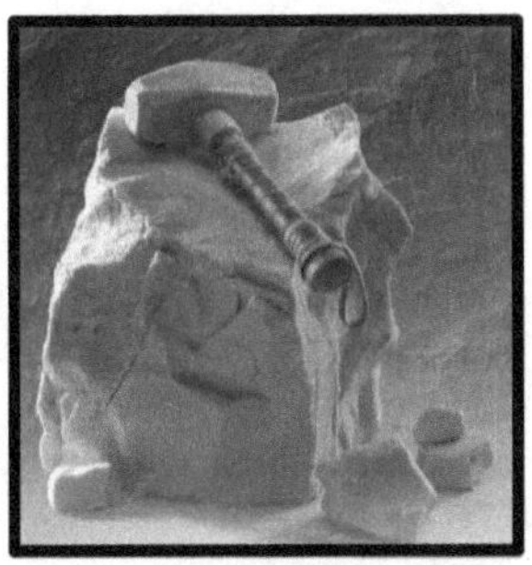

CHAPTER 28

onnor crouched across from the Powder House at the edge of the tree line above the far side of Loch Wick. The sun had fallen behind the Maclachlan Mountains and deep shadows filled the valley.

He could not suppress a thrill of excitement to think an army crouched in the darkness right behind him, led by Lady Shona and half a dozen Guardians. For a moment he could imagine himself a hero, worthy to stand with the Guardians of the realm in driving the Grandurians from his home.

Nearby, the man with the wide-brimmed hat and hunting leathers, who the captain had referred to as the Pathfinder, studied the area with his glowing eyes. He turned to Captain Rory, "No movement outside the wall."

Rory motioned Connor ahead. They rounded the loch and crossed the Upper Wick with no incident. Torches burned at the wall gate, but the Powder House stood dark and silent.

Tomas led two soldiers into the Powder House through a side door. Connor waited impatiently, excitement and nerves making him restless. The soldiers exited the Powder House a moment later and reported it empty.

"Where's the powder, lad?" Rory asked.

"I don't know. It's always kept here."

"We need to know where they've moved it," Shona said.

"We have to get into the town. I know how to find out," Connor said.

"Very well." Rory muttered a low command to one of his sergeants, and a dozen soldiers slipped into the darkness. They paralleled the base of the cliff toward the wall gate, led by the Pathfinder. The moon was not yet up, so they disappeared completely after only a few paces.

After half a minute, Rory followed, but stopped fifty yards away from the gate, well away from the pool of light cast by the torches. One mail-clad Grandurian stood guard at the entrance to the town.

Connor and the others waited in silence. A moment later, two long ropes shot out of the darkness. The noose of one settled over the Grandurian sentry. Before he could react, the rope yanked him off his feet and dragged him fast down the road and out of the light. The second rope disappeared into the darkness beyond the torchlight, went taut, and then dragged a second guard after the first.

Grunts and several low thuds echoed out of the darkness. Connor winced as he imagined the soldiers pummeling the guards, or worse. A moment later, soldiers appeared out of the darkness, bearing the bound and gagged prisoners, who they dumped at Rory's feet. The captain called for a shielded lantern and shone a single beam of light over the captives.

They both lay unmoving, beaten unconscious. Blood flowed down the scalp of one, and a bright new bruise shone on the other's face. Braided steel bands bound their hands and feet, and another length connected the bonds behind their backs and ran up to circle their throats. It took only a second for Connor to realize why. If the men awoke and began to struggle, or tried to straighten their legs, they would strangle themselves.

He shuddered at the brutal efficiency and some of the glamour faded. Rory's men were here to capture or kill the Grandurians. This was their job, and they would do whatever it took to succeed.

After shielding the lantern, Rory said softly, "Bring them. We may need the prisoners. Grahame, find the LongSeer."

The Pathfinder saluted and led a four-man squad forward.

Rory turned to the Strider. "Donald, find out if any more enemy patrol the village."

The thin fellow saluted and zipped through the gate and into the darkened town.

Rory led the rest of the company toward the gate at a brisk trot. "Where to, lad?"

Connor longed to go home, to let his mother wrap him in one of her wonderful hugs, but forced himself to go the other way, to the Healer's house. As they slipped through town like shadows, Connor couldn't shake a feeling of strangeness about the town, although he could not pinpoint why the familiar sights felt so odd.

He led Rory and Shona through the back door into Mhairi's bright kitchen that smelled like fresh-baked pie. Mhairi sat at the plain wooden table with Jean and Hamish.

Hamish saw them first, and his eyes nearly popped out of his head at the sight of leather-clad Shona. Jean came smoothly to her feet. If the sight of Connor in leather battle armor, flanked by the huge Rory and the curvaceous Shona startled her, she didn't show it.

She made a graceful curtsy to Lady Shona and gave Connor a little kiss on the cheek. He couldn't help grinning. Mhairi didn't even try to hit him.

"We've been waiting for you," Jean said. "Is this your entire army?"

"Ah, no." He introduced Captain Rory, who bowed over Jean's hand and kissed it lightly. Jean flushed, and Hamish's face turned red. He stood, but did not dare come around the table.

When Connor introduced Shona, Jean made a second little curtsy, joined by her grandmother. "It's a pleasure to meet you, Lady Shona. Connor's told us all about you."

Hamish came around the table, drawn to Shona despite his obvious fear of Rory. He mumbled, "He didn't tell us everything."

Shona smiled at Jean, "Did Connor tell you about our kiss in the river?"

Jean's eyes widened, Hamish's jaw dropped, and Rory rounded on Connor. "You didn't tell me about kissing the Lady Shona, lad."

Connor tried to stammer a reply, but couldn't figure out what to respond to first, the hurt in Jean's eyes, or the threat in Rory's voice.

Shona stepped up beside Connor and slipped an arm casually over his shoulder. "Relax, Captain. I nearly drowned when we were hiding from the Water Mocassin. Connor kissed me to share the breath of life."

Rory frowned, as if trying to find reason to remain angry. Jean recovered from her initial surprise and her face settled into the unreadable mask she assumed when treating injuries. Connor hated her knowing about the kiss, although he loved the fact that Hamish knew. He cherished the memory and wouldn't change it for the world, but he wondered why Shona would choose that one moment to bring up?

"Listen," Connor said to re-focus everyone. "We need to know where they put the granite powder."

"The powder?" Hamish asked. "Why?"

Jean frowned. "I'd think you'd want to know about the prisoners. They're still locked up in the manor."

"The granite's important," Connor said. Shona gave him a warning look, but after what she'd just done to Jean, Connor decided to pretend he didn't see it. "It fuels some of the Petralist powers."

"Really?" Hamish and Jean asked together.

Shona gave Connor a hard look. "These are things we don't speak of, so keep it to yourself."

"Not such a secret as you might think," said old Mhairi. She inspected the two of them critically. "You're both granite Petralists, aren't you?"

Connor stared. From the look on her face, Jean was just as surprised.

Hamish, who couldn't seem to tear his eyes away from Shona, said softly, "She doesn't look like granite to me."

If Mhairi's guess surprised Shona, she did not show it. "You can hold a secret. That's enough for now. Yes, I am a granite Petralist. Captain Rory is a granite Guardian, and Connor will become one."

"Enough chatter," Rory said. "Where is the powder?"

Hamish started out of his reverie. "They took it all up to the plateau. Had us store it in the big barn on the south side of the manor house."

"You saw it?"

"Yes, sir. They pressed several men into service, and I volunteered so I could see what was going on."

Shona gave Hamish a warm smile, and his face flushed beet red.

"That'll be their undoing," said Rory. "They should've moved it inside."

Shona shrugged. "They have plenty. Probably didn't consider it a risk."

Before Rory could answer, the back door opened and Donald, the Strider jumped inside. "Captain, the Pathfinder reports three men on the road to the plateau. Two locals and one Grandurian soldier. Running hard."

Rory frowned. "How'd they escape town before you found them?"

"I wasn't looking for soldiers hidden inside a local's home. They must have seen me pass and left before Grahame arrived with the other scouts."

"They go to raise the alarm," Shona said.

"Without a doubt. Sir, should I intercept?"

"No, said Rory. "The Longseer will see them coming." He muttered a curse, "No time for the careful assault we planned. Order the charge."

CHAPTER 29

s they ran for the upper gate at the head of the army, Shona called to Rory, "Captain, do you think this is wise?"

"Nay, lass. Not wise, but necessary."

Connor ran just behind them, wishing he'd had time to say good-bye to Jean. His stomach roiled with worry. This was not the careful plan that had sounded so good when they discussed it.

Instead of circling around to the south and approaching the plateau from the long slope that fell gently down toward the river, where the Grandurian Longseer would be less likely to spy them from afar, Rory was leading them up the main road. If Ilse wanted to kill the prisoners, she would have more than enough warning. Connor's father's life hung in the balance.

"Captain," he called to Rory. "Why do you think the soldier forced locals to run with him to the manor?"

"I doubt they were forced."

It took a few pounding strides for that to sink in. As they led the army through the upper gate and onto Manor Road, Connor said, "You can't believe villagers would willingly help the Grandurians?"

"There's always some who see profit for themselves in betraying others," Rory said, his voice grave.

"But …"

Rory glanced back at him. "Think, lad. Who in town might want to turn the situation to their own profit?"

Connor could not bring himself to answer. In his mind, he saw the foreman, Keith, and his shrew of a wife, Cinaed. They would do it. Could one of the runners be their son, Stuart? The thought turned Connor cold.

Outside of town they met the Pathfinder and his scouts. In the darkness, Grahame's eyes glowed and looked hard, like faceted crystal. Connor could not look into those eyes for more than a second, and he wondered what stone fueled his powers.

Rory slowed, and Grahame said, "I'm sorry, Captain. They fled before we arrived. Looked back often. They know we're here."

Rory nodded. "As we feared. Any sign of the Longseer?"

He shook his head. "Still too far, but I bet he'll be up in the tower atop the manor house."

"She," Shona said. "The Longseer is a woman."

Connor remembered the woman in the long blue dress whose eyes seemed to burn with an inner fire similar to Grahame's.

"She'll see us coming at least half a mile out," Grahame said. "No way around it."

"That'll give them at least two minutes to prepare, or to run," Rory said.

"They won't run," Shona said. "They might kill the prisoners, though."

Rory shook his head. "The prisoners are their only bargaining chip. They'll fetch them, but if we hurry, we can hit them before they're set." He raised his voice, "We run hard, men. Strike them down before they murder the prisoners."

"Ilse is mine," Shona reminded him.

Rory turned to the Strider, Donald. "At first sign of alarm, run ahead and scout their position."

Then the big captain broke into a run, with the entire army instantly on his heels. Connor wished he still had some granite powder. Since Shona had offered Patronage, he wished for the strength to fight through to his father.

Again the feeling of strangeness returned as Connor ran along the familiar road to the plateau. This time he understood it. He'd climbed this road hundreds of times. The sights, the clean night smells, the soft sound of wind along the mountain or the pounding of feet on the hard-packed roads, it was all as familiar to him as his own breathing. And yet it wasn't. Tonight everything was different. Tonight he ran to battle.

Everything was familiar, and yet it was all alien. As they ran hard up the long, gentle slope, Rory outlined his new plan to the sergeants, who fell back to brief their men. Connor wished Rory would assign him an important task, but feared at the same time that the captain might call his name. Rory never did.

At every stride, Connor expected to hear shouts of alarm or hear the bell atop the tower begin to toll the warning, but it remained still. That silence made Connor even more nervous.

They topped the final rise and pounded along the road that ran straight for the main entrance to the manor. No lights shone in any windows, and a fragile silence reigned, broken only by the steady gurgling of the fountain in front of the manor house. There was no sign of the men who had run from Alasdair to raise the alarm.

Unchallenged, they made for the manor house, with Connor's nervous tension growing at every step. Rory raised his hand, fingers spread wide, and several groups split off.

Shona and one of the Guardians led half a dozen soldiers to the right, assigned to secure the precious powder in the big barn on the far side of the manor. Possession of that powder might turn the tide of battle.

Another Guardian, with a score of soldiers at his heels, followed Shona's troop to the right, while an identical party ran left. Each group would assault the side entrances to the manor. The multi-pronged attack would hopefully fracture the defenders and overwhelm them.

Without slowing, the strike forces trampled through Lady Isobel's precious flowerbeds. Connor winced to see the prized plants crushed. She'd probably blame him for it.

With less than a hundred yards to go, the great brass bell finally began to toll high in the tower. Lights flared in several of the tall windows of the lower levels, and someone shouted an alarm inside the manor.

Rory laughed. "Fools! Caught 'em sleeping."

Two mail-clad Grandurian soldiers poked their heads out through the main entrance, spied the charging army, and pulled the thick, iron-banded doors closed again.

Rory shouted, "Charge!" and accelerated to a full sprint, headed straight for those recently closed doors. His skin faded to gray and his footsteps became heavy as he drew upon the strength of granite.

Grahame the Pathfinder shouted, "Strider, circle the manor. Identify defensive positions."

Donald shot forward, kicking up a spray of dirt as he raced past Connor's troop and then Shona's company.

As they closed on the manor house, Connor's fear only increased. The attack seemed too easy, and the towering building seemed more threatening tonight than ever before. He imagined enemies firing down on them from the crenellated parapet above, but he could see no movement up there.

What was Ilse planning?

He could not bring himself to share Rory's enthusiasm. They were overlooking something.

Five leaping strides from the doors, Rory shouted, "Obrion!" He tucked his head in to one shoulder, clearly planning to crash right through the doors and any defenders foolish enough to get in his way.

Tomas and one other Guardian flanked him. Connor watched in breathless anticipation, eager despite his uneasiness to witness them unleash their incredible strength.

Two long strides from the stairs, Captain Rory abruptly stopped mid-stride, as if he'd struck an invisible barrier. Tomas did the same, but the third Guardian bounced backward as if he'd run into a stone wall. He fell hard onto his back and lay motionless, stunned.

Rory and Tomas hung suspended in the air in mid-stride, as if frozen. Soldiers shared surprised, uneasy glances as they slowed to a halt.

One man whispered, "What devilry is this?"

Captain Rory's rear leg twitched, and his toe dug into the ground, as if trying to pull him backward.

Connor shouted, "Help him!"

He grabbed for Captain Rory's shoulders, but his hands struck the invisible barrier. It felt warm, and pulsed against his hand, but he could not penetrate it. It was almost as if the very air had turned to stone.

Rory was stuck more than halfway into it, with only part of his back and one leg free. Connor slid his hands across the barrier, but could find no gap. Standing this close, he could finally see the curving boundary of the barrier, shimmering just a little in the darkness, almost like a rippling heat wave. It created a half-circle, blocking the entire northern entrance of the building.

Soldiers grabbed straps on Rory's back, or yanked on his leg. Together they pulled, but Rory remained stuck fast. The Guardian who had bounced off the barrier shoved them all aside, grabbed Rory's battle leathers, and heaved mightily.

Rory popped free and the two fell in a heap with the burly captain on top. Rory gasped for breath, and only then did Connor realize with horror that Rory had been unable to breathe while trapped.

Rory sprang to his feet, "Get Tomas out of there!"

Soldiers worked together to haul Tomas out of the suffocating barrier. Connor circled the group and slid his hands along the invisible wall. He'd never imagined anything like this could be possible. Rory stood nearby, frowning at the barrier as other soldiers explored it with their hands.

This couldn't be a normal Petralist power if even the captain hadn't ever seen it.

A low humming sound drew Connor's attention. He peered through the barrier and there in the shadows, sitting on the lowest step, sat a gray stone about a hand span across and half as thick.

Shouting erupted from around the right corner of the manor house. Rory signaled the troop to follow, and ran in that direction. Lights from the manor's windows illuminated the entire strip of ground between the manor and the steep plateau edge, only fifty yards to their right. The assault force assigned to breach the side entrance had encountered the same kind of invisible shielding and pounded vainly against it with their swords.

Shona and her small band, looking like wraiths in the distant dim light, were just reaching the large barn situated a hundred feet south of the manor. Shona grabbed the handles of the huge sliding barn doors that faced toward the edge of the plateau, and heaved against them. Her skin glowed white in the darkness as she tapped her granite strength to throw the heavy doors wide.

Bright torchlight spilled out the open door, and Shona stood silhouetted against the light for a second, one hand raised to shield her eyes. She raised her sword and shouted a challenge.

Even as she took a step forward, an entire wagon, suspended by thick ropes, swung out through the opening and smashed her band aside like gnats. They tumbled into the night toward the edge of the plateau where they were lost from view.

Connor could scarce believe Ilse's audacity to use the wagon as a weapon. It meant she had known they would try the barn first. She'd planned for it.

As Connor took a step forward, intent on checking on Shona, Captain Rory shouted, "We need to find another way in."

Just then, Donald skidded to a stop nearby. "Captain, the barn is empty. It was a decoy all along. The strike force on the far side has encountered the same odd shielding."

Rory said, "This Ilse is proving resourceful. I look forward to learning how she did this."

Donald said, "Sir, some of the Grandurians are assembling at the rear entrance. No sign of the prisoners."

"Very well." Rory looked toward south and added, "she wants us to attack from the south. So be it."

He started jogging in that direction and called out, "Slingers to the front. Fast Rollers, tap and ready. Ware for ambush."

Soldiers fell in behind him, led by ten slingers and the Fast Rollers, whose bodies swelled with granite power as their skin faded to gray.

Connor ran with them despite his worry for Shona, filled with burning energy now that battle had been joined, but also consumed with worry.

Even he could see Ilse had planned her defenses well, and it unnerved him that her tactics surprised Rory. What else did she have in mind? What other trap still lay before them?

CHAPTER 30

ory led the army around the southern end of the Keep, intent on striking through the gap between the manor house and the big barn. He made it three strides before bouncing back from another invisible barrier.

Soldiers explored the shield that stretched in a slightly curving line all the way from the manor house to the big barn, sealing off that route of attack. Shona and her strike force staggered out of the darkness to join them, and Connor breathed a sigh of relief. She looked shaken, but not badly hurt.

Everything beyond the shield looked slightly distorted, as if they peered through a thin screen of water. Ilse stood at that southern entrance to the manor house where both doors stood wide open. Half a dozen soldiers, including the tall, shapely, Anika and her hulking brother, Erich, flanked her with weapons drawn. They stood in the doorway atop the four wide steps, as if the tiny advantage in height gave them any hope of defeating Rory's hundred. Torches illuminated the area with warm golden light and showed Ilse's face calm, unafraid.

She made a beckoning gesture to Rory.

Shona pounded on the shield and snarled, "I'll eat that woman's heart."

"I'll help you cook it," Rory said. He began circling the big barn and called out, "Look lively, men. She wouldn't force us this way without hoping for some advantage."

With weapons at the ready, the army jogged around the big barn until they faced the southern entrance to the manor house. There they paused to study the Grandurians' defensive position.

Connor moved to the right of the army, close to a single story carriage shed with a low, almost flat roof and an open front. About eighty feet separated the big barn and the carriage shed, framing a courtyard through which the army would be forced to advance before reaching the manor house. The huge sliding doors on the near side of the big barn stood open, revealing no threat, while the open front of the carriage shed showed it empty but for its usual complement of carts and wagons. A two-wheeled mule cart with a long bed sat just outside the shed, its twin shafts pointing toward the barn.

Connor took all that in with a single glance, but what drew his gaze was the double staggered row of tall haystacks set across the courtyard between the barn and the carriage shed, partially blocking access to Ilse's company, like a half-finished wall. The haystacks stood ten feet tall and were spaced about three strides apart, and Connor could not imagine what tactical purpose they might possess.

When Rory paused about twenty feet from the odd wall of haystacks, Ilse shouted, "Stand down, men of Obrion. We wish to --"

Rory did not let her finish. "Slingers!"

The ten slingers whipped their arms back to launch stones at the Grandurians, but Grahame shouted, "Ware, Captain. There are men up in the --"

Before he could finish, and before the slingers could release their missiles, blinding lights blazed in every one of the manor's wide windows. Grahame howled with pain and staggered, clutching his eyes. Connor joined the others in shielding his eyes, and his worry burst into full-blown fear of the Grandurians.

It was like the manor had somehow consumed the sun, which was trying to escape through the open curtains, making it impossible to look directly at the building. The doorway remained darkened where Ilse and her men stood, so he couldn't even search for their back-lit figures to orient on.

Rory cursed, but did not advance. "You can't hide forever!"

Ilse's voice replied from behind the light. "Don't be a fool, captain. No one has to die tonight."

Shona lifted her sword high and shouted, "You do!"

She charged.

Rory tried to catch her, but she moved too fast. He shouted, "Stand down, Shona. Those haystacks have to be a trap."

"Coward!" Shona paused and looked back. "Be a Guardian and lead these men!"

Rory sighed. "So be it."

Then he raised his sword and shouted, "Charge!"

Connor's heart sank as the army surged forward. He knocked an arrow, but could find no target. He feared the consequences of Shona's action, although he applauded her bravery and hoped she succeeded.

As Shona and Rory and two of the Fast Rollers raced through the gaps between the haystacks, a soldier shouted, "Wingrunner!"

A blur of movement above him and to the right drew Connor's attention. The skinny Grandurian with the narrow face who wore baggy pants like Donald was sprinting down the roof of the carriage shed. He moved faster than a galloping horse and when he reached the edge of the roof, he leaped high and soared to the closest haystack.

Without slowing, the Wingrunner zipped from one haystack to the next in enormous leaping strides. As each foot landed, he dropped a small, glittering object onto the hay.

Soldiers shouted for slingers to drop the man, but he crossed the entire courtyard in three pounding heartbeats and dove through an open window in the side of the big barn.

Before soldiers could turn to give chase, the first haystack erupted into flames, followed in turn by each of the others. Fire roared high into the night, and heat seared Connor's face. The roaring of the flames drowned out conversation, and the smoke smelled like lantern oil. He retreated with the rest of the army from the raging inferno. The soldiers who had stood closest to the haystacks clutched at burned eyes or beat at singed clothing.

Then Connor gasped as he realized only Shona and Rory and the two Fast Rollers had made it through the firewall before the Wingrunner triggered the trap. They alone faced Ilse and her company.

As the soldiers regrouped under the direction of the other two Fast Rollers, Connor ran up the sloping bed of the mule cart and jumped up onto the low carriage shed roof. From there he could see over the burning barrier and, despite the bright lights, managed to focus on the tiny strike force.

Rory and the others had nearly reached Ilse's company, who had formed into a defensive line to meet them. They ran up a low mound of dirt, only seconds away from closing with the enemy. Rory's battle cry echoed back through the fire and stirred Connor's heart as he silently urged on the burly captain.

In that second, two huge rocks plummeted from above and crashed into the ground three strides in front of Captain Rory. They struck with terrific force and, with a loud whump, sank halfway into the earth, driving down the ends of thick planks concealed in the dirt. The opposite ends of the planks, acting as levers, burst out of the ground under the feet of the charging force, catapulting all four of them high into the air.

They soared above Ilse's band and crashed with terrific force into the wall of the manor house. Connor was surprised they did not smash through the wall entirely. They hung for a breathless second there before sliding down the face of the manor, leaving indentations in the façade.

Connor raised his bow, but could not make himself shoot Ilse, even though he could now make her out through the blinding light. He'd never killed a person before, and as much as he hated her for threatening his father, her bold cleverness forced a grudging respect.

As the attackers fell, Anika and Erich caught the two Fast Rollers. Using their own momentum against them, they whipped the two men around and launched them back over the flaming barrier, onto the leading ranks of the army.

Connor raised his bow again. He didn't mind shooting Anika. She terrified him so much he preferred to shoot her from a distance. He still shuddered at the memory of clinging to her wildly twisting form as she crashed through the dark forest by the river. He could barely believe he'd bested her, and never again wanted to stand so close.

Rory leaped to his feet and shouted at Ilse, "I'll rip your heart out."

Anika stepped in front of Ilse and beckoned Rory on with a grin. "Take mine heart first, soldier man."

Erich moved to intercept Shona at the same time. All four of them swelled with granite power, so Connor lowered his bow. The arrow would do nothing against stone-hard skin.

Shouting down in the courtyard drew his gaze. Some soldiers had pulled two wagons out of the carriage shed and were moving them into position to try to drive them through the flaming wall. The Guardians had gathered closer to the flames, but Connor could not tell what they intended.

The shouting came from soldiers trying to intercept the Wingrunner, who had shot out of the big barn, making for the Fast Rollers. Slingers threw stones at him, but the skinny fellow moved too fast, and the stones missed.

The Fast Rollers turned to face the new threat, but the Wingrunner sprinted past before they were set, and whipped out a braided steel cable, capped with a studded ball. Driven by his super-human speed, it cracked the nearest Fast Roller in the side of the head.

The man tumbled to the ground, the granite-gray skin of his face webbed with cracks. He did not move.

The Wingrunner continued past, ran up the same mule cart Connor had used, and leaped up onto the carriage shed roof.

Connor tried to bring his bow around, but the Wingrunner sprinted past with a laugh before he could. The man leaped off the far side and, when he hit the ground, accelerated around the back side of the manor house.

Donald appeared on the roof beside Connor. He dropped the small pack he wore and said, "That one's mine."

Then he too jumped off the far side of the roof and accelerated after the Wingrunner, spraying dirt in his wake. In a single heartbeat, he surged from a jog to the speed of a diving pedra, and disappeared around the manor house. His legs blurred, moving faster than should be possible.

Back by the manor doors, Erich leaped down the steps and met Shona with an overhand blow driven by all his strength. The crack of the impact sounded above the roar of the flames. Shona stumbled back under the sheer force of the blow, and Erich moved in to finish her off.

In that moment Tomas, thrown by the other two standing Fast Rollers, flew through the top of the flaming wall. He landed in a roll and came to his feet already running. He tackled Erich, and the two pummeled each other with their stone-hard fists. Shona returned to the fray, and the three fought with reckless abandon, using fists as much as swords. They all took heavy blows, but shrugged them off without slowing.

Meanwhile, Anika and Rory collided with a resounding crack. Their skin shone white in the bright light, and their forms shifted as they increased their tap-rate. She seemed to glow, the picture of a perfectly formed goddess, while his every muscle rippled with power. They grappled together, and for a moment looked more like they were embracing than wrestling.

Connor stared as the Guardians and Petralists fought. The stories Bruce had told them for years had seemed fantastical, but they completely failed to capture the magnificence of these warriors.

He could do nothing to help in that super-human battle, but he had to do something. So he jumped back down to the ground and, as soldiers started driving the two wagons toward the flame wall, he ran through the big barn to see if he could help Donald against the Wingrunner.

Behind him in the courtyard, the soldiers who had started charging the wall of fire suddenly crumpled to the ground screaming. Connor could not see what new evil powers toppled them, but their cries of pain filled him with a need to strike back at the Grandurians.

As soon as he stepped out through the far doors of the big barn, he caught sight of the Wingrunner running south toward him, with Donald closing the distance between them fast. The Wingrunner veered around in a tight turn that pointed him straight at the steep western edge of the plateau.

Donald poured on the speed as he moved to intercept, and Connor held his breath as the two raced toward the edge of the plateau in intercepting paths.

Before they collided, the Wingrunner suddenly reversed direction and dug his feet into the soft grass. He leaned far back and braced his legs as he skidded to a stop.

Donald tried to do the same.

His legs flew up into the air, and he slammed hard onto his back. Connor gasped. It looked like he had slipped, as if in mud. Donald's momentum drove him on, sliding on his back, barely slowing even though he tore at the grass with his hands in a desperate attempt to stop.

With a long, angry shout, he shot out over the edge of the plateau and plunged into the night, out of sight. Connor prayed the spirits might grant he land in the river.

The Wingrunner gave the spot where Donald slid off the cliff a roguish salute, sparking a fresh wave of anger in Connor. As the man closed fast on his position, Connor raised his bow.

He felt no hesitation about shooting this man.

The Wingrunner raced past and made an obscene gesture at Connor.

Connor released.

The arrow leaped away to catch the irritating little man, but the Wingrunner heard the twang and accelerated away with unbelievable speed. He shifted a little to the right as the arrow caught him, and sped up again. For a moment, the two flew across the plateau side by side, then the Wingrunner snatched the arrow out of the air, gave Connor a wave, and rounded the big barn out of sight.

"Tallan take you!" Connor shouted. He cringed and instinctively looked around to make sure his mother hadn't heard him shout such a vile curse, even though the man deserved it.

Gripping his bow hard, Connor ran back through the big barn, but paused to stare in shock. The charge at the flaming wall had broken, and dozens of soldiers, many of them clutching bleeding wounds, huddled behind the toppled wagons, using them as barriers. Others lay unconscious as comrades dragged them back from the fire wall.

What sickened him most was the thought of what Ilse would do when Rory's force finally figured out a way through her defenses, or when the flames burned out. Would she then bring forth the prisoners and murder Connor's father in a last desperate attempt to save herself?

Just then, something struck one of the wagon barriers and bounced to land at his feet. He picked it up and examined the jagged piece of granite, a little smaller than an egg. The Grandurians were using the local stones of his homeland to support their invasion. The thought added fuel to his towering anger.

He needed to shoot someone.

With one leather-armored arm raised to protect his face, he sprinted across the battlefield. Soldiers shouted at him to get down, but he did not pause. The two remaining Fast Rollers appeared from the carriage shed carrying the bed of Lord Gavin's coach. They had ripped off the wheels, the canopy, and the plush seats, and carried the heavy base of thick planks reinforced with steel like a giant shield.

As they moved toward the flames, clearly intent on driving through the barrier despite the missile barrage that had stopped the previous attempt, Connor jumped up onto the overturned mule cart and scrambled up onto the roof.

He crouched there and reached for another arrow just as Verena stepped out of the shadows and joined Ilse on the steps in the doorway. Ilse pointed toward the flaming haystacks, and Verena nodded.

Even though she looked vulnerable standing beside soldiers dressed in battle leathers wearing her red silk blouse and black vest, she drew an opaque square stone out of the leather satchel she carried. It was about as long as her forearm and looked unremarkable.

Verena stepped to the side of the doorway, pressed her back against the open door, and held the stone flat to her stomach. There, she crinkled her face as if concentrating. With her cute little nose, and her hair bound in a loose braid, she looked adorable.

Gale force wind erupted out of the stone she held pressed to her stomach and howled through the haystacks forming the flaming barrier. It whipped the burning hay into a cyclone of fire that boiled up into the air and rolled over the army caught in the courtyard.

Screams ripped the night as soldiers fled the firestorm, beating at burning clothes or trying to drag unconscious companions out of danger. The Fast Rollers, who had been preparing to storm through the firewall, tossed aside their barrier and ran to assist their comrades. Their stone-hard skin offered some protection as they led the army back toward the southern lip of the plateau where it fell away into a long slope downriver.

Connor had to do something. His bow rose almost before he willed it, and the arrow came effortlessly to his ear. All the anger and fear building inside him since the attack began burned through him and filled him with a terrible resolve.

He'd never killed anyone before.

It no longer mattered.

He sighted on Verena.

CHAPTER 31

onnor took a deep, steadying breath. Somehow Verena had triggered the wind with that stone. He could not imagine how, but that didn't matter. The force of the air drove her back against the wall where she fought to hold the stone steady. Her big blue eyes seemed enormous as she stared in open amazement at what she'd done.

Connor released the arrow.

The bow twanged as the arrow leaped away, flashed over the wall of flames, and shattered against the bottom edge of the stone in Verena's hands.

The impact twisted the stone against her stomach, and she yelped. The stone dipped forward, and the wind blasted it up against her sternum.

The force of the wind drove Verena up off her feet and the pressure of the air scraped her up along the door. She shouted in pain or surprise and wrenched at the stone, and managed to twist it a little.

Connor winced. He'd flown the Heatstone oven. He knew what that meant.

Verena shrieked as the force of the wind drove her across the width of the door and then through the open doorway. She disappeared into the dimness beyond, her arms and legs trailing behind as she flew into the manor house.

The flames had driven the army back, but also destroyed the barrier. Rory's force quickly regrouped, and soldiers began shouting, "Obrion".

Part of Connor wished they would back off, but they never would. They were angry. So was he. They would charge again, and this time nothing would stop them.

Not far from Ilse, Anika and Rory fought hand-to-hand at the base of the steps. She stood as tall as he, and the two seemed equally matched. Of course, Connor knew nothing of hand-to-hand fighting, but they both looked impressive, and neither one had yet gained an advantage.

As Connor watched, Anika broke with Rory and punched him hard in the chest. Rory staggered a couple of steps back but caught himself and grinned. He looked like he was enjoying himself.

Anika grinned right back and spread her arms wide. "Come. Wrestle again. I break your heart."

Rory laughed. "We'll see who breaks what." He launched himself at her again.

Not far away, Erich caught Tomas under the arm with a mighty blow that knocked him a couple steps back. Even as Shona leaped at Erich's back, the big Grandurian side-stepped, caught Shona's arm, and slammed her onto the ground. She struck with terrific force, and Erich stomped on her face.

"No!" Connor looked around desperately, filled with rage at the sight. He prepared to jump from the roof to join the impending charge, but his eyes settled on Donald's small pack he'd dropped before chasing after the Wingrunner.

Hanging from the belt was a small leather pouch.

Connor dove for it, drove his hand in, and felt powder.

He concentrated hard, willing the power into his hand. Warmth spread up through his arm and he laughed. Then he frowned as he realized the power felt wrong somehow. Instead of the insect-crawly feeling of the Curse he was used to, this power slithered up his arm like a breath of wind and filled him with boundless energy.

Suddenly he could not stand still.

Down by the doorway, Shona cried out in pain, and the sound drove away all hesitation. With granite-hardened muscles, he could help her.

Connor charged.

The world seemed to tip suddenly as he shot forward far faster than he'd intended. Instead of muscles turning leaden with deadly granite power, his legs burned with the need to run.

He moved way too fast. The shingles of the roof whisked past, and even as the truth dawned on him, he sailed out over the edge.

He hadn't absorbed granite. The pouch held some other stone, the power that fueled the Strider's super speed.

The image of the Wingrunner leaping off the roof and accelerating around the manor without injury flashed into Connor's mind, and he focused on running. He landed hard, and accelerated faster than he'd ever imagined possible. But his legs tangled and he toppled forward.

With arms and legs flailing, Connor fell into a wild somersault. He hollered with fear and tried to plant his feet to regain his balance.

It almost worked.

Instead of regaining his footing, Connor vaulted up into the air. He sailed right past Erich, who was fighting Tomas again, missed Anika by inches as she grappled with Rory, and cleared three of the four steps up to the doorway.

His leading foot caught on the forth step and he tumbled forward again, right at a very surprised Captain Ilse. The captain managed to twist, and Connor scraped along her side as he tumbled past and sailed into the darkness of the manor.

Where he plowed right into Verena.

She yelped as he collided with her. The two of them somersaulted back into the dim recesses of the large room and fell hard together, a tangle of arms and legs. They rolled over each other several times before they finally came to a painful stop.

Connor groaned and blinked against the sudden darkness, amazed that he hadn't died. Every muscle ached, and all of his exposed skin screamed from being scraped against the hard stone floor. He tasted dirt, and his ears rang with the sound of brass bells.

Something stirred under him, and only then did he realize he'd ended up on top of Verena. He looked down and their noses nearly touched.

Suddenly he became intensely aware of how they lay together, of her soft warmth, of her gentle, earthy scent, and mostly of her big blue eyes that seemed to glow in the darkness.

"Connor? Where did you come from?"

Her breath smelled sweet, like mint. The fact seemed ridiculously incongruent given the situation, and Connor couldn't suppress a chuckle.

Verena giggled, and that made him laugh harder.

She grinned, and her smile seemed to light up the room. "Get off and help me up."

Outside, Ilse shouted, "Verena!"

"Coming!"

Connor clambered to his feet and helped her to stand. "What are you going to do?"

"You'll see," she said with a sweet smile.

Then she punched him right in the throat.

Connor gagged, and even as his hands rose instinctively to his throat, she slammed her palm into his stomach. Despite the protection of his leather battle armor, pain exploded in his midsection, and his knees buckled. His eyes watered and his stomach lurched like he might be sick.

He fought to hold down the urge to vomit. He didn't think anything could come up with his throat jammed closed, and didn't want to find out what would happen if it tried. He gasped for breath and fell to one side, unable to move or to stand.

How could Verena hit so hard?

She placed a gentle hand on his shoulder, "I'm really sorry." Then she turned and raced for the entrance, pulling something from her satchel.

Outside, Obrioner voices rose into a crescendo of battle fury. The army must be starting the charge that would sweep Ilse's tiny force away for good.

Verena stopped in the doorway and tossed something to the right, and then something else to the left. Connor's eyes were blurred with tears, but they looked like small stones.

A frightening rumbling sound, followed by startled cries of alarm sounded from outside. Somehow the rumbling sounded familiar, but Connor could not place it. His mind was fuzzy from lack of air.

He was just thankful Hamish hadn't seen him get beat up by a girl.

Silhouetted in the doorway, Verena shouted, "Now!"

Connor squinted at her and decided he should have shot her, not the rock. Maybe in the knee. That would've hurt a lot.

The Wingrunner whipped past, little more than an impression before he was gone again. Connor forced himself to his knees despite the roaring pain in his gut, and cringed at what he saw outside.

Long earthen walls ran out from the manor house, boxing in Rory's army like a herd of sheep.

They didn't seem to care and, led by the two Fast Rollers, continued their charge. As one, they lifted their voices and their swords, and came on like a flood.

Ilse and her men could not hope to stop them this time.

Soldiers fell screaming from the ranks, but the army did not falter under the fresh missile barrage.

Erich tackled Tomas, rolled over him and, using their combined momentum, launched Tomas out toward the advancing army.

Shona, who had regained her feet, shouted in victory and raced past Erich. Her face was caked with dirt, and blood seeped from her nose, but she sprinted up the steps, right at Captain Ilse.

Ilse sidestepped Shona's lunge and shoved her right into the door post. It cracked, and the heavy door sagged on its hinges. Shona bounced back, and before she could recover from the shock of the blow, Ilse grabbed her arm and yanked her around in a tight circle.

Shona shouted a curse as Ilse pulled her off her feet and sent her rolling down the steps. Erich caught her by the back of her battle leathers, spun again, and tossed her into the air.

She crashed into Tomas, who was just staggering to his feet.

The army had nearly reached the two, and the sight of the charging, unstoppable force filled Connor with wild elation. Despite all of Ilse's tricks, she was about to be overrun.

Erich threw himself to the ground right behind Rory just as Anika pushed him. Captain Rory stumbled and tripped over Erich. Erich kicked him in the face and then grabbed his arms. Anika grabbed his feet and, even as Rory struggled mightily to free himself, they tossed him like a sack of grain.

He landed in front of Tomas and Shona just as the army reached them. The entire group came on, a wall of steel that would trample Ilse, her small force, and probably level the manor house.

Verena had descended the steps to the low mound of earth where she faced the charging army alone. They were barely twenty feet away, closing fast. They'd never fall for her cute routine. They'd crush her.

Even though she'd just beat him up, Connor couldn't help shouting hoarsely, "Verena, get out of the way!"

She glanced over her shoulder and gave him a dazzling smile before turning back to the onrushing army …

… and dropping a stone onto the mound of earth.

Connor shouted, "No!"

A wall of earth erupted up out of the mound. It spanned the entire area between the first two walls she'd summoned, and shot up at a low angle. It slammed into Rory, Shona, and the other soldiers and tumbled the entire army back like rag dolls.

Connor winced. Shona was having a really bad night. Then he frowned as the army kept tumbling and sliding back and back away. They should have stopped already.

They didn't. The entire army kept sliding, arms and legs flailing on the smooth surface of the hard-packed ground until they slid right off the southern end of the plateau onto the gentle slope beyond.

The entire battlefield between the barn and the carriage shed glistened in the bright light, like ice on a sunny winter's day.

Verena gave a little hop and clapped her hands together like a little girl who just crushed her first spider.

Beyond the edge of the plateau, a single bugle call rang out.

Ilse raised a fist in triumph, "Well done everyone. Scouts, monitor troop movements. The rest of you, prepare secondary measures."

As soldiers scattered to their various assignments, Ilse turned toward Connor. She took a step toward him, but Verena raced past her to Connor's side. She pulled his arm over her shoulder and helped him to a nearby bench.

She smelled so good, and it felt wonderful to hold her like that, with her snuggled in so close to his side. For a second he forgot she'd punched him out in the first place.

"Are you all right?" Verena asked, real concern in her voice.

Connor glared. "I can barely move."

"Whew! I was worried I might've hit you too hard. That move causes permanent damage sometimes."

"You hit me plenty hard enough, thanks."

She eased him down on the bench, and Connor released her with mixed feelings. Part of him wanted to punch that cute face, but part of him wanted her to sit beside him.

A soldier brought a torch to illuminate the room, and Ilse moved to join them. This part of the manor house was as plain as the north end was ornate. This was the side where work was done. Six storerooms emptied into this big room, while wide stairs led to the lower levels crowded with soldiers' barracks and slaves' quarters, more storerooms, and various cellars. Three entire levels were carved into the plateau underground.

Verena plopped down on the bench beside him and took his hand in hers. She had tiny hands that were surprisingly warm. She looked right into his eyes.

"I didn't want to hit you, honest. It's just, I had to break that assault before anyone got hurt."

Connor barked a laugh. "You almost killed me, and from what I saw, you hurt just about everyone." In his mind, he again saw Shona and the entire army tumble back off the edge of the plateau, helpless to withstand Verena's single dropped stone.

"Well, I mean not seriously hurt."

"People might have died out there."

"Oh, I doubt it. Everyone tried to be careful."

Connor snorted.

Verena clapped her hands together and made a little squeal of delight. "Wasn't that incredible?"

"Not really."

She gave him a little push. "Don't be so sour. Sure it was. I mean, I hope no one got hurt too bad, but I've never worked that exact combination before. I bet they were surprised."

"And sore." Connor tried to see past the cute face, filled with childlike enthusiasm. "How did you do it?"

She grinned and squeezed his hands. "It's so exciting. It's an entirely new branch of Building. We don't even have a good name for it."

"You shielded the doors?"

She nodded.

"You made wind, and fire, and …"

"Yes!" She suddenly leaned in and kissed his cheek. "I love it how smart you are. No one else understands me."

If she thought his reaction was understanding, she was more deluded than he'd thought.

Ilse joined them, "Verena, good work tonight."

"Thank you, Captain." A frown cracked her excited façade. "Good thing it worked. I didn't really bring supplies for a long siege."

Captain Ilse nodded. "Good thing it worked."

"We need to find more stones."

Ilse turned to Connor and settled the full weight of her angry stare on him. He suddenly became acutely aware of his very dangerous position. Ilse and her tiny band had somehow just defeated Rory's entire army.

Connor was her prisoner. Again.

CHAPTER 32

onnor, you betrayed my trust."

To Connor's surprise, the criticism cut him to the bone, and that just made him angry. "Just like you betrayed mine."

"How so?" Ilse looked genuinely startled.

"I promised to show a group of lost strangers how to get back home. You never said you'd invaded our country or kidnapped our high lord's daughter. Do you really think I could let you drag her away to die?"

"You don't know what you're talking about. Now all these people's lives are at risk because of your rash action."

His rash action?

"You invaded our land. All you had to do was leave."

"It's not that easy."

"Adults always say that when they're making excuses."

"And children never want to realize there's a past before every present."

"You've made enough mess of the present. Why should I worry about what you did in the past?"

"It's not my actions that you should worry about."

Connor leaned back against the wall. These Grandurians made no sense. She spoke the Obrioner language well, but maybe she really didn't understand what the words meant.

Just then, the sibling Petralists entered the room. Tall, shapely Anika led, her long blond hair blowing out behind her as she walked, her beautiful face set in angry lines.

She advanced on Connor, one fist half-raised. "You! I should break you bones."

Connor pressed back against the wall and wished he knew how to control the speed he'd used to get into this mess. Anika looked angry enough to kill him, and after watching her stand toe-to-toe with Captain Rory, it wouldn't be hard.

"Easy," Ilse said to the angry woman.

Anika bared her teeth in a snarl. "You make me look fool. Erich no stop laughing."

She probably had looked ridiculous, with her hands bound by his leather jacket and her hair tied to that tree. Served her right for scaring him so bad.

Erich pushed past Anika, his broad face split by a wide grin. His blue eyes twinkled and he clapped Connor hard on the shoulder. "You good boy. No laugh so hard ever."

Anika said something angrily to Erich in Grandurian, and he only grinned wider. "I laugh so hard, break face. She angry face, look like monkey butt in tree."

Verena clapped her hands over her mouth but could not totally suppress a burst of silvery laughter. Anika's scowl deepened, and she took one angry step toward her brother, but Ilse restrained her with one hand. With the other hand, Ilse rubbed her face to try to conceal her own smile.

Connor looked from Erich to Anika, "What's a monkey?"

They laughed harder.

Anika shouted and pushed Erich away. He waved to Connor and headed down the central hall that led deeper into the manor. Anika then rounded on Connor, who shrank back from her fury.

Looming over him, she said in a threatening tone, "I beat you head unless you tell about man."

"What man?"

She gestured toward the steps outside. "Man I fight. Strong hands."

"Captain Rory?"

"Rory?" she repeated slowly, and her angry glare fell away, replaced by a little smile. His name sounded foreign and far more exotic in her strongly accented voice. "Captain?"

Connor was happy to talk if it diverted her anger. "Yes. He commands the army."

"Is very good. We wrestle again."

"I'm sure you will." She made less sense every second, but it seemed to make her happy. She might be trying to gather information to plan their next fight, but her questions seemed too general. He didn't think he'd revealed any of Rory's secrets, but she looked far too pleased. Maybe he had.

Captain Ilse said, "I hope this Captain Rory is as smart as he is brave." She gestured toward the outer door and Anika moved off in that direction.

Ilse turned back to Connor and gave him a long look that sapped his new-found good humor. He didn't regret anything he'd done, except maybe running in here and getting captured. Too bad the army failed.

"You are wearing Petralist battle leathers," Ilse said.

"Ah, yes. It's on loan."

Ilse cocked her head a little to one side. "That's the jacket of a Boulder, but you exhibited the speed of a Strider tonight."

"He didn't do a very good job of it," Verena said.

"It was the first time I tried."

"I'm surprised they gave you basalt in the middle of a battle if you'd never really tried it before."

So it was basalt that fueled the Striders' super speed. Probably the same for the Grandurian Wingrunner.

"Well, they didn't really give me the basalt," Connor said sheepishly. "I sort of borrowed it."

Verena laughed and Ilse said, "So they loan out Boulder battle leathers to untried Striders now? I find that unusual."

This conversation was going all the wrong directions. "Well, since I left my jacket with Anika, this was the only thing that sort of fit."

"I prefer granite," Verena said. "It's kind of bland, but not bad. Basalt just tastes like dirty socks."

"You sound like Hamish. He's the only person I know who thinks rocks taste different."

"Really?"

"Aye. He thought marble tasted spicy."

Verena smiled, a thoughtful look on her face, and said softly, "It does."

He was talking too much again. Then again, this might provide an opportunity. "I'll have to introduce you. You two can eat rocks together."

"We don't really eat them, you know."

Connor shrugged.

"I would very much like to meet this Hamish."

"Maybe later," Ilse interrupted. "Right now you have stones to prep."

Verena stood. "Be safe, Connor."

As she disappeared deeper into the manor house, Ilse said, "Connor, you present a unique opportunity."

"For who?" That didn't sound good. Were her torture skills getting rusty?

"For both of us. I'd like to throw you in the dungeon in chains for what you've done, but I need you."

"Really?"

Ilse nodded with a rueful grin. "We've driven this Captain Rory back for the time being, but he'll return."

Tallan's Eye, he would, and despite Verena's rocks and Anika's wrestling moves, they wouldn't take Captain Rory by surprise again.

"I don't want to hurt them, but if they don't keep their distance I will."

"It would be easier if you hadn't invaded our land and kidnapped a bunch of people."

"Be that as it may. Tell your Captain Rory to leave the town alone. He is not to attack again. We've already proven we can defend ourselves. Next time, we'll kill his men, not just scare them. We'll also kill all of the Cutters."

"Why?" Connor couldn't hide his dismay.

What if Rory attacked again? How could he not?

"Economics. With no Cutters, the production of the quarry would be cut by at least ninety percent. Rory won't risk that."

"Why are you doing this?" Connor asked angrily. "I thought you just wanted to go home."

"You interfered. That's not an option any longer. Rory knows the reasons behind our actions, and what he must deliver for us to withdraw."

Connor forced his hands to unclench, fought down the urge to punch her in the face. She would just beat him up. She'd made Shona look like a clumsy fool.

"I'll tell him."

Ilse leaned forward, her face hard. "If you betray me again, I'll flay the skin from your bones." Connor cringed away from the cold certainty in her eyes. "And I'll do the same to every person you know in this village."

"I won't," Connor assured, fighting not to let her see him tremble.

"Now go."

He bolted for the exit, but instead of following the army off the southern slope of the plateau, he rounded the end of the manor house and headed for the road to Alasdair.

Before anyone could give chase, he threw aside all restraint on the Strider curse that now filled him with restless energy. This time he kept his feet as he tripled his fastest speed and raced for Alasdair.

He would deliver the message to Rory, but first he had to talk with Hamish and Jean.

CHAPTER 33

hoa." Hamish shared an incredulous look with Jean after Connor finished relating the battle at the manor house. "Are you serious?"

"I can hardly believe it, and I lived it," Connor said. The three sat around Jean's kitchen table. Old Mhairi hadn't even threatened Connor with her tonic when he arrived, but left to tend to a patient while they talked.

"So you really are Cursed, aren't you?" Jean asked.

Connor nodded, and it struck him that although he'd experienced so much in the past two days, for his friends this was all still terrifyingly new. He studied Jean's face, trying to tell if she thought him a monster. She wore her hair loose and, although a single line of worry creased her brow, he could tell nothing from her expression.

"What does it feel like?" she asked.

Connor sat back in his chair and tried to find words. It was surprisingly difficult. How would one describe breathing, or walking? The Curse had been a part of him all his life, even though he usually tried to ignore it or suppress it.

"It's like ... "

Hamish leaned forward. "It's like tasting rocks."

"What?"

"It's like tasting rocks," Hamish repeated. "It's so real for me, but no one else really understands it. I don't think you can."

"You're right. I can't really explain it, although I did meet someone who tastes rocks."

"Who?"

"Verena. That girl I mentioned who drew power from stones and helped break the attack."

"Wow."

Jean, who looked annoyed for some reason, said, "But you can control your Curse, right?"

"I'm learning."

She placed a hand over his on the table, and her face became earnest. "I don't want you to get hurt."

"That's the thing," Connor said excitedly. "Now that I'm learning to use it, when I can control it, it will protect me. It's almost impossible for Guardians to get hurt."

Hamish snorted. "Tell that to the guy who fell off the plateau."

"Eat rocks, this is different."

"How is it different?"

"He uses a different stone."

Jean said, "Connor, this is serious business. These soldiers plan to kill each other, no matter what Ilse told you. It's a wonder you survived."

He did not want to admit how true she spoke, but he could not hide. He needed to prove himself to Shona.

"I know. That's why I came here first. Things are going to get bad, and I need you two to help prepare the village."

"How?" Hamish asked.

"Rory won't stop. If he fails in the next attack, Ilse will start killing people. If it comes to that, we'll need to get everyone we can to safety."

"That's going to be difficult," Jean said. "They already threatened to kill more people if everyone leaves town, and Lord Gavin threatened Daor for anyone who leaves."

"We have to find a way," Connor insisted. "Once they start killing people, do you think they'll stop just because people listen to Lord Gavin?"

To Hamish, he said, "Take any excuse to meet Verena. They may call for men to do work tomorrow. Volunteer."

"How will that help?"

"I told you how she unlocks powers in stones. She said it's something new, but I don't understand it. I think you might."

"She tastes rocks, too?"

"Yes, like you tasted the oven."

Jean gave Hamish a hard look. "You didn't tell me about the oven."

"It was an accident."

"Talk with her," Connor said. "She's already interested in meeting you."

Hamish grinned. "And she's a Grandurian magic girl?"

Connor chuckled. "I don't know what she is. She's very cute, but don't underestimate her. She's deadly."

If anything, that only made Hamish more eager to meet Verena.

Connor turned to Jean to explain what he wanted from her, but she was giving him a hard look.

"So, this Verena is cute, is she?"

Connor shrugged. "Sure." Behind Jean, Hamish started gesturing to Connor to stop talking. Too late.

Jean rose abruptly to her feet, "I have to see to my patients." She turned and walked quickly from the room.

Connor stared after her and Hamish punched him in the shoulder. "For the guy trying to outsmart two armies, you're amazingly dense."

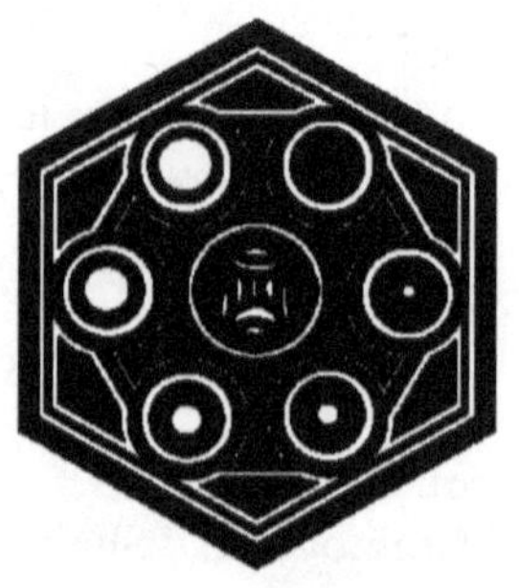

CHAPTER 34

onnor easily slipped out of town. In fact, most of the townsfolk probably could have joined him without Ilse learning of the escape until they were all free. He fought to control the seething frustration at how easily she'd gained control of the town.

He had to find Rory and deliver Ilse's message before Rory decided to attack again and his father paid for it with his life. Besides, there might be a Grandurian hidden somewhere in the village. Someone had helped the Grandurians escape Rory's scouts earlier, and Connor couldn't take the risk of it happening again.

Not yet.

Connor trotted south along River Road, parallel to the looming cliff of the plateau, until he met the gentle southern slope that ran the mile back up to the plateau. Downriver, the open slope met the tree line, and Connor moved off into the trees, looking for tracks.

It didn't take long. The army was camped near the banks of the river about two miles downstream in a large clearing. A sentry materialized out of the darkness, but recognized him and waved him on.

Large campfires burned in the corners of the clearing, with another in the center. Rows of groaning men lay on blankets at the far end of the clearing, waiting their turn with the Healer, who was busy working on a man with a badly broken leg. The end of the bone protruded up through the skin at a sharp angle.

While his beefy assistant held the soldier down, the Healer yanked the man's foot down hard to set the bone. The soldier screamed and writhed in the assistant's hands and bit clean through a leather-wrapped stick held between his teeth.

The Healer gently applied light brown mud, smearing it on liberally until the entire lower leg was coated. Then he wrapped the entire muddy limb in a canvas sack. Two waiting soldiers carried the man to a blanket.

Most of the soldiers not lying in the queue waiting for the Healer's attention sported bruises, scrapes, and burns. Few looked unscathed. Connor breathed a sigh of relief when he saw Donald sleeping near one of the fires.

Captain Rory, who sat conferring with Shona and Tomas at the central fire, caught sight of him. His craggy face split with a smile. "Connor, lad, I thought you'd gone and died on us."

"So did I."

"Glad to see you're back safe."

Shona turned toward him. One eye was swollen shut, and a deep bruise marred the opposite cheek. Her skin was scraped and puffy.

"How'd you get back here without a scratch?" She asked through swollen lips

"I got beat up pretty bad."

She huffed. "Doesn't look like it."

Only then did Connor realize he actually felt remarkably well. The wild tumble into the manor house had left him scraped and bruised and sore, but now he felt great. Even his throat where Verena sucker-punched him felt fine.

If his Curse healed him this fast, why hadn't Shona's?

He glanced around the fire at the battered army. "Did everyone else make it back?"

Rory frowned. "Lost four from the slinger missiles they used."

He tossed one of the jagged pieces of Alasdair White to Connor, who frowned over the missile. Granite was tough, but the soldiers' steel helmets and armor should have protected them.

Rory continued. "Seven men are in very serious condition. Hopefully they'll make it."

The Healer dropped to the ground next to Rory with a groan, "I told you, Captain, they'll live." At Captain Rory's raised eyebrow he added, "The rest can wait a minute. I can't heal if I'm too tired to stand."

He gave Rory a meaningful look, "If we had even a puff of granite powder left, I could still be working."

Rory frowned. "Leave off, Marcas. You're not the only one feeling the lack."

Tomas handed Marcas a tin cup full of water, which he gratefully accepted and slurped down. The burly Fast Roller said, "I tried pounding one of those missiles to dust, but it wouldn't break. They're harder than steel."

"How is that possible?" Connor asked.

Rory poked the fire with a stick, "One more mystery we'll beat out of Ilse when we take her." Then he forced himself to relax. "You've done great work tonight, Marcas."

"I've never seen so many broken bones from one engagement."

Tomas said, "Well, not on our side, anyway."

Marcas raised his cup in silent agreement.

"That wall struck hard," Shona muttered. "Half the army's unfit for battle."

"Not to worry. The bones will be mended by morning."

"You can't be serious," Connor said. He broke his arm once, and it took months to heal.

"Sandstone casts, boy. If I don't run out of sandstone afore I finish setting them all, those bones will be strong enough to fight on by breakfast." He gave Captain Rory another meaningful look. Rory only scowled at him. "My casts are the fastest way to heal a bone."

He gave Connor a thoughtful look and muttered, "Well, almost the fastest."

"Connor, where have you been?" Shona asked.

"Well, I was Ilse's prisoner for a while."

Shona's one good eye blazed with fury at Ilse's name, "How did you escape?"

"I didn't. She sent me to deliver a message."

At Shona's disappointed look, Connor wanted to hit himself in the head with a rock. She might appreciate not being the only deformed person in the circle of firelight, and he was such an idiot. He should have come up with a better story.

"Before we get to the message lad," Rory said, "I need to know, did you really use basalt or did I just take one too many hits to the head?"

"I did, sir. I took it from Donald's pouch."

Shona gaped. Given her swollen lips and battered face, it made her look ridiculous. "You did what?"

"I thought it was granite."

Shona scooted over on her log and gestured for him to sit beside her. "You really used basalt on your first try?"

He shrugged. "Wasn't very good at it. I fell right into their … hands."

"But you did it!"

"Aye. What's the first stone you used second?"

Marcas barked a laugh, and Rory rubbed his face to hide a grin.

"Connor, that doesn't make any sense at all."

"You know what I mean."

"I know what you mean." Shona scowled and added softly, "I've never achieved affinity with anything but granite."

"Most people can't," Marcas interjected. "Boy, what's got us all flummoxed is you used another igneous stone."

"I thought you said half the Guardians can do it."

"You weren't listening. Half can get a flicker out of a sedimentary stone as a secondary. Never a second igneous stone."

"Why not?"

He shrugged. "Why are young folks full of curiosity and stupidity in equal measure? It's just the way things are."

Rory said, "He's right. Using two igneous stones is as rare as the Tallan's own curse."

Connor shivered. He'd never heard of the Tallan's curse, but it had to be doubly evil.

Why would Rory even mention it?

Tomas added, "Maybe not quite that rare, although I haven't heard of a Guardian-Agor in a generation."

Shona shuffled closer to Connor, "Never mind all that. The fact that you did it, and while so new to granite, is nothing short of amazing. Dangerous, but amazing. Tell me how it felt."

He almost said, "Like tasting rocks," but that wouldn't work with her.

Wait a minute, how was it dangerous?

Before he could ask her to clarify, Rory said, "Later. Tell us about Ilse's force. Was there really a Sapper hidden among them?"

"A what?"

"A Sentry?"

"Ah, they were definitely keeping watch."

Shona took his hand. Her fingers felt cool and a little rough. "A Sentry is a Petralist with powerful slate affinity. A strong Sentry can move earth like they did tonight, raising walls, tossing us off the plateau."

Rory nodded. "Weren't expecting a Sentry, or Sapper as they call them. Changes the battle plan completely."

Connor shook his head. "They don't have a Sapper. It was Verena."

"Who's Verena?" Shona asked.

"You remember, the girl who brought me to their camp by the river." At her blank look, he added, "About our age, cute, dressed nice."

Shona frowned. "I remember her. She didn't look that remarkable to me, and you have terrible taste in clothes."

"Well, not dressed like a soldier."

"I thought she was a servant."

"Not hardly. She called herself a Builder."

Rory frowned. "A Builder? Are you sure?"

"You've heard of Builders?"

Shona said, "There hasn't been a Builder in Obrion since the time of the Tallan. The Speedcaravan's about the only artifact left. I'm surprised they risked one on this mission."

"They have a rare gift for working with stone," Rory added. "Talent was lost for centuries, and only just reappeared in Granadure a few years ago."

"One more reason to kill her," Shona added. "The king's law still calls for death to all Builders."

"Why?"

She shrugged. "I have no idea, but I'll enforce it."

Connor decided that would be a good time to mention Ilse's statement that they didn't want to kill anyone.

Shona laughed. "They shouldn't have invaded."

Rory turned to Tomas. "Spread the word. When we capture Ilse, we must take this girl too. It is imperative we understand what these new Builders can do."

"Then we kill her," Shona added.

Connor wished he'd kept his mouth shut, and he was deeply grateful he hadn't mentioned Hamish to them. Even though Verena had punched him, he didn't want her getting hurt.

Better to change the subject. "The Petralist, Anika, who you fought tonight, she was asking about you, Captain."

"What did she say?"

"She wants to wrestle again."

Rory grinned. Not an eager-for-battle grin or an I-want-to-break-her-in-pieces grin. It was a happy grin, and it looked completely wrong on his craggy face.

Rory rubbed his hands together absently, "She was something, wasn't she?"

Shona rolled her eye. "Please, Captain, stay focused."

The grin disappeared and he frowned at no one in particular, "I am focused. We can't take Ilse until we defeat her Petralists. I'm just ... planning how to do that."

"You're planning something," Shona said with a toss of her long hair. Then she added, "Wait till I get my hands on that big blond Petralist. I'll make him pay for stomping on my face." She fingered the bruise on her cheek.

"His name is Erich. He's Anika's brother."

"So if I subdue Anika, he might surrender," Rory said.

"Or rip your head off to free her," Shona said.

Connor nodded. "I second the rip your head off response."

"Better to kill the Grandurian wench when you get the chance."

Rory didn't look convinced. Connor hoped he knew what he was doing. Anika was quite a woman, but she'd break Rory in pieces if he underestimated her.

"Tell me Captain Ilse's message."

When Connor repeated Ilse's demand, Rory pursed his lips in thought and stared up at the star-lit sky. "She is a wily one, that Ilse. I am looking forward to questioning her."

"That's all you have to say?" Shona demanded.

"For now."

"What else does she want?" Shona asked.

"She said Captain Rory knows what needs to be returned before they'll leave. What did she mean, Captain?"

"It means she won't leave until we drive her out."

That was a completely useless answer.

Shona said, "She's bluffing. We should attack again immediately. She won't be ready for it."

Rory waved a hand at the campsite. "Our powder stores are gone. Half the men are injured, and we're facing unknown Builder powers. Attacking tonight is suicide."

"We could take them by surprise," Shona insisted.

"Who surprised who tonight?" When she pouted at the fire, he added, "No, Ilse's no fool. She won't be taken easily. We'll rest and recover tonight. Connor, tomorrow you'll lead Donald and Grahame and their scouts to the best vantage points to observe them."

"That's it?" Shona demanded.

"For now. Tomorrow is soon enough to decide the best way to route them from Alasdair."

"That's not good enough, Captain."

"I will not throw away the lives of my men. When I know how best to proceed, we will take the town. Not until then."

Shona tried to argue further, but Rory would not be moved. Connor was grateful Rory had the sense to wait. He didn't want to admit it, but even he could see Ilse held the upper hand at the moment.

As he sat near the fire, soaking up the warmth, he thought back over the battle and considered ways they could avoid similar disasters in the future. Then it dawned on him, he was already convinced they would launch a second attack, despite the risk to the prisoners.

And Ilse would be ready for them.

CHAPTER 35

onnor awoke to bustling activity just after dawn. Soldiers were hastily donning armor and assembling in squads in the center of camp. It took him a few seconds to realize virtually all of the sick beds lay empty but for piles of discarded bandages. Soldiers who had screamed as their shattered bones were set the previous night stood at attention, looking ready for battle.

Connor reached for his bow but realized the air was charged with excitement and a little nervousness, not the tension of impending battle. He found Rory standing with Shona near the central fire. Shona's face looked beautiful in the soft light, fully restored.

They stood talking with a slender man in chainmail armor. On his head perched a tight-fitting blue cap, and over his shoulder draped a cape of mottled forest-green.

"How many men?" Rory was asking.

"Five full companies, including an entire squad of Boulders, and a mixed company of support troops."

Rory blinked. "More than I expected."

"*He* cares for my wellbeing," Shona said with a satisfied little smile.

"No doubt your safety is General Carbrey's chief concern," Rory said with a straight face.

The soldiers nearby came to attention. Into the clearing marched a dozen huge warriors who towered over even Tomas and the Fast Rollers. They wore heavy plates of steel armor and carried gigantic shields. On their backs hung massive hammers with long, steel handles that looked like they must weigh thirty pounds.

At their head strode a hugely muscled warrior with a surprisingly youthful face. When he caught sight of Rory, he grinned like a little boy. "Rory, well met!"

The two clasped hands. The newcomer stood half a head taller and half again as broad in the shoulders. "Captain Peader, well met."

The giant warriors parted and a thick-chested man with short-cropped salt-and-pepper hair strode into the clearing. He took in the scene with one sweep of hard brown eyes. The two men who flanked him bristled with weapons. Twin swords hung on their backs, and they wore many daggers strapped to their torsos and limbs. They moved with the fluid grace of deadly nuall hunting cats.

As one, Rory and his men saluted. The thick-chested newcomer returned a smart salute, passed Rory without stopping for a greeting, and strode to Shona. He made a tiny bow, "Lady Shona, I am happy to see you safe."

"Thank you, General," Shona said graciously.

Only then did the general turn to Rory. "I hear you've botched things completely, Captain."

He spoke with formal, clipped tones in a voice that commanded compliance. Connor wished he'd hung back farther. The general exuded an aura of authority, and Connor felt like an ignorant country fool standing close to the great man.

Rory, his face expressionless, gave a brief but complete summary of the events of his excursion. When he mentioned Shona's return on the barge, assisted by a local lad, a Guardian-Agor, murmurs rippled through the otherwise silent force of newcomers.

Rory nodded toward Connor, and the general focused the full weight of his intense stare on him. Connor could not meet his gaze, but stared at his feet.

"He is confirmed Agor?"

"Aye, sir."

Connor glanced up and found the general regarding him with genuine curiosity. "Interesting." General Carbrey gave Connor a little nod of acknowledgement. "A pleasure to meet you, lad. I look forward to talking with you in detail later."

"Thank you, sir."

Rory continued his report, relating the assault on the town, the surprise tactics employed by the Grandurians, and their eventual retreat. As he detailed Verena's amazing powers and how they played a pivotal role in the entire battle strategy, the general's initial scowl of displeasure faded.

As Rory talked, more soldiers poured into the clearing, while still more packed the trail as far down River Road as Connor could see. They came by the hundreds, the majority of them dressed in chainmail like Rory's army. Scores of mounted knights flanked them, wearing steel plate armor and long lances, riding huge destriers with coats of chainmail shielding their flanks.

Still more men, dressed in the simple worker garb of Linn, moved into the clearing and started setting up tents, building fires, and establishing a far more elaborate campsite. Connor stood in the midst of it all, filled with a growing sense of wonder. He'd been impressed by Rory's small army, but they had been but the vanguard.

Did Ilse comprehend what she'd unleashed when she stole Shona away from Merkland? She should have run when she had the chance.

Rory finished his report by saying, "Given the situation, I recommend capture of Captain Ilse as well as the Builder Verena."

"I concur," General Carbrey said.

"Don't forget Kilian," Shona added.

General Carbrey's face lit up. "Kilian is here?"

"He is."

"Captain, on initial reports, I suspected you of gross negligence. However, now that I understand the full situation, I am revising that initial assessment."

"Thank you, sir."

"We must take Kilian as well as the two women. His capture would be worth even more than retaining the boy."

The general added loudly, "Captains, to me."

In less than a minute, seven men stood with him, along with Shona while the rest of the army was ordered back to give them room to converse privately. Rory stood beside Captain Peader, who towered over the others. The two soldiers with all the weapons looked tiny beside him, but did not seem fazed by it.

Another captain clearly led the cavalry, clad in steel plate and wearing a high-pointed helm with a blue and green cloth pennant affixed to the top. Another would be a Pathfinder, for he dressed in simple hunting leathers like Grahame, and wore a similar wide-brimmed hat that failed to conceal his glittering eyes.

Connor could not imagine what group the last Captain might represent. He wore no armor, but was dressed in a tunic of bright blue and linen trousers of deep green. He wore his flame-red hair shoulder length, and he looked sunburned, with a florid complexion.

The other soldiers stood at attention while the Linn scurried about working on the camp. Connor slid closer to Tomas and stood with the Fast Rollers. After several minutes of quiet conversation, the small group broke apart and General Carbrey faced the packed clearing.

"Men of Obrion, soldiers of Merkland, today we stand upon the path of duty. Today we rise up to reject the tyranny our enemies to the north would impose upon us."

Soldiers shifted and stood taller. Connor tried to mimic them, filled with resolve as the general's words rang through the camp.

"As you know, the peaceful town of Alasdair has been invaded by Grandurians, the same force that abducted our own Lady Shona only days ago." Shona moved to his side and stood tall, head high, looking every inch the High Lady.

General Carbrey raised his right fist high. "We will not allow this aggression to stand. We will shatter their forces and reclaim this land for liberty!"

As one, every soldier raised their fists in salute and shouted, "Liberty!"

General Carbrey's voice rose higher still. "You are the shield protecting our nation. You are the sword against oppressors. You are the men of Merkland!"

Again all voices raised in unison. "Merkland!"

Connor shouted loudly with them, filled with the fires of patriotism like he'd never felt before at the thought that he, a simple Linn, was privileged to stand with these men, to prove himself alongside them.

General Carbrey lowered his fist and, as silence settled over the army, said calmly, "Today we will see victory.

"Today we route the enemy and capture three prisoners. Your Captains will brief each squad on your specific missions. Fulfill your duty and preserve the freedom of Obrion."

Connor's raging enthusiasm faded a little. He didn't hate Ilse, even though he probably should. He wished she'd just leave so no one had to get hurt. He really wished Verena could escape the coming battle unharmed, but that was unlikely. She would stand with Ilse and share a common fate.

When he thought of Kilian, he again saw the Water Moccasin skating across the surface of the river in the pre-dawn dimness, with sword drawn. He shivered at the memory. Maybe they'd all be safer with Kilian captured. Then again, without Kilian, he'd never have gotten the chance to kiss Shona underwater.

The general raised a second finger. "Our second mission today is to secure the quarry. It is a strategic asset that must be protected. Third, we secure the safety of the prisoners taken by the Grandurians. We will see to the release of the Cutters and Lord Gavin and his family."

Did the general mean to place the Cutters first, or did he only mean to lump all of the hostages into one group? And did he really consider the quarry more important than those hostages?

General Carbrey raised his voice. "I am proud to stand with you and lead you into battle. I know you won't fail."

Connor stood tall with the Guardians, filled with pride at the general's words. He would not fail. He would do his duty. He would prove his worth and claim his place as Guardian.

General Carbrey looked Connor right in the eye, as if able to read his thoughts, and beckoned him forward. Honored, and a little nervous, Connor advanced.

"You're a local hunter, lad?"

"Aye, sir."

"Very good. Rory tells me good things about you."

"Thank you, sir."

"Describe the lay of the land."

Connor explained how the forest gave way to the open slope that rose gently north for a mile up to the plateau upon which the manor stood, the layout of the manor house and its outbuildings, the town on the far side, and even the steep switchback road that led past the deep lochs and on to the quarry itself. Carbrey asked several clarifying questions.

"Very well," the General said finally. "We will attack up the slope."

"They'll see us coming," Connor said. "They might murder the prisoners."

"They will see us. They will see their cause is hopeless. Our numbers are overwhelming. This Captain Ilse has demonstrated tremendous ingenuity and resourcefulness. I respect that. Such a captain is no fool. She will surrender to save the lives of her men. They will be in our custody before lunch. I look forward to speaking with her."

"So do I," said Shona. "I have a score to settle."

General Carbrey frowned, "Lady Shona, you must learn to see past the personal insult. Captain Ilse will indeed suffer, but not out of spite. She has proven herself a capable adversary, and is therefore worthy of respect."

"How can you say that?" Shona asked angrily.

"How can you not admire her ability as a soldier? With such a small strike force, she has accomplished much and has stood against tremendous odds. My respect for that does not change the need to destroy her force, take her prisoner, and force from her the secrets she holds."

"I'll help with the forcing," Shona said. "I'll pay respect over her coffin."

"If you wish."

Carbrey began issuing orders. Companies moved to the base of the long open slope that rose to the plateau, and there assembled into tightly packed units.

As the army moved out, Linn appeared with pouches of powdered stone. Rory's Fast Rollers eagerly applied generous quantities of granite to their removable battle plates. Connor was just trying to figure out how to remove his plates when Rory handed him a small pouch of powder.

"Don't worry about the plates, lad. This will be over before you get to use it. Save it, and we'll practice some this afternoon after your town is freed."

Connor reluctantly tucked the precious granite into his belt. A moment later, Shona approached and handed him a second small pouch.

"I grabbed you some basalt," she said with a happy grin. "This is so exciting. We'll practice some this afternoon after we capture that Grandurian wench."

Connor tied it to his belt next to the pouch of granite.

Shona noticed the other pouch, "Connor, there's something else I need to tell you about using two igneous stones."

"All right."

Before she could answer, a soldier summoned her to speak with Carbrey.

Connor said, "I know, after the battle."

She flashed a warm smile and headed off after the soldier. Connor could not help but watch how she walked in those battle leathers.

He stepped out of the forest in a good mood and looked out over the gathering army with wonder. He'd never imagined he'd see such a sight in his life, let alone stand in the midst of a sea of armored men.

Rory and his Fast Rollers flanked General Carbrey in the center with Captain Peader and the gigantic warriors under his command. Tomas had told Connor that all dozen of them were Boulders, granite Guardians like the Fast Rollers, but who consumed vast quantities of granite for years to permanently enhance their bulk and strength. These men pushed the far limits of granite strength and stood as living embodiments of all the marvelous legends Bruce had ever related.

The slender fellow with the bright chainmail armor and mottled green cape turned out to be another Strider. He led a company of regulars up River Road to block any attempted escape by Ilse and her force. It was a waste of time. She'd never flee that way. At least they'd be able to take back Alasdair easily while Ilse's troops were beaten atop the plateau.

Two hundred-man companies of mail-clad soldiers flanked Rory and Peader's forces, while the company of cavalry remained in the rear. Dozens of scouts held the perimeter all the way back into the trees.

As the companies gathered, General Carbrey summoned Connor and pointed up the slope. Tiny in the distance, Connor could just make out a long earthen wall spanning the top of the plateau that blocked the view of the manor house. It probably stood a good dozen feet tall.

"I take it that wall is new," General Carbrey stated.

"It wasn't there last night."

Verena had been busy. She really had a knack with those walls. Connor thought back to the Wallstone she'd given him the first night they met, and he slipped his hand inside his belt pouch to feel the smooth slate.

A Strider raced up to the group. Connor itched to reach into the pouch of basalt powder at his belt and run the open plateau with this man. He'd consumed the last of the basalt he'd absorbed from Donald's pouch in his run down to Alasdair, and he missed its wild freedom.

"General, the eastern flank of the slope is impassable." The Strider pointed toward the right hand side where the gentle slope met the base of the far steeper flank of Mount Alasdair. "The entire length is soaked."

Carbrey glanced to Connor. "Is that normal, lad?"

"No. It's always been dry that far from the river."

"More meddling from this young Builder, no doubt."

The huge Captain Peader said, "She should've tried to soak the entire slope. Would've given them a big advantage."

"Perhaps, but I'd be surprised if she could raise so much water," Carbrey said. "Still, inform the cavalry to stay on the left flank."

Connor doubted the horsemen would like riding along the outer edge of the slope, close to where it fell steeply down to River Road and the Lower Wick.

"Send for Gregor," Carbrey ordered.

A moment later, a bear of a man approached. He stood almost as tall as the giant Captain Peader, thick of limb, with a bull neck and dark-brown eyes with almost no whites. His skin was deeply tanned, almost matching his hair. He radiated a permanence that rivaled the bulging strength of the Boulders and made the Fast Rollers seem insignificant. He wore a coat of heavy chain armor made of thick steel links that must have weighed two hundred pounds but didn't slow him.

"How may I serve?" Gregor's voice rumbled like the moving of earth, and made Rory's deep voice seem childlike by comparison.

"These Grandurians possess unusual powers. Check the hillside before we commence the attack. I want no surprises."

Gregor nodded and moved a little way apart. He crouched and scraped away the grass at his feet with thick fingers, rolling back the turf as easily as Connor would wipe granite dust from his father's worktable in the Powder House. He drove one massive hand into the earth to the wrist.

The ground shook and the earth directly under Gregor's feet rose and lifted him ten feet off the ground. He stood atop the pillar, hands embedded in earthen posts that flanked him like a rail.

Connor gaped. Verena's Wallstones were impressive, but this was awe-inspiring. If the man was not a Builder, what was he?

Then it dawned on him. The man was a Sentry.

Gregor bowed his head in concentration and everyone nearby stood silent and watched the giant atop his high earthen tower. After a long moment, he called down, "General, I sense no Sapper. There is movement behind the wall. It appears they plan to defend the plateau.

"I applaud their optimism," Carbrey said. "What of the wall?"

"No active control."

"Can you remove it?"

"It is possible, although difficult from this distance."

"Very well, we'll wait until we close on their position. Dropping it then will magnify the impact."

The earthen column settled back into the ground with a rumble that Connor felt through his feet. The air smelled like springtime after planting, and filled Connor with restless energy. He could scarce take in all the wonders.

Carbrey turned to Connor. "Lad, stay at the rear with the reinforcements."

"But sir, I can help."

"I appreciate your enthusiasm, but you are as yet untrained." He swept his arm across the gathered army. "These men are professionals. We'll set things to right. I will wish to speak with you at length later."

Connor reluctantly moved back to the trees. Shona gave him an encouraging smile, but it did little to cheer him. She was going to battle with the army while he had to watch like a Linn.

He didn't want to be Linn any more. He wanted to be a Guardian, but how could he prove himself if they wouldn't let him fight? Just in the past couple of days he'd learned so much, gained so much more control over his Curse. He'd do whatever it took to prove himself. He would find a way.

General Carbrey made a chopping motion with his hand. "Advance."

The army began to move, hundreds of men marching in unison, and the sound of their cadence reverberated back through the ground to Connor. Ilse probably felt it all the way up on the plateau.

Did it fill her with terror? Did she face her imminent defeat with the same calm resolve she'd faced Rory's army last night? Connor had no doubt whatsoever that she would.

He'd bet Hamish every desert for the next year that she'd also planned a brilliant surprise for Rory's army.

Unfortunately, there was no way she could know Carbrey would show up this morning with so many reinforcements. Whatever Ilse might be planning, she could not hope to win.

Somehow, he knew she wouldn't agree.

CHAPTER 36

arbrey led his army up the slope toward the plateau at a steady march. Connor scrambled up a tall oak tree to better witness the battle, so he had a clear view of the awesome sight of hundreds of men marching in step, weapons at the ready, armor gleaming in the clear morning sunlight.

If only Ilse and her tiny band, hidden behind Verena's single wall, would run. Instead, they'd stand boldly and fight, somehow convinced they could win against so many. Connor only hoped Verena surrendered before she got hurt.

Nervous anticipation grew in Connor at every step the army took until he could barely contain it. The crisp air smelled of pine and earth and river. Somehow it seemed wrong that everything felt so normal.

The army covered half the distance to the plateau with no sign of Ilse or her troops. Connor expected to see the wall tumble down under the power of Gregor the Sentry at any second.

Instead a thick, fifty-foot-long tree trunk, stripped of branches, sailed over the wall. It thundered down onto the slope and bounced wildly as it bore down upon Carbrey's army.

"They're grouted," Connor whispered, horrified at what was about to happen.

The army was too far away for Connor to hear more than a muted roar as soldiers shouted warnings. Regulars started running cross-slope to try to escape the deadly missile.

Rory's Fast Rollers and Peader's Boulders ran straight toward it. They formed a wall of stone-hard warriors in front of General Carbrey and braced themselves with shields raised to meet the tree head-on.

The tree smashed into them, and the line staggered back a pace. Two soldiers crumpled to the ground. The memory of the Fast Roller who met the stone pedra the same way flashed into Connor's mind. He winced and hoped the men up on the slope had avoided shattering their ankles.

The tree bounced up and over the line of Guardians, sailed over Carbrey and his retinue, and continued tumbling down the slope. Most of the soldiers had already cleared a path for it.

A few did not.

The tree scattered those hapless few like corn before a scythe. It continued down the hill, leaving broken bodies strewn across the slope in its wake. All around Connor, soldiers of the rearguard exclaimed with dismay and anger.

They should have known better. Captain Ilse was not one to be underestimated.

He could not sit still, not after battle was joined. So he slipped down from the tree and shoved one hand into the pouch of basalt on his belt.

He concentrated, and the warm energy of the powdered stone began flowing into his hand. It slithered up his arm and filled him with boundless energy, with the need to run.

So he ran. He angled upslope and to the right. Carbrey had ordered him to stay behind the army, but not by how far. He had to get closer, had to get a better view.

Connor grinned as he poured on the speed and tore up the slope. He'd planned to stop when he hit the soft, muddy ground on the eastern edge of the slope, but before the change in ground even registered, he was racing across it. He laughed. He was running too fast to sink in the mud!

Emboldened by his success, Connor increased his tap-rate and accelerated. Water and mud sprayed out behind him as he shot up the slope and across the muddy bog to where the slope met the base of the mountain.

Connor spied a shelf of rock protruding from that steep mountainside about fifty feet up, and raced toward it. Running on his toes, he shot up the side of the mountain, hardly slowing. With a final leap, he landed on the shelf.

"Yes!" Connor raised both hands in victory and hopped up and down several times in exultant glee.

Basalt was so much fun. Why hadn't he been cursed with this all his life?

He looked upslope toward the plateau just as the long earthen wall collapsed and sank into the ground. Connor stood high enough that he could see the top of the plateau all the way to the manor house.

Several figures stood near the edge of the plateau, tiny in the distance, but he thought he recognized Captain Ilse and the sibling Petralists. Luckily, he did not recognize any of the Cutters. Ilse must have expected her wall to hold off the advancing army longer.

He fervently prayed his father would live out the day.

Movement behind the small group drew his gaze. Connor blinked a couple of times to make sure he was not imagining the sight. A tiny figure who had to be Verena stood atop a wide platform along with another stripped tree trunk. They were flying up the side of the big barn. Connor squinted to see better, but the distance was too great and he could not see what lifted them up the side of the tall barn.

He'd sort of flown the Heatstone oven, and Verena had been propelled back into the manor house by her air blasting stone, but he'd never imagined anything so graceful, so controlled as what he witnessed.

How was it possible?

When Verena reached the roof, several soldiers rolled the heavy tree trunk off the platform and onto a complex contraption he could not clearly make out. Then they scurried to the side.

"Look out!" Connor shouted, even though the soldiers in Carbrey's army could not hear him.

A pair of tall fir trees that flanked the big barn, that had been cranked dangerously far over backward, sprang upright.

The tree trunk, lashed to those bent-over trees with a series of ropes and pulleys, shot up into the air.

They built a catapult in one night?

The tree-become-missile sailed gracefully high over the edge of the plateau, slammed down onto the slope, and careened down the hill. Most of the soldiers were already clear of the path of destruction, but several of the fallen still lay where they had fallen. Men were racing to pull them aside lest they be crushed a second time.

They shouldn't have bothered. The second tree did not follow the same track as the first. Somehow the Grandurians had launched it at an angle, and it barreled down the slope directly at a full company of surprised infantry.

Rory and his Fast Rollers had already moved to the opposite side of the slope, along with half of Captain Peader's Boulders. Only six Boulders stood forth to meet the tree and its thousands of stone weight, in a desperate attempt to save the lives of the men who scrambled to get out of the way.

Shona stood with them.

"Look out!" Connor shouted again, so loud his voice cracked.

How did Shona end up there, directly in the path of destruction? Had Ilse targeted her specifically?

She looked like a child standing next to the hulking Boulders, but she did not retreat.

Please spirits, let the tree bounce over them.

The tree bounced high, and for a second Connor exulted.

With a sickening feeling of dread, Connor realized the truth. The tree came straight down at Shona and the six Boulders. The Boulders braced their shields, and Shona lifted empty hands to ward against the unstoppable force. Surely they max-tapped their powers.

It did no good.

The tree plowed through the heroic group without slowing. Shona and two of the Boulders collapsed to the ground under the tree's awful weight, while the other four tumbled aside like chaff in a strong wind. Without slowing, the deadly missile smashed through the remnants of the column that were too slow to dodge.

This time, Connor clearly heard the screams of pain as men were crushed. The tree continued on until it ground to a halt in the mire of the eastern edge of the slope, a little north of where Connor perched safely up on the mountain slope.

Healers and soldiers pressed into service to help them raced up the slope to pull the wounded from the battlefield. Connor stared at the carnage, at the broken bodies, and the crimson smears marring the brown slope. Mostly he stared at Shona's leather-clad form that lay unmoving on the hillside, and clenched his fists in helpless rage.

Ilse might claim all she did was defend her people, but she was the aggressor in Alasdair. It was her fault these brave men were hurt and dying.

For the first time Connor hated her, and wished with all his soul that Carbrey would reach the plateau and utterly destroy the Grandurians. He felt sad for what would happen to Verena, but she'd chosen her course.

Connor leaped from the shelf and slid down the steep slope. Just before he landed in the mire, he tapped his basalt speed and pulled deep from the boundless energy raging through his limbs.

He nearly over-ran his balance as he sprang forward, but managed to right himself. His legs moved so fast he dared not look at the ground as it shot under his feet for fear of stumbling. He'd never dreamed of such speed.

Deep in his bones, his hips and upper legs burned with a need to move differently, to shift in impossible directions. Sharp pain spiked through his hips and thighs and for a second it felt like his bones began to crack under the onslaught of the basalt.

He panicked and eased back, reducing the tap-rate. He hadn't realized it was possible to draw too deep from the basalt and break his own legs.

Was that one of the dangers Rory was trying to warn him about?

Easing his stride a little seemed to work. He slowed just a fraction, and his bones solidified again. Maybe the Curse he'd grown up with wasn't so bad after all.

Something loomed in Connor's vision, and only then did he realize he'd been sprinting up the slope, so distracted by the basalt that he hadn't realized his course had started to wander.

The tree that just crushed Shona to the earth lay right in front of him. Connor tried to leap over it.

He almost made it. His leading foot caught the top edge of the trunk, and he tumbled forward, out of control. He started shouting, but then his face struck the muddy ground and his mouth filled with mud. He gagged and then spewed mud as he somersaulted like a Sogail competition ball up the slope.

He finally came to a stop, face down, spread-eagled in the mud. After a moment, he rolled over, gasping, his heart pounding with fear and elation. He'd nearly died.

But he hadn't. He couldn't stay there. He had to reach Shona, so he forced himself to unsteady feet. Mud and water cascaded off. He tasted mud, and one of his nostrils was plugged with it, as were both ears.

Connor shook himself like a wet dog in a vain effort to dislodge the mud, blew it out his nose, and dug a muddy finger into his ears. That didn't help as much as he'd hoped. He spat a few times, but the taste clung to his mouth, and all he could smell was wet dirt.

Connor carefully tapped basalt again and leaped forward.

And fell right onto his face.

He spat a new mouthful of mud and looked down at his feet. They were stuck up to the ankles. All he'd managed to do was trip himself.

One boot almost came off as he pried his feed out of the mud. Upslope a third tree trunk began its wild, tumbling assault on the left flank of the army this time. Rory and the Fast Rollers, assisted with Captain Peader and his Boulders, and by a lucky bounce of the tree, knocked it high enough that it sailed completely over the company that huddled right behind them.

Connor breathed a sigh of relief and, with his feet finally free, tapped basalt again. This time he quickly gained speed until he rippled across the muddy ground, like a rock skipping across a pond.

Mud and water sprayed far out behind him as he found his pace, and Connor laughed at the thrill of moving so fast.

Within seconds, he passed the scattered remnants of broken companies, altered course, and closed on Shona, who was sitting up, attended by a couple of soldiers.

Connor, gratified to see she still lived, slowed and dropped to his knees beside her. She sat awkwardly, as if in great pain. Her light brown hair was matted with blood and covered her face as her head lolled forward onto her chest.

One of the soldiers was saying, "We need to get you to safety, Lady Shona."

She tried to push him away. "Where's my sword?"

"Broken."

"Help me up," she commanded and lifted one hand that wobbled in the air. "We need to attack the … thing, and beat … the other one."

The soldier shared a helpless look with his companion.

Connor took Shona's upraised hand, "Lady Shona, are you all right?"

"Connor?" She slowly lifted her head.

He gently brushed her hair back from her face, and stared in shock. Her skin still bore the gray sheen of granite power, and a series of fine cracks spread across the side of her face. Her eyes stared at him dully, as if not quite able to focus.

"Have to fight," she muttered.

"Shona, you can't. You're cracked."

One of the nearby soldiers said sharply, "Watch it, boy. That's Lady Shona you're talking to."

Shona frowned and blinked a couple of times, finally bringing her eyes into focus. "How dare you say that to me, you ungrateful Linn?"

"I didn't mean it that way, not like you're mentally cracked. It's your face, you're really cracked."

She pushed at him. "You're hopeless. Get away from me. You're filthy, and you stink."

She tried to rise, and fell back to the ground with a strangled cry of pain. The soldiers moved to help her, but

Connor waved them back.

"I've got this."

One soldier snarled, "Watch it, kid, or you'll be cracked."

"No, seriously. She granted me Patronage. It's my duty to help."

As they regarded him suspiciously, he drove his hand into the pouch of granite powder at his belt. Instantly the insect-crawly feeling of granite power skittered up his arm. He'd show Shona who was useless. Connor drew upon the Curse and focused it throughout his body.

White-hot agony exploded through Connor's entire being. Every muscle convulsed, and he collapsed to the ground beside Shona, shaking, his feet pattering on the ground. His skin faded to gray, then to white, and began to flake and peel. Every inch of skin burned as if someone scraped it raw with burning irons.

Connor tried to scream, but his throat closed, and he lacked the ability to even writhe under the agony of it. His vision blurred, and his body faded from burning agony to a dead numbness so deep he might never wake again.

Beside him, Shona said weakly, "Who's cracked now?"

Connor could not even groan.

As blackness flickered at the edges of his blurry vision, he dimly heard General Carbrey.

"Cavalry charge!"

CHAPTER 37

onnor's head fell forward against his chest, and the movement dragged him awake. He groaned and blinked eyes that felt coated in sand. Every muscle ached so deep, he wondered if they'd been ripped from the bones.

"What happened?" he whispered.

Two soldiers had lifted Connor and draped his arms over their shoulders to carry him downslope. One of them said, "Easy, lad. We'll get you out of here. Don't worry. Cavalry is charging. The battle is almost won."

He doubted it.

Connor didn't voice his fears, but he had too much grudging faith in Captain Ilse to expect an easy victory at this point. Too bad she wasn't an Obrioner. The country could use such a brilliant leader.

The thunder of a hundred galloping destriers shook the ground as the cavalry charged up the slope. Connor looked across slope and noticed the two soldiers who had been trying to help Shona before he interfered were leading her toward the Healers. She argued with them every step of the way.

I should be a cavalry knight, he decided. That wouldn't hurt so much, and they looked amazing.

With cloaks and pennants streaming behind them and lances held high at identical angles, the knights galloped up the hill in perfect formation. At the top of the plateau, Ilse's force had gathered into a single body that looked pitifully inadequate to stand against so many mighty chargers.

Maybe Ilse really had run out of surprises.

"What's that?" A soldier cried.

The two men dragging Connor pulled him around with them. His legs still weren't working, and he could barely feel his deadened body, but his eyes worked, and the sight helped him forget about the rising fear he'd somehow permanently injured himself.

About a dozen large, gray birds descended out of the clear morning sky and speared into the ranks of charging horses. They flitted nimbly between the riders and steeds, tearing at faces and digging at horses' eyes.

At first, it looked like the cavalry would ride right through the distraction, but then one horse in the lead reared, with a bird clawing at its eyes. It stumbled as it came back to the ground and its rider almost fell from the saddle. They careened right into the paths of several other riders.

As the formation wobbled, more horses reared or bucked, and the charge collapsed into a wild melee. Men tried to strike the gray birds, but they moved with startling speed, and the close-packed knights ended up hitting each other.

One of the soldiers holding Connor by the arm said, "Hey, those are bats."

"I've never seen bats that big," said his companion.

Connor realized then the truth. These bats were conjured, like the stone pedra. Kilian was at work again.

A group of knights broke free of the tangled mess of men and horses and resumed the charge. A bat flew past them and dropped something from its claws.

An earthen wall shot up from the ground in front of the lead riders. They yanked hard on their reins, but could not stop. Horses and riders alike plowed into the wall and sank deep into it. Most fell back to the ground, but a couple remained stuck in the wall like flies to honey paper.

A second bat dropped another stone behind the massed knights, and another wall shot out of the ground. As it reached its apex, a brilliant light exploded to life in the middle of the pack of riders. Its blinding light added to the mayhem, so bright it had to be the same thing Ilse had used last night to blind them at the manor house.

General Carbrey's voice carried over the battlefield. "Gregor!"

At the same time, another tree shot off the catapult atop the big barn and careened down the slope, directly at a densely packed company of soldiers. The men scattered, but many could not escape the wildly tumbling missile. Their screams filled the air, and the tree left dozens of their broken bodies strewn across the battlefield.

"Let's finish with this one," one of the soldiers holding Connor by the arms said. "Looks like we'll be needed again." The soldiers dragged Connor downhill, and soon the lower wall blocked his view of the struggling cavalry.

General Carbrey's voice rang out again. "Infantry, retreat. Gregor!"

Companies of foot soldiers began retreating down the hill after Connor, bearing with them the wounded and the dead. Shouts and screams still rang from beyond the wall where the cavalry still apparently fought to free themselves.

At the foot of the slope, the Healers, led by old Marcas, had set up field cots for the wounded, and waged their own battle against death and pain.

Marcas took one look at Connor and ordered him dropped on a blanket near the tree line until someone could check on him. Marcas turned to Shona, clutched his little sandstone pendant, and placed a hand on Shona's cracked cheek.

The earthen walls blocking Connor's view of the cavalry collapsed, and the blinding light sank into the ground. Only then did Connor locate Gregor. The Sentry stood near Carbrey, one hand buried in the ground.

Even as Connor watched, Gregor huddled with Captain Peader and Captain Rory. The air nearby burst into rainbow light that flashed blindingly for a second.

When the light disappeared, two miniature nuall cats stood beside the captains. Instantly, the nualls sprang toward the cavalry.

The nualls leaped impossibly high and each caught a granite bat in their jaws. The bats exploded into muddy water, and the nualls leaped again, catching more bats, allowing the cavalry to re-group.

A loud crack echoed across the valley from up on the plateau beyond Connor's sight. Carbrey's voice rang out over the battlefield. "Catapult is down. Cavalry, charge! Infantry, charge!"

The army reversed course and every man not wounded, and not bearing the dead and dying, broke into a run. The cavalry launched into a gallop, more a mob of angry horsemen than a disciplined formation of glorious knights.

They'd kill Ilse just as dead.

Nearby, a soldier pointed. "Look, the bats crashed and shattered!"

Connor frowned. Why would Kilian surrender his one good weapon?

At the lip of the plateau, Ilse's tiny force, looking like miniature dolls in the distance, shouted war cries, and charged onto the slope, directly toward the onrushing cavalry.

This was it. They recognized defeat and ran to meet it, hoping for the glory of death in battle. The sight sickened Connor. What a waste. He wanted to look away from the imminent carnage, but could not.

How could they throw their lives away after fighting so bravely? There had to be some dignity in surrender.

Then a geyser of water shot up from the ground, halfway between the two converging forces, and spread over the slope. The cavalry charged right through it. Knights raised swords to strike down the hated Grandurians, or lowered lances to skewer them.

The water covering the slope turned to ice.

It changed so fast, in less than a heartbeat, that most of the knights probably never realized what happened. Their destriers' delicate ankles snapped by the hundreds as hooves failed to break free of the thick ice, and the incredible weight of horse and rider drove the hapless animals forward against the restraint.

Horses screamed in agony and the entire company collapsed. Knights crashed to the ground into jumbled heaps of armor around and beneath the thrashing, screaming horses.

As one, the entire army cried out in dismay at the sight of the cavalry felled by one evil deed. Men shouted in rage and discipline fled as the army sprinted up the slope, seeking vengeance.

The Grandurians reached the fallen knights first. While Carbrey's army was still half a minute's run away, the small force of Grandurians descended on the stunned and helpless knights. They struck without mercy, clubbing knights with heavy maces or hammers. Anika and Erich grabbed knights like toys and tossed them from the melee into a pile, or finished off injured horses with mighty blows of their granite-hard fists. Soldiers surrounded the mass of injured soldiers.

As Carbrey's army closed, Ilse's voice rang out over the battlefield.

"Stand down, men of Obrion, or every knight dies!"

The army kept charging, with Carbrey in the lead.

Ilse shouted again, "And Lord Gavin and his family, and every Cutter dies with them!"

She pointed up the hill where several of her men stood behind Lord Gavin, Lady Isobel, the Cutters, and even Moira. Right beside Lord Gavin stood Hendry, Connor's father, easily recognizable to Connor, despite the distance.

He and the other prisoners stood in a row, bound together, helpless as babes under the Grandurians' knives. Seeing his father, who had always seemed so powerful, so unbreakable, standing helpless tore at Connor's heart.

With barely ten strides between the armies, Carbrey lifted his hand and shouted, "Halt!"

The army slowed to a halt almost close enough to touch their fallen companions and the Grandurians who stood above them, sharp blades at the knights' throats.

Connor could barely breathe through his rage. He tried to stand, but his body still refused to move.

He was such a Tallan-cursed fool! How could he be so stupid? He wasn't a Guardian yet, and had done something wrong, although he couldn't fathom what. He should have been able to use his granite strength.

Carbrey and his battered army that still outnumbered Ilse's tiny force many times over seemed to lean uphill, as if barely restraining the urge to leap forward and destroy the Grandurians. Ilse appeared calm, flanked by the big, blond Petralist siblings.

Deep silence settled over the battlefield, and voices carried clearly all the way down to Connor and the other wounded.

"You must be Ilse," Carbrey said.

"I am."

"I am impressed by your bravery and by the ingenuity used to prepare the battlefield."

"Thank you, General. I regret we meet under these circumstances, and it grieves me to see such loss of life. Had you heeded the warning I delivered to Captain Rory, your men and horses could have been spared."

"Do you really expect us to do nothing while you invade our lands?"

"I expect you only to return that which was stolen so we can withdraw."

Connor yearned to join the army, to understand what they talked about. What could have possibly been stolen that would drive Ilse's company to such feats of desperate bravery?

"I applaud your dedication, young lady. Surrender now and I'll kill your men quickly."

"At the moment, you do not hold the advantage, General. I recommend you withdraw or people will die who should be allowed to live."

"Your life is forfeit," Carbrey said. "You must understand that."

"We shall see." Ilse looked unafraid.

"Name your terms."

"They are three. First, as I stated before, that which was stolen must be delivered. Second, you hold two of my men, taken prisoner last night in Alasdair. They must be returned. Third, we must be allowed safe passage back to Granadure."

"You demand much, Captain."

"In return, Lord Gavin and his family live. The Cutters remain undamaged, and peace can be restored between our nations."

Carbrey nodded, as if reaching a decision. "Enjoy this victory, Captain, while it lasts. I agree to the prisoner exchange. Release your prisoners and I will return your men to you."

Ilse smiled but shook her head. "I will give you all of these brave knights, plus the so-called Curse Finders and their attendants for my men. Lord Gavin, his family, and the Cutters remain here until my other terms are met. You will order your forces to withdraw from Alasdair."

"Very well."

The army reluctantly withdrew to a safe distance while the two Grandurian sentries captured the previous night were fetched. Connor kept expecting to see some kind of bold, unexpected attack sweep Ilse and her men off the mountain, but nothing came.

They completed the exchange within minutes. Ilse and her small force returned to the plateau while Carbrey's army began the arduous task of carrying the injured knights down to the already-overwhelmed Healers. Very few of the knights walked down the hill unassisted, and none of them rode.

Connor couldn't stand the sight of all those slaughtered horses. How could Carbrey just walk away from the battlefield after taking such losses?

It was the right move as far as the prisoners were concerned, but part of him yearned for the chance to join the next assault, which must surely come.

As he watched Captain Ilse's men lead his father and the other prisoners back from the lip of the plateau, he raged against his helplessness. He had to stand, had to help.

He couldn't move. He watched the Healers, hoping to catch an eye and somehow coax one of them over, but they ignored him. Long lines of wounded with far worse injuries waited for the Healers' limited attention.

As Connor watched old Marcas work, the sandstone figurine the Healer clutched in his hand crumbled to dust.

Marcas did not seem surprised, and his burly assistant handed him another. He turned back to the wounded man he was treating, gripped the new sandstone pendant, and placed his other hand over the man's injured torso.

Something clicked in Connor's mind and he again remembered the odd conversation he'd had with Marcas after the battle with the pedras. He'd said it was rare to show a secondary affinity without training. Secondary affinities were established with sedimentary stones, either for healing or light. He'd also been terribly interested in Connor's sandstone pendant gifted to him from Aunt Ailsa.

It could not hurt to explore the connection, so he focused hard. With agonizing slowness, he inched his right hand up to his throat and weakly clutched the pendant, an intricately carved image of a bear. Its rear legs were looking worn. He wasn't surprised. He'd tumbled and fallen enough to have broken the little pendant in half.

Connor focused on the pendant. Although not a powdered igneous stone like granite or basalt, there must be a way to use its power. Sandstone healed and he needed healing, so he closed his eyes and focused, although he could barely feel the pendant in his numb fingers.

For long minutes, nothing happened, but it wasn't like he had anything better to do, so he stubbornly kept at it. As his concentration deepened, the constant aching of his muscles faded, as did the sounds of men moving nearby or screaming as shattered bones were set. Eventually Connor reached a place of deep meditation he'd rarely found even while sitting atop barren mountain tops.

In that moment, gentle warmth began flowing into his hand from the sandstone pendant. Like the rising of the sun melting the early morning frost, the fragile warmth eased his pains and revitalized his limbs. The dead numbness faded, and he breathed deep for the first time since his Curse struck him down.

Connor lay like that for several minutes, drinking in the wonder of the magical healing. The flow increased as his affinity with sandstone grew. Then it changed to a flood, as if some hidden door sprang open in his soul.

Connor gasped and sat up in one convulsive move. He dropped the sandstone pendant and stared in awe at his hand. It still tingled with the healing warmth that spread throughout his body. He'd never felt so good.

Grinning like a fool, Connor leaped to his feet. The rear legs of the pendant looked much more worn than before, so he carefully tucked it into his jacket.

He'd done it!

He'd proven Marcas right. He really did have an affinity for sandstone. This had to help his chances of confirming Patronage.

He found Marcas just as the old Healer set a soldier's badly broken leg, drawing the bone smoothly back into the torn flesh. The man screamed and writhed in Marcas' assistant's strong grasp.

Marcas glanced at Connor, then looked again. "I thought you were hurt, boy."

"I was."

"I'm glad someone found the time to tend you."

"They didn't. I tended myself."

Marcas gave Connor his full attention. "You did now, did you?"

He held out the sandstone pendant. "You were right. I can reach this."

Marcas gestured at the injured man lying on the cot.

"Show me."

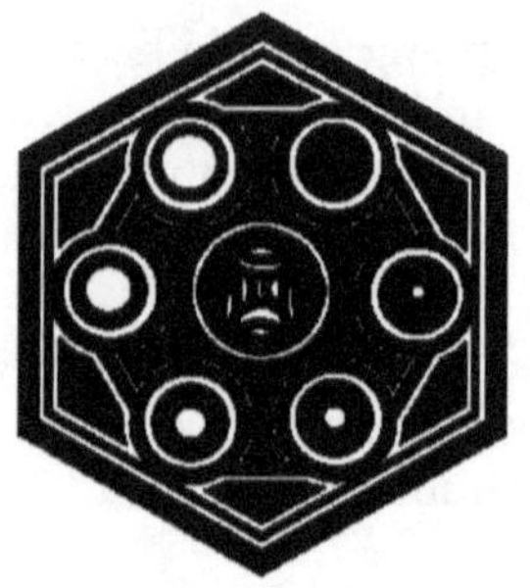

CHAPTER 38

don't know how," Connor said.

"I will guide you," Marcas assured him.

"Can't it wait?"

Marcas shook his head. "This is a rare opportunity, boy. No one heals so quick without training. Your pendant there is a wondrous gift, and I believe it's unlocked talent you might never have known."

Connor hesitantly moved to Marcas' side. The soldier lying on the cot moaned, "Stop jabbering, and just fix my leg!"

"Shush," Marcas said, "and we might just get you healed faster."

The soldier's trousers were cut away to reveal a deep gash in his thigh where the bone had burst through the skin. He looked pale from loss of blood, and pain lines etched his face.

"Grasp the leg here beside the wound," Marcas directed, and moved Connor's left hand to the soldier's leg. He placed his own right hand on the opposite side and pressed inward. "Hold it closed."

The soldier gasped, and Marcas shushed him. "Now, focus."

"On what?"

"Spirits preserve me. On the pendant, of course."

Connor did so, although he was deeply aware of Marcas' intense stare, the soldier's distrustful one, and Marcas' assistant's curious one. He tried to return to the solitary, quiet place in his mind, but found it all but impossible.

The soldier's skin burned fever hot under his hand, and warm blood trickled between his fingers. Every pained breath of the man only heightened his tension. He tried to reach past that, to will the healing magic into his hand from the pendant. He'd done it for himself, he could do it again.

After half a minute that seemed to take an eternity, a gentle whisper of warmth flowed through his fingers. He grinned and drew upon that tiny trickle.

Suddenly he connected with the pendant, and the flood gates opened again. Warm healing power burst in upon his soul and filled him to capacity. It washed away his tension and fear.

"I feel it."

"Good. Now, focus on the wound. Feel that."

Connor closed his eyes and concentrated. Somehow, filled with the gentle power of sandstone, he could feel the soldier's wound, as if he could see with his fingers. Hopefully it wouldn't prove to be a permanent effect because there were lots of things he did with his fingers he really didn't want to see that clearly.

Marcas spoke gently, and explained what Connor saw through his hands. Together, they explored the jagged gash in the skin until Connor understood it to a degree he'd never have imagined. He saw how the bone had ripped the skin, how the muscle had swollen from the wound, and how the pieces needed to connect back together.

Carried on the current of the old man's voice and whispers of healing magic that flowed from his hand into the soldier's leg, Connor's mind probed deeper. There he found the bone, snapped in half, with the pieces now re-aligned under the Healer's hand. He noted the torn tendons and ripped muscles.

He'd field dressed many kills, but had never seen the pieces of a body so clearly. To do so while the patient's skin still remained intact and he still breathed was a wonder unimaginable even moments before.

Marcas continued speaking, and under his direction, Connor focused the healing power into the wounded soldier. He molded it with his will like clay inside the man's leg, binding it to the broken leg, the rent flesh, and mending it together like his mother might mend a ripped shirt.

Some time later, Connor stepped away from the soldier, and almost fell as he returned to his normal senses. He stared in wonder at the new flesh that replaced what had been broken and torn. "Wow."

Marcas laughed softly and clapped Connor on the back. "Wow indeed, boy. I've never seen such a gift, nor such a grasp of the concepts."

"You showed me."

"A guide can show a path, but you walked it."

The soldier looked up at them, "So, I don't feel so bad any more. I hear sometimes that's a bad sign."

"Not this time." Marcas grabbed the soldier's hand and hauled him upright. The man shouted in delight as he stood on his own feet. "I can't believe it," he laughed and gave Marcas a bear hug. "Thank you!"

"Thank the boy. He did the work."

The soldier stared at Connor and then glanced back at Marcas, as if expecting some kind of joke before laughing again and pumping Connor's hand. "I am in your debt, lad."

Then he ran along the line of injured soldiers, exclaiming that he'd been completely healed. That triggered an avalanche of questions and pleas for help.

Marcas faced him. "Looks like we have a busy day ahead of us."

"Us?"

"Would you let people suffer when you can help?"

"Of course not."

"Then come. I'll teach you how to check for internal bleeding."

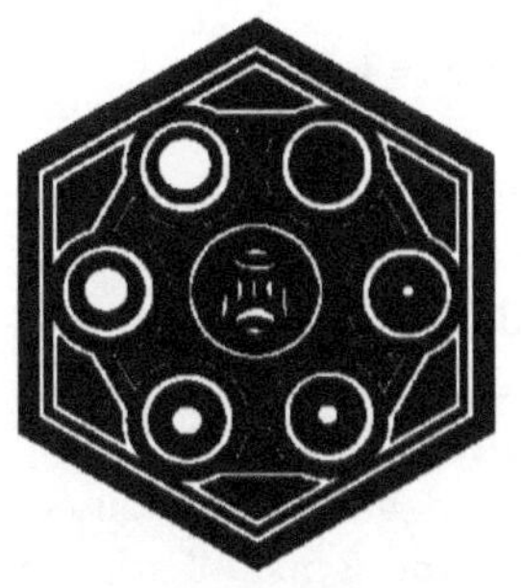

CHAPTER 39

he day passed in a blur for Connor who got lost in a wide new world of tiny proportions. He set more bones than he could count, learned the major organs and where to find them, and how to identify damage, then to repair it.

Without the constant gentle guidance of Marcas, Connor would have been hopelessly lost. He learned to trust the magic, to send it through a patient like feelers. Areas of hurt drew the healing power, and even led him to wounds Marcas had not expected. It did most of the work of healing. All Connor had to do was focus it and bind it to the wound.

"How is it possible?" he asked Marcas after one particularly delicate case, a soldier whose insides had been all but crushed by a tree, and who even Marcas doubted would survive.

Marcas stared after the soldier, who still called loud thanks to them as men bore him to a quiet recovery spot. He might have been able to stand, but he'd suffered such trauma, Marcas insisted he rest until the next day.

"You have a wonderful gift," Marcas said.

"I'm not that special. The sandstone does most of the work."

"Aye, in this case it does. That pendant of yours is a marvel."

"You keep saying that. What do you mean?"

Marcas drew him aside and gestured to his assistant to fetch them food. Connor only then realized noon had already long passed, and he was famished.

While they ate a thick stew, Marcas said, "Know this, Connor, that pendant you wear around your neck is probably worth more than your entire village."

Connor choked, "How?"

"It's affinity-sculpted."

"What's sculpted?"

They both turned as Shona joined them. She looked healthy and whole, although she hadn't managed to wash her blood-matted hair. She sat beside Connor, "You have a lot of explaining to do."

"I do?"

She barked a laugh. "Oh, come on, Connor. I'm no cracked Linn. This morning, you were comatose with full-on double-tap sickness, and now I hear you're some kind of miracle worker."

"The boy's had a busy day," Marcas said with a wide smile.

"So you just woke up this morning and decided being a normal Guardian wasn't enough for you?" She spoke irritably, as if somehow he'd offended her. He couldn't imagine how, so he decided to pretend he didn't notice.

"Looks like I have a sandstone affinity."

"Clearly," Shona said with a shake of her head, as if that was the dumbest thing he could have said. "But no one who just 'figures out' they have a sandstone affinity heals like the Tallan's own guardian."

"I'm just trying to help," Connor shot back. "It's not my fault I'm good at it."

"He's had some help," Marcas interjected as Shona gave Connor an angry glare.

"I know, old man, you've been his shoulder angel all day."

"That's not the half of it, Lady Shona. He has an affinity-sculpted pendant." He gestured at the sandstone bear hanging around Connor's neck. The lower legs were worn completely away, and the front legs looked like they'd soon follow. It pained Connor to see it disintegrating as he drew upon its power, but he could not refuse it to the brave men who were hurt today trying to free his home.

Shona gasped and snatched at the pendant, but Connor caught her hand. They shared a startled look, and Connor quickly let her go.

Shona gave him a hard, regal look, but surprisingly didn't scold him or beat him up. She reached out more slowly and cupped the pendant in one hand.

"How is it possible?" she said in an awed voice. "Even my father only has two affinity-sculpted stones."

"So, they're different than regular sculptures?"

Shona sighed and then gave him a little smile. "I forget sometimes how clueless you are."

"Thanks."

"It's not your fault." She patted his hand. "Statues or carved stones are very common. When we say a stone is affinity-sculpted, we mean something entirely different."

"So my Aunt Ailsa, who sent me this pendant, doesn't carve other statues?"

"Oh, she most likely does, and that's probably most of her business. The king only allows a small number of sculpted pieces to be crafted each year." Shona gave him a thoughtful look, "This is probably an unauthorized crafting. Your aunt could get into lots of trouble if anyone ever found out."

Connor held out his hand, and Shona released the pendant back to him. He watched her carefully.

Would she really turn in Aunt Ailsa? He still didn't understand the crime. Or was she trying to maneuver him into a position where he'd feel obligated to gift the pendant to her?

Would he? Could he, now that he'd discovered what good he could do with it?

Shona laughed, a rich, honest sound. "You should see your face."

"Stop teasing the boy," Marcas said sternly. "It ain't right with how much good he's done today."

"You're right, Master Healer," Shona said. "I was only teasing, Connor. I don't really care if this was authorized, but be wary of how many people learn about it."

Connor glanced at the bustling camp and his heart sank. "The entire army knows about it."

"No," Marcas said. "They know you're an unusually gifted healer."

"But you could have done it all yourself, couldn't you?" Connor asked. "All you needed was the pendant."

"Perhaps." Marcas held up the worn sandstone pendant he wore around his neck. "These carvings carry adequate power for most common healings, but that sculpted pendant of yours holds at least ten times as much power, in a far more concentrated form."

"How is it possible?"

"That's what makes sculpted items so rare and so valuable, and so closely controlled," Shona said. "A gifted affinity-sculptor, like your Aunt Ailsa must be, can look into a power source stone and see patterns. Some stones contain vortexes of power, concentrations of whatever gift they grant. Sculptors can craft those stones to focus and magnify those vortexes. The resulting pieces grant powers no regular stone could hope to match."

"So you're saying without this pendant I wouldn't have been able to heal?"

"You have a rare, strong talent, lad. But that pendant triggered it far earlier than otherwise possible, and magnified it beyond your natural ability without years of learning." Marcas tapped the pendant, "So aye, perhaps I could have done as much as you did today, perhaps even a little more." He sat back and gave Connor a little smile. "Then again, perhaps not half so much."

Connor slipped the pendant over his head and held it out to Marcas. "Do you want to try?"

Shona's eyes widened in surprise, and she opened her mouth, but snapped it shut again. She looked at Connor with an expression that made him feel like she was weighing him, judging him. It made him deeply nervous, but he did not lower the pendant.

Marcas stared at it like it was a poisonous snake. His hand twitched, as if he barely restrained the urge to take it. Finally he shuffled a little further away and shook his head. "Nay, lad. It's yours. Common hands like mine were not meant to wield a sculpted stone."

"Why not? You're more Healer than I could ever hope to be."

"My reasons are my own, but have a care. Tasting power this strong, standing in the very threshold, exposes one to inherent dangers."

Shona shot Marcas a warning look, and Connor swallowed the questions he wanted to ask about the dangers. He sensed she would refuse to elaborate, but forced down his frustration.

So he only asked, "What do you mean?"

Marcas hefted his worn pendant. "I know my limits, lad. No need to take such a leap of faith at my age."

As Connor placed the pendant chain back over his head, Shona said, "Marcas, you're a man of uncommon wisdom."

Marcas snorted. "And you, lass, have a gilded tongue when you wish."

She rose and drew Connor to his feet. "Come. Carbrey wants to meet with you."

Chapter 40

onnor was surprised when Shona led him out of the camp and took River Road downstream.

"Where are we going?"

"To the main camp."

"I thought that's where we were."

"Rory's army barely fit in that clearing. You think Carbrey's army could?"

Connor shrugged. "That was the biggest clearing this side of the river for a long way."

"It was."

About a mile downriver, Shona led him into a clearing that he'd never seen before. No stumps remained, and even the earth looked solid instead of pockmarked with holes where Boulders might have ripped trees from the ground.

A large command tent dominated the center of the vast clearing. Smaller tents and cook fires dotted the ground, surrounded by racks of weapons, piles of armor, and huge tables where Linn worked to prepare the evening meal. Shona led Connor directly to the command tent.

The inside was spartan, with several folding chairs drawn up along the outer walls and a military bunk in the far corner. A wide, round table dominated the center of the room, holding a large map, edges held down by piles of parchments. General Carbrey and his captains stood around the table.

"Come in, lad," Carbrey said. "I hear you've found a gift for healing today."

"Yes, sir. Healer Marcas was kind enough to teach me some."

Carbrey looked pleased. "You show great promise, Connor. I'm looking forward to exploring that talent of yours when this business is over. Lady Shona's conditional patronage is a little unorthodox, but appears to be justified in this case."

"Thank you, sir."

"Now, to business. You know these mountains?"

"Better than anyone."

"Don't try to impress me, lad. I don't like boasters. Just tell the truth."

"It is the truth, sir."

Rory cracked a smile, as did the hulking Captain Peader, but the other five captains all remained expressionless.

"Very well," Carbrey said. He pointed at the map and said, "Let's see if that confidence is justified. Take a look and tell me what you see."

That was the first map Connor had ever seen. It showed a wide land with mountains along the northern border and the western side. Large sections, dotted with cities, divided it. One name drew his eye. Raineach. That was where Aunt Ailsa lived.

Carbrey pointed to the northern section, "We're up here, lad."

Connor scanned the map, trying to memorize as much as he could. This was the first time he'd ever gotten an idea of what Obrion really looked like. He found Merkland on the northern end of the map, up near the mountains. Carbrey traced the Wick River up from Merkland and pointed to a spot in the mountains that read Alasdair Quarry.

Amazing that the land could be drawn like this. He started tracing the mountains around the quarry with his fingers, trying to reconcile the drawing with what he knew.

He frowned. "This map is wrong, sir."

The Captain with fiery hair barked a laugh. "How many maps have you read, lad?"

"This is the first."

"Then what makes you think it's wrong?"

"Here, sir. Just look at Mount Ingram." On the map, he pointed to a peak to the northwest of the quarry and explained how it should have been set directly north of town. And to the east, the map showed one unbroken peak instead of the multiple mountains in the range.

He finished by saying, "It's more incomplete than actually wrong, sir."

Carbrey said, "Tell me then, lad, can you lead a force around Alasdair without being spotted?"

"I can."

"Tell me true. Lives of your own loved ones are at stake."

"I know it, sir. It'll be a hike, but we can come out of the mountains up by the quarry and take Quarry Road right down onto the plateau."

Carbrey smiled, "Very good." To the captains, he said, "We will muster at the foot of the slope. Light watch fires and make sure we are seen."

To Rory, he said, "You will lead the assault force on the manor. This is to be a precision strike."

"Understood, sir. My team is already assembled."

"Excellent. That woman made me the fool today, Carbrey added with a rueful smile. "This insurrection must end tonight."

"We'll take her alive, sir," Rory promised.

"And the Water Moccasin, Kilian," Carbrey added.

"And the girl Builder," the flame-haired soldier said. "I'm looking forward to interrogating her." His eyes seemed to glow as he talked, and Connor worried more than ever for Verena's safety.

"Focus, Aonghus," Carbrey said. "Take those three, and we'll have won an intelligence coup like this country has never seen." He stood tall, "Gentlemen, the fiasco this morning proved that times are changing. We must be nimble, adapt to the situation, and change ever faster. Tonight, we take the first step forward into a new world."

CHAPTER 41

After they left the command tent, Shona drew Connor to a far corner of the field. Soldiers filled the clearing, either eating dinner or sleeping in neatly assembled rows of small tents, cots, and blanket rolls. They passed Rory's company, slipped between a row of large water bladders hanging from tripods, and stopped at a cheery little fire. It burned in a ring of stones, with a couple of logs nearby for benches. No one else was around.

Shona sat on a log and drew Connor down beside her. The afternoon was fast fading, and shadows lay over the forest. Even with hundreds of soldiers within earshot, for the moment they were very much alone. Connor felt intensely aware of Shona's presence close beside him. He blessed the spirits for granting him so much time with her.

Shona handed him a cup. "Drink this."

Connor gulped the contents. Water, but filled with grit, as if she'd scooped it from the bottom of the river.

He grimaced. "What was that?"

"Soapstone."

Well, at least it wasn't sand, but no one had mentioned any special properties of soapstone yet. Then he laughed at the thought that he'd been teasing Hamish all along for sucking on rocks while now he was drinking them.

Shona frowned. "This is no laughing matter, Connor."

"I'm sorry. It's nothing. You wouldn't understand."

"Oh, so not only am I absurd, but I'm also slow-witted?"

How did the conversation get so twisted around so fast?

"No, of course not. It's just ... my humor is so far beneath you, Lady Shona."

She sniffed airily then flashed a warm smile. "That's very good, Connor." She slid a finger down his cheek, setting his skin tingling and his body glowing with warmth. "I like a man with a good tongue."

He matched her smile. *She thinks I'm a man.*

She leaned a little closer and her eyes sparkled in the firelight. "Connor, in the past couple of days, you've gone from not even knowing how to fully tap your ... curse, to demonstrating a powerful secondary affinity with basalt."

"You said that's rare, right?"

She placed one hand on his arm. "It is. Maybe one person in a generation can achieve affinity with dual igneous stones. We call them Guardian-Agor."

Shona scooted still closer until her thigh pressed against his. She seemed unaware of the close contact, but Connor found it very distracting.

"Then today you decide to trigger an unprecedented affinity for sandstone. Do you know what this means?"

"No."

Her face glowed with excitement, and he had to fight a sudden urge to touch the smooth skin of her cheek. Amazing to think only hours ago it had been cracked like a fractured granite block.

He might be a Guardian-Agor, but she was still a high lady. He could not forget his place, especially not with his Patronage still unconfirmed.

"I gave you that soapstone to try something."

"Like what?" He'd be willing to try just about anything she suggested.

"It's a metamorphic stone. Maybe one in twenty Guardians who achieve strong affinity with a sedimentary stone can reach any kind of affinity with a metamorphic. We call it the tertiary power."

Sounded like one of the diseases Mhairi would make you drink tonic for.

"Most metamorphic affinities are formed after years of training and practice. But you're special, Connor. I believe you can do it, right now. If you can … " Her voice trailed off into a squeak of excitement.

Sitting there, with Shona leaning close, face shining with excitement, eyes sparkling with firelight, well he'd have run out and pantsed Captain Peader for her.

He grinned and tried to sound casual. "There's only one way to find out. How do I do it?"

Her excitement faded just a little, "I'm not entirely sure." She squeezed his hand, "How did you use sandstone?"

"Do they work the same?"

She shrugged. "I have no idea, but it can't hurt."

He'd held the sandstone pendant in his hand. Trying that with the soapstone would be unpleasant, so he just said, "Well, I just focused on it and willed it to work."

"Really? That's it?" She looked disappointed.

"Well, I concentrate really hard."

"Try it."

Connor took a deep breath to calm his nerves, and only then remembered she hadn't bathed since the battle. Better to breathe shallow for a while.

With his Curse, he didn't have to think about how to unlock it. It was always there, rippling just under the skin, although right at the moment he didn't feel it. Then there was the basalt, which felt so similar to granite, although that was missing too.

"Wait a minute, what's that double-tap sickness you mentioned earlier? That's not going to happen again, is it?"

"No, don't worry. That happened because you absorbed both granite and basalt at the same time. Don't do that again."

"Can't Guardian-Agor use two igneous stones?"

"Not at the same time."

That sort of made sense once he thought about it. Kind of like not shoving your fork and your spoon into your mouth at the same time.

He frowned. "So, on the battlefield today, I should have just kept running in circles until I used up all the basalt?"

Shona laughed. "Of course not. Just purge."

"Is that like throwing up?" Old Mhairi could purge a patient faster than they could make the run to the outhouse.

Shona punched him lightly in the shoulder. "Stop it. I'm serious."

"All right. Pretend I am too. How do I purge?"

"It's pretty simple. You focus all the power into the center of your chest." She placed her hand over her heart, closed her eyes, and said softly, "Then you drive it out."

"Does it hurt?"

"Not really. It pushes out through the skin and forms a white powder called lamacal."

That seemed weird, but then he remembered the odd ritual the Grandurians had performed at the camp by the river, just before he helped Shona escape. So, not only were Petralist and Guardian powers similar, but they purged them the same way.

"So you just use it again later?"

Shona gave him a disgusted look. "Of course not. It's just waste."

Made sense. He'd never tried to re-use anything else he'd ever purged.

"Now focus," Shona commanded.

"But I don't know what soapstone does yet."

"Affinity to water, same as Kilian."

The Water Moccasin scared Connor, but the thought of maybe skating on water thrilled him.

"Focus," she repeated.

Connor tried, but sitting so close, he found it even harder than when old Marcas had been standing right beside him, whispering in his ear. Shona's voice was definitely more pleasant.

Maybe she'd whisper in his ear? Maybe she'd punch him in the face if he asked.

As he tried to focus, his blood pounded in his ears, louder than he'd ever known. It was a wonder Shona couldn't hear it. He tried to force the annoying distraction aside, but the more he tried to focus, the louder the pounding of his own blood drowned out all thought.

For a moment he wondered if he might have a cracked blood vessel or a stuttering gallbladder, or ... that wasn't right. He couldn't think clearly or remember what Marcas had just taught him with all that noise. It was like a river flowing through his body.

Then it hit him. Blood was water, so it must be tied to the soapstone. He opened himself to that pounding, rushing sensation, and only then did he become aware of a pulsing energy that flowed all through his veins, in time with the pumping of his heart.

As soon as he felt it, he became aware of Shona's heartbeat and the pumping rush of her blood right next to him.

Weird.

Beyond Shona, he felt a powerful connection with the water bladders hanging in a row on their tripods.

Connor grasped at the surging stream of power and willed it to manifest itself. He wasn't sure how to focus it, but he just tried to release it like his long-hated Curse. The rushing strength surged to greater intensity until it felt like he was going to pop.

The connection to the distant water bladders sharpened, and in a desperate attempt to release the power, Connor reached through the link to those water bladders, and willed all the soapstone power out through that link.

With loud rips, the water bladders ruptured simultaneously. Connor and Shona spun, and gaped in identical open-mouthed amazement at the five columns of water that leaped into the air and arced toward Connor.

For a moment, he felt it, connected with the water, and it became an extension of his hands. He could direct it, extend it through the air. He grinned as the columns of water responded to his will, reared higher still, and flowed into delicate arches that met directly over their heads.

Shona shouted, "You did it, Connor!"

The connection with the water wavered, and Connor yanked on it to try to get it back.

He pulled too hard.

Shona's triumphant shout turned into a shriek that ended in a gurgling protest as the water blasted her off her seat and sent her sprawling. It doused the fire in a gout of steam and flooded the area.

The drenched Shona staggered to her feet, and Connor moved to help. Only then did he realize he was completely dry. Thankfully, she didn't seem to notice.

Captain Rory and several of the Fast Rollers came running at the sound of the shout. Rory frowned. "What's going on here?"

Shona waved a dismissive hand. "We're fine, Captain."

Rory dismissed his men with a gesture, but he remained. Shona ignored him. She grasped Connor's hands and he cringed, expecting her to be angry.

She laughed. Her rich voice pealed forth in joyous laughter, and after a second, Connor joined her. She looked so pretty when she laughed.

"Connor, you did it!"

She kissed him squarely on the lips.

It only lasted a couple seconds, barely enough time for Connor to freeze in terror. Rory was going to punch him to the moon.

Shona released him and gave him a wet hug. Connor couldn't help but hug her back. If Rory was going to kill him, might as well enjoy the moment first.

Captain Rory, looking less than pleased, said, "Lady Shona, may I suggest you dry off?"

"Of course, Captain. Good idea." Shona giggled, kissed Connor's cheek, and left him. Connor stood beside Rory, watching until she disappeared into the darkness.

"You have a rare gift, lad."

"Thank you, sir." Connor wondered if the beating was about to begin.

"A word of caution."

"Please."

"Tread carefully around that one."

"Shona?"

"Aye, lad. I don't want to see you get hurt."

Connor frowned. "She's just helping me explore different affinities."

Rory nodded. "A worthy effort, but ask yourself why."

"I don't understand."

Rory paced away, "It's not my place to interfere with Lady Shona. Just have a care. There are dangers inherent in what she's doing with you."

"What dangers?" Other than maybe execution for kissing High Lord Dougal's daughter.

"Best I leave that for Lady Shona to explain." After a brief hesitation, he added, "I'm sure she's planning to." He gripped Connor's shoulder. "Just promise to talk with me before trying another stone."

He turned and left. Connor sank back down onto the log beside the drowned fire and stared at the dead coals. He could scarce believe he'd experienced so many wonders, and witnessed so much destruction all in one day.

It scared him more than a little to wonder what tomorrow might bring.

CHAPTER 42

onnor paused at the top of a steep incline and drew in a deep breath. The air tasted cool and fresh in the still hour before dawn. The waning moon did little to illuminate the mountainside, but Connor easily picked out the nearby landmarks.

"Are we there yet?"

He turned to help Shona up the last few steps of the steep slope. She lingered close, and slid one hand up his arm as the rest of the company reached the summit.

"That was quite a climb, but you're not winded at all."

He grinned. "Basalt was the right choice. I feel great."

Connor had led the strike force downriver a mile to where they could climb a saddle between peaks. There, Shona arrived unexpectedly and declared she would join the party. After overruling Rory's strenuous objections, she handed Connor pouches of both igneous stones he'd established affinity with, and he'd chosen to absorb basalt. As they climbed, he'd barely tapped the boundless energy that burned in his legs, and still leaped up the steep slope like a mountain goat.

Rory joined them, still frowning. "Lady Shona, please reconsider. If anything were to happen to you, it would mean my head."

"Drop it, Captain. I am here on my own authority, and I will see to securing Ilse for interrogation." As she spoke, she patted the canvas pack she carried slung over one shoulder.

Rory scowled and turned to Connor. "Where do we go from here, lad?"

Within the hour, Carbrey's army would rouse and assemble at the southern end of the slope beneath the plateau to draw Ilse's gaze. Timing would be tight, and they could not waste any of it arguing. Connor enjoyed Shona's presence and attention, but he worried that Rory might be right that she would be wiser to stay in camp.

"We're on schedule, Captain. We follow this ridge for a solid hour to a game trail that will lead us right down to the quarry road."

"Very well. Let's move out. You and Donald scout ahead."

Connor eagerly agreed. The strike force included Tomas and three other Fast Rollers, Grahame the Pathfinder, Gregor the huge Sentry, and Donald the Strider, as well as a full score of regular infantry.

After getting the company pointed in the right direction, Connor trotted ahead with Donald. The slender fellow offered some advice before they tapped their basalt and poured on the speed.

"Lean forward as you accelerate or your legs can literally run out from under you."

He explained how to alter course by shifting weight more than by actually trying to turn his feet. "The faster you run, the smaller the movements to avoid a crash."

They broke out of a thicket of fir and the ridge ascended to a hidden valley. The slope lay open and unobstructed under the moonlight so Donald said, "Let's go. Start small and accelerate gradually."

Connor opened himself to the power of basalt, and his legs quivered with the need to run. He bounded forward into an effortless sprint, and within seconds raced across the slope faster than one of Lord Gavin's horses. Laughing with the thrill of it, he increased his tap-rate. His legs blurred and, as he topped small rises, he literally flew across the slope for dozens of yards.

Donald kept pace with him all the way up the ridge and across the hidden valley. There, the trail wound up a steeper slope to a long bluff that would take them along the flank of the mountain to the game trail.

Shadows deepened as they entered thick stands of trees, and Connor started to slow. Donald pulled ahead and called back, "Come on, lad, where's your spirit?"

Connor accelerated again, but Donald pulled even farther ahead. He wanted to laugh again as he increased the tap-rate. Although he'd only just established affinity with basalt, flying across the landscape on stone-enhanced legs felt as natural as if he'd done it his whole life. The boundless energy rippled through his legs like a constant wind, lifting him and easing the strain until running felt easier than breathing.

The two of them entered a series of tight turns, with trees looming out of the shadows so fast, he avoided them by pure instinct. Even though he should be rightly afraid of crashing, Connor grinned with the thrill of it. Buoyed by the basalt, he tried to match Donald's grace, tried to shift his weight to pull his body around turns, but found it far more difficult at greater speed.

One large bush appeared suddenly, and Connor's balance was off from the last bend. He tried to turn hard, but lost his footing, tripped over the bush, and tumbled into the nearby forest. He crashed through branches and barely missed hitting a large tree.

Donald must have heard the racket because even as Connor staggered to his feet, shedding branches, the Strider slid to a halt nearby.

"Shoulda had that one," Connor said.

Donald grinned. "Those so-called Fast Rollers have no idea what speed really means."

Connor blew out a breath. "It's amazing." His heart beat fast, but he barely felt winded. His body ached from the wild tumble into the brush, but the battle leathers had protected him from the worst of it.

"You've barely touched what you can do," Donald said. "I'll warn you now of the danger."

"You mean more than just watching out for trees?"

"No lad, the real danger lies in finding out how fast you can really go."

"Why is that a problem?"

"Because once you hit your top stride you'll never be satisfied with walking again." He paused and gave Connor a long look. "Basalt opens a door you can never return through completely. You can never live life slow like the rest of the world. There's a need burning in your heart to always push the limits, reach the ultimate boundary of your speed, the very cusp of the threshold."

"It can't be all that bad," Connor said, struggling to comprehend how running fast could prove such a danger.

Donald shrugged. "Don't say I didn't warn you."

As they walked out of the thick brush, Connor clutched the sandstone pendant tucked under his jacket and drew a whisper of healing strength from it, just enough to wash away the worst of the bruising. Donald's warning slipped to the back of his mind as he looked forward to the freedom of super-human speed.

Donald led him at a slower pace up to the next open slope that would top out at the trail. "Let's race to the top."

"If I win, you get me a long-knife like yours."

Donald barked a laugh. "Never going to happen. You haven't tasted real speed yet."

"But what if?"

"Better to get one of the meteor hammers like that Grandurian Wingrunner used."

Connor thought of that long steel cable, capped with the spiked ball the Wingrunner had used to clobber one of the Fast Rollers. "I hope you have one handy, because I'm going to win it."

Without waiting for a response, he sprinted up the trail and drew deep from the basalt. He accelerated so fast, he almost outran himself, and had to ease off for a second to regain his balance.

In that second, Donald caught up. Connor poured on more speed, but could not pull ahead. The ground blurred past as they raced up the slope, faster than an arrow.

Connor grinned with the challenge of it, but then Donald called out, "See you at the top."

The Strider shot forward, so fast Connor might as well have been crawling on hands and knees. Connor stared for a second in wonder, and then increased his tap-rate as far as he could.

He accelerated again, but deep within the very bones of his thighs and hips, pain started throbbing, and then spiked to sharp intensity. His legs felt like they were fracturing.

Connor eased off and the pain faded. Donald waited for him at the top of the slope, leaning against a tree, a grin on his face.

"How did you do that?" Connor asked.

"Have to draw deep, so deep it hurts."

"It started to. Felt like my legs were cracking."

Donald nodded. "The official term is Basalt Max-Tap Joint Displacement Shift, but we just call it The Fracking."

"Fracking?"

"Aye, when you go Fracked, or fractured." He gestured at his baggy pants. "It's the reason Striders and Wingrunners wear these. The Fracking is when the tap-rate triggers a physical change."

As he spoke, the top several inches of his thighs suddenly bent outward with loud pops until they shifted nearly horizontal. His lower legs bent abruptly downward, as if he'd grown new joints.

Connor grimaced. "What did you just do?"

Donald bounced where he stood. "It's hard to stand still like this." With another loud pop, his legs snapped back to normal. "The Fracking changes us so we can move faster. You've already hit the limit for moving your legs back and forth. When we go Fracked, that extra joint allows our upper legs to rotate in full circles without our lower legs having to move so far. That's when you find out what fast really means."

"I think I'll just take your word for it tonight."

Donald grinned. "I don't blame you. Took me weeks to build up the courage to break my legs."

Connor wondered if he'd ever dare to do it.

CHAPTER 43

he rest of the company caught up with them an hour later. Connor led everyone to the trail, then down to Lookout Rock where he liked to enjoy the panoramic view of the valley.

Down on the lower plateau, the manor sat dark, with only a couple of lights gleaming in the lowest windows. Even as they watched, tiny fires sprang to life beyond the manor house, far away at the base of the slope where Carbrey's army moved into position.

A growing sense of excitement mixed with dread in Connor's heart. Ilse had proven herself more than clever. If she had a larger army, Connor would fear they'd never force her out. But despite her courageous stand, she could hold no hope for long-term victory.

This had better work. Connor trusted that Carbrey knew what he was doing, and trusted Rory even more, but he wondered what Ilse had prepared.

If the attack failed, would she really follow through on her threat to kill Lord Gavin and his entire family? Would she really kill Connor's father and the other Cutters? Were they wise to take that chance?

Connor led the party down to Quarry Road, and Grahame indicated no one patrolled nearby.

Before they reached the deep lochs of the ancient flooded quarries perched near the edge of the cliff, Gregor called a halt. As the party gathered around him, the powerful Sentry crouched and drove one hand into the hard-packed road. The ground rippled out from his hand and pulsed against Connor's feet, flowing halfway up his boots.

He shifted, and the earth moved with him, but did not release its hold. He shook his foot harder, but the ground did not fall away.

"Stop it," Gregor said in a deep, low whisper beside Connor. "It is the plan."

Connor jumped. He hadn't noticed the big man rise. The rest of the company stood quietly, as if not bothered by the ground's strange behavior.

"Try to stay in step," Gregor said softly. "It eases the burden of masking so many." Then to Connor he added, "In case that Builder can listen through her wall stones too."

The group moved out slowly and settled into a steady march, everyone moving in step. The ground flowed under their feet even as they walked, and seemed to catch them at every step and lower them gently to the surface of the road.

After the first few steps, Connor lost his unease, and resumed scanning the area. For whatever reason, Gregor felt this important, and Rory didn't seem surprised by it. He had to admit, traveling with Guardians was never boring.

They began descending the steep switchback road down the cliff to the plateau. Protective darkness wrapped around the manor like a blanket, but the Grandurians stationed on the far side, along the rim of the plateau, were exposed and easily noted.

Halfway down the face of the cliff, Grahame called a halt with a raised hand. He pointed at the manor house and made a series of gestures to one of the soldiers. The man moved to one side, pulled out a sling, and fitted a round stone.

He stared at the manor house intently, and Connor followed his gaze. Only then did he notice the Longseer standing atop the tower, which sat only a little lower than their position. She was turned profile to them, intent on Carbrey's army downriver.

The slinger whipped the sling around his head and released it with a soft snap. The Longseer pitched to the side and crumpled silently.

"Good shot," Rory whispered.

As the group resumed their march, Connor glanced over at the soldier and wondered if he might have another sling handy. Connor was the best stone thrower in Alasdair, but he'd never imagined such a shot.

As they reached the plateau and began moving toward the northern entrance of the manor, Grahame pointed out two sentries lurking in the shadows. Two slingers stepped forward this time and launched rocks simultaneously.

At the same time Donald leaped forward, so fast he must have Fracked. The stones struck true against the Grandurians' helmets with distant pings.

Donald caught the Grandurians even as they fell, and dragged them around the manor house. By the time Rory's company trotted up to the house, he already had the men gagged and securely tied.

Connor led the group along the eastern wall to the kitchen entrance. Gregor remained there while Connor led the others inside. As he slipped into the kitchen, lit only by a single candle and the dying embers of the fire, Connor fought to control a rising tide of tension.

They'd made it to the manor house. He prayed they'd succeed in freeing his father.

Rory looked at the blackened walls, shattered shelves, and the rubble. "What happened here?"

Connor hadn't seen the devastation of the kitchen since he left it wreathed in flames. The destruction was even more complete than he remembered.

"Curses and Heatstone ovens don't mix very well."

Rory coughed, and his face reddened as he tried to suppress a laugh.

Shona gave him a withering glare, and then frowned at Connor. "Where's Ilse?"

"She might be upstairs, but I bet she's at the south entrance watching Carbrey."

Rory turned to Grahame, who would be leading the regular soldiers and one Fast Roller into the basement levels in search of the prisoners. "The Petralists should be focused to the south. Listen for Gregor's signal if anything goes wrong."

Grahame saluted and led his men north through the formal dining room toward the main stair on the far side. Connor led the main strike force out the kitchen through another door to the south hall that split the rear half of the manor house all the way back to the southern entrance. This half of the manor was filled with pantries, storage rooms, and workrooms.

Before they reached the great room at the southern threshold, Ilse's voice echoed down the hall.

"You two, fetch the prisoners. We might need them after all."

Rory motioned everyone back down the hall to a pair of doors they'd just passed that faced each other across the hall. Tomas led half the party into the buttery on the left hand side while the rest of them took the opposite door into the garderobe.

Connor glanced back at Tomas' group across the hall and noticed several of them casting glances in his direction. He wondered if they were considering breaking open one of the casks of ale there.

By the smell in the garderobe, Ilse's men used the latrine frequently and had not bothered to close the lid to the cesspit. After hustling into the room, Shona covered her nose with one sleeve, rounded on Connor, and made furious motions with her other hand.

"I don't think now would be a good time to use it," Connor whispered.

Rory barely suppressed a coughing laugh, and his shoulders shook for several seconds.

Poor guy was having a hard night.

Shona folded her arms with an angry glare and leaned against the wall close beside the door.

Footsteps announced the approaching soldiers. Rory moved to the doorway beside Shona, while the rest of the team slipped into the deeper shadows.

Two soldiers approached down the hall and passed between the groups hidden on both sides. Rory lunged out of concealment, grabbed the closest soldier, and yanked him out of the hallway and into the garderobe. Tomas mirrored his move, pulling the other soldier into the buttery.

The soldier tried to shout the alarm, but Rory punched him in the head, knocking him out cold. Other team members bound and gagged him. The entire process took less than five seconds.

Across the hall, Tomas signaled success on his side. They then crouched by the doors and listened. No sounds of alarm. So far so good.

Rory turned to Connor and Shona who crouched beside him and whispered, "Now we wait and see what other fish we can catch."

As one minute slowly became two, Connor fought to suppress his nervous energy as he thought back to the last time he'd been in the manor.

Was it possible only a couple of days had passed since he'd run from Lady Isobel?

Connor's entire world had changed in that time, and he'd learned more about his Curse than in the whole of his life to that point. He prayed the spirits would grant them success. He had to save his father and free his village, had to earn his patronage.

He glanced at Shona, who crouched beside him with one hand still pressed over her nose. Even like that, she looked beautiful. It seemed impossible that he'd kissed her in the river, and that she'd willingly kissed him just hours ago. She was a High Lady and as such should consider him lower than dirt.

Could she really care for him, or was his Curse all she cared about?

Ilse's voice again echoed down the hall, cutting short his musings. "Where are those two? Don't they have any concept of time?"

Verena's girlish voice answered. "I'm sure they're hurrying."

"We'll see about that."

Rory made a circling motion with one hand, and Connor stepped to the side of the door as Rory and Shona crouched, ready to spring.

A few seconds later, Ilse and Verena approached from the southern end of the hall and passed between the two lurking parties.

This time Shona struck. She grabbed Ilse and yanked the woman into the room. Even as Ilse fell, her body hardened into the perfectly sculpted lines of a Rumbler.

It didn't matter. Fast Rollers pinned her to the ground while Rory tied her hands. Shona pulled a nasty looking contraption out of her pack and began strapping it around Ilse's head. The sight of the metal cage and long attached lever made Connor shiver. That was no ordinary shackle.

A muffled shout from across the hall drew Connor to the door just as Verena came pelting out the buttery. Behind her, Connor caught a glimpse of Tomas shooting through the air with a small stone pressing into his stomach. Air whistled out of it in a thick, visible column, blasting Tomas through his close-packed squad, sending men tumbling, before finally crashing right through the outer window.

Verena skidded to a halt in the corridor facing Connor. She gave him a wide smile and a little wave.

Connor jumped out to grab her, but she threw herself to the side and landed on her knees. Despite the odd move, she shot down the hall faster than a running man, sliding on her knees like the floor was a steep, ice-coated mountainside and not flat stones.

"Catch her," Rory shouted behind Connor.

Connor sprinted after Verena and tapped basalt, blurring down the hall. Verena slid across the large room at the end of the hall and staggered to her feet.

Connor could not stop in time, and slammed into her back. The two of them fell forward and tumbled over one another, down the steps, and landed in a heap together at the bottom.

Verena landed on top this time, and the hard landing drove most of the breath from Connor's lungs. He lay for a second, gasping.

Verena pulled herself up to her elbows and brushed her hair from her face. Her eyes glittered with mirth and she said with a little giggle, "Connor, we have to stop meeting like this."

Connor started to smile back, but Verena's eyes hardened and Connor cried, "No, don't hurt --"

Verena elbowed him hard in the face, and pain exploded through his cheek and nose. Stars danced in his eyes, and he gagged and tasted smoke.

Even as he tried to weakly paw at her to ward off another blow, she jumped to her feet and shouted, "We're under attack! The manor! The Captain!"

Connor forced himself to roll to his hands and knees and squinted through the pain. Grandurian soldiers, led by the burly Erich and his terrifying sister, Anika, charged from the far side of the big barn.

Connor tried to retreat, but his legs still felt like jelly. He glanced back just in time to see Shona and Rory appear in the doorway at the head of their strike force.

Between them they held Ilse prisoner, with hands and feet shackled to a short chain that prevented her from standing erect. The shackles on her feet only allowed her to take tiny steps, forcing her to toddle forward like a child.

The contraption Shona had strapped on covered Ilse's head, neck, and chin. It vaguely resembled a cage, all steel bars and leather straps. One long bar extended from the base of her skull two feet out to the side. Shona clutched the end of it.

"Stop," Shona commanded, "or your captain dies!"

The Grandurians slowed their advance and stopped at the end of the big barn.

Shona gave them a wolfish grin. "Careful. Even if she tries to tap her power, I can rip her head off."

Connor stared, horrified. The worst part was that he believed Shona would do it without hesitation.

"Connor, grab the Builder."

Connor jumped to obey Shona's command. Verena stood nearby, staring in open-mouthed dismay, but had already thrust a hand into her ever-present satchel.

Connor rushed over and grabbed her arm before she could withdraw whatever mischief-causing stone she was searching for. She looked so devastated as he led her back toward the steps that he wished he could say something to comfort her.

She gave him a sad smile. "Sorry about hitting you again."

"Next time, try something different, less violent."

Like kissing him again.

"I'll try," she whispered, although she had to know there would never be a next time.

Shona ordered, "Send the signal."

One of the black-armored Fast Rollers produced a short bow and an arrow with an odd, fat head wrapped in cloth. Another soldier leaned over the arrow and struck flint with steel until, with a shower of sparks, the tip of the arrow burst into flame. The soldier aimed high and released.

The flaming arrow arced into the night. Down at the base of the slope, Carbrey's army started charging up the long slope.

"You will all stand down," Shona said, "You have lost. We have won. This conflict is over."

They'd done it. Carbrey had outfoxed Ilse. It really was over.

Anika strode forward a couple of steps, her face livid. "We no surrender without wrestle again."

Rory grinned, "I promise lass, I'll see to you in just a minute."

Just then, a light exploded to life above the manor so bright it looked like the return of the sun. Darkness fled, and everyone clenched eyes against the blinding brilliance.

Rory wouldn't get a minute.

CHAPTER 44

onnor, who was looking toward Shona, was the only one to see a pair of shadowy forms race super-fast out of the darkness behind the strike force. Even before he could open his mouth to shout a warning, they struck.

The two Wingrunners ripped through the small strike force, dragging a rope between them and yanking soldiers' feet out from under them. As they closed on Rory and Shona, they dropped the rope and whipped out meteor hammers. One struck Rory in the back of his helmeted head. The impact rang like a gong, and the captain, whose skin had already faded to gray, tumbled down the steps.

The other struck Shona's hand where she held the long lever against Ilse's skull. She also had instantly tapped her granite at the appearance of the bright light, and the blow rang out with a sharp crack.

Shona shrieked in pain and staggered, clutching her hand to her chest. The two Wingrunners raced past Connor, and even as he struggled to decide between chasing them and going to Shona, two more Wingrunners raced out of the darkness behind her.

"Look out," Connor shouted this time.

Shona turned, but the Wingrunners were just too fast. They leaped the mass of fallen soldiers who were struggling to rise, and one of them shouted something in Grandurian.

Ilse stiffened and pulled her elbows in tight. The Wingrunners grabbed her by the arms, dragging her from a dead stop into a full run in the blink of an eye.

Shona tried to strike one of the men, but he rammed a shoulder into her. He apparently hadn't noticed her leathers or her gray skin.

Shona rocked back slightly from the impact while the Wingrunner tumbled away in a wild spin and fell unmoving into a heap thirty feet away, beside the barn.

The other Wingrunner ran Ilse down the steps. Connor moved to intercept, but Verena tripped him and helped drag Ilse into the safety of her gathered force. Soldiers immediately began tearing at the straps securing the contraption to her head while Erich and Anika moved to face Rory and Shona.

Before the groups could close, Gregor appeared around the corner of the manor and called, "Captain, we must retreat."

"Now's not a good time," Rory said. His fingers flexed in anticipation, and he did not tear his eyes from Anika.

"It never is." Gregor crossed the courtyard in a blink, sliding across the hard-packed ground like water, and grabbed the captain by the shoulder. "Play later. We have a hostile force closing fast on our position. They number in the hundreds."

That got Rory's attention. "How is it possible?"

"I do not know. Their full numbers are shielded from me. I caught only a glimpse."

Rory's eyes widened, and he glanced back, as if he could see through the manor house.

Gregor nodded. "Aye, Captain. They have a Sapper. Played me like a newborn. Gave me just a taste to distract my attention while he shielded those Wingrunners." He added in a tone of wonder, "He shielded Wingrunners in full sprint, Captain. Only one man I know of can do that."

"Anton."

"Aye."

"Captain, we can take this rabble," Shona said. "Carbrey's almost here. We can win this."

"No lass. If Anton's masking an army, we cannot hold. We retreat to Carbrey and make our stand there."

He spoke as if it were they who would be fighting for their lives. The abrupt change in his demeanor chilled Connor to the bone. Never mind how impossible it was for such a huge Grandurian army to descend on them here.

Down on the lower slope, Carbrey's army had already advanced more than halfway to the plateau. They only needed a few minutes to secure the entire area.

They didn't have minutes. The ground started to shake, and Connor did not need Gregor to tell him hundreds of running feet were the cause.

Just then, Grahame and the secondary strike force appeared in the southern entrance, running hard. "Captain, I heard the signal. What happened?"

Connor ran up the stairs to Grahame. "Did you free my father?"

He shook his head, "Not enough time."

Connor's heart fell. How could the carefully planned assault be falling apart? They were so close to victory!

He pushed past Grahame and ran for the southern stairs. The prisoners were probably being held in the second sub-level. He only needed a few minutes to free them.

Outside, Rory shouted, "To me! Retreat!"

The company formed up, drew weapons, and ran straight for the gathered Grandurians.

Connor snarled and ran after the retreating army. Every step farther from his father drove a dagger of guilt into his heart.

Outside, Anika scowled at Rory. "Maybe I no let you run."

Rory called out, "Next time, lass."

Anika glanced at Erich, who motioned to the rest of the company to stand aside, but then she snarled, "No. We fight now."

She charged at Rory.

Before she took two steps, the ground caught her feet and she fell forward hard. The earth buckled and rolled her unceremoniously aside.

As the company ran past, Gregor called out, "Next time, listen to your brother. You can play with Rory later."

Connor ran to catch up, but Verena moved to block him, and he said, "Look, Verena, I'm sorry about all this."

She gave him a sweet smile, "No hard feelings."

Then she tried to punch him in the face.

He was expecting it this time, and caught her arm and they struggled. Under that cute face and soft voice, she was tough as steel, and Connor barely held her off. Finally he twisted her arms hard behind her back and pulled her close so she couldn't knee him between the legs.

"Stop trying to hit me all the time." He gave her arms another hard twist to punctuate his growing anger.

She yanked against his wrists, despite how much it must hurt, and he had to pull her hard against him to keep from losing his grip. They stood there for a moment, faces inches apart, bodies locked tight together as they swayed and fought for dominance, and Connor suddenly became aware of her in an entirely different way. This was so much like how Rory and Anika had wrestled, that he felt his face flush.

If anyone looked at them right now, would they see them fighting or embracing?

Verena's minty breath washed over his face and, staring into her wide blue eyes, he was suddenly struck by just how pretty she was. It triggered a sudden urge to kiss her grimacing little mouth.

Before he could decide if he really wanted to, she relaxed against him and said, "Connor, please."

Surprised, he slackened his grip a little.

Verena slammed her forehead into his nose. Connor staggered back, blinded by pain, but he didn't need to see to know she was about to hit him again.

He tapped basalt and leaped away.

"Hey, no fair!" she shouted.

His blurry eyes focused on the raging Anika who stood directly in his path. She reached for him, and he had no doubt she'd rip his arms off.

He leaned right, and his wildly churning feet dug into the ground and whipped him in a tight turn right through the open big barn doors. He flashed through the barn, and for a second hoped to race out the far side to freedom.

The far doors stood closed.

Connor tried to plant his feet and skid to a stop, but slipped on the straw-covered floor, and tumbled end over end across the barn before slamming to a halt against the closed doors.

After coughing and spitting blood, Connor clutched the sandstone pendant at his neck and drew heavily from its healing warmth. He only allowed himself a few seconds. He had to escape.

He rolled to his hands and knees, but he'd already lingered too long. Half a dozen soldiers poured into the other end of the barn, led by Anika. Connor pressed himself against the closed doors and wished he'd absorbed granite. At least then he could break through the doors.

Before Anika could wreak vengeance upon him, Verena darted past and blocked the angry Petralist's way.

"Enough, Anika. See to Ilse. I'll deal with Connor."

Amazingly, Anika stopped. After a final glare in Connor's direction, she spun and pushed through the soldiers.

Verena ran to Connor, slipped under one of his arms, and pulled him to his feet. Again he was struck by how perfectly she fitted into the crook of his arm. This time he was smart enough to drive the thought away immediately.

He groaned as bruised muscles complained against the abuse. "Please don't hit me again."

Verena pushed hair out of her face, "Of course I won't hit you, silly. There's no point now."

She led him slowly out of the barn where a huge army marched past and massed along the southern lip of the plateau.

He was trapped, prisoner.

Again.

CHAPTER 45

onnor stood with Verena as soldiers flowed past until at least a hundred men, and even a few women, assembled. Most were chainmail-clad regulars, but at least eight of them wore the leather armor of Rumblers.

One tall man with broad shoulders, white hair, and a long, drooping mustache stopped beside Ilse, who had been freed from her cage. The man wore a simple brown uniform but no armor. A long, slightly curved sword swung at his hip.

Ilse saluted smartly, despite her dirty face and one swollen eye. "Thank you, General."

"I am glad to see you safe, Captain."

"You arrived just short of too late."

On the slope, Carbrey's army slowed, and a trumpet sounded a long, clear note.

"Good," the new general said. "They seek parley. Who leads their forces and what is their disposition?"

"Carbrey, with a large force of regulars and a nearly full complement of Guardians."

The General blew out his mustaches and nodded. "I should have known. This complicates things."

"Do you think he'll attack outright?"

"If he sees me now with the battle lines drawn, most likely."

"We still have hostages," Ilse offered.

The general shook his head. "What I need are communication channels. How have you been negotiating?"

"A local boy."

The trumpet sounded again.

The general said, "Let us hope he sends the boy soon or many will die tonight."

Verena pulled Connor toward the general, "Over here, sir."

"What happened?" Ilse asked.

Verena shrugged. "He runs faster than he thinks."

"That's not fair," Connor said, but did not dare argue further as they stopped before the tall general. Up close, the man was even more imposing.

Behind the general, a huge man the equal of Gregor for sheer mass, rounded the end of the manor house. He radiated power, despite gray streaks in his dark brown hair, and when his dark eyes swept over Connor, the force of his gaze nearly buckled Connor's already weak knees. The man exuded a sense of vast age and wisdom.

This had to be Anton.

Immediately Connor began to understand Gregor's concern. He would risk much to avoid facing this man.

Two other men followed Anton and moved to flank the general. They looked familiar in their leather and steel armor, with two swords sheathed on their backs and myriad knives strapped all over. They could almost pass as the brothers of two captains in Carbrey's army. These men moved with the same deadly grace.

The general regarded Connor with warm blue eyes. "You are the liaison, are you, boy?"

Connor shrugged. "I just carry messages."

"That is exactly what I need right now." The general extended a large hand, "I am Wolfram." Like Ilse, he spoke with barely a trace of accent.

Connor nervously took the man's hand. He had a strong but not overbearing handshake. "I'm Connor."

General Wolfram started to speak, but paused. His gaze sharpened, and his grip tightened. But before Connor wondered at the pause, the hesitation disappeared and the general's smile returned.

"It is a pleasure to meet you, Connor."

"Thank you, sir."

General Wolfram looked disapprovingly to Verena, who still stood with Connor's arm draped over her shoulder. "You and I will speak at length once the current crisis is abated, young lady."

Verena shrugged out from under Connor's arm and made a little curtsy. "Of course, General."

Wolfram turned back to Connor. "Tell Carbrey to stand down."

He was interrupted by a trumpet calling three quick notes.

"Blast the impatient fool," Wolfram said. "He means to attack."

"I'll deal with it." Kilian, the Water Moccasin strode past, carrying a bucket of water.

"This, I have to see," General Wolfram said.

Connor, Verena, and Ilse followed the general to the battle line. The general stopped in the second rank of soldiers but Connor pushed to the front with Ilse.

He wished he hadn't.

Staring down the slope at hundreds of armored soldiers charging uphill made his knees start to shake. They were barely a hundred yards away. Two steps in front of his men, Carbrey led the charge from the center, sword raised and face set in hard lines.

All across the lip of the plateau, armor creaked as soldiers set themselves to receive the charge. On the flanks, soldiers raised heavy crossbows, while others began unbuckling large, bulky canvas packs resting on the ground in front of them. The Rumblers in the center of the line swelled with granite and hefted massive weapons or huge rocks.

Connor was standing on the front lines of what was about to become a pitched battle. He'd seen enough of battle in the past couple of days to know he didn't want to get caught in the middle of one.

He started to back away, but Ilse grabbed his shoulder.

"Stand with men and watch."

Verena pulled a small stone out of her satchel and flashed him a wide smile. "Don't worry, Connor. I won't let them hurt you."

He glared at her, and prepared to tap basalt as soon as Ilse eased her hold. They might all be crazy, but he wouldn't die with them.

On the far left flank, Anton the Sapper rolled up to the line, standing atop a high tower of earth that flowed over the ground like a living thing. But it was Kilian who stepped beyond the lines to stand alone before the charging horde.

Whistling to himself, he threw the water. It arced up and out of the bucket, trailing a thin streamer that remained connected to Kilian's hand. It sailed in a glittering silver arc toward the charging men, gaining speed and thinning as it fell.

It struck Carbrey in the face.

He tried to side-step, but the water followed his movement and whipped out like a snake. The impact knocked him from his feet.

Behind him, the charging soldiers parted to avoid running him over. Rory and Shona, who had been flanking him, tried to lift him to his feet. The rest of the lines kept advancing.

Carbrey convulsed, struggling and writhing around as water frothed in his nose and mouth. They barely held onto him.

The ground shook under Connor's feet from the thudding tread of the charging army. He glanced sidelong at Verena, wondering when she was going to throw a Wallstone or something. She did not move.

Carbrey thrashed harder, his antics drawing Connor's gaze from the terrifying sight of the charging army. It looked like he was drowning.

Rory scooped at the water with his hands, but it flowed around his fingers. Carbrey heaved, clearly trying to vomit, but nothing came out. The water continued churning into froth around his face.

Connor had nearly drowned once in the wild Upper Wick. Seeing Carbrey writhing and unable to clear his lungs brought that remembered panic back with terrifying clarity. He glanced at Kilian, who stood with one hand half-raised, the thin stream of water connecting him to Carbrey holding steady in the air like a solid arc of silver.

"Stop it! Don't kill him," Connor shouted.

Kilian glanced back and winked.

Carbrey convulsed again, and the water disappeared. He'd swallowed it. For a second, Carbrey seemed to be all right, but his face went ashen and he grabbed at his stomach.

Then he screamed.

He writhed on the earth, twisting and pounding at his own chest, screaming in pain. Connor looked from Kilian to Carbrey and shuddered. He'd learned much about various Petralists, but he'd never imagined anything like this.

The charging army was barely fifty yards away and closing fast when Rory snatched a trumpet from a nearby soldier and blew two loud notes. The army skidded to a halt. Within three running strides, they went from a full charge to parade rest. Silence descended over the battlefield. Carbrey's cries of pain echoed clearly across the slope.

In the center of the lines, Connor recognized many of the soldiers, including the hulking Captain Peader and several Fast Rollers. Several of them recognized him, and he breathed a sigh of relief. They knew he'd been captured again. If the armies did collide, they could help free him.

Maybe Ilse had planned this all along to plant the seeds of doubt in their minds. Would they fall for it, and wonder if he'd sided with the Grandurians?

Rory blew two more notes, and the army retreated down the slope until they stood behind their leader, who had stopped struggling. The two captains with all the knives moved to Rory's side, and appeared to be arguing.

Shona's voice carried across the field, "Stand down. I support Rory's decision."

With Rory's help, Carbrey climbed shakily to his feet, but then doubled over. In a single, convulsive heave, he spewed the water out.

It splashed to the ground, but instantly gathered into the air. A long tether reached back to Kilian.

Connor thought back to the water bladders he'd burst back at camp. Did that mean he was a Water Moccasin too, or whatever they called that affinity in Obrion?

The possibility disgusted and fascinated him in equal measure. To one day skate across the surface of the river would be wondrous beyond imagining. And yet, look what pain Kilian could inflict.

Shimmering like liquid silver, the water flowed into the shape of a sword and floated across the front lines of the army. Every soldier drew back from it, and it returned to face Carbrey.

Kilian spoke, his voice calm and loud enough for everyone to hear. "Return to your camp and await our messenger."

Shona lunged forward and slashed at the liquid sword. Her blade passed through it and she stumbled. The liquid blade swept toward her face. She shrieked and retreated.

Rory stepped in front of the liquid blade and held up his hands in a sign of peace. "Send your messenger." Then he turned his back on the liquid threat and barked a few orders. The army began a slow retreat back to the trees.

Kilian turned to Ilse and made one of his extravagant bows before throwing a cocky salute.

Ilse smiled, "You can't resist, can you?"

"What? Stopping a massacre? Saving hundreds of lives? No ma'am, I cannot."

"Show-off."

Kilian began pushing through the ranks of soldiers but paused next to Connor, "The trick, boy, is not in how much force you bring to bear, but in knowing where to apply it for the greatest result." Then he winked and disappeared through the ranks of soldiers.

Connor looked after him, completely torn. Should he hate the man for torturing Carbrey, or should he applaud him for stopping a battle?

"Come," Ilse said to Connor, and drew him back to where the general waited for them.

"I owe that man a medal," the general said.

"He'd prefer a good steak."

"Done."

To Connor, the general said, "We have much to discuss."

CHAPTER 46

olfram led Connor and Ilse back to the manor and up to Lord Gavin's study on the second floor. The big man moved with confidence, as if he'd lived in the manor for years and not just arrived. Wolfram rounded the huge desk, stood beside Lord Gavin's chair, and motioned Connor to sit in one of the leather seats facing the desk. Ilse remained by the door.

"How did a local boy become the messenger of choice between our forces?"

When Ilse didn't speak, Connor said, "I just sort of fell into it, sir."

"I am glad you did, Connor. We meet at a difficult time. Fate has placed us on opposite sides of this conflict and by rights we should be enemies." He leaned forward and said, "But in you, I see no enemy. I see a brave lad who wants only the safety of his family and village."

How could Wolfram possibly know?

Wolfram continued. "With your help, I believe we can avert pitched battle and save many lives. Will you help me do this?"

Pride stirred deep in Connor's heart that such an important man would show so much confidence in him and treat him with so much respect. "I will, sir."

"I knew I could count on you." Wolfram turned to the western window that looked over the river, hands clasped behind his back, as if deep in thought. After half a minute like that, he turned, "Tell General Carbrey these are my terms for peace. He must maintain a buffer of at least two miles from the village and this manor house. More importantly, he must return that which was stolen. If he does, we will leave peacefully and no one gets hurt."

Ilse had mentioned the cryptic stolen item. It must be worth a fortune if they would risk open warfare to retrieve it.

He licked his lips and whispered, "And if he doesn't?"

Wolfram gave him a look of both sorrow and determination. "I will flood this quarry and kill all the prisoners."

Connor recoiled, horrified by the words, and by the matter-of-fact way in which he said it. "But you can't," he blurted. "They didn't do anything to you!"

"I am afraid that is not the point." Wolfram looked genuinely sorrowful.

Connor looked from Wolfram to Ilse, angry and confused. How could they talk about being friends and in the next moment calmly threaten to kill and destroy?

"That's not right," he finally said.

"War is never right," Wolfram said. "But it is necessary. The choice is Carbrey's to make. We do not wish for bloodshed, but we will not allow his aggression to remain unanswered."

His aggression? Carbrey wasn't the one threatening Connor's family.

"The situation is more complicated than you know," Captain Ilse said, speaking for the first time.

"You keep saying that, as if it justifies the terrible things you've been doing, but it doesn't!" Anger drove Connor to his feet to face Ilse.

"We didn't start this, but we'll finish it," Ilse snarled.

"Start what? You invaded."

"That was not the beginning of this conflict," Wolfram said, drawing Connor back around to face him. "This conflict began when a small boy was kidnapped by agents of your High Lord Dougal. All the suffering, all the death that has resulted is guilt he bears responsibility for."

"You lie," Connor said softly, but thought of Carbrey's strange comment about a boy when he first entered the camp.

Could it really be true?

"Open your eyes, Connor," Wolfram said, his gaze boring into Connor, "and you will see the truth."

He clapped Connor on the shoulder and said, "Deliver my terms and make sure Carbrey understands my determination in this. On his shoulders lies the fate of many. Go now. Be brave."

Connor retreated to the door as if in a fog, his mind whirling with Wolfram's revelation. It had to be a lie. They had to be twisting the truth somehow. He lacked the knowledge to see through the lie, but he swore to find it.

As he reached the door, Wolfram added with another friendly smile, "Stop by the kitchen on your way out. Young men your age are always hungry."

The general clearly hadn't visited the kitchen yet.

Connor didn't trust his voice, but stepped into the hall. Wolfram called after him, "Be wary of Carbrey. He is a very dangerous man."

The man's view of events was so twisted, Connor could barely comprehend it. "If I may, sir, isn't that something an enemy would be expected to say?"

"But we are not enemies."

"I don't understand, sir."

"In time, I hope you will. Consider what you've learned, and with the Tallan's blessing, you will see the truth."

Connor recoiled, pulled the door closed, and leaned back against it. Why did they insist on invoking the devil's name? It only confirmed that their point of view was too corrupted for him to understand.

He wanted to pound something to relieve some of the tension. Every time he felt like things were going to be all right, something happened to show him just how powerless he really was.

Wolfram's words rang in his mind with terrifying finality. He would kill Connor's father. With an entire army here to reinforce Ilse, Connor wondered how Carbrey would ever be victorious.

How could the general claim they weren't enemies? Could he be telling the truth about the kidnapped boy? Connor suddenly wished he'd asked more questions.

Ilse's voice drifted through the door to him. "When Carbrey learns you are here, he will strip the garrison at Merkland and flood this valley with troops."

Connor pressed his ear against the door, and barely caught Wolfram's soft reply. "That is my fear."

"This could be an ideal time to attack Merkland directly with our main forces."

"Perhaps."

Footsteps sounded on the polished wood floor down the hall, so Connor pulled away from the door and trotted toward the stairs. He almost ran into Verena at the landing. He recoiled, and lifted a hand to protect his face and throat.

Verena smiled and took his hand in her warm, little one. "Oh, Connor, you're so funny." She pulled him to the end of the hall to the wide window overlooking the southern slope. She turned to him, and in the soft light, her skin seemed to glow and her eyes to shine.

Still holding his hand, she said, "Connor, I'm real sorry about what happened. You must be so frightened."

The intensity of her gaze made it hard to concentrate. "I'm more worried for my family. I don't want anyone to get hurt."

"Me too."

Even though she'd hit him and helped capture him three different times, he felt a surprising connection with the amazing young woman. "Verena, do you think anyone can stop the fighting before lots of people get killed?"

She leaned her head against his shoulder and whispered, "I hope so."

"How?"

She met his gaze and squeezed his hand. "I don't know yet, but I'm more confident knowing that you're helping."

Connor snorted. "There's not much I can do."

"You're already doing it." She reached into her ever-present satchel, and he tensed. Instead of throwing some evil rock in his face, she withdrew a small, ornately carved wooden box.

She extracted from it an oblong white stone about the size of his thumb and handed it to him. "This is special."

"I thought every rock you touched was special."

She smiled, her face radiant in the dim light. "You can be really sweet sometimes." She closed his fingers over the rock. "This is quartzite. A gift, for you to remember me by."

"What does it do?"

Instead of replying, she smiled, and her blue-eyed gaze became so deep he worried he might sink into it and lose himself. "I'm glad you're safe, Connor." She leaned forward and kissed him softly on the cheek. "Keep it with you, and think of me."

CHAPTER 47

t was nearly dawn by the time Hamish arrived with Lilias at Jean's back door. Connor jumped up from the table where he sat with Jean, and his mother swept him into her arms. She held him for a full minute, and he lost himself in the comforting strength of her embrace. The fears and confusion melted away for that moment.

Once they returned to the table, Connor related events of the two failed assaults, and some of what he learned about various Petralist and Guardian powers. He left out most of the details of his own growing affinities. He'd concealed his Curse for so many years, he still struggled to speak openly about it with his friends.

When he told them about the arrival of General Wolfram and his army, Hamish frowned. "Wait a minute, how'd they get an army here?"

"I've been wondering about that. I can only guess that Ilse somehow found the trail across Mount Ingram."

"There's no trail," Jean said.

"Yes, there is. I found it just this summer. It's narrow though ... . " Connor trailed off.

"What is it, son?"

"The trail. It wouldn't be hard to wipe it off the mountain."

"That would trap the Grandurians here," Jean said.

"I know. It might force them to surrender."

"Or fight all the harder," Hamish said.

"I'll let Carbrey decide the best course."

Lilias frowned. "This General Carbrey, I'm starting to wonder about him."

"Don't blame him, mom. How could they know Verena would have all these new powers with her Builded stones? And how could we expect another army would show up? The attack tonight would've worked."

"Easy, son. I know there's reasons for it, but a good commander should foresee problems and work to avoid them."

"I want to meet this Verena," Hamish said eagerly. "I'm on the work crew today, if they don't cancel it now that the army's arrived."

"Find her if you can." Connor's feelings for Verena were so jumbled, he was not sure what he wanted to tell Hamish about her. "Be careful. She's dangerous."

Hamish laughed. "What, is she going to hit me?"

"She might."

His smile faded. "But she tastes rocks, right?"

"Yes. Find out how it works. Any information you can gather might be very important."

"Don't worry, Connor, I'll ferret it out of her."

Jean placed a hand on Hamish's and said warmly, "No offense, Hamish, but you're not exactly the ferreting kind. More like the fall at her feet kind."

"Hey, no fair," Hamish frowned.

Connor smiled with them, but in his mind he heard Verena saying the exact same words, and the sound of her voice warmed him. He shook the memory away. He needed sleep. He was getting cracked.

Jean said, "I'm summoned to the manor house tomorrow too."

She explained that Lady Isobel had sent word that three ladies would be allowed to visit for an abbreviated Women's Circle meeting.

Connor frowned. "Mom, shouldn't you be chairing that meeting?"

She nodded and patted his hand. "Normally, yes, but I don't have access. Cinaed somehow convinced Ilse she spoke for the circle, and no one else has been allowed in to see Lady Isobel."

"Now's not the time for her games." Connor's simmering anger easily focused on Cinaed. "People are getting hurt."

Hamish spoke up, "Stuart's been bragging that his mom's going to take over as chair, that she's the only one showing leadership during the crisis."

Lilias said, "She sees only a chance for personal gain through this tragedy."

The truth of it saddened Connor, and further fueled his rage.

"I could just skip it," Jean offered.

"Oh no, dear. You must go. You're the one person we can trust to bring us word about what they're plotting."

"And while you're there, try to locate where they keep the prisoners," Connor added. "I expect there will be another battle soon, and I'm going to try to free dad and the others."

"How could you do that when the entire army can't?"

"I'm still working on it."

He hadn't really thought about it until he said it, but he realized that's what he had to do. He could no longer count on anyone else. He had this rare ability to establish affinities with multiple stones. He had to explore it further, learn all he could, and figure out how to rescue those prisoners.

"I'll try to come visit again before nightfall."

He rose and gave his mother another hug, traded shoulder punches with Hamish, and turned to say good-bye to Jean. Instead, she led him to the door.

"Connor, we need to talk."

He followed her outside. "I thought that's what we were doing."

She smiled, just a little, but it quickly faded. Whatever was on her mind, it was serious. Connor tried to imagine everything he might have done to upset her. He stopped after thinking about kissing Shona twice, wrestling so close with Verena, and ... well, there was no way she knew about all that, did she?

Jean drew him away from the door and tucked her long, blond hair behind one ear. Connor hadn't seen her much in the past couple days, and drank in the sight of her. As much as Shona dominated his life right then, she could not match Jean's pure, innocent beauty.

"Connor, this may not be the best time to talk about this."

"All right. I'll see you later," he said, hoping she'd wait until he had more time.

As he turned to run, Jean grabbed his hand. "Don't be such a grout-for-brain. This is important."

"Jean, there are armies preparing to kill each other, and maybe all of us too. Just tell me what's bothering you and I promise to help."

She touched his cheek. "That's one of the things I love about you, Connor. So eager to help, no matter the cost."

Love? It suddenly felt very hot in the cool, early morning breeze.

She cocked her head to one side a little, like she did when puzzling over a healing mixture. "You're to be a Guardian." She sounded sad.

"I am." He had to be Guardian. It was the only way. He reached for her hand, but she slid her fingers from his.

"Connor, Guardians aren't allowed to have families."

He blinked. That's not where he had hoped the conversation was going.

Jean met his gaze, and her face suddenly looked anguished. She continued in a rush, "Connor, I can't promise to you, not Cursed, not even if you become Guardian. I couldn't have children, knowing Teagair would be refused, that they'd be taken."

She threw herself into his arms and sobbed, "Connor, I'm so sorry."

He held her awkwardly, at a loss for words, as confused emotions battled for dominance. Part of him exulted that Jean confessed she cared for him, that he was holding her close, that she seriously considered promising to him.

At the same time, her words tore at him, proving his worst fears. She could not see past his Curse, no matter her feelings.

Then again, his growing affection for Verena confused him all the more. Did he really love Jean? He had always assumed he did, but how could he feel so attracted to Verena?

What about Shona? Could she really care for him, or was he just a curiosity to him? He couldn't make head nor blade out of any of it, and that just made him want to Curse-punch something.

How had life gotten so complicated?

After a moment, he pushed her gently away and brushed tears from her cheeks. He turned her face up until their eyes met. "Jean, I don't know what's going to happen in the next day or two, but you must know you'll always hold a place in my heart."

She smiled weakly and rubbed at her face. "You're not angry with me?"

"How could I be?"

"Oh, Connor, you are a special man."

She kissed him tenderly on the lips.

CHAPTER 48

n the manor house, Verena stepped into the study where Wolfram stood by the window. He moved to greet her, and she handed him a small, ornately carved wooden box that he placed on the desk.

"Is it well shielded?"

"Yes."

"That was a masterful performance, Verena. Despite your father's disapproval of your presence here, if you weren't so valuable as a Builder, I would recommend you as a foreign operative."

"Thank you, sir," she said softly, her eyes downcast.

He squeezed her shoulder. "It's always hardest when we're forced to work through those we genuinely respect."

She nodded. "Why is that?"

"Because they probably wouldn't understand."

"Yes, sir."

The words comforted her a little, and she tried to hide the powerful conflicting emotions that burned in her heart. She believed in this mission, but couldn't help think of Connor's strong hands holding hers, of the trust in his eyes as he took the little stone.

What would he say when he learned the truth?

A man in a simple green coat entered the room and took up the box. Wolfram said, "I want someone listening at all times. Bring me hourly reports."

"I will see it done, general."

Verena excused herself and climbed to the empty third floor where she paced for a long time.

CHAPTER 49

hen Connor reached the camp, a soldier ushered him directly to Carbrey's command tent. The general was sitting on his cot, still looking pale and weak. Shona sat in a chair nearby, wrapped in a thick, blue cloak, flanked by the various captains.

When Connor entered, Rory clapped him on the shoulder. "Glad you survived, lad."

"Thank you, sir."

"Where have you been?" Shona asked. She shifted and her cloak fell open a little to reveal her bandaged hand held gingerly in her lap. Her concern warmed his heart and eased some of his concern.

"They captured me again."

"That's becoming a bad habit," Captain Rory said.

"I'll work on it."

General Carbrey moved to a hard-backed wooden chair beside the large map table. "I take it they sent you as messenger."

"Yes sir. I bring word from General Wolfram."

"Wolfram!" Carbrey snarled. "Are you certain?"

"Yes, sir."

Carbrey took a steadying breath. "I should have expected this. Tell me lad, what did you see of his army?"

"I saw about a hundred regulars, maybe eight Rumblers, the four Wingrunners that attacked Captain Rory and Lady

Shona, the Sapper Anton, and two fellows who look a lot like you two."

He finished by pointing to the two captains with the twin swords on their backs.

The two exchanged grins. "Aye, we know the Allcarvers," said one.

The other flexed his hands. "Might be this time'll do it."

Carbrey said, "Only under the right conditions."

"Of course," they replied in unison, but the glint in their eyes suggested they'd close with the others if any chance presented itself. Connor decided he wanted to be standing far away when that happened.

Carbrey barked a laugh and leaned over the table and the map on its center. He pounded the surface with a fist, "The old wolf has over-extended himself this time. He won't escape me again."

Connor's heart sank. The general's face brightened with anticipation for battle, making him look younger, despite his salt-and-pepper hair. Connor hadn't yet delivered Wolfram's message, but he worried how Carbrey would respond.

Carbrey, still staring at the map, said, "Where did he come from? How could he bring such an army into Obrion without detection?"

"Sir, I believe they crossed directly from Granadure, from the far side of Mount Ingram."

"That mountain is impassable."

"No, sir, I'm afraid it isn't."

Shona spoke. "Connor found a way through. Initially he was going to show them so they could leave."

"I think they must have found it," Connor said.

Carbrey frowned. "It is the only explanation that makes sense." He looked over at Connor, "How is it that you found this trail when no one before you ever has?"

Connor shrugged. "I've hunted all over these mountains. I go places no one else goes. I almost missed it."

"Explain."

"It's a tiny trail, barely more than a scratch across a cliff. Most people wouldn't even realize it was a trail. It's very dangerous."

"Then it would be hard for an army to cross."

Connor nodded. "Very hard." He thought of those huge plate-armored soldiers with their massive weapons and shields, and shuddered at the thought of trying to traverse the mountain weighed down with all that gear.

A little smile played across the general's lips. "Then he cannot easily get reinforcements." To his captains, he said, "We will strip the garrison at Merkland and flood this valley with troops. We'll cut him off and destroy him."

"General," Connor said, talking over one of the captains, who was speaking about troop dispositions.

Without turning around, Carbrey said, "Never interrupt your superiors, boy. You delivered your message. Don't pretend to greater honors."

Connor's face reddened with the rebuke. For a moment, he'd felt accepted here, believed that his opinion mattered. He should have known better. He was still an untested Linn, not even a full Guardian, despite his rare affinity. Still, Wolfram's words rang in his mind, and he hadn't even delivered the terms yet.

"But sir," Connor said, pushing the words through the fear. "There's something else you should know."

"You presume to interrupt a second time? Do you really think it is you who should decide what I need to know?"

"No, sir," Connor stammered. "I'm sorry, sir. I just thought you'd want to know Wolfram is planning to attack Merkland."

"Why would Wolfram tell you that?"

"He didn't. I overheard him and Captain Ilse discussing it. Ilse figured you'd strip the garrison and recommended they invade and attack Merkland while its defenses were weak. I didn't get to hear the final decision."

Shona moved to stand beside Connor and placed her good hand on his shoulder. "I told you he was useful to have around."

Carbrey considered the news. "Wolfram is a crafty devil. He would attack Merkland, especially now. What better way to gain what he wants than to lure our army out here to this forsaken land. He'd be free to attack at his pleasure." After a pause, he continued softly, "It fits. Until now I could not see why he would focus so much energy here despite the quarry. Good work, lad."

"Thank you, sir."

The general pointed at one of the captains. "Dispatch a Strider downriver immediately. Order the garrison to full alert, and bring the prisoner to me under heavy escort."

The captain saluted and left the tent.

"Do you think it wise to bring him here?" Rory asked.

"He's safest with me. Let Wolfram break his army against Merkland's walls. He won't find what he's after." He paced from the table and spun back to the group. "We'll play his game and make him think he's tricked us."

Connor yearned to ask about the prisoner, but dared not interrupt Carbrey again.

The general stood, "I've sparred with Wolfram for years across the border. He's a crafty son of the Tallan like no other, but this time he's committed himself too far. His faith in this Builder girl will be his undoing. This time, I'll destroy him."

"What if Wolfram brings in more reinforcements?" Rory asked. "We outnumber him, but it would not take much to shift that balance."

"Boy," Carbrey motioned for Connor to join him at the map. "Tell me about Mount Ingram. Where is the best place to station a company to deny them access to this trail of yours?"

The map was a complete waste of time. Connor knew what had to be done. He did not want to say it, but could not think of another option.

"Sir, there is another way. The mountain can do the work for us."

"How?"

"I can tell a company of your men how to trigger an avalanche to wipe out the trail entirely."

CHAPTER 50

hen Jean returned from saying good-bye to Connor, Lilias noted her tear-streaked face. Her heart went out to the young woman, but she could not offer wisdom and comfort right then, especially not with Hamish loitering about. Besides, she was not entirely sure what to say.

Her son was growing, changing. She'd dreaded this day all of Connor's life. Already she saw him becoming a man who might save many lives, but he was also growing apart from the town. He no longer fit in, and that tore at her heart.

She motioned Jean to resume her seat, and called Hamish over from where he was rooting for food in Mhairi's cupboards. The boy never stopped eating.

"We have plans to make."

"I thought we did that," Hamish said. "I talk with Verena, Jean finds Hendry and the other prisoners and spies on Lady Isobel, and you …"

His voice trailed off and Lilias said, "And I orchestrate our little revolution."

Jean perked up from her quiet sorrow. "Revolution?"

She gave them a long look. They were so young, and yet who better to entrust the future of the town to than the rising generation? Besides, she trusted no one more completely. At least, no one she had such ready access to.

She took a sip of her rapidly cooling cider. "Armies gather around our town and open battle will probably be joined before nightfall. Do you think we'll remain safe?"

"They only said they want the Cutters," Hamish protested. "Why would anyone hurt the rest of us?"

"They may not plan to, but do you honestly think they'll hesitate if battle dictates the destruction of our town to grant them some advantage?"

Jean shook her head. "They'd slaughter us without a thought."

Hamish paled and pulled a carrot stick from his mouth. "What can we do?"

"First, we follow our plan. Connor needs the information we can gather for him."

"We need to prepare," Jean said. "Despite the threat of Daor, we might need to run before it's too late."

Lilias smiled. Such a smart one. The boys only saw her beauty, but this one had real promise. She really needed to pull the girl aside for a little talk.

Hamish looked stunned. "But we can't. Lord Gavin said."

Jean said, "Lord Gavin's a fool."

Hamish gaped, and Lilias spoke. "Jean is right. We cannot bury our tools and hope the mountain splits for our good. We may need to orchestrate our own escape."

"But what if he rescinds Teagair?"

"We'll deal with that when the time comes." She spoke the words with confidence despite the paralyzing fear at the thought of losing her children. "Better to risk living as slaves than accept death without fighting for freedom."

"No one will go," Hamish said.

"They will if we prepare them, if we flee together, at once, before the Grandurians can stop us."

"They'll kill us," Hamish said.

"Not if we do it right. They don't have the numbers to fight a battle and chase us at the same time."

"They might kill the prisoners," Jean said.

Lilias took a deep, steadying breath. "They might."

"Then how can we do it?"

"How can we not?" Lilias surprised herself by the heat in her voice. Hamish rocked back in his chair under the intensity of her gaze, and she held him with it.

"Those prisoners, my husband, are a bargaining chip. They will die if they ever lose their value, not if we escape." She forced herself to say it coldly, despite the screaming terror that tore her heart at the possibility.

"How can we be sure?"

"We cannot." She took each of their hands and met their worried gazes. "I can't promise anything but this. Freedom is always worth fighting for. If we give up, if we stop fighting, we've already lost. We must trust to the army to save our families."

"No," Jean said with tears glistened in her eyes. "We need to trust Connor. He'll save them."

She finished in a whisper.

"He's a Guardian."

CHAPTER 51

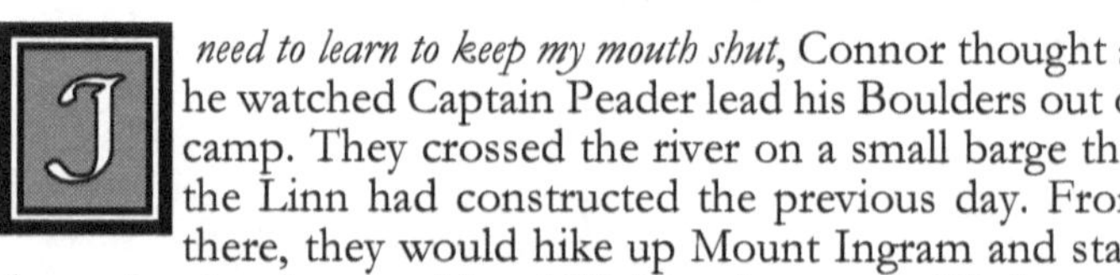

need to learn to keep my mouth shut, Connor thought as he watched Captain Peader lead his Boulders out of camp. They crossed the river on a small barge that the Linn had constructed the previous day. From there, they would hike up Mount Ingram and start the avalanche that would seal Wolfram's army in Obrion.

Wolfram would become desperate, and any hope for peaceful resolution would die in flames of bloody battle. Or, as General Carbrey predicted, they would see the hopelessness of the situation and surrender. He had dismissed Wolfram's terms with barely a moment's consideration, confident of victory.

The Grandurians would never surrender.

Connor could not believe they would. Ilse had proven she'd stand calmly against impossible odds, and the little he knew of General Wolfram suggested he was cut from the same stone. They would fight, and many would die.

Connor had no idea how to stop them. Why hadn't he kept his mouth shut?

Because he owed it to his country, that's why. Then why did he feel like such a betrayer for doing it?

Despondent, he shuffled across camp to where Tomas and the Fast Rollers were gathered around a small fire at the edge of the clearing where Rory's strike force bunked. He'd been so sure in town that he could make a difference, but he wondered if he was just kidding himself.

If full-scale battle was joined, his father would surely die. His family might be killed also, as would Hamish and Jean. So many people depended on him. He could not just give up. There had to be a way.

Connor dropped to onto a log near the fire beside Tomas, and the big soldier said, "I'm surprised you chose to sit with us lowly Fast Rollers, lad."

"Why wouldn't I? I'm one of you, aren't I?"

"Are you?" Tomas' voice was not entirely friendly. Neither were the looks cast at him from the other men. The unexpectedly cool reception on top of everything else triggered Connor's anger.

He snapped, "I am, unless you want to show me why I'm not?" At that moment, he would have eagerly fought the big Guardian.

Tomas laughed and clapped him on the shoulder. "That's the spirit of a Fast Roller, lad." The other men in the group seemed pleased by his reaction too.

They were all insane.

Connor's anger faded, "Look, Tomas, if I've offended you all somehow, I apologize. It's been kind of a rough day. I don't understand most of what's going on."

Tomas said, "Not to worry, lad. Guess I'm just too thin-skinned."

One of the other Fast Rollers piped in, "Aye, and dim-witted too."

Tomas barked a laugh. "Ha, Cameron! And you're the one who actually thinks the granite powder comes from beating on rocks with a hammer."

Connor looked from Tomas to Cameron's wide, brutish face, to see if they were making fun of him. "Uh, he's right."

The look of shock on Tomas' face drove Connor into a fit of laughter, joined by all of the other Guardians. Tomas' disbelief turned to outrage.

"That's not how they do it where I come from!"

Connor wiped his eyes. "Where are you from?"

"Raineach. It's a city far to the south."

"What do they quarry there?"

"Well, nothing really, not in the city. It's a trading center. But there's sandstone mines to the west, and a granite mine northwest. Lots of stones come to Raineach for processing."

"So how do they process granite down there?"

Tomas looked from Connor to Cameron, who was still wiping his eyes and said in a far more subdued voice, "Well, I always thought … oh, never mind!"

Connor decided to change the subject, although he made a mental note to draw Tomas aside at some point and ask him more about Raineach. "So why did you think I didn't want to be a Fast Roller?"

Tomas spoke around a bite of roasted meat. "You chose basalt." The other Fast Rollers looked disgusted at this. "Figured you were turning your back on granite."

"How could I? I've been Cursed with granite all my life."

"That long?"

"As long as I can remember. Why?"

Tomas waved aside the question. "Now you know what it is, why not stick with it?"

Connor paused as all of the fears rushed back, fear of not gaining Patronage, of losing control, of hurting others. Fear of having to leave his family. Forget the new fears for his family's safety. Suddenly he was relieved to get a chance to talk with this solid warrior.

"It's just, my Curse has always been a problem. The few times I tried to use it I only made things worse. I didn't want to do that again last night."

"I can respect that lad, but it's not the curse that brings the luck."

"No, it ain't," agreed Cameron. "The luck comes with how you use it."

Connor didn't believe it. He'd seen what his Curse did to discount it too easily. "Anyway, looks like I've got this Guardian-Agor affinity to explore too. I wanted to try out different things."

Tomas leaned in closer and said in a low, serious voice. "Have a care with that, lad."

"Why?"

"Captain Rory's warned you of the dangers."

"He said there are dangers."

"Aye. Use caution. For sure you've got to explore what you can do, but have a care. We know you, and we'll stand with you." The other Guardians all nodded assent. "But don't count on other companies doing the same."

"Why not?"

"Don't be daft, boy. It's human nature to resent success that comes too easy. You don't want enemies here in Carbrey's camp."

Connor wanted to scoff, but then he thought of Cinaed and her long-standing jealousy of his mother.

As he considered, Tomas continued. "Only a fraction of all Guardians gain even a weak secondary affinity. I've been trying for years, and I can barely light limestone enough to see my way on a cloudy day."

Cameron opened his mouth, but Tomas turned and snapped, "Leave off."

Cameron muttered something about Tomas' mother and confusion about which end to wrap with the swaddling clothes.

Tomas ignored him. "Don't you see the problem, lad? You walk in here and start healing like you're born to it."

"It's not that simple."

"Be that as it may, lad, keep your eyes open. You have a rare talent, and it'll come in handy in the war, no doubt. But don't make enemies where you could make friends."

"You make it sound easy."

"Hardly that. Just don't flaunt your talent so much." Tomas clapped him on the shoulder and gestured toward the roasted meat. "Help yourself, lad. We're in for a long wait."

After eating for a few minutes, Connor glanced at the distant command tent, "Tomas, what do you think they're talking about?"

"Battle strategy, of course."

"Won't they just launch a full attack like last time?" He inwardly cringed to say it aloud. So many lives hung in the balance.

Tomas surprised him by shaking his head. "Can't. Not yet anyway. Don't know the enemy well enough."

"I saw them. We outnumber them by at least four to one."

"Aye, but it's not the regulars that win battles, lad." Tomas tapped the side of his nose with one finger, "Battles with Guardians and Petralists are different. It's all about strategy, about which side best allocates their talent."

"I don't understand."

"Think about it, lad. That clever Captain Ilse, Tallan take her eyes, gave us a solid thumping, and we outnumbered her by lots more. How'd she do that?"

"She prepared, and she used Verena's powers."

"Aye, that Builder's proven to be a real thorn. She's a new element to the whole puzzle, and makes it more complicated, but doesn't change the basic challenge. Ilse beat us because she applied her powers best."

Tomas nodded toward the command tent. "Now Carbrey and his captains need to outwit the Old Wolf. General and he have been playing this game a long time. There's no one better than Wolfram at deploying his Petralists."

Connor had already seen how much damage Kilian could do, and he expected Gregor or Anton could destroy entire companies of regulars if left unchecked. Then again, if Tomas and enough Fast Rollers could ever close with Ilse, surely they could finally beat her.

He sat back and considered the challenge, and his head swam with all the variables, and he didn't even know all the stones and their powers yet.

"So how will he do it?"

Tomas shrugged and spat into the fire. "Reckon I don't know. Strategy's never been my strength."

Cameron piped in, "Can you even count to five?"

"Shut it, or I'll crack your face."

Cameron laughed. "Couldn't do nothing but make me prettier."

Tomas leaned closer to Connor and said softly, "When I'm not wearing gloves I can get to ten, no problem." He poked the fire and spoke more to himself, "It's no easy chore. That

Kilian'll be a problem. We got no Spitter to counter him. Gregor's good, top of his game, but he's got Anton to deal with." He made a low whistle.

"They got Wingrunners, at least four," Cameron said.

"Striders'll do for them." Tomas grinned at Connor. "That's a sight, lad, mark my words."

"Aye, you get a chance to see a running battle, make sure you do," Cameron said.

Tomas wagged a thick finger at Connor. "Mind, now. Just cause you run fast don't make you a Strider. Don't meddle in a running battle. Ain't no place for one not knowing what to do."

Connor wondered what it would be like to see Wingrunners and Striders racing full tilt across the plateau, slinging stones or whipping meteor hammers at each other. One Wingrunner alone had played a huge part in blocking Rory's first assault.

How much damage could a full squad do?

Cameron said, "You saw them good, lad. See any Flameweavers?"

"I have no idea."

"Captain Aonghus could handle it if they do," Tomas said, "but trick's in ferreting them out."

Cameron added, "I'm glad we got Blades. Sounds like Wolfram brought his Allcarvers."

"Blades?" Connor asked.

"Them Captains with twin swords."

Tomas shuddered, "That's a pair I'd not mess with."

"What's their affinity?"

"Obsidian." Cameron said. "Enhances their natural talents."

Tomas nodded, "Aye, those two are among the best swordsmen in the realm. When they tap obsidian they could cut down every last regular to a man."

"Could even drop a few Rumblers, probably," Cameron said.

"But you've got granite," Connor protested.

"Gainst them, don't matter," Tomas said with a snort. "They'd carve out your eyes, and while you're screaming, they'd shove a sword down your throat."

Cameron pointed a smoking stick at Connor, "You can't imagine how fast and how accurate they are. I've seen one cut a granite statue clean in half."

Tomas gestured at the gathered Fast Rollers. "We've been trained to deal with them, but I'd still not want to face Wolfram's Allcarvers with just the six of us. We might win, but we'd pay dear for it."

Cameron jammed his stick back into the fire. "When the Blades meet the Allcarvers, just stay clear."

Tomas pulled more meat from the spit. "Well that's it, lad. All their strategizing boils down to them questions."

"So that's all the Petralists?" Connor asked.

"Nay, lad, but all we expect to see from your description. Still, general needs to figure out how to draw out Wolfram's Petralists and shut them down, and we get our bash-fight and win this war." He punctuated the last sentence by slamming one heavy fist into his other palm.

Cameron saluted the distant command tent. "Here's hoping General gets it right!"

Connor raised his fist with the others, winning approving nods, but his heart wasn't in it. As the Fast Rollers started talking amongst themselves about the best strategies for beating Grandurian Rumblers, Connor couldn't shake a growing conviction that a simple bash-fight would be the last thing they'd get.

CHAPTER 52

ou're Hamish, right?"

Despite the pleasant tone of the voice, Hamish jumped. The pitchfork load of manure he had been throwing toward a two-wheeled cart missed and struck Stuart in the side of the head. The brawny fellow rounded on Hamish, but an angry curse died on his lips.

Hamish was surprised to find a very cute girl with huge blue eyes, dressed in the fine clothes of a noble, standing behind him. Her friendly smile and slight inquisitive tilt to her head eased some of the tension knotting his muscles since reporting for service at the manor house an hour ago.

He bowed. "I am Hamish, my lady."

She flashed a dazzling smile and took his hand. "I've heard so much about you. Come."

As she led him toward the south side of the manor, Hamish glanced back. Stuart stared after him, disbelief on his manure-covered face.

Hamish grinned, straightened his shoulders and walked more confidently behind the cute Grandurian.

She passed the sheep pen, and led him into one of the small storage sheds on the far side. Normally it held farm tools and miscellaneous supplies for working the gardens along the eastern edge of the plateau. They had been replaced with all kinds of rocks piled high on the shelves. The air was thick with the smell of earth and dust.

He recognized some of the rocks, stone figures or carvings from the lower levels of the manor house, including a couple of large, cube-like crystals a hand span thick. He'd never figured out what they were supposed to be. On one shelf at about shoulder height, he was surprised to see chunks of diorite. They looked like the broken pieces of the Ashlar's hammer.

The noble girl turned to him and said, "I've met your friend, Connor."

"You must be Verena."

"How did you know?"

"Connor told me about you."

She grinned, looking ridiculously pleased. "Really, what did he say?"

"He said you're dangerous."

"I am."

Hamish's smile faded. He wasn't sure if he should believe her. She looked so nice.

Verena crossed the small shed and picked up a couple of tiny chunks of blue marble that had once been part of a statue's arm. She handed one to him and popped the other into her mouth. "Tell me what you taste."

Finally, someone who understood.

He sucked on the rock, but didn't need to bother. He'd always liked marble, more than ever since tasting the oven. "Spice."

He'd been practicing so much with marble in the past two days that he instinctively pried open the stone's power and released a tiny jet of flame. Then he yelped and spit the rock out as it started burning his tongue.

Verena caught it, but instead of dropping the flaming rock, she held it up and the flames winked out.

"How did you do that?" Hamish asked.

"In a minute." She picked up a couple of pieces of granite, handed him one, and spit out her piece of marble exactly the way he usually did. She got good distance with it, and it clattered down onto one of the shelves. He was starting to like this girl.

Granite was as familiar to Hamish as his own family. "Crackers."

"Uh-huh." She picked up a couple of crystal-like stones that had been sitting on one of the cube crystals he'd noticed earlier.

"What's this?" he asked.

"Quartzite."

He knew the taste, just hadn't known what to call it. "This one tastes like a summer breeze."

Verena laughed, a simple, happy sound. "Yes! That's the perfect way to say it." She turned serious. "You're a Builder, Hamish of Alasdair, and I'm going to teach you what that means."

"Really?" He'd dreamed he might learn something from her, but dreaded it too. If he really shared similar powers, would she call the soldiers to take him away? "Why would you do that?"

"Call it a favor to Connor."

Hamish couldn't help grinning, and he tentatively explored the quartzite stone in his mouth. There. He found a tiny crack like he did with the marble. He pried at it, and was thrilled when it cracked open a bit.

The stone blasted out of his mouth, propelled by a jet of air. It struck Verena in the forehead and she stumbled back with a cry.

Oh, no.

Hamish leaped forward to help, but Verena tripped over a rough stone on the floor and fell to her backside. Hamish tripped over her and crashed into one of the shelves piled with rocks. It splintered, and he fell in a heap amid an avalanche of small stones.

Hamish pushed rocks out of his face and tried to rise. Rocks rattled and bounced as they rolled off him like water. Verena, who sat a couple feet away, started laughing. Hamish couldn't help but join in.

They stood and Hamish retrieved a piece of marble from the pile at his feet. He held it up and triggered a little flame. "Can you show me how to turn it off?"

Verena covered his hand with hers, and the flame winked out. "That is only the beginning."

CHAPTER 53

onnor left the Fast Rollers and moved through the camp, driven by a restless energy. He avoided the masses of regulars who were resting, playing at dice or cards, sharpening weapons, or fixing armor. He declined an invitation from Donald to sit with the Striders, and slipped into the forest to avoid Marcas, the old Healer.

Not only did worry about the upcoming battle unsettle him, but he couldn't help thinking about the prisoner Carbrey mentioned. Could it be the same boy Wolfram told him about? Could this entire conflict really be a result of the taking of a boy? Why would High Lord Dougal order such a thing? Was there more history he did not yet know about that would justify it?

His wandering steps led him north of camp, to the smaller clearing where Rory's army had camped the first night and where he'd helped Marcas heal so many soldiers. He passed several scouts along the way, but no one challenged him.

In the northern clearing, Gregor the Sentry stood atop a full tower of earth that reared twenty feet and stood eight feet in diameter. He faced north, his hands embedded in rails connected to the top of the tower. A man in the baggy pants of a Strider, along with half a dozen soldiers dressed in hunting leathers, sat around a small fire not far away.

As soon as Connor saw Gregor, he realized he'd been looking for the man. Ever since the conversation with Tomas, another nagging worry had tugged at his mind.

He strode to the tower and, as he reached the base, Gregor spoke without turning around. His deep voice seemed to flow down the tower with great weight. "You seek knowledge, boy."

Now that he stood close to the tower, looking up at the giant of a man standing so far overhead, Connor's determination wavered. He took a deep breath and said with forced confidence, "I want to know about Sentries."

Gregor glanced down, "And what if I told you I want to know about cutting granite from the mountain?"

"I could tell you all about that."

"Please do so."

"Now?"

Gregor nodded.

Such a simple request. Even though he'd never be Ashlar, Connor knew everything about cutting granite. But as he opened his mouth to speak, he paused, unsure where to start.

Gregor stood there, unmoving like a statue, and appeared willing to remain there all day. Under his heavy stare, Connor felt compelled to speak.

"Well, there's actually quite a bit. Do you want to know everything, or just the basics?"

"Exactly."

Without warning, the high earthen tower sank smoothly into the ground. Connor stepped back as the ground shook and the air filled with the heavy scent of tilled earth.

"That is the question, is it not?" Gregor asked. "To learn of the Sentry is to learn of the earth. I am a student of the earth and yet lack understanding in many things."

He sure chose a long way to say 'Be more specific'.

Connor considered his next question a little more carefully. "What is your affinity?"

"Slate."

"Do you absorb it like granite, or just hold it like sandstone?"

"Neither. Slate is a metamorphic stone." Gregor sat back, and the ground flowed up behind him into a huge chair to catch his weight. "What drives this interest?"

Connor shrugged. "I'm trying to learn everything I can while I have the time."

"Why is that?"

Connor's frustration flared under the barrage of deflecting questions. "Because I can't save my family in ignorance!"

Gregor leaned back in his earthen chair, "Ah. Atop the foundation of truth, useful knowledge may be laid."

"So does that mean you'll tell me about Sentries?"

"It does." Gregor's calm façade cracked for the first time into a genuine smile. "Few bother to ask. Metamorphic stones are the tertiary affinity, and few there are who attempt such a long road. Fewer find success. To be a Sentry is to be alone, and at the same time it is to be the servant of all."

It sounded miserable.

"Why do it then?"

Gregor's smile widened and he tapped one arm of the earthen chair upon which he sat. "The earth grants many gifts to those willing to learn its secrets. Are you willing to pay the price to learn?"

The unending cryptic answers drove Connor to change tracks.

"I heard you talking about Anton. Do you think he'll be hard to beat?"

Gregor chuckled. "Aye, lad. That he will be."

"Can you do it?"

"Not one to mince words, are you?"

"My family's in danger. I can't afford to."

Gregor leaned forward and pointed one thick finger at Connor's heart. "Keep the knowledge of your purpose close. It will guide you."

"I will."

"Anton has stood alone against entire armies. He is the most decorated Sapper ever to live, a true disciple of the Tallan."

"He didn't seem that evil to me, just kind of old. Like weathered granite."

"He is not evil," Gregor said. "Not in the true sense."

"I didn't know there were different senses of evil."

"There are many, including true evil of the heart, as well as evil by association."

"You'll stop him though, won't you?"

"I must. It is my duty."

"What are you going to do?"

Gregor chuckled. "Keep pondering on it." He gave Connor a thoughtful look and added, "They say you are Guardian-Agor, and powerful even for such a one."

"I've heard that too."

"Are you willing to test yourself against the earth?" His voice reverberated around Connor like a landslide.

"If it'll help, I'll try anything."

Gregor rose. "Good. Increase knowledge at every opportunity and your foundation will ever be solid."

From his jacket pocket he drew a thin wafer of stone and handed it to Connor, who slid his fingers across the smooth, greenish-brown surface.

"Do I bite it, or something?"

"Put it in your shoe."

"Really?"

"Metamorphic stones are unique. They enable affinity with the elements. This is their power, and a truth many fail to grasp. Raw elements are untamed and untamable, but we who establish this affinity may learn to walk with them. When successful, they will lend us of their strength in direct measure to our capacity. Thus slate is placed closest to the earth."

Connor felt more than a little foolish as he removed his right boot. Before he could slip the wafer inside, Gregor said, "For the first attempt, better to leave your shoes off."

The huge man pulled up the thick turf as easily as Connor might brush aside a cobweb. In seconds, he cleared a wide, bare patch of earth and motioned to Connor to stand in it, with the wafer of slate under one foot.

"Concentrate on the slate, reach through it with your senses to the earth beneath. It is the gateway to the element."

Connor closed his eyes and focused. The earth felt cool under his feet, and surprisingly soft. His toes dug into the loose soil, and the smell of turned earth and grass drifted on the breeze. He wondered idly how slate would taste to Hamish.

Despite the soft buzzing of insects and the occasional trill of birds, the clearing fell quiet. Connor felt for the slate under his foot, and reached for it like he did the sandstone pendant. He tried drawing strength from the slate like he did healing, but even though he tried for several minutes, nothing happened.

Gregor spoke softly. "The bucket does not command the river to flow. It is filled only when placed in the waters."

He really needed to get this guy together with Bruce. Bruce knew more sayings than any ten people Connor had ever known. One of his favorites was 'roost with the pedras, wake with the spirits.' It had come to mind several times over the past days.

Still, Gregor might prove his match.

Instead of pulling at the power of the slate, Connor tried pushing against it, tried to reach out to the earth, through the stone.

The response came immediately. His thoughts seemed to sink through the thin wafer, and touch something vast. It was like leaning off the edge of the stone pier at Loch Wick and plunging his face into the still waters of the loch.

After the initial shock of contact, his senses radiated outward in an expanding circle. It was like gaining an additional limb, one that had been numbed his whole life.

An awestruck grin spread across Connor's face as he connected with the land all around. Even with his eyes closed, he knew exactly where Gregor stood beside him, where the soldiers lounged around the campfire, where trees thrust mazelike tangles of roots into the ground. A squirrel skipped across the earth from one tree to another, and the movement pulled his attention, like a bug crawling across his skin.

Connor became aware of strength flowing up into him with the enhanced senses. Completely unlike the itching numbness of granite, this power connected him to the earth, united him with the earth's immovable strength. He felt like nothing under heaven could knock him over. It would be like trying to knock over a tree, or a mountain.

He opened his eyes and laughed. "It's amazing!"

Gregor grinned like a little boy. "I am impressed. You are more than Agor, perhaps even Dawnus."

"What's that?"

"A topic of great weight, and one for another day."

The guarded answer didn't even faze Connor. He just grinned and reached farther, exploring that enormous new part of himself unlocked by the slender wafer of slate.

Gregor guided Connor in learning to focus his will, concentrate on specific areas of interest so he could recognize things that contacted the ground even briefly.

"Sentries with deep affinity with the earth who learn to walk with it as a friend, receive endowments of strength and of longevity."

"How long can you live?"

"I have passed eighty."

Connor gaped at the mighty Sentry. He was no decrepit old man.

Gregor shrugged, "It is said Anton survived the Tallan Wars, lived in the dark days when Granadure split from Obrion."

"They used to be part of the same country?"

Why hadn't anyone ever taught him that?

Gregor nodded, his face solemn. "Much knowledge is lost of the past, truths that might help shape the future."

"You must have learned a lot, though," Connor said, wondering at the ability to live so long.

"Aye. Over time, Sentries learn to mold the earth, shape it to their will. We can raise fortifications for armies or shelters against the rain. When connected with the earth, little may approach without detection."

Connor frowned. "You said something about Anton shielding the army from you. How was it possible?"

"It is a delicate skill, and difficult to master." As he spoke, Gregor's presence faded from Connor's earth-sense. Connor glanced over at the big man to make sure he hadn't floated away. He stood, feet sunk half into the soft earth, but he remained invisible to Connor's earth senses.

It took a long moment of focused concentration on the spot where Gregor stood before Connor recognized a subtle shifting of his senses, as if feeling were somehow re-directed around Gregor, leaving him in a hole, a numb spot. Connor pushed against that spot. It was like ramming his nose against a glass jar, and he could not penetrate.

"How did you do that?"

"You show great promise to sense what is missing. Time only will grant mastery of this skill."

Connor turned his attention from the invisible giant and threw his senses out beyond the clearing. To the south, he felt the heavy weight of the army encampment, and to the east, the towering heights of the mountains. High above, he even felt the rapid passage of a hunting nuall. Then it passed onto solid rock and faded from his senses.

"Why can't I feel through the stone of the mountain?"

"It depends on which stones form the mountains. This area lies heavy with granite, which is a power stone foreign to slate."

"But I have affinity with granite."

"Were you to tap granite while connected with the earth, you could walk with it as you do the loose earth."

Connor did not entirely understand, and was tempted to absorb some granite to experiment, but decided not to pause. There was so much more to explore.

To the west, a shimmering wall blocked his senses, and he frowned until he realized it must be the Lower Wick. "I can't pass the river."

"Water and earth are ancient rivals. Water nourishes earth, but will not yield its secrets."

Connor tried exploring to the north, but a long, invisible wall blocked his passage. Not like the impenetrable presence of water, this was an invisible barrier, just like the one hiding Gregor's presence.

"You're blocking the entire valley?" The scope of Gregor's reach made Connor feel very small.

"From the river to the mountain. Just as we can feel others, so can the enemy."

Connor had never imagined the enemy sensing their every move through the earth. The knowledge that they could made him shiver.

What else could the Grandurians do that he'd never imagined?

A heavy weariness grew upon him and he retracted his senses. He wanted nothing more than to lie down and take a nap.

"How do you make those chairs?"

"You attempt to run before you can walk, my friend."

"I fall a lot. I'm all right with that."

"Very well. Form in your mind the image you desire. Focus your senses on the piece of earth you wish to shape, and pour that shape into it."

"That doesn't make any sense."

"Think of it as inviting that piece of earth to try a new shape."

Connor really wanted to sit down, so he forced aside his doubts and created an image of a simple chair. Holding that image in his mind, he focused on the ground under his feet and tried to drive the ground up into that image.

For a second the earth responded, and he felt it beginning to move. It rippled under his feet, but then the image of the chair wavered in his mind.

The ground exploded upward right under his feet and sent him somersaulting into the air, and the abrupt feeling of loss wrenched at his mind. It was like having his leg yanked off.

He shouted and wind-milled uselessly. As he fell, a slender finger of earth flowed up to meet him. It caught him as gently as his mother's embrace and lowered him to his feet.

Gregor said, "You show great promise, young one. You may yet learn to walk with the earth."

"Thanks for showing me a little. I'd like to try again some time."

"You know how to find me." Gregor extended another wafer of slate.

Connor gratefully accepted the small stone and slipped it into his belt pouch. As he headed back toward the main camp, the ground lifted Gregor onto his tower.

Connor considered all he learned from the mighty Sentry and he grinned at the wonder of it.

"What are you smiling about?"

He looked up, surprised, to find Shona standing before him in the forest, her hands on leather-clad hips, and her heavy cloak thrown back over one shoulder.

"Just thinking about all the great things I've seen today."

She took his hand, "Come on, and maybe you'll find another reason to smile." She drew him off the trail and deeper into the woods to a small clearing under a couple of towering oaks. They were alone, but Connor's thoughts jumped back to Gregor.

Was he watching them through the earth right now?

So he climbed onto a large rock thrusting out of the ground nearby. Shona joined him and opened her hand to reveal a small, rather ugly gray rock only about the size of his thumbnail.

"What's this, another experiment?"

She smiled. "You're a quick study, Connor." She hesitated for a second before pressing it into his hand, and then shuffled closer, chin in hands, elbows propped on drawn-up knees. She looked unusually vulnerable, not the commanding high lady she normally projected. Connor found it uniquely appealing.

"Am I supposed to swallow this whole thing?"

"No. It's quartzite, one of the metamorphic stones."

"Really?" He thought back to Verena in the manor house and the pretty white quartzite stone she'd given him. She'd said it was just a token, something to remember her. He shouldn't be surprised that she'd choose a power source stone even for that.

"What does it do?"

"It's absorbed through the mouth. You stick it in your cheek and suck on it."

Connor almost laughed as he thought of sucking on a rock like Hamish, but he schooled his face to remain impassive. Shona could not learn about Hamish. She'd already stated she would execute any Builder, and he suspected Hamish shared that ability with Verena.

"Well for you, if your amazing talent lets you achieve affinity with quartzite as easily as it did soapstone ..." Her voice trailed off, and her face glowed with excitement. "It should give you the gifts of the Pathfinders."

"They see really well, right?"

Shona nodded and leaned closer, a mischievous smile on her face. "They say quartzite enhances all the senses. Sight, smell, taste, and touch, every experience is said to be magnified." She leaned closer still. "Won't it be fun to explore that?"

Connor felt his face flush, and the air became suddenly stuffy and warm. Shona's attention flattered him as much as it bewildered him. What would her father think of her consorting with a common Linn?

Before he could formulate any kind of response, a distant bugle sounded two quick notes from camp.

Shona grimaced, "Keep it for later." She slid off the rock.

"What's going on?"

"Time to attack."

CHAPTER 54

On his belly, Connor peered over the edge of a rocky bluff on the flanks of Mount Alasdair. Directly below his position, the manor looked like a dollhouse, and Wolfram's army like a group of toy soldiers. Bright noonday sun flooded the valley, but its comforting warmth did little to dispel his apprehension.

Shona and Rory crawled up to either side of him.

"Has it started yet?" Shona whispered.

"I don't think so."

Connor looked left, across the panoramic view of the slope south of the plateau. In the distance, some of Carbrey's army had assembled, while large numbers of soldiers moved in formation along the near side of the river, about a mile from Alasdair. He had expected Carbrey to attack up the slope like last time.

Why divert so many men along River Road?

The truth struck Connor like a physical blow and he gasped. "He means to attack Alasdair!"

"Shush," Shona said.

They might be over a thousand feet above the plateau, but their mission relied on stealth, and Rory had explained they had to be careful not to alert the Longseer to their presence.

Connor forced his voice to a whisper as he watched the tiny figures moving toward his town. Carbrey had ordered Connor to take Rory, Shona and the Fast Rollers back along the secret route to the rear of the plateau. Even though

Connor doubted Ilse would be taken by surprise again, Carbrey seemed confident.

"We'll give them a distraction they can't ignore," he'd told Rory. "Once all of the major players are committed, we'll signal. You'll only have a few minutes to complete your mission, Captain."

Only after they crested the first long summit above the river did Rory explain their mission. "We mean to free the prisoners. Without that leverage, once he learns the pass back to Granadure is blocked, Wolfram will have no choice but to surrender."

Connor doubted it.

He wondered at Carbrey's plan. Those men hiking along the river could surely be seen by Wolfram's Longseer. There was nothing preventing Kilian from washing them all downriver before they ever set foot in Alasdair.

"Look," Shona pointed northwest toward the distant Alasdair. "Movement just downriver of the loch."

Connor strained his eyes to see people running right across the Lower Wick.

"That's not possible," Rory said. "There aren't that many Spitters in all of Obrion."

"They'll reach the town in under a minute," Connor said.

How could this be happening? Why would they fight in Alasdair instead of attacking the enemy atop the plateau?

All along, he'd been comforted by the fact that the town would be spared the worst of the fighting.

All along, he'd been wrong.

Shona drew him close and whispered, "Connor, the quartzite."

He had forgotten about the little pebble she'd given him. He fumbled in his belt pouch, but pulled out a small wafer of marble that the flame-haired Captain Aonghus had handed him before they left for their respective assignments.

"Catch," the captain had called without warning. "Pop that in your mouth if you can handle the burn."

"I've tasted marble. Tastes like any other rock."

Aonghus shook his head. "I heard what you did with soapstone. Let's see if you're the Dawnus Shona claims. Slip it under your tongue and give it a moment. Suck through the pain, and that's when life really gets hot."

He hadn't dared try yet. The wild look in Captain Aonghus' eye when he talked about it made him wonder at the wisdom of ingesting marble.

After he fished out the pebble of quartzite, Shona said, "Grahame said wedge it into your cheek and suck on it."

"Whoa! What are you doing?" Rory snatched the quartzite away from Connor.

"We need to see," Shona said, defensive.

"Are you mad? We can't risk quartzite now."

"Why not?" The burly Captain's open concern surprised Connor.

What was Shona trying to do to him?

"It's dangerous and reckless."

"I need to know!" Shona hissed.

"Not like this, lass. You could sunder his other affinities and waste his talent."

"What do you mean?" Connor asked. That sounded really bad.

"He can do it, I know it," Shona insisted.

"Why risk all his potential so recklessly?" Rory asked.

"That's none of your business, Captain," Shona declared, and assumed the angry, regal look like when she spoke with Ilse.

Despite her imperious glare, Rory shook his head. "No, lass. I cannot allow this folly."

"Cannot allow?" Shona's eyes bulged with indignation. "How dare you presume such authority?"

Unfazed by her growing wrath, Rory said, "Please, lass, wait until we have time to ensure the proper safety –"

"I don't have time," Shona hissed. "I'm to be included in the pairings this year, and ..." her voice fell to a whisper and her anger evaporated. "Without a secondary affinity, I cannot guarantee ... "

For a second, Rory looked embarrassed. "I am sorry, Lady Shona. I didn't think –"

She waved aside his apology and met his gaze with a fierce look. "With my Patronage of Connor, if I can confirm him at least Dawnus, then I regain control."

"Still, you risk much, for both of you."

"What are you talking about?" Connor interrupted.

Shona flushed and said quickly, "Nothing we have time to discuss."

"If you are determined," Rory said, "at least try marble first."

"Before we try anything, I need to know what you're talking about," Connor said, irritated. "And what's Dawnus? Gregor mentioned it yesterday when he taught me slate, but wouldn't elaborate."

Shona gasped, and Rory cried, "You established affinity with slate?" They both looked at him with such awe that he wished he'd kept his mouth shut.

"Gregor said I did good for a first attempt."

"I can't believe it," Shona whispered.

Rory balled his hands into fists and exclaimed, "I told you not to experiment with any more stones without talking with me first. You have no idea how dangerous that was!"

"Well if you hadn't been so cryptic, maybe I would have," Connor shot back. He was tired of being the only one who didn't understand anything. "What's wrong with me using slate? I already proved a tertiary affinity with soapstone."

"The important thing is you did it," Shona said, pulling Connor around to face her. She beamed at him and touched his face, a wondrous look on her face. "You really did it."

"So, does that mean I'm this Dawnus thing you were talking about?"

"Oh no, Connor, you're something far greater." She smiled so wide, her face nearly split.

Rory rejoined the conversation. "Few Guardians manage a tertiary affinity, even after years of work. Of those, perhaps a handful in an entire generation demonstrate gifts powerful enough to become Dawnus."

"They possess the rare gift of establishing affinity with a second tertiary stone," Shona added.

"But that second affinity with metamorphic stones must be with the opposite elemental power of their first," Rory added.

"I don't understand." The rapid explanation had lost Connor.

"You connected with soapstone first," Shona said. "Water. So to be Dawnus, you should have next tried marble."

"Fire," Connor said in understanding.

"Trying anything else could have set you back years, if not burned out your existing affinities altogether," Rory said.

Connor gaped, but Shona laughed, "But it didn't. You're more than Dawnus, Connor. You're something we haven't seen since the Tallan Wars over three hundred years ago."

He tried to ask what that was, but Shona pressed a finger to his lips. "Before I tell you, prove me right. Try quartzite."

Rory said, "It's too late to show caution now, lad, might as well. But hurry up, the assault on Alasdair has begun."

A quick glance back over the edge of the cliff showed the attacking Obrioner soldiers had somehow crossed the Lower Wick and were converging on the town.

Quartzite was supposed to enhance senses. He yearned to see the distant impending battle, to confirm his family and friends remained safe, so he popped the ugly little pebble into his mouth.

He sucked on it for a few seconds while Shona and Rory watched him expectantly. At first, all he tasted was rock, and that made him think of Hamish and wonder what his friend would taste in the stone.

All of a sudden a river of warmth flowed up through the flesh of his jaw and pooled in the center of his head. A low humming began vibrating in his skull. It wasn't uncomfortable, but more than a little distracting.

Then the liquid warmth flowed into his eyes. His vision clouded and his eyes burned, as if he'd gotten pepper in them. He flinched and rubbed one eye.

What in the name of the Ashlar's Hammer?

His eye had changed. Through his eyelid, it felt hard, faceted, like a gemstone.

He opened his eyes and gasped at the riot of color screaming for attention. He'd never seen such brilliant depth, and he stared out over the valley of Alasdair in startled wonder.

Whatever he looked at snapped into focus with a clarity he'd never dreamed possible. A fish jumped in the Lower Wick, and the movement drew his gaze. As he focused on the distant river, his vision swooped down as if he was a diving pedra, and he braced himself against the solid rock upon which he lay.

After that initial gut-twisting shift, he marveled at the exquisite detail of the fish as it slipped back into the clear waters of the river. Every scale reflected the sunlight with dazzling intensity, a riot of rainbow colors that took his breath away.

Shona tipped his face toward her, and his vision snapped back into close focus with another wrenching shift. He blinked, and then stared at her, transfixed.

He had always thought Shona lovely, but now he could barely breathe as he drank in every detail of her smooth skin, and looked so deep into her hazel eyes, he felt he could see into her soul.

She laughed, and the rich sound triggered another shift in the liquid warmth of quartzite pooling in his head. Some of it touched his ears, and something popped.

Sharp pain stabbed deep through his ears and he flinched and grabbed his head. Then he frowned and felt around. The lobes of his ears were longer and stuck out farther from his head.

He wiggled them.

He'd never been able to do that before, but it was as easy as snapping his fingers. He twisted them impossibly far out, and then up and down.

Shona laughed along with him and touched one elongated lobe. The rich sound of her laughter reverberated through his enhanced ears with unbelievable richness.

How was it possible? Would they change back when he ran out of quartzite? Would Shona care? What about Jean?

Surprisingly, he wondered what Verena would think too.

Other sounds crashed in on his mind and for a second all thought fled under the onslaught. A flood of indecipherable noises clamored for attention, scattered his thoughts, and sparked a massive headache.

Then Shona's voice filtered through the jumble.

"Connor, you are Blood of the Tallan."

He gasped. He'd never heard of such a terrible curse, but it stunned him by its potential for evil. "I thought you were happy."

"Oh Connor, but I am."

"How could you say such a thing then?"

"Sometimes I forget how much you have to learn."

"What's there to learn? You just called me a devil."

"You don't understand. There hasn't been such a gift since the Tallan himself." She cupped his face in her hands and said with triumphant joy. "Together, we'll make history."

He wanted to protest.

She kissed him first.

Connor forgot to breathe as her lips pressed hard against his and overloaded every one of his enhanced senses. So close, he could count the minute ripples in her skin, map the curve of her cheek, see himself reflected in her half-closed eyes.

The rosewater scent she wore filled him with thoughts of springtime and Sogail laughter. The slide of her fingers against his skin sounded loud as trumpets blaring to the world the wonder of this High Lady's affection.

He could feel her skin heat with passion that echoed through him and drove aside fear of the curse she'd just pronounced over him. He dared clutch her head and draw her lips tighter against his.

After what seemed an eternity, she released him and leaned back, a look of triumph on her angelic face.

He started to grin in reply, but a flash of crimson light behind her drew his gaze. With another stomach-wrenching flip, his vision swept in on the town until he could see every detail, as if he were standing right in front of the wall, right down to individual cracks in the stone. It was amazing. He could see everything, including …

… men burning.

He looked away from the grisly sight of soldiers stumbling back from the wall gate that was engulfed in flame. Movement drew his gaze to two figures flowing down the steep slope from the plateau toward the southern wall of Alasdair.

Anton and Kilian were moving to succor their forces. Anton rode half-reclined on an odd-shaped chair of earth that sported branches to hold his feet just off the ground, with hands extended. The entire seat smoothly descended the slope, sliding right along the surface of the ground. Kilian stood with feet planted wide, legs bent, hands extended for balance. He slid down the steep slope on a cascading sheet of ice that formed just in front of his fast-sliding feet and then faded away behind him. His hair blew in the wind of his passage, and several times he bounced high into the air, but always landed on sure feet.

For a second, Connor forgot the horror of the pitched battle raging up the streets of Alasdair as he watched the two powerful Petralists rushing toward Alasdair. He'd slid down every conceivable slope within walking distance of town in the winter, but the rough planks they used seemed laughable compared to the Petralists' elegant descent.

He couldn't wait to try it.

More Grandurians were descending the road from the plateau, while another force of Obrioners raced up River Rod toward the town. It looked like they'd arrive at about the same time

Would Alasdair survive the approaching storm?

CHAPTER 55

amish shoved the last quarter-loaf of honey-laced oat bread into his mouth as he and Blair reached the opening to the flood-under passage near a small shed up against the outer wall. Moments ago, all the Grandurian soldiers had rushed for the wall gate, giving them the perfect opportunity to scout the area for a potential break to freedom.

As they discussed the best way to marshal the townsfolk, and how fast they could slip everyone through if an evacuation proved necessary, Hamish popped a piece of soapstone into his mouth. It tasted cool and refreshing in the warm noon sun, like a sip from a mountain stream. In the short time he'd spent with Verena, she had taught him so much. He couldn't wait to see her again.

A thunderous roar sounded from the wall gate, followed by screaming. The two shared a surprised look, and jogged down Wall Street until they could see the wall gate around a row of homes.

Billowing flames filled the opening, and burning soldiers were fleeing the inferno. Many of them beat at flames that blackened skin, burned hair, and melted uniforms.

Hamish gagged while Blair retched. A pair of wagons that had been overturned to block the gate collapsed into cinders. Even as they watched, the flames condensed into a tall, writhing pillar before leaping skyward, only to plunge onto the cartwright's warehouse close to the gate. Fire enveloped the building, turning it into a gigantic torch.

"What's happening?" Blair gasped.

Soldiers shouting "Obrion!" rushed through the gate and fell upon the disorganized Grandurians and, without mercy, began cutting them down.

With a sinking feeling of dread, Hamish realized their peaceful town had become a battlefield.

"Come on, we have to warn everyone."

The fighting concentrated along central Market Street, but some of the Grandurians retreated away toward distant Cliff Street, with Obrioner soldiers in close pursuit. The two forces fought savagely, and soldiers fell screaming from both lines.

Such brutal death shook Hamish to the core. He'd never been a hunter like Connor, never been comfortable around blood. The screams and terrified faces of men who fell dying in the streets of Alasdair spurred him to run faster.

He led Blair up Wall Street, shouting for everyone to stay inside.

Then a soldier climbed atop the burning cartwright's warehouse and, laughing like a madman, stood within the inferno. Either he was insane and committing suicide, or he was a Guardian.

When the fire didn't consume him, Hamish whispered, "Guardian." Connor had explained some of what the Guardians could do.

Terrible things were about to happen.

The soldier, who had to be a Firetongue, threw his arms out wide, and the fire that enveloped him convulsed three times. Each time, it vomited a huge ball of fire.

One arced toward distant Cliff Street, while the second splashed down onto Market Street. The last thundered into the Grandurian soldiers fighting at the corner of Wall Street not far behind Hamish and Blair.

Screaming men scattered under the brutal onslaught, beating at the fire or trying to roll to put it out. Obrioner soldiers rushed in to finish off the wounded. Flames flowed through the street like water, and fastened upon the nearest houses.

Hamish pushed Blair farther up the street, "Tell everyone to gather at the Ashlar's. It's made of more stone."

As Blair rushed off, Hamish ran back to the two burning houses and pounded on the back doors. They were Cutter homes, and with the fathers imprisoned, both families were huddled in their family rooms.

Once they realized the danger, they followed Hamish out of the burning homes, and he led them at a run up Wall Street toward the Ashlar's house at the far end. Ahead of him, Blair was evacuating other families.

The few remaining Grandurians were charging after them, with Obrioner soldiers close behind. At the sight of the blackened, bloody soldiers with drawn weapons, Hamish spurred the villagers on.

If the soldiers caught up with them, would they pass by, or cut down the villagers who got in the way?

Then more fire rippled up the street past them on both sides before blocking the way and rising into a wall of flames. The women and children huddled around Hamish as the soldiers closed in from behind. The wall of fire began sliding toward them, as if the insane Firetongue didn't care that he'd kill them all along with the Grandurians.

Smoke choked Hamish, and he fell to his knees, unable to breathe. His eyes burned, and he tasted cinders. The hot air dug at his exposed skin like hundreds of tiny fingernails. There was nowhere to run.

He tried sucking harder on the soapstone, but felt nothing. In desperation, he felt with his Builder senses for the tiny crack in its core that would unlock its power.

Verena had said soapstone connected to water, and he needed water more than anything.

There! Hamish found the crack and wrenched it wide open.

Almost instantly, a fountain of water exploded up from the well in the square, and reared high above the town before thundering down upon the buildings of the square.

Despite the smoke choking him, Hamish howled, "No! Not the bakery!"

The street began to rumble, and a cresting wave of water, eight feet high, rolled into Wall Street and plunged into the flames blocking their way.

Water exploded into clouds of super-heated steam as the water extinguished. Hamish snapped the stone's power closed, fuming at Verena. Why hadn't she warned him something like this could happen?

Why did it have to be the bakery?

As soon as the dangerous clouds drifted high enough, Hamish led the way up the street at a run. Behind them, the Grandurian soldiers split through a side street.

A moment later, they reached Lilias, who was ushering everyone inside.

Stuart, who lived next door, shouted, "Some of you can hide in here."

When people kept crowding into the Ashlar's house, Cinaed appeared in her doorway and beckoned, "Come on, you'll be crowded in there. Our house is secure too."

No one paid her any heed, but all pressed into the Ashlar's house. Lilias called, "Once they calm down, I'll send some over."

Cinaed spun without a word and stalked back into her house. Stuart remained outside a moment longer, staring out at the spreading destruction.

At that moment, the ground rumbled outside the town, and arches of earth shot up over the wall from outside and crashed down onto the recently evacuated housed of Wall Street. Homes were knocked off their footings, and the advancing Obrioner soldiers swept away like kittens in a hurricane.

At the same time, a pillar of water surged up from Loch Wick, rearing a hundred feet before cascading down onto the cartwright's burning warehouse. The explosive hiss of steam shrieked through the town like a death knell.

Hamish wondered if the Firetongue survived. Even though the man was supposed to be an ally, he terrified Hamish more than the Grandurian soldiers ever had.

Instead of following everyone inside, Hamish rushed for the square.

"Where are you going?" Stuart called.

"I have to check on Neasa. Come on."

The brawny youth stepped out onto his porch, but his mother's voice pulled him up short. "Get inside before you get hurt!"

He shrugged apologetically and turned back to the house, shoulders slumped.

Hamish was so glad Cinaed was not his mother.

As he ran, he vowed that if Neasa was hurt, he'd never taste another rock again.

The square lay in shambles, with splintered wood and chunks of stone littering the area. The bakery and tavern were shattered, and several nearby buildings heavily damaged.

Hamish crawled through a narrow opening into the devastated interior of the bakery. Timbers and debris blocked much of the front room, and the heavenly smell of sweetbreads mingled with the clinging dust.

Neasa lay under an overturned table, with fresh baked bread in piles around her. As Hamish carefully moved the bread aside, Neasa groaned.

Thank the spirits. He could still suck on rocks.

He vowed instead to help her restore her oven as soon as possible. The town could not long survive without her breads and rolls and desserts. Maybe his mother would let her bake in their house?

"What are you doing, lad?" the fat baker mumbled as he moved the table. "The roof could collapse any second."

"I'm here to help." He tried to lift her to her feet, but she cried out and fell back, clutching at one leg.

As Jean so often pointed out, Hamish lacked any healing sense, so he decided to get Neasa to the healer's house.

He tried carrying her, but could barely lift her, so he dragged her by the arms out of the rubble, with her thanking him and urging him on. Then he rushed off to the blacksmith's shop and retrieved the wheel barrow. It took only a moment to load her into the barrow and then stack bread high in her lap.

"Leave the bread, lad," Neasa said through teeth gritted against the pain.

"You're hurt. You're getting delirious." He tucked a few more sweetbreads around her and gave her a reassuring smile. "Don't worry, I'll save as much as I can."

A dozen Grandurian soldiers rushed past the square, sprinting in full retreat toward the eastern gate. Hamish hoped the fighting was ending, and shoved a few dusty sweetbreads and two loaves of honey bread down his shirt. Then he heaved on the handles of the overloaded barrow.

They crossed Market Street as fast as Hamish could maneuver the delicate load. To his right, beyond the eastern gate, a large force of Grandurians was advancing on the town, led by a man who shone so bright, Hamish could not look right at him. To his left, a score of Obrioner soldiers ran toward the square, donning odd-looking darkened goggles. Two other groups of Obrioner slingers split off Market Street, heading for Wall Street.

The Firetongue, who Hamish now remembered Connor had called Captain Aonghus, stood atop the western wall beside the wall gate, facing a man who stood atop the southern wall.

Aonghus' laugh echoed all the way across town to Hamish, and sent shivers of fear racing down his spine. Fire rolled out the man's mouth and enveloped his hands as he brought them together sharply, and sheets of fire ripped through the air toward the other man.

Hamish wanted to look away, but couldn't, even though he didn't want to see the man die.

The man lifted his hands, and pillars of water erupted up out of the ground behind him, wrapped him in an upward-flowing waterfall, and deflected the flames away.

That had to be Kilian. Flames and water arced back and forth overhead as the Guardian fought the Petralist. Sheets of water exploded against spiraling columns of flames, while curtains of fiery rain battled whirling mists. Dense, super-heated steam drifted all through the battered town and clouded the entire scene in thick haze.

"Move, lad!" Neasa yelled, startling Hamish out of his stunned immobility.

They crossed to Cliff Street and approached the Healer's house, where a crowd of people were already gathered, pushing for a chance to get in. Hamish caught another view of the wall gate between buildings, and paused to watch the insane Captain Aonghus.

Just then a wave of water knocked Aonghus off the wall. He fell, but with a blast of fire from his clenched fists, drove himself back into the air, just like the flying Heatstone oven with Connor riding on it.

He landed on the granary tower.

Hands lifted high, fire erupted all over him and flowed down over the building. The dust-filled granary, always carefully guarded from the tiniest spark, exploded.

Hamish lost sight of Captain Aonghus as the man tumbled high over the wall toward Loch Wick.

"No, not the grain!" Hamish shouted, nearly dropping the barrow with its precious load of bread.

"Careful, lad," Neasa snapped.

"But the grain is gone."

She wiped a tear and said, "We'll manage, somehow."

In mournful silence, he pushed her to the Healer's house, where Jean helped him position Neasa on the kitchen table for lack of any other place.

As Jean tended to her, she asked, "What's happening outside? Reports are contradictory."

She seemed so calm, despite the flood of injuries, and that calm helped Hamish center his thoughts.

"It's worse than you could imagine. They're destroying all the food."

She turned to give him her full attention, her face disbelieving.

He hardly believed it himself. It was a disaster.

"Believe it," Hamish assured her. "They just blew up the granary, and the bakery ... got wrecked. They're trying to starve us out!"

"Forget about the food, grout-for-brain. There's more important things to worry about."

"You won't be saying that when you start getting hungry."

Through the open window, the distant sound of a bugle rang from outside of town.

"I wonder what that means," Jean said.

Hamish snapped his fingers with sudden realization.

"Lunch time."

CHAPTER 56

o!" Connor shouted and beat a fist against the unyielding stone of the cliff. "They're destroying the town!"

"It has to be done," Rory said gravely. "The Petralists need to be drawn out."

Before Connor could snarl a reply, a trumpet blew from Carbrey's camp.

Three Striders catapulted out of the trees at the base of the slope, already at full sprint, and raced in parallel courses up the long slope toward the plateau.

As the Striders tore up the slope, five Wingrunners sprinted down the slope from the manor and moved to intercept.

The two groups closed at phenomenal speeds. The Wingrunners whipped out long meteor hammers, while the Striders threw daggers or spiked granite balls. Both groups ducked or swerved as they raced close by each other.

At the last second, Donald swerved in toward a Wingrunner, so close Connor thought the two would collide. They didn't, but the Wingrunner staggered and fell, clutching at his abdomen where a bright streak of red blossomed. He hit the ground and tumbled before coming to a stop.

Connor recognized the fallen Wingrunner as the man who had lured Donald to the muddy trap and sent him flying off the edge of the plateau.

The remaining runners changed course and began an intricate, high-speed ballet, closing briefly before splitting and circling around for another pass.

Connor watched, captivated. From where he crouched, he could see the complex patterns the runners made as they crossed and then re-crossed each other's paths, each side trying to maneuver the other into a compromised position where they could deliver a death blow.

Blood pounded in his enhanced ears, and his breath quickened. He could see them so clearly, their faces locked in deadly concentration while their legs blurred. It was almost as if he stood among them. The sound of their footsteps was like the pattering of steady rain. Their torsos swayed sometimes almost horizontal as they tore through tight turns. Connor clenched the bare stone upon which he lay, and part of him wanted to rush down there and pit his own speed against theirs.

"Never seen a running battle so clear," Rory muttered.

"Are we holding the town?" Shona asked.

Connor checked. Gregor faced the legendary Grandurian Anton, and both had risen upon their earthen towers outside the long southern wall of Alasdair. Anton's tower stood a little taller with a crenellated top, while Gregor's was stouter. The ground between the two rippled and shook, as if unseen titans did battle just below the surface.

With Aonghus still swimming for the shore of the loch, Kilian moved along the southern wall, probably planning to meet up with the advancing reinforcements.

"Can we go yet?" Shona asked.

"I don't see the signal," Rory said.

"What are they waiting for?"

"Not everyone is committed. Still need the Rumblers and the Builders," Rory said.

As if in response to his words, Captain Peader and his dozen Boulders broke out of the edge of the forest and started up the slope in a ponderous charge. Not far behind, Carbrey himself followed, flanked by the two Blades, and a handful of soldiers.

Atop the plateau, the hulking Rumblers in their plate armor, huge shields, and massive swords, started down to meet Captain Peader's force. Ilse led the group, but Connor could not see Anika or Erich. With them came Wolfram with a small company almost identical to Carbrey's.

"Any time now if the generals are committed," Rory said.

Connor hoped they'd send the signal before fresh fighting erupted in the streets of Alasdair between the approaching reinforcements from both sides.

The Grandurian force was led by a tall, thin fellow wearing only leather armor and no visible weapon, but who blazed like a living sun. He led his force at a run toward the eastern gate.

"A Solas," Rory said. "Light bringer. Strong one, too. Even I can see that light."

Meanwhile, the subterranean duel of the earth movers suddenly erupted. A thin spear of earth shot out of the ground at Gregor's tower. Connor caught his breath, expecting to see the tower shattered, but the entire tower swayed to the side as if blown by an invisible wind, and the spear of earth only struck a glancing blow.

Half a heartbeat later, a gigantic claw of earth exploded out of the ground at the base of Anton's tower, connected to a trunk almost as wide as the tower itself. The claw ripped a huge chunk out of the middle of the Grandurian's tower, and the structure swayed dangerously.

Before Gregor could finish off his opponent, three more thick spears of earth shot out of the ground on different sides of Gregor's tower. They drove deep into the structure, and the entire thing collapsed into a pile of rubble.

Gregor fell hard, but instantly slid sideways as if dragged by an invisible hand. A wave of heavy earth crashed into the space he just vacated and would have buried him alive.

Then the slingers struck.

A force of Obrioners lunged out from behind cover, wearing strange, darkened goggles, and let fly at the Solas, barely thirty paces away.

Four missiles struck him, and he buckled under the assault, his face crushed. His blinding light abruptly winked out.

More slingers joined the attack, and rocks slammed into the advancing Grandurian lines. Few of them carried shields, and men fell senseless to the ground. The entire charge wavered.

At the same time, two other groups of slingers, previously hidden along the inner side of the southern wall, attacked. One group pummeled Kilian with half a dozen stones, and he toppled off the wall.

Other slingers launched an attack against Anton in his tower. Several stones struck the huge Sapper, but they bounced off without apparent effect.

Before a second wave could strike, the front face of his tower flowed upward to block the missiles. A wave of earth reared up over the wall and thundered down onto both groups of slingers, burying them and shattering several more buildings along Wall Street.

Connor worried for the families living in those houses, but breathed a sigh of relief to see the onslaught missed his home.

The ground under Kilian rippled, and his body slid along the south wall until it rested near Anton's tower.

No wonder Gregor worried so much about him. Anton was a one-man army.

Even he wasn't impervious. The distraction afforded by the slingers gave Gregor time to launch another attack. Countless spears of earth drove into the tower, shredding it and forcing Anton to leap from the top.

Even as he fell, a column of earth reared up to catch him, and a new tower formed under his feet. The ground that had been heaving and rolling only seconds ago flattened and calmed.

Down on the slope below the plateau, a single burning arrow shot high into the air.

Rory rose. "Our turn."

CHAPTER 57

s they rejoined the rest of the Fast Rollers and started running toward the junction with the hunting trail that would lead them down to Quarry Road, a single bugle sounded from far below on the battlefield.

"What is that?" Connor asked. He'd released the power of quartzite and removed the much smaller pebble from his mouth.

"Parley," Rory said.

"I thought Carbrey planned to keep fighting?"

"Once we confirm we have the prisoners, I guarantee they will. Now, run."

They ran hard, and Connor wished for basalt. He'd only been exploring his Guardian-Agor powers for a few days, but he'd already come to rely on them despite a lingering distrust. That distrust, built up over a lifetime of suppressing his Curse, would take time to overcome. Maybe when he understood his powers better, he could fully embrace them.

They raced down to the lookout rock. Tiny in the distance, Carbrey and Wolfram met in parley while their forces waited, poised to resume battle.

Connor led the group past the deep lochs at the very edge of the cliff above the plateau, and then down the steep switchback road. As they neared the manor house, a man in a simple tan coat stepped out of the main entrance.

"Take him," Rory said, and the group charged.

Instead of fleeing, the man stepped to meet them and dipped a hand into a leather satchel at his waist.

"Builder," Rory said.

Sure enough, the man tossed a small stone at them when they were but ten leaping strides away. The ground shuddered, and a wall of earth shot up to block their way.

Without slowing, two Fast Rollers crouched and cupped hands together. Tomas stepped into their waiting hands, and the men heaved, sending him soaring up over the wall.

A startled voice called from the far side, "Hey, you're not supposed to ..."

It cut off abruptly.

The rest of the company circled the wall and found Tomas tying up the unconscious Builder. Shona removed the man's satchel and threw it far across the plateau toward the road to Alasdair.

"Hurry." Rory led the group through the main doors into the great hall.

The huge room, spanning the width of the manor and rearing two stories high, stretched halfway down the length of the building. The giant fire pit was cold, and the torches dead. Nothing moved in the gloom.

"I don't like it, Captain," Tomas said. "Too quiet."

Rory nodded. "Be alert."

Connor led them at a run across the huge room and down a flight of stone steps. The last time they assaulted the manor, Grahame had explored the first sub-level without finding anyone, so he headed for the second.

As they descended into the gloom, two of the Fast Rollers held up small limestone pendants that glowed brightly. Tomas held one, but the light shone so dim, Connor wondered if he was imagining it.

"Told you," Tomas said.

As soon as they reached the second sub-level, Connor knew his guess was right. Torches burned here, and he heard Lady Isobel's shrill voice.

They stopped at a root cellar, with doors of heavy oak with thick steel hinges. It didn't matter.

Tomas and Shona ripped the doors off their hinges. Inside, they found Lord Gavin and his slaves and servants, including Bruce, sitting on the hard stone floor.

Rory kicked open the next locked room where Lady Isobel and Moira and a gaggle of female servants and slaves sat in wooden chairs.

As soon as the doors opened, Lady Isobel sniffed, "About time, filth. I will have you know, I am not one to tolerate this kind of abuse."

Shona frowned, but Connor shrugged. "She's always like that."

Then Bruce jumped to his feet. "Connor, is that you, lad?"

He grinned, "Have I got some stories for you."

As the prisoners filled the hall, Connor caught sight of Moira. She looked tired and dirty, but her eyes glowed with warmth when she saw him.

As soon as Lady Isobel exited her cell, she exclaimed, "You! Don't think for a moment I've forgotten how you tried to murder me, how you destroyed my beautiful oven."

"I didn't try to murder you," Connor said with forced calm. He was surprised to find the sight of an angry Lady Isobel no longer scared him. Instead he felt more pity for her than anything. What a tiny, unhappy world she lived in.

"Don't you contradict me, you ingrate!" She rounded on Captain Rory and shouted, "You, sir. I don't know why you allowed this criminal inside my house, but I demand you arrest him at once!"

"Keep it down," Rory said, "Or this rescue attempt may end very quickly."

"You mean you haven't driven the invaders out of my house yet?"

"We're working on it."

"Well, you're taking too long. Now arrest that boy and take me from this place."

Shona winked at Connor, "Lady Isobel, we've risked our lives to free you. Instead of insulting Captain Rory, I think some thanks are in order."

"And who are you, girl?" Lady Isobel demanded. She looked down her nose at Shona's battle leathers and sniffed.

"High Lady Shona."

Connor wanted to kiss Shona right there for the wonderful gift of witnessing Lady Isobel wilt before Shona. She dropped into a curtsy so deep, she almost fell over. "Oh, my lady, I didn't recognize you."

"No, you were too busy complaining so loud it's a wonder you haven't alerted the entire house."

"Well, I … "

"And did I hear that this boy destroyed a Heatstone oven you possessed?"

"He certainly did," Lady Isobel regained a little of her offended dignity.

"I will make sure to thank him properly later."

Lady Isobel's mouth fell open and for the first time in Connor's life, she was left struggling to find words.

Shona added softly, "Since the king himself has ordered any such contraband destroyed, I am sure you've planned to reward Connor handsomely for this act of patriotism."

Lady Isobel stammered, and Lord Gavin came to her rescue. "Of course, Lady Shona. As soon as we get out of here."

"See that you do it soon, before he leaves for Merkland to begin service as Guardian."

Lady Isobel looked from Shona to Connor, her mouth moving silently. Lord Gavin patted her hand.

"Come," Rory said. "We have to leave, and quickly. Where are the Cutters?"

Connor said, "They must be at the far end, the only other good place for cells."

"Lead the way, lad."

Moira moved to stand beside Connor and took his hand despite a glare from her mother. "Can it be true, Connor?"

"It's good to see you, Moira."

He squeezed her hand, then left to lead the way south to free his father and the other Cutters. He glanced back a couple of times, and wondered. It warmed his heart to see Moira, but seeing her near Shona drove home just how different they were. Moira was a simple, country lady and he would always see her as a friend, but he'd changed a lot in the past few days, and no longer felt the same allure from her.

As he struggled to understand the change, he led the group down a long corridor with storerooms spaced evenly down its length. He stepped through the door on the far side and started through a huge open room.

Only when Lady Isobel exclaimed, "Where are all my treasures?" did Connor really look where he was going. The room was normally packed full of furniture, trunks of clothes, and other trinkets. She rarely used any of it, but seemed to take joy in simply piling it as high as possible.

The room stood completely empty but for a small table standing against the closed door on the far wall.

"What type of treasures were housed here?" Rory asked.

"All sorts of things. My things." She stepped away, hands out, as if to touch the missing possessions.

"Were they important?"

"Of course, you brainless lout."

"Keep your voice down," Rory said off-handed, but he looked to Connor and raised an eyebrow in question.

Connor shrugged. "She never actually used any of it."

"They were heirlooms," Lady Isobel exclaimed. "And don't you take that tone with me, you filthy Linn murderer."

Shona said, "You're not dead yet, but if you don't shut your mouth, that may change."

"Hurry, lad," Rory said with a frown. "Men, on the alert."

The Fast Rollers drew weapons, which startled the prisoners into a tight group in the center of the party, with Bruce in front. They hurried for the far door, but before they got halfway across the room, it opened and someone stepped through.

Verena.

CHAPTER 58

ressed in her usual silk blouse, Verena gave Connor a wide smile, "Hello, Connor. That's far enough."

Behind her, a pair of soldiers placed a wide, square stone on the small table beside the door.

Connor's heart sank. It was all another trap.

"Hi, Verena," he said in a resigned voice.

Shona gave him an angry glare and stepped to the front of the group. "I'll handle this." She raised her sword and charged.

Connor moved to stop her, but Rory caught his arm. "Don't interfere, lad."

Shona closed fast on Verena, but the Builder raised one eyebrow, turned, and touched the stone sitting against the wall.

A ferocious wind blasted out of the stone. It struck the entire group and drove them back a step. Lady Isobel shrieked as the wind caught in the many folds of her skirts and tumbled her across the room, with her servants scrambling to help.

While Connor and the others fought to hold their ground, Shona snarled like a lioness and, one heavy step after another, drove forward through the wind.

Verena, still smiling, reached back and accepted a small leather sack from one of the soldiers. She dumped it into the wind.

Flour.

White powder exploded into the room, and most of it hit Shona in the face, instantly coating her in white. She muttered something vile and rubbed at her eyes. She stumbled, and the wind instantly tossed her back. She fell and slid despite slapping uselessly against the smooth stone floor until Rory caught her and helped her back to her feet.

"Are you willing to surrender now?" Verena asked pleasantly.

"You're dead," Shona spat. The threat would have been far more effective if she hadn't been covered in flour.

Verena whistled, and the door behind them opened. Anika and Erich, the sibling Petralists, stepped into the room, followed by half a dozen crossbowmen.

Anika smiled happily. "My Rory, we good time wrestle now."

"I'm all yours, Anika."

"Oh, please," Shona said. "We're at war here, Captain."

The hulking Erich scowled from his sister to Rory and said, "Surrender or many hurts. I beat you two times."

"I am sick of all the talking," Shona snarled, and her body hardened into the perfect lines of granite power. "Captain, I want to … chugga … doo."

"What was that?"

Her voice trailed off into a groan and she toppled slowly forward and fell hard on her face.

On the far side of the room, Verena clapped her hands, "I just love it when she does that."

"What did you do?" Connor dropped to the floor beside Shona.

Verena waved the sack she'd dumped into the wind. "Wasn't just flour she ran into."

"Weakening agent," Rory said.

"Think it got us too, Captain?" Tomas muttered, and spat on the floor.

"Don't know, but we can't risk it. Untap, lads."

"Those crossbows are looking pretty ugly right now, sir," Tomas said.

Rory nodded. "Anika's going to break me in half."

Erich tossed several pairs of steel shackles into the room, and their clanging on the floor sounded to Connor like the slamming of prison doors.

"Surrender, or many hurts."

Anika shrugged and blew Rory a kiss.

Rory looked from Verena to the Petralists, and their crossbow-wielding troops, to the shackles, clearly torn. Connor checked on Shona and found her breathing, but unconscious.

They'd failed. So many people had died to give them a chance to free the prisoners, to end this conflict. So many more would be endangered if they failed.

Would his own family die?

The thought enraged Connor. He looked from the unconscious form of Shona to Moira, who huddled with her family. She looked back at him, terror in her eyes, but trusting him to help.

He couldn't let her down. He had to act, had to do something.

He slipped a hand into his pouch, although he wasn't sure what he could do. Quartzite wouldn't help, and he didn't have any igneous stones. There had to be something.

His fingers closed around the wafer of marble.

The crazed look he'd seen in Captain Aonghus' face was exactly what he needed. He leaned over Shona, as if to check on her, and slid the wafer under his tongue.

Erich took a step into the room. "No wait. Put on bracelet."

Verena giggled, "Erich, just don't talk."

Connor sucked hard on the marble, but it was a rock. It tasted like rock.

Then it didn't.

A jolt of spicy heat erupted into his mouth from the stone, and Connor gasped at the intensity of it. He loved spicy food, but even the spice roots he ate during the Sogail failed to match the riot of flavor exploding across his tongue.

Verena said, "Connor, what are you doing?"

He couldn't answer. The heat intensified until it felt like his mouth was actually burning.

Erich lost patience and said, "Shoot Captain."

Rory snarled, "Max tap, lads!"

As one, the Fast Rollers' skin faded to gray and their bodies swelled with power.

"Shoot all!" Erich roared.

Crossbows shuddered as bolts leaped into the room. Lady Isobel shrieked and pushed Moira aside to throw herself to the floor, followed by her entire retinue. Moira stumbled, right in the line of fire.

Not Moira.

Time slowed and Connor did the only thing he could. Despite the pain, he drew heavily upon the marble power and shouted in agony and fear and anger.

A jet of fire exploded from his mouth.

It shot past Moira, so close her clothes smoldered. She screamed and threw herself to the side. The flames boiled onward and consumed the crossbow bolts.

Erich and Anika leaped back into the mass of hapless soldiers as the flames reached for them. The entire group fell back through the far door and slammed it shut. The fire beat against the door and it ignited.

Connor's breath failed, but the flames continued to pour forth. He couldn't stop it, did not dare close his mouth for fear of burning off his own lips. He remembered all too clearly how trying to smother the Heatstone oven had failed.

He couldn't breathe through his mouth, so he tried using his nose. The hairs in his nostrils singed.

Heat blistered his face. The air smelled like sulfur, and the flames roared like a nuall.

And still the fire poured from his mouth.

Connor couldn't see. The fire filled his vision and drowned out all sound. He screamed with fear and pain as the flames continued to drive out of him across the room.

Then strong hands grabbed his shoulders and spun him around. Voices shrieked as people dove again to the floor under the fiery stream. Connor tipped his head back to avoid killing anyone, and the flames tore up into the ceiling, setting ancient beams alight.

Rory's voice shouted in his ear, "Turn it off!"

Connor shook his head, and winced when the motion sent flames splashing around the room.

"Don't!" Rory shouted. "I'll guide you."

The Captain spun him until he faced Verena. She retreated and slammed the heavy door shut.

Facing directly into the wind blew the fire back toward them. The air was filling with smoke, and the heat was rising to dangerous levels.

Out of the corner of his eye, Connor saw Rory cock his arm back and throw his sword. A second later, something crashed, and the wind stopped.

Rory took Connor's shoulders, "Forward lad, through the door."

As they walked, Connor aimed the stream of fire at the floor to try and see. It blackened the floor, and through the crimson sheets, he saw Verena's air stone lying on the floor, blasting air up into the ceiling. The door beside it crackled and popped, and then collapsed in a cloud of glowing cinders.

Rory shouted, "You, girl, show us the nearest stairs, and someone grab that wind stone."

Moira edged close, her face streaked with soot, and her eyes staring wide with fear. He wanted to comfort her, but couldn't do anything but vomit fire.

There had to be a way to turn it off, but even though he tried to will the fire to cease, nothing seemed to work. He tried to spit it out, but the searing-hot marble burned into the skin under his tongue and stuck fast. Fire raged through his mouth in an unstoppable storm. He could barely breathe the charred air, and his limbs trembled with suppressed fear.

No wonder Aonghus acted crazy. Using marble pushed one to the brink of self-destruction.

Under Moira's direction, Rory guided Connor through the manor house, setting room after room ablaze. A raging Lady Isobel had to be forcibly restrained from assaulting him. Connor didn't blame her. He wanted to beat himself.

Every step tore at his heart. They were leaving his father behind.

When they reached the kitchen, Lady Isobel shrieked anew, "You filthy Linn demon! Not again."

Connor turned until he could see her out of the corner of his eye and shrugged. The movement of his head sent boiling sheets of fire spewing across the kitchen, instantly re-igniting the already blackened walls.

Connor tried not to feel so satisfied with such a fitting revenge, but couldn't quite manage it. If Lady Isobel hadn't been such a vicious, thieving petty woman, he never would have been on that barge.

He never would have been captured.

Never would have met Verena. Never would have saved Shona.

His village would not have been invaded. Probably.

As conflicting thoughts warred in his brain, he let Rory guide him toward the final door. Outside and in the wide open space, Connor could see a little better. The group broke into a run, with his fifty foot tongue of fire leading the way.

At the top of the switchback road, Connor caught sight of Loch Sholto, the flooded quarry situated close by, right at the very edge of the cliff. He shrugged off Rory's hands and dove headlong into it.

The shocking cold of the loch embraced him. He savored it, but the flames didn't stop. They only set the water boiling around him. A little water finally slipped into his mouth and loosened the marble wafer's hold against his skin. Risking the burning of his lips, he spat the wafer out.

Still burning, it fell into the deep blackness of the loch. Connor hung there in the water for a moment, exhausted, letting the water fill his mouth and ease the pain. He watched the marble sink further and further along the outer wall of the loch, until it glimmered hundreds of feet below.

For a second, it illuminated something dark that clung to the outer wall of the loch, and then it hit the bottom and winked out.

Bruce helped Connor climb onto the bank. Far below, the manor house burned. Even farther, Carbrey's army was retreating, while on the plateau a group of soldiers had broken off from the main force and approached the road leading up to their position.

Rory clapped Connor on the shoulder, "You are full of surprises, lad. Come on, we'd best get out of here."

Tomas slung the still-unconscious Shona over one shoulder, and the group moved to follow Rory toward the trail into the mountains.

As Connor moved to the front of the party, he met Moira's gaze. She regarded him with fear and awe, and looked away after only a second. Barely a trace of their old friendship remained in her eyes.

She knew he was Cursed, and nothing could ever be the same.

CHAPTER 59

ooks like the fighting is over for now," Hamish said as he entered the healer's kitchen. "The Grandurians have been driven out."

Jean breathed a sigh of relief, and Neasa banged a fist onto the tabletop. "Tallan take those warmongers for wrecking our town before leaving."

"How is it out there?" Jean asked.

Hamish rubbed dirty hands across his grime-coated face. The whites of his eyes stood out against the dirt and lines of exhaustion. "Not good. They're still digging soldiers and people from the rubble. A lot of them are injured pretty bad." He spoke fast, his words spilling over each other, his eyes wild. "We can't salvage anything from the granary."

Jean noted the signs of growing hysteria and moved to his side. She took his face in her hands and forced him to look at her. "It'll be all right. We'll get through this."

He relaxed under her touch. "The army Healers aren't keeping up."

"Jean can go."

An exhausted but determined Mhairi stood in the doorway. "We've stabilized everyone here. Go with Hamish and see if you can help."

Hamish scooped up Jean's healer bag while she tied on a fresh apron and checked the many pouches of supplies in her various pockets.

Mhairi hugged her, "I'm proud of you, girl."

"I'm just trying to do what you taught me."

"No, dear, you've exceeded your training. Be safe out there. Have Hamish help. Off with you, now."

Jean followed Hamish into the rubble-filled streets, and the sight made her gasp. She'd been too busy to venture outside since the battle, and stared with horror. The Healer house remained untouched, but most of the houses on Cliff Street either bore marks of fire, or leaned on unsteady foundations, suffering heavy damage.

Mud and rubble clogged the streets as they made their way toward the square, passable only by scampering along planks laid across the roads in meandering paths. Gray haze hung heavy in the air, tasting of ash and smelling of wet cinders. Breathing proved difficult, and she covered her nose with one sleeve.

As bad as Cliff Street looked, Market Street was far worse. The fighting must have concentrated there, because no building stood unscathed. Many of the shops and warehouses lay in ruin, some still smoldering.

In the square, mud and debris had been pushed back to make space for the wounded. Neasa's shop was reduced to little more than a pile of rubble, and most of the other buildings surrounding the square had fared little better.

Dead bodies were stacked near Neasa's shattered bakery, while row after row of injured lay across the square. Three Healers, dressed in brown, were working on the most severe cases. Jean's eyes scanned the long rows, and the calm, calculating part of her mind catalogued the injuries and began sorting them by severity.

After taking a steadying breath to center her mind and lock away the horror that threatened to overwhelm her, Jean moved across the square to where injured men moaned on cots or jackets or bare ground while waiting to be treated.

One soldier, who stood nearby as a sentry, motioned Jean and Hamish away, but Jean said, "I am a local healer. I came to help."

He frowned, "Not much you can do here, lass. Better to stay inside."

"We'll see about that." Jean dropped to her knees beside the nearest injured soldier, who held a blood-soaked bandage over his shoulder. She gently peeled it back and bit her lip at the sight of the torn flesh.

The sentry took a threatening step forward, "I told you to move off, lass."

"Hamish, see if you can find some clean water."

He rushed off, and she spared a glance at the irritated sentry. "If you have nothing better to do, find me some clean bandages."

Then she set to work.

The next half hour passed in a blur as Jean stitched wounds, set broken bones, and worked to alleviate some of the overwhelming anguish. She refused to acknowledge the suffering and focused only on diagnosis and treatment, moving with practiced efficiency.

Cries of alarm drew her attention from her current patient, a local girl with a badly broken jaw. Thick, white mist billowed into the square from the eastern edge of town. It was clearly not natural, as its leading edge was too defined, too thick, and it rolled forward with implacable purpose.

More Petralists.

Soldiers reached for weapons, and villagers shrank back with cries of fear. Jean hushed the frightened girl lying before her. There was nothing else she could do but wait and see what devilry the fog carried with it.

In seconds, it rolled over her, consuming the square and obscuring all in billowing white. Jean could not help but hold her breath, her body tense against some kind of assault.

Instead, the mist pulsed against her exposed skin like hundreds of tiny, soft brushes that scrubbed way the filth and grime and clinging reek.

Voices called out in fear all around her, but Jean tipped her face up and threw her arms wide, exulting in the wonder of the moment. After so much destruction, she welcomed this tiny mercy. The mist smelled like new-washed clothing and the air on a crisp winter day, and for a second the horrors of battle faded away.

The mist rolled on through town, leaving the square sparkling in its wake. Rubble still lay piled everywhere, but blackened timbers now glistened with a thin sheen of dew. Many of the soldiers and injured looked after the mist with fear and made signs of warding against the Tallan, but Jean breathed deep the air scrubbed clean of ash and smoke.

Hamish entered the square, and Jean moved to join him watching the mist roll toward the wall gate. He grinned, "That tasted just like soapstone."

"It felt wonderful," she agreed. "What do you think it means?"

Before Hamish could answer, a sharp cry of alarm drew their attention to the eastern length of Market Street. At the far end, a solitary figure strode through the gate, straight toward a group of half a dozen soldiers, who drew weapons and charged.

Hamish sucked in a sharp breath. "Kilian!"

Jean stared closer at the man who Connor had called a Water Moccasin. His hair was dark and he wore loose-fitting trousers and tunic over his lanky frame. A sword and long dagger swung at his side, and fingers of water that glistened like quicksilver flowed along the granite streets in front of him.

He looked angry.

Even from a distance, Jean trembled at the sight of him. He approached the onrushing soldiers with an implacable stride, and she wanted to scream at them to run away. Couldn't they see they didn't stand a chance against him? She didn't know what a Water Moccasin was, but something about the man Kilian filled her with dread.

He looked like an approaching storm.

The soldiers closed on Kilian, and their war cries rang through Alasdair.

Instead of drawing his sword, Kilian made a shooing gesture. The fingers of water slipping along the ground at his feet surged up like living serpents and struck faster than Jean could follow.

Soldiers cried out in alarm, and one of them cut wildly at the striking ropes of water, but to no avail. The liquid tendrils wrapped the soldiers in glistening bonds, lifted them high, and tossed them tumbling down Market Street back to the square.

Jean winced at the sight, but could not help but catalogue the host of broken bones, contusions, and concussions. None of those soldiers would be fit for duty for a long time.

Without slowing, Kilian advanced down Market Street as more soldiers massed in the square. Jean could not believe they meant to face him after what happened to their comrades.

Hamish caught her arm and dragged her to the side. "Best get out of the way. I saw him fighting Captain Aonghus, but I don't think the slingers will get lucky again."

She followed his gaze to a group of slingers concealed among the ranks of soldiers.

A wild shout turned her back to the western side of town. A fiery blur raced up the devastated Market Street, moving faster than a galloping horse. By the time she realized the onrushing apparition was a man, wreathed in flames, laughing wildly, he was already shooting into the square.

As soldiers dove out of the way to let the super-fast, burning man through, Hamish cried, "That's Aonghus!"

Jean spun to follow Aonghus, who left streamers of fire in his wake, as he closed on Kilian.

"Boil in your own cauldron, devil!" Aonghus bellowed, and vomited an enormous gout of flame that blasted forward to fully engulf Kilian.

For three heartbeats, the crimson fires roared around Kilian, obscuring him from view. Aonghus skidded to a halt in the center of the street, burning hands thrown wide, laughing like a madman. Jean felt queasy, and feared what they would see when the fires subsided, but could not look away.

Then with the sound of a crashing wave, the thick column of flames winked out of existence.

Kilian stood unharmed in the street, his eyes blazing with living fire, while flames trickled out his grinning mouth.

Stunned silence fell across the town, and Aonghus' shocked whisper echoed all the way back to the square.

"Impossible."

Kilian said, "You have no idea."

Then he brought his hands together with the sound of a thunderclap. A wave of water rose to engulf Aonghus, whose fire hissed like a hundred angry snakes before the waters snuffed them out.

The wave knocked Aonghus off his feet before coalescing into a roiling sphere that rolled back toward the square, scattering soldiers again. Jean caught sight of a laughing Aonghus tumbling wildly inside the sphere before it bore him out the far side of the square, down Market Street, and out the wall gate. She doubted it would stop before crashing into the wick.

Kilian stalked forward, all trace of fire gone, with fingers of water again leading the way. As he approached the square, he called out, "Men of Obrion, we can do this the hard way if you prefer, but know my patience is at an end. Resist me at your own peril."

They didn't listen.

Slingers unleashed a volley of stones, and two dozen soldiers charged in unison.

A blur of water overwhelmed the soldiers. Their war cries changed to screams that were cut short into gurgling protests as the entire force of soldiers was carried away in a churning flood right through town and out the far gate.

Unopposed, Kilian strode into the square.

Townsfolk panicked. Men, women and children, who had come for healing, fled screaming. Jean was buffeted by the mob, powerless to help or to calm them.

Across the square, she caught sight of Connor's younger brother Blair, who had just entered the square carrying an injured child. The fleeing mob knocked him stumbling into the shattered remnants of the tavern where he fell hard against the front wall.

A heavy timber that had been balancing over the door, fell with a shriek of protesting wood.

Jean cried out in horror, powerless to do anything but watch. Before the timber could crush the children, a tendril of water whipped out and caught it. Then another wrapped gently around the children and lifted them from the rubble.

Jean turned back to face the approaching Kilian and studied him more closely. Despite his angry expression, for the first time she noticed the laugh lines around his eyes and mouth, and the slight bluish tint to his hair.

The inconsistency of his act of mercy startled her and left her feeling shaken, unsure of herself. How could this man, one of the violent invaders responsible for so much destruction, care what happened to a pair of children in a stampede he had triggered?

As Kilian approached, people began begging for mercy, and Jean moved to intercept him.

"What are you doing?" Hamish hissed.

Kilian noticed her advance, and paused, one eyebrow raised in surprise. Jean continued her advance despite the fear that set her limbs shaking, trying to focus on the act of mercy he'd shown Blair instead of his terrifying violence.

Before she could speak, Kilian surprised her by making an extravagant bow and giving her a dashing smile. "What can I do for you, little lady?"

Jean felt her face flush, and for a second she struggled to find words. That irritated her, and she drew herself up tall. "I will not allow you to harm my patients."

Kilian smiled, and his eyes twinkled with mirth. "You're a brave one, aren't you?" His voice was strong and clear, and he spoke with just a hint of an accent that Jean found surprisingly pleasant.

She reminded herself that he was part of the reason so many people had suffered that day. "Call it what you like, but I warn you not to cause any more suffering here. I didn't work so hard to treat these people only to have you murder them."

Kilian's face hardened with anger. "Don't blame me for the stupidity of your general."

"I blame you for your actions, and the destruction you caused here."

"Don't judge before you know the facts," he snarled.

How dare he echo one of the creeds by which Jean lived her life!

She advanced a step and pointed an accusing finger at him. "Don't try justifying your cruelty. The suffering here is entirely your fault."

"Your boldness is turning to folly, girl."

Hamish appeared beside Jean then and hefted a broken plank. "You lay a finger on her and I'll kill you."

Jean wanted to slap Hamish for interfering. She'd already pushed the man pretty hard.

Kilian surprised her again by laughing. He threw Hamish a cocky salute and winked at Jean. "I'm liking this town more and more. I'm glad to see Connor's not the only Obrioner worth knowing."

"You know Connor?"

"I do. He's a frustrating young man, with more bravery than good sense."

Jean smiled, "I'll tell him you said that."

"You tell him to look deep. He's in a position to do much good."

"I will."

"And I will respect your wishes, my brave young healer."

Kilian made a sweeping gesture with one hand. Fingers of water slithered across the square to each of the injured soldiers, spread beneath them, and gently lifted them a finger's width off the ground. Then they began floating across the square and down Market Street on those rippling beds of water.

"Those men will reach their camp safely. What happens to them after that is out of my hands."

He turned to the three Healers and said, "Remove your forces from this town. You have two minutes."

The men saluted and headed for the wall gate.

Kilian turned toward the far side of the square, but paused and made a gesturing motion. A finger of water appeared bearing a soldier's sword belt, complete with sheathed sword and dagger.

The Water Moccasin brought it over and handed it to Hamish. "If you're going to defend your girl, you need a real weapon, boy."

Hamish took the sword with a look of wonder.

Jean frowned, "I can take care of myself."

"Be that as it may," Kilian said gravely, "allow the young man to do his duty too."

He gave her another extravagant bow and walked away.

Near the wall gate, a trumpet sounded as the remaining soldiers in Alasdair began their retreat.

Hamish, clutching his new sword close, said, "So it was all for nothing, then?"

"No," Jean said. "We learned something. Lilias was right. It's time to make our own freedom."

CHAPTER 60

onnor startled awake and sat up on his blanket. Night had fallen, and the camp lay quiet. He felt surprisingly good, despite the long day. He patted his worn sandstone amulet and wondered what he'd do when its healing powers ran out.

He looked around, trying to figure out what had awakened him. He guessed he'd slept maybe a couple of hours after a long afternoon spent helping Marcas. He'd tried to learn as much as he could without showing off the power of his sculpted pendant.

As night fell, he'd learned from Tomas that the general considered the day's foray a success. The Grandurian Solas and one Wingrunner had died while none of the Obrioner Guardians perished. He did not seem to count the many men who died fighting in Alasdair.

What angered Connor the most was news that Kilian had driven the army from Alasdair. After paying such a high price to take it, he'd been furious that they'd left the broken town to the Grandurians.

Tomas had explained, "More fighting there would have been pointless and cost both sides many lives. Better to leave them in peace."

"In Grandurian hands!"

"Would you prefer they kept fighting until everyone lay dead, and the town shattered to ruin? Because that's what would have happened."

A little later, there was a stir among the Fast Rollers. Tomas had explained that the prisoner had arrived from Merkland and was being held in a tiny cave in the mountain nearby, reachable only via a narrow ravine.

Connor knew the area well. He and Hamish had played there as kids, storing their 'treasures' as part of a game of Guards and Robbers. He wished he could see the heavily guarded prisoner who General Wolfram wanted so badly.

Could they really be a child?

A voice called his name so softly he barely heard it. It sounded like Verena, and his heart quickened to hear her.

He slipped into his boots and moved toward the trees, searching for her. He was surprised by how much he wanted to see her big blue eyes, but worried what could have driven her to risk approaching so close. How did she pass the scouts? How did she pass Gregor?

Her voice came again, faint but close. "Connor, come to the river."

He slipped past sleeping men and into the deep shadow along the banks of the Lower Wick, but saw nothing.

How could Verena speak so softly and still remain unseen? Was this another of her powers?

Down by the river, when he was sure no soldiers lurked in the shadows, he called softly, "Verena, where are you?"

Nothing. He waited for three long minutes, but saw nothing in the darkness, heard nothing but the steady gurgle of the Wick, and the normal night sounds of frogs and insects.

Frustrated, he moved further downriver, scanning the bank for any sign of her. It was too dark to look for tracks even though the moon had risen.

After a few more minutes of steady searching, Connor was about to turn back when he heard a splash and what sounded like a girl humming.

The underbrush grew thick there along the river, so it took him a few minutes to find a narrow passage. He ghosted through, not wanting to scare Verena away.

He stepped through the last screen of brush into a narrow space right at the water's edge. Thirty feet out in the river, a woman surfaced and threw her long hair back over her head.

It wasn't Verena.

It was Shona.

Her skin glowed softly white in the dim moonlight, and Connor stared until she dove again. Only then did he realize she wasn't wearing her battle leathers.

They were piled right at his feet, close to a white towel that hung from a nearby branch.

"Connor, are you spying on me?"

She had surfaced again, much closer to shore this time, and stood in water up to her bare shoulders.

Instead of shrieking or shouting for him to leave, Shona was smiling. She took a step forward and rose a little out of the water.

Connor threw out a hand and cried, "Wait. Stay where you are?"

Shona's rich laugh floated over the water and caressed his ears. "Why so shy? We've floated this very river together."

"That was different."

Panic set his hands shaking. Even though he and Hamish had tried to spy on Jean this summer, they hadn't actually expected to see the girls bathing. He liked kissing Shona, but the thought of seeing her unclothed terrified him.

She was beautiful, but she was a high lady. When her father found out she'd kissed him, his life would be in enough peril.

If he found out about this …

Connor started to back away.

"Don't you leave me, Connor," Shona snapped and took another step toward shore. The water slid lower, and her skin glowed brighter. His heart pounded in his ears, and his face flushed with rising heat.

"Fine, but stay where you are."

Shona cocked her head and smiled again. "You dare command me?"

"Of course not. It's for your own good, though."

"I know what's good for me, Connor."

She leaned forward, "You either come in here and kiss me again, or I'll come out and kiss you."

I am so dead.

CHAPTER 61

onnor found it hard to think.

He should just run and risk Shona's wrath. Then again, if her father was going to kill him anyway, why not really earn the old man's wrath?

The sight of Shona standing in the water, with the soft light playing over her shoulders was rapidly convincing him to accept her offer.

Before he could decide, the night sky suddenly lit, and the trees shook with thunder that pealed through the forest out of the clear night sky.

Connor spun. The source of the bright light came from the direction of camp. Worse, a billowing fireball burst up into view from behind the trees.

"The camp is under attack," Shona hissed.

Startled, he spun back to find her standing beside him, already wrapping a cotton bath robe around herself.

He wasn't sure what to feel. Part of him breathed a sigh of relief that he'd escaped Shona's ultimatum, but part of him raged at the interruption.

Shona scooped up her battle leathers and ran barefoot through the brush back toward the trail. "Come on."

The way the robe clung to her, he'd follow her just about anywhere. Still, he forced his mind to work a little. "How do you know it's an attack? Maybe Captain Aonghus burped in his sleep."

"That's not funny." She set a fast pace upriver and back to camp where they stepped into a scene of chaos.

Carbrey's command tent was simply gone, replaced by a blackened crater. Smaller tents and equipment lay strewn across the clearing, tangled amongst many unmoving bodies. Fires burned wild all through camp. Men were running and shouting and trying to don armor and grab up weapons and fight fires and give directions all at once.

Thick smoke rolled through the clearing, making everything look ethereal, like ghosts moving through a nightmare.

Shona ran through the press to Rory's camp on the far side. Connor followed, already coughing. They found Rory and most of his unit gathered. The rest of the Fast Rollers were sprawled unmoving on the ground.

Connor stared in horror. What devilry could have dropped those powerful warriors? Fear began replacing his initial shock.

"Captain, what's going on?" Shona called.

Rory looked relieved at seeing Shona, and didn't bother commenting on her appearance. "We've been attacked. I didn't see it strike, but the fumes are poisonous to Boulders."

"Nonsense. I'm tapping my powers now and they are … unna … fudda."

Connor leaped forward to catch her as her voice slurred just as it had in the manor house. He almost made it.

Shona fell hard onto her face.

He dropped to his knees beside her, and found her unconscious, breathing shallow. He arranged her robe to cover her a little better, brushed her hair from her face, and his eyes lingered on the curve of her cheek, the soft glow of her skin. Even though many might think him cracked, he was glad he'd told her to stay in the water.

His feelings for Shona were strong, but not entirely clear. Her motive for taking such an interest in him were cloudy, and having accepted her offer by the river would have played into whatever scheme she was developing. Her attention flattered him, but he didn't trust it yet.

Rory pulled him from the brief reverie. "Don't use granite, lad."

"I don't have any."

"Good." He gripped Connor's shoulder. "Join the defenders and watch yourself, lad."

"Defenders? From what?"

Distant screams and the clear ringing of clashing steel sounded from the north. Rory grimaced.

"Grandurians."

Then he strode purposefully through camp, shouting orders, driving back the bedlam with a growing circle of restored discipline. Within seconds entire companies were catching up weapons and running north toward the battle.

Connor raced through the mobilizing camp, dodging soldiers still strapping on armor, trying not to inhale the acrid smoke too deeply. He found his small bedroll and scooped up his bow and arrows before following Rory.

The army rushed north through the forest, bearing Connor along like the current of the Upper Wick. As he ran, Connor reached into his belt pouch and found the basalt Shona had given him. He absorbed it all.

A moment later they reached the northern edge of the forest and, as soldiers shouted battle cries and surged forward, Connor paused to stare.

Wolfram's army had attacked down the slope and initially cut down the small company of soldiers who first responded. Light blazed like miniature suns in several places around the perimeter of the battlefield, bathing the entire area in a patchwork twilight.

Hundreds of newly mobilized Obrioner soldiers, led by Captain Rory, charged toward the much smaller Grandurian force, and it looked like they would smash through Wolfram's lines without pause.

The ground shook and walls of earth burst from the ground to block the way. They towered fifteen feet before toppling forward. Rory, who could not tap his granite strength, scrambled with his soldiers to escape the sudden danger, but some of the men did not react quickly enough, while a couple fell. The entire charge degenerated into a mass of milling men, unable to run.

With a shout of defiance that echoed over the battlefield, Rory reversed course and charged straight at the falling wall.

Connor took an involuntary step forward, his eyes locked onto the big man, one hand raised in a useless gesture to help. Hundreds of stone weight of earthen wall fell upon the defiant warrior.

Rory burst through the far side amid a spray of earth. The wall to either side of him disintegrated as it hit the ground, melting back into the earth. The breaking wave of earth tossed dozens of soldiers through the air to crash down onto their comrades.

Rory saluted to his left. Connor followed his gaze and noticed Gregor. The giant Sentry nodded gravely, and Rory raised his sword to resume the charge.

In that second, something fell from the sky. Connor caught the barest hint of movement before it exploded into the very center of the closely packed army at Rory's heels.

Fire blasted in every direction, tossing men aside like chips of stone under the Ashlar's hammer. The entire company disintegrated into a jumbled mass of burning soldiers.

Then the flames leaped skyward in a single pulsing column that arced north and thundered down upon the smaller Grandurian army.

Captain Aonghus stood near Gregor, hands raised, fire dripping from his mouth.

Screams rent the night air from both armies, and the stomach-turning reek of burned flesh and hair clung to Connor's nose.

Rory's army resumed its charge, but a small group of hulking Rumblers broke from the Grandurian line and moved to intercept. The six giant warriors, encased in heavy armor and bearing gigantic weapons met Rory and his two hundred.

The Rumblers, who had come from the north and therefore had not breathed the poisonous fumes that prevented Rory's army from tapping granite, shattered the leading edge of the army. Soldiers flowed around them and encircled them in a wall of steel, but the Rumblers tossed men aside like babies and shattered them with heavy blows.

For a moment, Connor lost sight of Rory in the crush. Then, as the Rumbler who held the very center of the line smashed three soldiers aside with a single blow of his hammer, Rory dove in close and punched the huge Rumbler in the side of the knee.

The leg buckled, so he must have tapped granite despite the danger. The Rumbler toppled, and Rory surged to his feet, his roar of victory echoing across the battlefield.

Then he too collapsed.

Soldiers tackled the mighty Rumbler and fought to pin his arms and legs while two of them attacked his eyes with thin bladed daggers. The Rumbler convulsed off the ground and shed soldiers like a man bursting up through the surface of a loch. Then he fell lifeless to the earth next to the motionless Rory.

Other Rumblers plowed through the ranks of soldiers and wreaked terrible vengeance on them.

Captain Aonghus unleashed a barrage of pulsing fire against the Rumblers. Whip-like streamers snaked over the Obrioners to drive at the Rumblers' eyes, or wrap them in pillars of billowing flame.

The giant soldiers fell back under the onslaught with armor melting to their stone-hard bodies. Meanwhile, the ground under the entire battlefield groaned and shifted ominously underfoot as Gregor fought Anton for dominance of the earth.

Even though his arrows would do little against the Rumblers, Connor drew and fired faster than he ever had in his life, driven by rage at the horror of battle, and by Rory's heroism. The fighting raged a good hundred yards away, a long shot for perfect accuracy, but he didn't care.

His first arrow ricocheted off one Rumbler's helmet and, although it did not damage, the soldier raised a hand to shield his eyes.

The eyes.

That's why Rory dared tap granite, despite the heavy price, to give his men a chance at the Rumbler's eye.

Connor ran for higher ground where his arrows could

prove most deadly. Battle rage coursed through him, an urge to leap into the fray despite the danger. The feeling thrilled as much as terrified him, amplified by the screaming of men, the clear ringing of steel on steel, and the sickening sound of steel rending flesh. The sharp scent of burning hair and the stomach-wrenching aroma of cooked meat joined in his mind with bright blood that seemed to coat everything, particularly the unmoving bodies of fallen soldiers.

Connor passed behind General Carbrey who stood calmly amid the chaos of battle, shouting orders that his Striders raced to deliver. The two Blades flanked him, but even as Connor caught sight of them, they moved toward the right flank of the battle line.

Connor finally saw General Wolfram, surrounded by a small personal guard, including his remaining Wingrunners. The two Allcarvers, so similar to Carbrey's Blades, advanced at a trot to meet their deadly counterparts.

As the pairs closed on each other, soldiers scattered out of the way. When only ten strides separated them, all four drew their twin swords and charged.

Their swords leaped like living things, slashing so fast they blurred. The four men pivoted and twisted around each other, swords clashing with showers of sparks. In seconds, Connor lost track of who was who as they turned, slashed, and spun in an intricate, graceful dance that moved so fast Connor could not follow individual strikes.

Connor ran past it all to the flank of Alasdair Mountain that formed the western boundary of the valley, and climbed about thirty feet up. Just as he turned to find targets, movement above him caught his attention, and he cringed, expecting another exploding fireball.

Instead something huge swooped out of the night sky in a steep dive just above the mountainside. It would pass to his right, about a hundred feet up. Could it be another great stone pedra? Connor knocked an arrow and took aim despite the futility of the gesture if it proved to be another monster.

It wasn't a pedra.

It was a wagon.

CHAPTER 62

wagon?

Connor blinked a few times to try to clear his vision. The incredible sight of a large wooden wagon did not change. Could the Grandurians have pushed it off the flanks of the mountain, or constructed another giant catapult?

No, it wasn't falling. Instead it dove steeply, like a bird, not a falling stone. It swooped overhead and continued its steep descent to the south, headed toward the main campsite. As it passed, it banked slightly, revealing a glimpse of several people riding inside.

Connor spun back to the battlefield, but no one else was looking in his direction.

He turned back and, after a couple seconds scanning the night sky, found it again. The flying wagon had all but disappeared in the deeper shadows of the night sky to the south, but he caught a whisper of movement at the edge of vision.

Connor didn't hesitate. He reached for the boundless energy of basalt and raced after it.

The wagon glided fast, but Connor ran faster. He poured on the speed, drawing deep from the basalt, to the point where his legs started to ache in the early stages of the Fracking. He held that tap-rate and angled his course up along the steep slope until he hurtled just above the tree line, so fast he tore across ground so steep he'd normally never maintain purchase.

Brush clung to this part of the slope, little more than deeper shadows in the night. Using the skills learned from Donald, he shifted his shoulders, altering course by tiny degrees, and he closed on the wagon, avoiding collisions by sheer instinct.

He risked occasional glances into the sky to confirm the wagon maintained its course. It leveled out about fifty feet above the slope, just barely higher than his position, and he closed further. Within seconds, the fires of Carbrey's camp glowed from his right.

If the wagon banked in that direction, they'd reach the mostly deserted camp in seconds. Why would they go there?

Shona.

She and the Guardians who had tapped their granite power would still be lying helpless on the ground. Connor's blood ran cold as he realized that must be their purpose. If they murdered the granite Guardians, they'd shift the balance of power firmly to Wolfram's advantage.

The wagon began to slow, but instead of turning toward the camp, it banked to follow the curve of the mountain farther east around a rocky outcrop. As it did so, it tipped toward the slope where Connor ran, giving him another glimpse of those who rode inside.

Verena sat at the very front, while Kilian sat in the back with Anika and Erich and a handful of soldiers.

He should have known. Somehow Verena had given the big blocky wagon wings and flown it down the mountain.

What else could the very cute, very dangerous girl do?

Another group of torches beckoned from the slope of the mountain ahead. It had to be the destination.

The lights illuminated the cliff where lay the hidden cave Connor and Hamish had played pirates in. The cave that held the prisoner.

The cliff rose out of a clearing at the western edge of the forest, reached by a tight ravine where two towering Boulders stood guard. The ravine, little more than a narrow cut in the cliff, led up to a small ledge about twenty-five feet above the ground. The narrow cave mouth marred the cliff face like a black scar, flanked by two more hulking Boulders. One of them was the youthful-faced Captain Peader.

As the wagon entered the torchlight, the two Boulders stationed at the base of the ravine stared in shock for just a heartbeat. It was enough.

Even as they raised weapons, a thin trickle of water spilled over the edge of the wagon to the earth, glistening in the torchlight like a stream of silver. Half a heartbeat later, geysers erupted under the feet of the Boulders. Water rolled up their torsos and encased them to their necks.

The water hardened to ice, and the soldiers' shouts of challenge changed to cries of alarm. The mighty Guardians strained against the ice encasing them, and cracks started to form. They would break free in seconds.

More water fused to the columns until the Guardians stood imprisoned within a wall of ice a dozen feet thick.

Archers seated in the rear of the wagon loosed a volley at Captain Peader and the other boulder stationed upon the ledge as the wagon floated closer. The Guardians ignored the arrows that bounced off armor and skin, dropped their swords, and reached for stones to throw.

The wagon swept closer, and the sibling Petralists leaped off and tackled Captain Peadar and his companion. The four collided like an avalanche and commenced beating on each other.

Connor tapped his basalt again and raced past the entrapped Boulders, whose lips were already turning blue from the cold. He wished he had granite so he could shatter their prison, but couldn't think of a way to free them fast enough to help with the fighting.

So he scampered up the narrow ravine and peeked over the edge just as Captain Peader's companion staggered from a particularly heavy blow and slipped off the ledge.

The mighty siblings tackled Captain Peader and, although he struggled valiantly, they inched him steadily toward the edge.

Connor ground his teeth and had to resist the urge to raise his bow. The arrows would not hurt the Rumblers. He could shoot Kilian or the archers in the wagon, but that wouldn't help.

He had to do something!

Then Connor remembered the quartzite. He still had a little. He wasn't sure how it would help, the only other stone he carried was marble, and he didn't dare use that again so soon after the fiasco at the manor house. Quartzite was metamorphic, so he should be safe from double-tap sickness.

He popped the quartzite into his mouth, and within seconds the pool of warmth bled into his cheek from the tiny stone and gathered in the center of his head.

Connor tapped it a little, and the warmth flowed into his eyes and ears. After a brief flash of pain in his temples, and a wave of disorientation, his vision sharpened and a tumult of sounds crashed into his mind.

Connor focused, but instead of zooming in on the struggling Peadar, his gaze centered on Verena. She sat on the front seat of the wagon, hands flickering across a series of crystal-like levers.

His gaze flowed over her face and he couldn't help but drink in the details of her eyes narrowed in concentration, of her cute button nose, and the curve of her cheek.

She bit her lower lip, and he grinned at the innocence of the gesture. Then she spoke, and her sweet voice sounded loud in his enhanced ears, even though she talked in a normal conversational tone.

"Wolfram, ten seconds out."

How could she speak with Wolfram? Connor had seen him in the battle facing Carbrey? What new power was she using?

The attackers shouted in victory and heaved the struggling Peadar off the ledge.

He shouted, "Tallan take you all!"

Then he disappeared over the edge.

Connor caught a glimpse of the captain's furious expression before he fell from view, and for a split second, he *felt* the captain slipping through the air.

At the base of the ravine, a sharp crack of shattering ice, followed by running feet rang loud in his ears. The other

Boulders were coming, but would be too late.

The wagon floated right up against the ledge, and Kilian rose to join the two Rumblers on the ledge even as they moved toward the mouth of the small cave.

They were about to free the prisoner.

"No!"

Connor jumped to his feet and lifted his bow to shoot Kilian, but in that second, as rage burned through him like marble fire, he *felt* everything. The wagon, the Rumblers, Kilian, everyone. It was like the air all around became an extension of his senses, and he could feel everything around him as if with fingers of thought.

Connor did not understand how it was possible, but if he could touch them, he could push them.

In the wagon, everyone turned at his cry. Kilian looked surprised, and Verena started to smile.

Connor pushed against them all as hard as he could. He threw out his hands and shouted, "I can't let you do this!"

Violent wind roared up through the ravine and knocked Connor to the ledge. It rippled past him and drove the Rumblers back to the edge of the ledge. They teetered and grabbed for the wagon for support.

The wind tumbled Kilian back into the wagon, knocked the four archers on top of him, and tumbled Verena right off her seat.

She cried out in surprise and grabbed for any handhold to catch herself. She yanked a couple of the crystal-like levers, lost her grip, and fell from sight.

The wagon lurched away, dragging Erich and Anika with it. They clung to the side as the wagon accelerated to the right and started to descend.

The wind died, and Connor climbed to his knees just as the wagon crashed through the tops of several trees before disappearing from his enhanced vision. A few seconds later, a loud splash echoed from the direction of the river.

Angry voices muttered from that direction, but Connor didn't bother to listen. Instead he scurried to the edge of the ledge.

Verena lay on the ground not far from the shattered ice, with Captain Peader moving toward her. Verena looked up and their eyes met. Her glare could have melted ice.

"Are you all right?" he called down to her.

"How did you do that?"

He had no idea, but she didn't need to know that. "I wanted to make sure no one got hurt."

"I think you broke my leg," she snapped.

"I wanted to make sure no one got seriously hurt."

She opened her mouth to shout an angry retort, paused, and glared again. "You are the most annoying boy I've ever known."

Just then, Captain Rory and a score of battered soldiers ran into the torchlight.

"Captain, you're all right!" Rory was the last person Connor expected to see.

Captain Rory grinned up at Connor. "Must've taken a mighty small dose of whatever that weakening agent is because it wore off pretty fast."

He joined Captain Peader who stood above Verena. "You've caused a lot of hurt, lass."

Verena flashed him a charming smile. "It was my pleasure, Captain."

Rory grunted and motioned one of the soldiers to lift her.

Connor half expected her to punch the man, "Careful. She's more dangerous than she looks."

"I'm not speaking to you, Connor."

"You just did."

"Well, not any more."

"Are you sure?"

Silence.

Rory motioned a couple of soldiers up the ravine. "Connor, you'll need to report what happened here."

"Of course. The other attackers are in the river."

"We'll see to it." He made a gesture, and a soldier rushed off toward camp.

"What about the battle?" Connor asked.

"Grandurians withdrew. Impressive maneuver, that. We might've pursued, but Donald brought word of the surprise attack down here."

Two soldiers reached the top of the ravine and joined Connor on the ledge. They pushed aside a black curtain blocking the mouth of the cave, and stepped into the lighted interior. Connor followed, eager to see the truth of the prisoner Wolfram risked so much in the failed attempt to free.

The soldiers re-appeared a moment later, leading a small boy. He looked to be about six, with classic Grandurian blond hair and blue eyes. He looked frightened, a little dirty, and terribly vulnerable walking between the two soldiers.

Connor dropped to his knees, unable to stand on suddenly shaky legs. His stomach lurched as the truth struck him like a physical blow.

Wolfram had been telling the truth.

"Are you all right?" one soldier asked.

"No." Connor clutched his head as he fought to reconcile the truth with everything he'd experienced over the past few days.

A small hand touched his shoulder, and he looked into the boy's eyes. Only then did he notice the unnerving intensity to the boy's gaze. He regarded Connor with far more maturity than a six year-old should have.

"You'll be all right," the boy said with a little smile.

The soldiers pulled the boy along, and Connor rose to follow, filled with a granite-hard resolve.

He would learn the truth, no matter what.

CHAPTER 63

amish burst into Mhairi's kitchen where Lilias and Jean waited at the round table. "There's definitely a battle going on south of town."

"What did you see?" Lilias asked, her face calm although she clutched Jean's hand.

"I made it half a mile down River Road." He gripped the pommel of his sheathed sword where it hung at his waist. The unfamiliar weight had slowed him some, but he'd vowed never to face another soldier unarmed. "No guards anywhere. Looks like they took everyone to the fight."

"Did you see Connor?" Jean asked, her face worried.

Hamish shook his head. "I didn't get close enough to see anyone clearly."

He paused as images of the battle played through his mind. If only he'd stayed farther away. He'd seen too clearly the burning bodies, heard the screams of the dying. He shivered at the brutality of it.

"It was even worse than when they were fighting in the streets. They …" His voice trailed off, and he stared unseeing at his feet. The hard bread stick he'd been chewing on tasted like ash in his mouth.

He spit it out and breathed deep the clean scent of herbs that always hung in Mhairi's kitchen. He wondered how Connor could handle it. Despite having a sword, Hamish didn't want to go to battle.

Lilias surprised him out of his reverie by taking his hands in her warm grip. He hadn't even noticed her rise from the table. She drew him to it, pressed him down into a chair, and passed him a mug.

He started to raise it to his lips, but paused and frowned at Jean. "Is this your grandmother's tonic?"

"Of course not. You don't need that yet. It's just water."

He sighed. Water tasted so bland after power rocks. He was tempted to drop a bit of marble into the mug to spice it up.

Lilias sat across the table from him, her gaze intense. "You're sure the Grandurians aren't watching the town?"

"I didn't see anyone."

"All right. They must be counting on everyone cowering in their homes."

"That's not a bad idea," Hamish said.

She patted his hand. "No, Hamish. We have to leave. All of us."

Jean leaned forward, her blue eyes glittering with excitement. "Are you sure we should?"

"Yes. I doubt we'll get another chance this good. You both know the plan. Small groups. We'll gather in the wood beyond the Lower Wick."

Hamish's throat felt dry and he gulped more water. They were really going to do it. He gripped his sword and rose. If Connor could be brave, so could he.

Before they separated, Lilias said, "No lights. Keep everyone quiet. Be quick." She gripped Hamish's hand and then hugged Jean.

While Jean ran to tell Mhairi, and Lilias moved toward the west side of town, Hamish bolted for his own home. He'd start with his family and, with the help of his seven siblings, gather the eastern side of town.

Ten minutes later he returned to the square after sending several groups toward the wall gate. No cry of warning had sounded. As soon as he met up with Jean, they'd head to the meeting place together.

The square lay empty, cloaked in shadow. While he waited, he reached for his belt pouch and felt for the tiny pieces of stone Verena had given him. She'd taught him so much, praised him for figuring out how to tap marble, and had taught him how to adjust the amount of power, and even how to shut it off again.

She'd explained that the more of a stone's power he unlocked at once, the greater the effect, but it would burn out more quickly. Once a stone's power was consumed, it crumbled to dust. He'd been surprised at the pang of sadness he'd felt as remains of the piece of marble he'd been practicing with had blown from his hand.

Lilias appeared across the square with Jean, followed by a group of a score of villagers. He moved to meet them.

"Did you get everyone?" Lilias asked.

"Everyone that would leave."

She frowned. "We can't force anyone to take the risk for freedom. All we can do is give them the chance."

She raised her voice. "Listen to me, everyone. We don't have much time. The battle may be over soon. Stay quiet, stick together, and follow Hamish."

"I don't think so."

A universal gasp swept the group as a bright light appeared above the rubble where Lord Gavin's pavilion had stood, held aloft by Captain Ilse.

Limestone. It had to be.

Despite the flash of fear at knowing they were discovered, Hamish couldn't help but wish he could get a piece of limestone. Verena had told him a little about it, but they hadn't had time to practice with it.

Lights blazed to life in each of the entrances to the square, illuminating more than a score of Grandurian soldiers. Hamish drew his sword with a shaking hand. He would fight to protect these people, but he'd hoped to actually learn how to use the sword first.

Then his heart sank as everyone he'd sent toward the wall gate trudged into the square, herded by yet more Grandurian soldiers.

How had the Grandurians found out?

Captain Ilse raised her voice, "You people will return to your homes immediately. My men are positioned along the wall and at the town gates. Anyone caught attempting to leave town will be executed along with their entire family."

Many villagers cried out in fear, and most of them broke for their homes without further urging. Hamish wanted to shout for them to stop, to stand together, but could not. His parents ushered the rest of his family toward their home, and he very nearly ran to join them. His father glanced back once, and in his eyes, Hamish saw terrible fear.

Hamish was one of the leaders of the revolt. He could not run with the others, could not abandon Lilias.

She was right! They couldn't just give up.

He and Jean both drew closer to Lilias, who stood like an island of calm in the center of the rapidly emptying square.

Beside Captain Ilse walked Cinaed. In the blue-white light of the limestone, the blocky woman's red-blond hair looked like blood. Behind her walked Stuart, looking uncomfortable.

"I told you I'd see you fall," Cinaed said to Lilias.

"How did you know?"

Hamish wanted to drive the woman through. How could she be so mean? They'd purposefully left her for last. While he and Jean were to lead the last group toward the wall gate, Lilias had planned to invite Cinaed to join the exodus. They had figured that even had she wanted to thwart them, it would have been too late.

"You're not the only one with spies in town," Cinaed gloated. "You would have sacrificed our husbands, risked Daor for everyone! I will guarantee everyone remains safe."

"You can't promise that."

"I can!" She pointed at Captain Ilse, who stood nearby, her face impassive. "She promised. As long as everyone obeys me, I will save this village."

"You're a fool," Lilias said. As Cinaed sputtered with rage, she spoke to Captain Ilse, "I hold you responsible for what you've unleashed upon this town."

"I do what I must, and I cannot allow insurrection here." She gestured at Lilias, and two soldiers carrying shackles moved toward her.

Hamish brandished his sword and jumped in front of Lilias. "Stay back, or you're dead!"

They dropped the shackles and whipped out their swords. Hamish tried to hold his ground, to set his weapon like they did, but he couldn't keep the tip from shaking. Actually, it looked like he was trying to point it at both of them at the same time, so he snarled and pretended that was what he intended.

His hand started to cramp, and his legs shook. His mouth had gone dry, and he struggled to breathe normally.

Behind the soldiers, Stuart looked shocked that he'd stand his ground, and the sight of the big traitor bolstered Hamish's courage. If only he'd hit Stuart with more than manure earlier.

Captain Ilse said, "Boy, you don't want to die tonight."

"I won't let you hurt her."

"If she comes quietly, she will not be harmed. She will join her husband at the manor house."

Lilias pushed his sword gently down. "Thank you for standing with me, Hamish, but I will not allow you to suffer in my stead." She pulled him close and kissed his forehead. "I assume full responsibility."

Jean drew Hamish aside, and he let his arm drop to his side. He didn't dare try to sheath it. The soldiers would just laugh at him. He fingered his belt pouch.

Should he unleash his new-found powers on them?

Jean pulled him closer and whispered, "Stop it, Hamish. Trust me."

He could not deny her, and squeezed her hand. It broke his heart to see Lilias shackled.

Cinaed gloated. "You've fallen, Lilias. You're through. I've been granted full authority here!"

Lilias looked upon her with pity. "You think tyranny leads to salvation? Your ignorance is going to kill us all."

Cinaed laughed. "Who's in chains?" She turned from Lilias and pointed at Hamish. "Boy, give me that sword!"

"No!"

Cinaed glared, but Jean spoke first. "I'll deal with it."

"You? You've betrayed me," Cinaed said to Jean. "I had such high hopes for you."

Jean took the sword from Hamish's surprised grip and moved toward Cinaed. "What choice did I have until now? I couldn't stop her. All I could do was hope you'd set things right."

"What?" Hamish exclaimed. He stared at Jean in open-mouthed astonishment. "How can you say that?"

She gave him such a look of scorn that Hamish retreated a step. "You're such a fool, Hamish. Did you really think we could escape?"

"Yes." His voice sounded weak even to him, and he hated her for it.

"That's why I couldn't confide in you." Jean turned to Cinaed. "I know all about their plans. I can help you make sure no one tries anything like this again."

Cinaed grinned, "Well done, Jean. You really are worthy."

Jean made a little curtsy and moved to stand beside Stuart. He tentatively draped a meaty arm across her shoulders and she grinned up at him.

Hamish couldn't take any more. Lilias in chains, their plan ruined, Jean and Stuart together!

Jean's betrayal burned through him like a piece of swallowed marble tapped wide open. He'd risked his life for her, swore to protect her from all harm. He'd never dreamed she'd do this.

Even as he struggled to comprehend how she could betray them, how he'd missed seeing her for what she was, Stuart said, "Better run home, Hamish, before you get hurt."

It was too much. Hamish bolted.

Stuart's laughter followed him out of the square, but Jean's words cut like daggers through his heart.

"Stuart, you're so brave. I'm glad you're here."

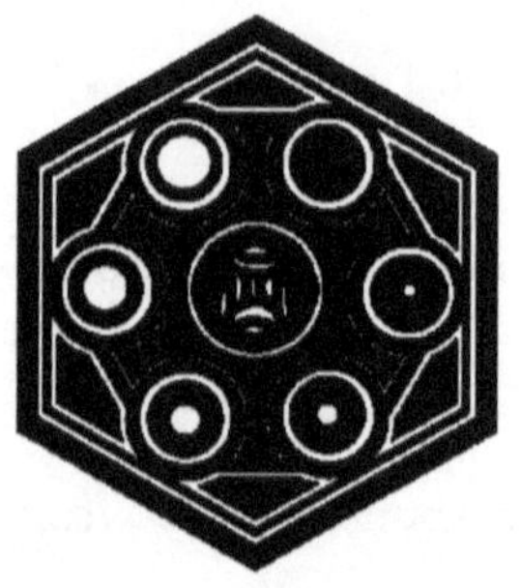

CHAPTER 64

onnor descended from the ledge, and had to help the boy over some of the bigger rocks. The lad had a strong, sure grip, and he walked unafraid, scanning the area as if trying to take in as many details as possible.

As they headed back to camp, his thoughts and emotions whirled. How could Carbrey accept so much death and pain, all to keep a little boy prisoner? Even the wonder of the flying wagon faded under the onslaught of questions.

Verena sat near a small fire in the center of the camp, her broken leg extended awkwardly, her face set in a mask of pain. Rory sat on an upturned log across the fire from her. Twenty soldiers, including two of Rory's Fast Rollers cordoned off the area, but they let Connor through.

Connor crouched next to Verena. "You were right all along."

She shook her head slowly and grimaced with pain. "Oh, Connor, I wish you'd believed me sooner."

"Hasn't the Healer looked at your leg yet?"

Verena snorted. "Not hardly."

Rory said, "Lots of good people died and were wounded tonight. The Healers are swamped. It'll be a while."

"If ever," Verena said. "I don't blame them really."

Seeing her in such obvious pain tore at Connor's heart. She was their prisoner, and he shuddered to think what would happen to her. He'd done this.

All she'd been doing was trying to save a little boy.

He could help. Connor reached for her leg with one hand, and pulled the sandstone sculpture from under his shirt with the other.

Verena cringed and grabbed his hand. "So this is how the torture starts, is it?"

He gently pushed her hand away, "You know me better than that, Verena."

"Do I?"

Her wide blue eyes seemed to glow in the firelight, and the honest question in her gaze saddened him.

"I'll show you."

He placed a gentle hand on her leg again, and this time she did not try to push him away. He gripped the pendant, closed his eyes, and drew heavily upon its warm healing power.

"Is that sandstone?"

"Shush."

Healing power rolled through Connor's arm, and buoyed by its gentle tide, he focused on her leg. His senses expanded, and he could see the jagged break and multiple cracks that spiraled through her bone. He slid his healing sight along her ripped tendon and bruised flesh.

He surrounded the wound with healing power and guided it inward. The bone began to fuse, cracks faded, and the tendons sewed themselves together.

Verena gasped and placed her hands over his. The warmth of her skin seemed to magnify the heat of the healing power, and rolled back up his arm.

He kept his hold on her leg for a full minute after the healing had completed, reluctant to break the moment. He opened his eyes and found her staring at him, her face scant inches from his own, her eyes wider than ever and somehow deeper.

She leaned across the inches that separated them, and her lips pressed softly against his, warm and gentle, and somehow incredibly intimate. Connor barely allowed himself to breathe, but when he did, he breathed deep the smell of her. She smelled of dirt and sweat and fear, and at the same time, like mint and clover.

Tomas whistled, and Rory said, "Enough of that, lad."

Connor cringed as Verena broke the kiss. Rory had seen him kiss Shona. Kissing the enemy in front of him risked a severe beating.

Still, he did not regret letting Verena kiss him. His heart sang, and his lips continued to tingle long after she broke contact.

"You're the most amazing man I've ever met." She gave him a dazzling smile, leaned back and said loudly, "You healed my leg."

"But you didn't bother healing me."

Shona stood across the fire from them, dressed in battle leathers, hands on her hips.

The memory of her in the bath robe flashed through his mind, followed by her standing in the river, skin glowing in the moonlight as she beckoned him into the water for a kiss.

The memories wilted under her angry stare.

Before Connor could move, Verena wrapped an arm around his neck and kissed him again on the cheek. She gave Shona a friendly smile, but spoke to Connor. "Thanks again."

When she released him, Connor moved to Shona's side. "Are you all right?" If he pretended the kiss never happened, maybe she'd forget about it.

She glared at him.

"You know we're going to have to torture her."

"Is that really necessary?" He tried to keep the worry from showing on his face. He didn't want Shona hurting Verena out of pure spite.

"I doubt she'll share her secrets willingly."

"Not with you," Verena said with a scornful look. Then she gave Connor a sunny smile. "But I'd give you anything you want, Connor."

He felt his cheeks grow hot under her intense stare, but fought to hide it since Shona was watching so close.

Time to change the subject.

"Shona, is there anything I can do to help you feel better?"

Her glare subsided and she slid one finger down his cheek. In a much calmer tone she said, "Oh, I can think of a couple of things you can do to help."

"Not now." General Carbrey marched into the circle. "So, this is the young Builder we've heard so much about?"

Verena rose smoothly to her feet and executed a graceful curtsy despite the dirt and the fact that she wore trousers instead of a skirt. "It's a pleasure to meet you, general."

He grunted. "Cooperate, and it may be." Then he turned to Connor and extended his hand. "I owe you a debt for thwarting that attack, lad."

"Thank you, sir. I was just doing my duty."

Gathering his courage, he added, "Sir, may I ask who the boy is?"

"Information you don't need to know, lad. Right now I need you up that hill to Wolfram. Tell him we have his Builder. I applaud his tenacity. The attack tonight was well orchestrated, but we all know he's trapped."

Carbrey's gaze bored into Connor, "I order him to surrender by dawn tomorrow, or this young lady dies by public execution."

Verena's face paled, and Connor barely bit back a cry of protest.

"After that, I guarantee I'll wipe his force from the earth, no matter the cost. This game is over."

CHAPTER 65

onnor passed through the battlefield on his way up to the plateau to deliver Carbrey's demands, and stared at the devastation. The ground lay in rippled folds from Gregor's battle with Anton, while wide swatches of scorched earth marked where Aonghus had struck. Charred bits of armor and twisted weapons testified of his effectiveness.

Bodies lay stacked in piles, waiting for burial. Blood soaked the ground, and the entire area smelled of vomit and smoke. The taste of ash clung inside Connor's mouth. Deep shadows covered the area, driven back occasionally by the flickering torchlight of men still gathering the dead and hunting for survivors.

Connor tapped his basalt and raced past, onto the slope up to the plateau. There he slowed to think.

Verena had spoken the truth right from the start. The Grandurians were sincere in their desire to free the imprisoned boy, but Connor still did not understand why the boy was taken in the first place. There had to be an explanation.

Besides, no matter how they claimed to want nothing but justice, the Grandurians had caused the death and suffering of many, and brought war to Connor's peaceful town.

The more he thought, the more frustrated he became, until a towering anger churned through him. Driven by that anger, he extracted the piece of marble from his pouch and popped it into his mouth.

He sucked deep, and the explosion of spice drove away the ash taste of battle, and triggered a wave of icy fear. He welcomed the growing pain and sucked harder. The last time he'd used marble, he'd burned down the manor and failed to rescue his father. It fit his mood perfectly.

The pain rippled from his mouth into the rest of his body. He deserved it. After all, it was his fault Verena was captured, his fault so many things had happened. He mulled that over as he walked, but could not figure out how he could have responded differently. He still hadn't figured out how to explain everything to General Wolfram by the time he arrived at the plateau.

The burned-out shell of the manor huddled amid its undamaged outbuildings like a corpse surrounded by mourners. The roof had collapsed and only individual blackened timbers remained standing above crumpled stone walls. A pall of smoke hung around the building like a funeral shroud, and the stench of cinders hung heavy in the air. A large command tent almost identical to Carbrey's had risen nearby, and Connor was ushered inside immediately.

The interior of the tent almost perfectly mirrored Carbrey's. Wolfram sat in a ladder-back chair behind a round table laden with maps and parchments. The general still wore his dirt-smeared armor. His long mustache drooped around his mouth, and furrows lined his brow where none had been before.

As soon as Connor entered the tent, Wolfram rose and came around the table, his face grim. "I am deeply disappointed in you, Connor."

The rebuke cut him deep. Connor tried to stand tall, tried to meet the angry general's stare, but couldn't.

"I am sorry you feel that way, sir. Maybe if you hadn't been so busy killing people I could have been of more service."

"You shame yourself," Wolfram said, his voice angry for the first time. "Do you have any idea what you've done?"

"Sir, I don't understand what's going on enough to have any idea what I'm doing."

Wolfram regarded him for a moment before saying, "Perhaps you are right."

He returned to his chair and motioned Connor to take a camp stool. Connor settled hesitantly onto it. He needed to deliver Carbrey's ultimatum, but did not want to risk angering Wolfram.

Captain Ilse entered, but Wolfram motioned her to silence. "Connor, you are in a unique position. Kilian returned only moments ago and reported how you foiled the rescue attempt."

At least Kilian was all right. "I was just defending the camp, sir."

"Perhaps, but you prevented Kilian from freeing the boy."

"I know that now."

"You saw him?"

Connor nodded. "But I don't understand."

"You need to." Wolfram leaned forward, his face intent. "His name is Nicklaus. He is distantly related to the king of Granadure. Agents of your High Lord Dougal kidnapped him exactly twenty-seven days ago."

"Why? What makes him so important?"

"The reasons are complex, and delve into arcane matters even I barely understand. Nicklaus is the product of a unique bloodline and shows potential for an exceptionally rare Petralist gift. I believe your High Lord Dougal intends to use that gift to unleash terrible destruction upon my people. It is worth more to him than any other treasure."

Connor rocked back as if struck as everything snapped into clarity. Was that why Shona favored him with such attention? Did she see only his gift, the potential gain she might reap by leading him to her father?

No. She didn't need to play such games. He had been traveling to Merkland when they met. She knew his deepest desire was to obtain Patronage.

"I don't believe you." Connor tried to sound confident, but he couldn't see through the lies. What else weren't they telling him?

"Yes, you do."

"That's why we took Shona," Ilse said. "To exchange her for Nicklaus."

So many people dead, so much suffering. The Grandurians were responsible. They had to be. He fought to reconcile everything he'd seen, everything he'd learned.

One of Jean's favorite sayings came to mine. Look deep, see clear. He tried, but couldn't pierce the haze.

Ilse added, "It's true, Connor. Unfortunately, we ended up here instead of back in Granadure. Then you helped her escape before we could exchange her for Nicklaus."

"I didn't know."

"Be that as it may," Wolfram said. "This situation is entirely a result of those events. We are here to free Nicklaus. I will not allow him to remain prisoner another day, nor suffer under Dougal's hands."

Connor slumped, unable to argue that much. "I stopped you tonight."

Ilse said, "Connor, you might just be our worst enemy."

She was right. He'd spirited Shona out of their hands, blocked the attempted rescue that very night. If not for him, they might have succeeded in their plans.

The thought should have elated him as a loyal Obrioner.

Instead, it only left him feeling confused. He did love his country. He wanted only to protect his town. And yet, after seeing Nicklaus, he wanted to see the boy set free too, wanted the Grandurians to return home in peace.

He was dreaming.

"I didn't mean it. I was just trying to protect my family."

"Ask yourself why Carbrey insists on pursuing this war," Wolfram said.

"He can't let you invade our country."

"He invaded ours first."

Connor didn't know what to say. He couldn't argue with Wolfram. He was too confused, needed time to think.

He stood. "General Wolfram, I bring word from General Carbrey."

"Very well."

Connor took a steadying breath and related Carbrey's terms. The tent felt hot, and the constant smell of cinders was making him queasy. He needed to finish, to get outside and clear his head.

Wolfram shook his head. "No, Connor. We both know those terms are unacceptable."

"I am finished being reasonable. Here are *my* terms. Carbrey will deliver Nicklaus and Verena, and we will withdraw. Otherwise, I will no longer show restraint. My forces will raze Alasdair and kill everyone who resides there."

"You'd murder everyone?" Connor exclaimed, horrified. "Where's your mercy now?"

Wolfram continued, his voice ringing. "We will flood the quarry and fight with no quarter given. We will see who wins the day, but I swear to you, boy, that I will not allow Carbrey's aggression to go unanswered. I am in my wrath, and you have yet to see me begin to fight."

Connor quailed back from Wolfram's fury. Gone was the pleasant control the general normally projected. For the first time, Connor saw his true power, and it terrified him.

He spun to flee, but just then Kilian threw the tent flap aside and strode in. At the sight of Connor, he glared and advanced, one hand outstretched as if to throttle him.

Connor dodged to the side, but Ilse stood there, and she too looked angry.

"Boy, I'm going to flay you alive," Kilian growled.

There was nowhere to flee. Enemies surrounded him on all sides. Connor sucked deep on the marble stone under his tongue, and the flash of pain triggered his anger.

He shouted at Ilse, "It's your fault!"

"What are you talking about?"

"Why didn't you tell me about Nicklaus sooner? All you had to do was tell me the truth!"

He rounded on the angry Kilian, "Why did you let Verena fly the wagon? Now she's prisoner, and they're going to kill her!"

"Don't you try to deny what you did," Kilian snarled. "You knocked her off the wagon. You kept us from rescuing my nephew."

"Your nephew?" Connor's anger withered, replaced by deeper confusion.

He looked from Kilian to Wolfram. "I thought you said Nicklaus was related to the king?"

"He is."

Kilian said, "And he's my nephew too. So now you know the truth. Now you see you've been helping men who kidnap little children for political gain. Now you understand a tiny part of my rage."

"Killing people doesn't help," Connor shouted back.

"I know what I'm fighting for. Boy, you don't even know who you are."

"I'm a Guardian!"

"You're a willing slave, nothing more."

"And you're a liar."

Kilian snarled, and water burst from a barrel in the corner of the tent. Before Connor could react, it shot across the tent and splashed at his feet. Even as Connor tried to retreat, the water rippled up his torso to the shoulders and hardened to ice.

Connor gasped as searing cold encased him, stabbing into his muscles. He struggled, but lacked the strength to shatter the ice. He hadn't dared absorb any granite.

Kilian advanced and said in a dangerous voice, "Perhaps we'll see what value Carbrey places on his messenger monkey. What do you think, Connor, will he trade Verena or Nicklaus for you?"

"I doubt it, General Wolfram said. "Kilian, let the boy go."

Kilian drew closer until he stood scant inches away. "How do you like having your freedom robbed, boy?"

"You're worse than you claim Carbrey is."

"If I'm that bad, maybe I should raise that ice just a little higher and cover your face. How would you like that?"

"I have a better idea."

Connor tapped the burning marble fire in his mouth and blew a gout of roaring flames straight into Kilian's face.

The Water Moccasin howled and tumbled back, clutching at his face with both hands. Connor twisted his head, spraying fire at both Wolfram and Ilse and forcing them to dive out of the way.

Cold was burning at his limbs, so Connor fought against it with the raging fire. Flames poured out his open mouth and flowed down his torso like a river. The ice prison shattered under the onslaught, and Connor staggered free.

Ilse's body hardened into the perfect lines of granite power, while Wolfram shouted for help.

Kilian rolled to his feet, his face livid. He popped something into his mouth, and instantly flames ignited in his eyes.

"I'm not done with you yet." He stalked forward, murder in his blazing eyes.

Connor retreated and sprayed flames in every direction. Papers on the table incinerated, and fragments whipped into the air. The inside of the tent became an inferno.

Then the flames condensed into a tight ball that floated above one of Kilian's hands, while a second ball of water floated above the other. The fire spewing from Connor's mouth winked out.

He couldn't imagine how Kilian managed it, but the sight of the angry Water Moccasin somehow also controlling fire terrified him.

"Do you really want to play with fire?" Kilian laughed, and for a second sounded as crazy as Captain Aonghus.

Connor spun and slashed his dagger through the outer wall of the tent. He stumbled through, tapped basalt right to the Fracking point, and shot away.

He passed half a dozen soldiers, but scores of men blocked the way south. He leaned so far over and almost lost his feet as his legs blurred and shot loose earth and rocks in a wide arc as he banked hard and zipped past the burned-out shell of the manor house. Even as cries of alarm grew throughout the camp, he headed for Alasdair.

As he reached the northern edge of the plateau, he glanced back.

A shadowy form blurred out of the darkness behind him. A Wingrunner, legs Fracked, closed with terrifying speed, his meteor hammer raised to deliver the killing blow.

Connor dug his legs in hard, and slid across the hard-packed ground. His legs shuddered, and he gritted his teeth against the pain. He cut hard over, then he poured on the speed, straight toward the edge of the plateau.

The Wingrunner was moving too fast to match Connor's abrupt course change, and his deadly hammer whistled inches past Connor's head. He leaned hard over and started a tight turn to come after Connor.

Connor tapped basalt as deep as he dared, to the point where his hips and thighs started throbbing with a deep ache. He didn't dare tap any more. He'd never gone Fracked, and didn't think he could handle it.

So he raced for the edge of the plateau with the Wingrunner closing rapidly. He didn't dare turn, or the man would cut the distance even faster. So he seized upon the one desperate option open to him, and ran straight ahead.

The Wingrunner closed fast and shouted, "Stop or I'll kill you, boy."

Connor didn't turn as the edge of the plateau neared with dizzying speed.

"So be it," the Wingrunner called. "It's your ... look out!"

Connor risked a glance back. The Wingrunner had apparently just realized their position, and leaned far over, legs whirling in their altered circles as he fought to avoid the edge.

Connor didn't. He launched off the edge of the plateau.

This time no Heatstone oven drove him into the air. Instead, he soared like an eagle out over the dark valley. River Road flashed beneath him, while to his right the light of Alasdair winked, as if in surprise. Air whistled past, its roaring drowning out all other sound, and its cool embrace relieving the burning of his lips. The stench of smoke and battle and fear washed away, replaced by clear familiar scents of river and forest.

In that moment he experienced freedom like he'd never dreamed possible. Connor shouted aloud at the wonder of it as he began a long, graceful arc toward the Lower Wick that glowed like a silver ribbon in the darkness.

He extended clenched fists above his head, and struck the river at a steep dive angle. The impact jarred him from knuckles to toes as he drove deep into the chill waters. He'd dived several times from the cliffs above Loch Sholto, so he knew how to set himself to handle the shock, but even so it rattled him to the core. He'd never struck with such speed.

Some parts of the Wick were shallow, so Connor angled his body, and even though his speed bled away fast, the change shot him back toward the surface in a graceful arc. He breached into the air like a heavy trout on a line.

Connor splashed back down and floated on his back. He stared up at the stars visible through the clouds and laughed. High above, torches moved along the top of the plateau, and Connor whistled in wonder.

Had he really just done that?

Then his smile faded. Yes, he'd really just learned the truth. The situation really was more twisted than he'd imagined. Wolfram really had just promised to murder everyone Connor knew.

What could he possibly do about it?

Hamish stared toward the plateau and wondered what might have happened. He'd seen the bright billowing flames for a moment from where he sat atop a shattered building in the outskirts of Alasdair.

He hadn't returned home yet. How could he? He couldn't pretend things were going to be all right, and that would only frighten his family. Had it been only earlier this evening that he'd felt so confident? He'd thought he knew Jean, believed that everyone would work together for their freedom?

He wondered if it might be better if the Grandurians just destroyed the town. He felt so heartsick from the betrayals, particularly Jean's, that he doubted the town would recover.

Maybe they deserved the pain and suffering.

Jean did, for sure. Cinaed deserved to be flayed alive for her wickedness, but the rest of the town didn't.

Hamish sat up straighter and looked again toward the darkened plateau. Despite the evil of a few, he would still fight. For his family, he had to.

There had to be something he could do.

CHAPTER 66

top the plateau, Wolfram stood near the big barn and watched the clean-up efforts of the command tent and allowed himself a little smile. The boy was proving far more resourceful than he'd hoped.

Ilse joined him, followed by Kilian. "Sir, do you think that maybe that went a little too far?"

Wolfram shook his head. "He needed the push."

Kilian stared southwest toward the river. "That was a great dive." He looked up into the night sky and his voice became distant. "That boy bears the stamp of history." His voice trailed off, and for a moment he looked far older.

Then he straightened and the years seemed to trickle off. "Poor kid. He thinks he's afraid now. He'd be useless to us if he knew everything."

Wolfram said, "He now understands enough. Our success may hinge on what he does now that he does."

"And if he doesn't?" Ilse asked.

"Then many people will die tomorrow."

CHAPTER 67

ou burned his tent?" General Carbrey laughed and clapped Connor on the back. "I wish I'd been there to see that."

"They were pretty mad about it. I had to run off the cliff and dive into the river to escape."

Carbrey laughed again. The assembled captains joined in, and Aonghus shook Connor's hand. His eyes glowed with just a hint of fire, and flickering crimson stained his teeth. "There's nothing like running with the flames, eh lad?"

"It sure was something," Connor agreed uneasily. Captain Aonghus' breath smelled like brimstone, and his hand felt hot as if he burned with fever. Despite having unlocked marble fire, Connor didn't like standing so close. The captain looked like he might explode at any moment.

"You're lucky you escaped Kilian," Captain Rory said.

"I caught him by surprise. Next time might not be so easy."

Rory cracked a smile. "Hope there's no next time, lad."

Shona, who wore her silk skirt and blouse instead of the battle leathers, walked around Connor and slid a hand along his shoulder. She smiled, and her face shone with excitement. Her eyes seemed to smolder, and the look triggered the memory of her standing in the river.

Was it just earlier that evening?

"I told you, General. He's more than Agor. Dawnus at least."

"Aye, he has a rare gift," Carbrey said. "Just as well we won't need to send any more messages."

"Why not?" Connor asked, shaken out of his rapture. They couldn't find a peaceful solution without more messages.

"There's nothing left to say. Wolfram is clearly growing desperate. He is not one to threaten innocents lightly. We are beyond talking. At dawn, we strike."

"What of the threat against the Cutters?" Captain Rory asked.

"The Longseer reported seeing them yesterday, but no word on where they are currently being held."

Connor had been deeply relieved to hear that his father and the other Cutters survived the manor house fire, but yearned to know where they were. They would probably be the first ones killed before Wolfram destroyed the town.

Carbrey shifted to the large table and stared down at the map laid out there. "The threat to the kingdom is too grave to ignore." He stood tall, "Our duty is clear. We must root this enemy out of our lands, learn the secret of this weakening agent they've used against us, and remove the threat posed by General Wolfram once and for all."

The captains all nodded agreement, but the flicker of patriotic fire that stirred in Connor's heart at the general's words wilted under fear for what Wolfram would do.

He couldn't help blurt out, "Can't we just give them the boy so they'll leave everyone alone?"

"It's not that simple, lad."

"Why not? They promised to leave if we sent that one little boy to them."

"Connor, you can't believe they'll keep their word," Shona said.

He shrugged. "Maybe they will. Even if they don't, we're no worse off. Isn't it worth the risk? Isn't one little boy's life worth the lives of everyone in Alasdair? Isn't it worth preserving the quarry?"

As Carbrey considered the question, Shona said, "Maybe Connor's right. I'm sure my father would agree the situation demands some compromise."

Connor tried to share his deep appreciation with a look. With Shona on his side, maybe the general would listen.

General Carbrey shook his head slowly, dashing his hope. "Your father is not here, Lady Shona, and his orders are clear. We must destroy this enemy incursion.

"We attack at dawn."

Connor wanted to howl with frustration. The answer seemed so simple, why couldn't General Carbrey see it? Or maybe he did, and just didn't want to accept it?

Maybe Wolfram was right about him.

"How did the boy come to be your prisoner?" he asked before he could stop himself.

Carbrey frowned. "That is information you do not need to know, lad."

"I think I do," he protested, despite a cautionary shake of the head from Captain Rory. "It's my family and friends that are going to die because of him."

"Don't press me on this," Carbrey said, his voice hardening. "You've given valuable service, but don't test my patience."

"But, sir --" he began.

Shona stepped in front of him. "Connor, I think you've said enough." She took his arm and tried to push him toward the tent flap.

"No, I haven't."

Why didn't she stand with him? If she insisted, Carbrey might relent.

"Yes, you have," Carbrey said. "You are dismissed."

Even as Connor tried to protest again, Shona and Rory dragged him from the tent. He wanted to strike out at them, but they already looked sad, as if they agreed with him but didn't dare argue.

Why should they? Their families weren't about to die.

Rory said, "Cool off, lad. Level heads win in the end."

After the captain disappeared back into the tent, Connor caught Shona's arm before she could follow. "Come find me later. I need to speak with you."

She squeezed his hand, then followed Rory back into the tent.

Connor paced through the crowded camp. Soldiers lay sleeping in long rows, or clustered around cheery fires swapping stories, gambling, or drinking.

He needed space, so he headed to the riverbank to watch the Lower Wick flowing slowly past. The quiet gurgle of the river could not drown out his thoughts, and they rose in a great tide in his mind.

One crazy possibility floated to the surface and no matter how he tried, he could not shake it. The audacity of it, the pure risk, sent a chill creeping down his spine. He looked out over the river again. This same river had borne him to safety just an hour ago.

Could he risk returning? If he didn't, would anyone he loved live out the next day?

Connor went to find Donald.

CHAPTER 68

After procuring more basalt to replenish his diminished reserve, Connor headed north. As soon as he passed the second row of sentries posted on the road, he tapped basalt and surged into a triple-fast sprint. Most of the clouds had drifted away, leaving the night sky clear. Glittering stars, along with a sliver of moon, barely illuminated the way, but the road lay empty ahead, and Connor knew the land.

He increased the tap rate, and as his legs began to ache, he gritted his teeth, and max-tapped. Sharp pain spiked through his hips and thighs, and he clutched at his legs.

He shouldn't have.

Under his hands, between steps, his legs buckled and shifted. His upper thighs snapped outward and the bone about eight inches down fractured into a new joint.

Connor howled and stumbled forward, but did not fall. His lower leg rotated down faster than he'd ever imagined possible, and caught him.

The pain faded quickly, and he reached down to touch his legs again. The place where his thighs had fractured rotated like a second hip socket, whipping his lower legs around in tight circles.

It felt bizarre. In his mind, he was running normally, but his legs were working so different than he imagined, that he second-guessed the movement and stumbled. He fell hard and bounced along the hard-packed road. He hadn't realized how fast he'd been running.

Connor climbed to his feet, but could not stand still even to catch his breath. Basalt energy coursed through his legs, setting them quivering uncontrollably.

He decided not to think about it, leaned forward and started to run. His newly Fracked legs whipped him forward far faster than he'd anticipated, and he fell again.

"Stones take it," he muttered as he climbed back to his feet. It wasn't supposed to be this hard.

It took four more tries before he finally managed to run without falling. He forgot the pain of new bruises as he flew up the road faster than one of his arrows.

Connor laughed with the pure wonder of it, and then he tried to outrun his own laughter.

He poured on the speed and stopped trying to see individual trees and bushes on either side of the road. They passed too quickly. He focused straight ahead and prayed no one's goat or pig wandered into the road tonight. He'd never stop in time.

In seconds, the open lands to his right sloped up steeply to the plateau, and he rounded a slow bend and came into view of the lights of Alasdair.

Connor slowed and reduced his tap rate. His legs snapped back to normal, and the fresh wave of pain rippling through his legs and hips tumbled him back to the ground.

With legs still throbbing from the abuse, he jogged the rest of the way to Alasdair. Two guards patrolled the wall, so he slipped in through the flood-under tunnel.

He ghosted through town, but headed for Hamish's house instead of Jean's. He yearned to see her, but there was too little time, and he needed Hamish's help.

Hamish gaped when he opened the door to find Connor on the step, then waved him in quickly and, after a furtive glance out the door, closed it tight.

"What's got you so jittery?"

"It's a long story. Why are you walking so funny?"

"Longer story."

Hamish's siblings were asleep, and his parents greeted Connor with far less than their normal enthusiasm. After a moment, they disappeared into their room.

"Are they mad that I came so late?"

"No. They're afraid."

"Of who?"

"Cinaed." Hamish explained about the attempted flight from Alasdair, Cinaed's betrayal, and the threat to execute entire families if anyone tried to escape.

"Connor, they took your mother away in chains."

Connor dropped into a wooden chair. He felt like he might be sick, and his head pounded so hard he groaned.

He'd been worrying so much about his father, he hadn't ever considered something might happen to his mother. He looked up sharply. "What about my brothers and sister?"

"They're all right. Neasa's with them. In fact," Hamish added with a grin. "With how well they're probably eating, they may not want you to come home for a while."

Connor managed a smile, but his heart wasn't in it. He doubted he could eat any of Neasa's sweetbreads even if Hamish had managed to steal some.

His red-headed friend dropped into another chair and his humor drained away. He said softly, "Connor, Jean betrayed us."

"How?" Connor struggled to process the revelation. He'd always hated Cinaed, but Jean ... Jean couldn't turn against them.

"I almost don't believe it myself." He met Connor's gaze with a look of profound hurt, then rose and paced away. "I would've died for her, Connor. I was prepared to."

His hands clenched into fists so tight, his fingers drained of color. His eyes burned with fury like nothing Connor had seen in him. "She took my sword, Connor, and called me a fool. She betrayed us, and people are probably going to die because of it. If that happens, when this is over, I'll kill her."

Connor didn't know what to say. He still could scarce believe Jean had done it. She was the smartest of them all. There had to be a reason.

"I'm trying to make sure no one else dies, and I need your help."

Hamish forced his anger down with an obvious effort. "What can I do? If anyone is caught out, they'll be arrested."

"I have to risk it. I'm going up to the manor."

"Might not be a good time," Hamish said. "I saw something blow up a while ago."

"Yeah, they're probably still mad about that."

"You did that?"

Connor related his disastrous last visit with Wolfram to Hamish. When he finished, Hamish said, "You can't go back there. They'll kill you."

"They might, but if I don't try, everyone could get killed tomorrow."

"What can you accomplish?"

"I have an idea how to end the fighting. I have to try."

Hamish regarded him for a moment, and it struck Connor that his friend had changed as much as he had in the past few days. The thought saddened him. He'd hoped to spare Hamish and the rest of the townsfolk.

"All right, Connor. I'll do what I can to help."

"Come on, and I'll explain on the way."

CHAPTER 69

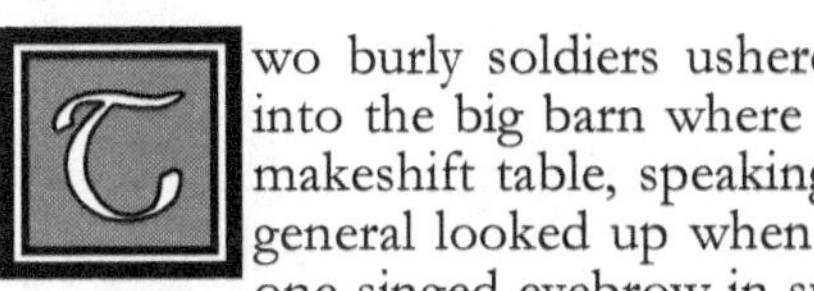

wo burly soldiers ushered Connor and Hamish into the big barn where Wolfram stood beside a makeshift table, speaking with Captain Ilse. The general looked up when they entered and raised one singed eyebrow in surprise. His uniform still bore the marks of ash and dirt from the scramble to escape the burning command tent earlier that evening.

He made a sweeping gesture at the large open space. "You might find this structure a little harder to burn down."

"I am sorry about your tent. I'm glad you weren't hurt."

Kilian stepped out of the shadows that clung to the far side of the large barn. "You've got a lot of nerve returning here, boy."

Connor had hoped to avoid Kilian. He tried to mask his fear with boldness. "I thought I'd give you a chance to be a better host."

Kilian laughed.

Connor just barely kept from sagging visibly with relief.

The Water Moccasin dropped into a nearby camp chair and slapped one leg with an open palm. "You've got spirit, boy. No brains, but plenty of spirit."

"Your friend can wait outside," General Wolfram said. "I imagine you have another message from Carbrey."

Hamish quickly departed, and Connor silently wished him luck. "No message, general. Just a proposition."

"A proposition from Carbrey?"

"No, from me."

Captain Ilse spoke. "What could you possibly propose that might be helpful if you lack Carbrey's blessing?"

"I believe you about Nicklaus."

"That's a good start," Ilse said.

"I want to help return Nicklaus to you, but I need something in return, a show of good faith."

"Such as?"

"The weakening agent you used against the Boulders."

Captain Ilse barked a laugh. "Nice try, Connor."

"I'm serious."

General Wolfram stroked his dirty mustache. "Why would we share this secret with you?"

"I can use it to barter for Nicklaus' release from General Carbrey."

Captain Ilse stared at him, hands on hips, her face incredulous. "You think after sacrificing so many lives, we'll just hand over the powder Carbrey's so desperate to obtain?"

"It's a powder?"

Of course it was. Why hadn't he thought of that? Powdered stone granted strength. Why not a different stone to remove it?

General Wolfram said, "Even if I believed you acted in good faith, how can I know Carbrey will support you instead of just taking the powder?"

"Don't tell me the name, just give me some of the powder. You can give me the name when I return with Nicklaus. And I swear, General, that I won't give the powder to Carbrey until he promises to exchange it for Nicklaus."

"And for Verena," Kilian said.

"And for Verena," Connor said with more confidence than he felt. He quivered with cautious hope as he waited for Wolfram's answer.

Captain Ilse said, "I don't think we can trust you, Connor. You've hurt us more than anyone."

"Perhaps," Wolfram said, "but our primary objective is Nicklaus' freedom. If we can obtain it through this exchange, I cannot ignore the possibility."

"I advise against it," Ilse said.

"Noted. Now fetch the powder."

"Carbrey might be able to determine the name of the powder once he obtains the sample," Kilian said.

"I will take that risk," Wolfram said. "If Carbrey betrays the deal, I will see him dead and his army shattered."

Captain Ilse left the barn and Wolfram said sternly, "Connor, I am trusting you."

"You won't regret it sir. Promise me that when Nicklaus is returned you'll leave."

Kilian said, "Don't you know the trail has been blocked?"

"That hasn't worried you before," Connor said with sudden realization. "You can leave whenever you choose to, can't you?"

Kilian grinned. "Maybe not so dumb after all."

"We can leave, and we will," Wolfram said. "Return the prisoners to us, and you have my word."

"I will."

Wolfram extended his hand, and Connor took it. The general held him in a firm grip, "If you betray me, Connor, your entire town will suffer the consequences."

Connor forced himself to meet the general's stare. If he failed, everyone might die anyway. Still, the weight of responsibility settled heavy on his shoulders.

"I won't fail, General."

"Then we have an agreement."

Captain Ilse returned with a small pouch. She handed it to Connor, and he gripped it tight.

"May the Tallan guide you," Wolfram said.

Connor cringed. "I'd rather he didn't."

"Some day, you may change your mind," Kilian said softly.

Connor left, and as he rounded the burned-out remains of the manor house, Hamish caught up with him.

"Did you get it?"

Hamish patted a leather satchel that hung over one shoulder. "Got it." Then Hamish stopped dead in his tracks.

Connor followed his gaze and was stunned to see Jean round the blasted ruins of the manor house. For a second, his heart sang with the sight of her. She couldn't have done what

Hamish said. It must have been a misunderstanding.

Jean saw them then, and her face reddened with shame. She turned away to pass wide around them.

"Jean," Connor called. He ran after her, but she threw out a hand for him to stay away.

"Don't come near me, Connor." She looked so frightened, he stopped.

"Jean, what happened to you?"

Her fear vanished, replaced with anger. She glanced back in the direction of Alasdair and said, "I grew up, that's what."

Then she ran around the manor house.

Connor stared after her for a long moment until a sharp hiss from Hamish drew his attention. Cinaed, flanked by two Grandurian soldiers, was approaching from Alasdair. It didn't look like she had seen them yet.

Hamish growled, and his hands tightened into fists.

"Easy, we can't start a fight right now." Connor said.

With an effort, Hamish controlled himself, and they moved far to the edge of the plateau where the deeper shadows concealed them.

After Cinaed passed, they headed back to Alasdair. "I hope this works," Hamish said. "But I'm starting to wonder if Alasdair can ever be saved, even if the Grandurians leave."

Connor gripped Hamish's shoulder. "It'll work. Don't ever give up."

"Good luck, Connor."

"If I fail ..."

"You won't."

Hamish handed over the satchel, and Connor tapped basalt and raced south, with the pouch of precious unknown stone gripped tight in his fists.

He barely winced when his legs Fracked, and he didn't fall this time as he raced south, bearing with him the one hope of salvation for Alasdair.

CHAPTER 70

s soon as Connor passed the last sentry outside camp, Donald the Strider found him. "Connor, Lady Shona is looking for you. Down by the river."

Perfect. Connor grinned, "Donald, I Fracked tonight."

The thin fellow clapped Connor on the shoulder. "You're still walking. It's a good sign."

Connor's grin faded. "What do you mean?"

"Just kidding, but you should've waited till I was with you. Sometimes it's a little freakish the first time."

"You can say that again."

"Tell me all about it later."

Connor waved and headed for the river. He found Shona standing alone near the bank, draped in her deep blue cloak. In the darkness, her face glowed and her finely sculpted beauty filled him with the same awe he'd felt when they first met.

"Connor, where have you been?"

"Running."

She smiled and took his hand. "Are you feeling all right?"

"Actually, I feel great right now."

"I'm glad. I was worried you still doubted Carbrey."

Connor took her hands in both of his. "Shona, we have to stop this war before more people are killed."

"If only it were that simple."

"It is simple. We just need to return Nicklaus and let them go."

She slipped her hands from his and stared out over the silver ribbon of the river. She wrapped her arms around herself, and even in the shadows, her face looked troubled.

Connor said softly, "You know it's the right thing to do."

"My father ordered the Grandurians defeated."

"But what if we can't?"

"You have so little faith in us, Connor?"

"It's not that. They're not fighting fair. Besides, is it worth the cost when all they want is one little boy? If we sent Nicklaus back to them, they'd leave, I know it."

"How can you be so sure?" She turned to him and slid one hand down his cheek. "What drives your faith?"

"It's the right thing to do."

She smiled sadly. "The right thing."

"Yes." If only she could see. "You feel it, Shona, I know you do."

"What I feel doesn't decide the fate of this war, Connor. Carbrey's in charge and he will not be swayed by feelings."

With a triumphant grin, Connor held up the small pouch of weakening powder. "He might be swayed by this."

At her questioning look, he made an extravagant bow and said, "Lady Shona, I present the weakening powder."

"Powder?"

She extended a hesitant hand. "How … ?"

Connor forced down a flutter of unease, pressed it into her hands. He had to trust Shona in this. Together they could save the town, and he could know her heart for sure.

If she betrayed him, he had already lost.

"I told you I went running. I ran back to the plateau, and Wolfram gave this to me."

"Why?"

He laughed at her stunned look. "Because it's the right thing to do, of course."

Shona laughed too and then pulled him close and kissed him hard on the lips. She smelled like roses and clean summer nights, and radiant joy rippled through Connor.

Shona broke the kiss and said in a breathless voice, "Connor, you're amazing! This is the top priority, and he just gave it to you?"

"In exchange for Nicklaus and Verena."

At Verena's name, Shona's exuberance faded.

"I promised an exchange."

"I can work with that. The weakening agent threatens the viability of the entire army. Knowing its source is priceless."

She gave him another kiss. "Carbrey needs to know about this."

She led him quickly through camp, past the guards outside the command tent, and swept through the flap without slowing. Inside, Carbrey and his captains stood at the table. A new soldier stood with them, a giant of a man who rivaled even Captain Peadar for size. He wore such thick plates of steel armor Connor wondered how he could stand without tapping granite.

"General, the weakening agent is a powder," Shona declared.

"How do you know that?" All eyes followed the pouch that she lifted high.

"Because we have it."

The captains all exclaimed at the news, but Carbrey rounded the table and reached for the pouch. "How is it possible?"

Shona withdrew the pouch just a little, and Carbrey frowned but did not pursue it.

"Connor obtained it."

Despite the heavy weight of everyone's stare, Connor stood tall. This was the moment he'd worked toward. He would be strong. "I returned to the plateau to give Wolfram another chance for peace."

"You are not a negotiator, lad."

"Well, I got it, didn't I?"

Carbrey reached for the pouch again. "What stone?"

"I don't know the name yet." Connor stepped between Carbrey and Shona. "Wait. I agreed with Wolfram that if you take the pouch, you accept it in trade for the prisoners."

Carbrey hesitated for a second, and Connor did not dare breathe.

Would he take it? Would he accept the deal and end the war and spare so many lives?

Carbrey took the pouch.

Connor grinned and his heart soared.

"I am not bound by terms you set."

His hopes shattered at his feet. "That's not right!"

"You are not authorized to bind me or this army. How could you ever assume otherwise?" Carbrey hefted the pouch and smiled. "But I thank you for this prize."

"It's not a prize. It's an exchange."

"There will be no exchange."

Connor stared, astonished. How could Carbrey do this?

Shona, who looked equally surprised said, "General, I think you should reconsider. Connor acted in good faith."

"Enough. The situation has changed. At dawn we rid the kingdom of Wolfram's threat."

"That's not right," Connor repeated through clenched teeth.

"It's in the best interest of the nation, boy, so that makes it right. We have the Builder, and now we have the mysterious powder. In a few hours we'll have Wolfram and Kilian, and the greatest victory in a century."

"I wouldn't count on it," Connor retorted. "Wolfram said he has more weapons you haven't seen yet."

"I will deal with Wolfram."

"Like you did today? Or yesterday?"

Carbrey's calm cracked for the first time and he took an angry step forward. "Don't dare question me, boy. Wolfram isn't the only one with surprises."

"What do you mean?" Shona asked.

Carbrey nodded toward the giant newcomer. "Our reinforcements have arrived. We will launch the Stone Rain at dawn and overwhelm them in a single stroke."

"You stripped the Merkland garrison?"

"The battle is here." Carbrey turned back to the table and surveyed the map. "All things are aligned for my victory."

"Except they'll kill my family and everyone in Alasdair," Connor said. He advanced, driven forward by anger and fear for his family. Things weren't supposed to turn out this way.

"That is a risk we must take."

"That's easy for you to say," Connor cried. "It's not your family that's going to die."

Carbrey hefted the pouch of weakening powder. "I'm in your debt for procuring this secret. You'll be well rewarded for your service, but you will follow my commands in the future. Is that clear?"

"You don't care that everyone in Alasdair will die, do you?"

"War demands hard choices, lad. That's something you'll have to learn as Guardian. Don't put your future at risk."

There it was, laid out so clear that even in his anger he could not miss the threat. Toe the line, obey without question, and his Patronage was secure.

Fail to do so, and ...

Connor looked to Shona for help, but although she looked frustrated, she only shook her head slightly. He ground his teeth and when Carbrey turned back to the table, he strode angrily from the tent. The cool night air outside the tent helped ease his fury. The camp lay silent as soldiers with fewer worries tried to catch as much sleep as they could before the upcoming battle.

Connor envied them. All they had to do was fight. None of their families lived in the path of battle. None of their parents were held prisoner, doomed to be the first victims of Wolfram's wrath when he learned of Connor's failure.

Realization struck like a bolt of lightning. Connor stood quivering as the truth rattled him to the core. Carbrey had betrayed his trust, but that didn't mean he'd failed.

With stone-hard resolve, Connor went to find some powder.

CHAPTER 71

onnor crouched at the edge of the forest and stared across the clearing at the base of the steep slope where the prisoner cave cut into the mountain. Torches ringed the area and bathed it in warm, flickering light.

Half a dozen soldiers stood at the base of the small ravine, barely ten feet from the cliff, and two more stood on the ledge up by the mouth of the cave. Connor clenched a long length of heavy rope he'd acquired in camp, and weighed a pair of small leather pouches. One held basalt and the other granite.

He could only use one.

Part of him yearned for the familiar, cursed itch of granite. He'd hated it all his life, but in this desperate moment, its familiar irritation would be welcome.

Besides, those were trained soldiers out there. But at least one of them was a Boulder, so maybe granite wouldn't help.

Slate would prove useful against a bunch of soldiers, but his best defense against Gregor was in not alerting him that anything was amiss. Shifting earth around would draw the Sentry's attention faster than anything.

So he tucked the granite away and dumped the basalt powder into his palm. He closed his hand around it and focused. Rippling energy flowed up his arm as he absorbed the stone, and it became difficult to remain still.

Time to move.

Without giving himself more time to think about how crazy this entire plan was, Connor tapped basalt and leaped from hiding.

He shot across the clearing, and breathed deep from the rush of cool night air that bore the distinctive scent of Alasdair Mountain. It helped, a little.

Before the soldiers standing guard could more than shout a warning, Connor raced past them on the right, and threw out the looped end of the rope.

The loop fell around the nearest soldier and Connor poured on the speed and leaned hard over. Dirt and grass sprayed out behind him as he made a tight turn.

He didn't turn hard enough.

For a split second, as the steep slope loomed in front of him with the promise of painful impact, Connor panicked. Then he leaned farther over.

And ran up and across the face of the slope.

The world shifted abruptly sideways, and he almost stumbled, but with a renewed burst of speed, he outran the fall. He leaned farther over, until his shoulder almost scraped the earth, and descended to level ground again.

Still leaning far over, Connor completed a tight circuit of the soldiers, who were reaching for weapons even as they tried in vain to turn and keep him in sight. He played out the rope behind him and, as the soldiers bunched into a group in their attempt to watch him racing past, he drew the rope tighter.

Too late, one soldier shouted a warning.

Connor completed the circuit and, knowing what to do, increased his tap rate. The first circuit took three seconds.

The second took two.

So did the third, and the fourth.

Soldiers cursed as the rope tightened and bound them. The two Boulders in the group tried to break the bonds, but when they strained against the ropes, their companions cried out in pain from the increased pressure.

Connor completed six circuits of the soldiers before running out of rope. He skidded to a stop and tied off the end.

"I'm sorry. I hope I didn't hurt any of you."

"I'm going to break your head, boy," one of the Boulders growled.

Time to go. Connor headed for the steep ravine that climbed to the narrow ledge and the prisoner cave. Just before he reached it, the ground surged upward to block his path.

Connor collided with the wall of earth and bounced back a step. Chill dread sickened him as he slowly turned.

"You may not pass." The deep voice drew his gaze up the side of the steep slope to a shadowed area he hadn't noticed.

Atop a column of earth pressed right against the steep slope stood Gregor.

CHAPTER 72

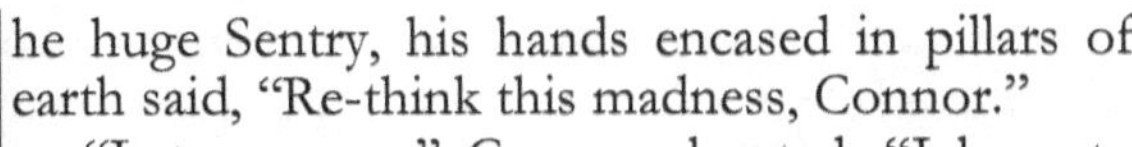

he huge Sentry, his hands encased in pillars of earth said, "Re-think this madness, Connor."

"Let me pass," Connor shouted. "I have to free them or everyone I love is going to die."

"I applaud your motives, but I cannot allow it." Why did everything have to be so difficult?

Gregor terrified Connor, but since he'd started down this road, the rightness of it drove back fear. It had to be done.

He retreated a couple of steps and tore away a section of grass to reveal the soft earth beneath. He pulled a small wafer of slate from the satchel Hamish had given him, a satchel full of stones pilfered from the pile Verena had shown him in one of the sheds.

Connor dropped the wafer of slate, kicked off one boot, and stepped onto the rock. He focused, and the deep strength of the earth flowed up through his feet, fusing him to the earth. He extended his hands, and the earth rose to encase them.

"You have talent, lad, but do not do this. It is a hopeless gesture."

Connor's senses expanded through the earth. The ground under him rumbled, and a column of earth lifted him into the sky to face Gregor.

"I can't let them die. You will let me pass."

Unlike the last time he practiced with Gregor, this time he found the Sentry's location almost instantly. Gregor was not even trying to hide.

Connor took it for a good sign and gripped the earth under Gregor's column with fingers of thought. The ground shifted below the Sentry, and for a second Connor exulted. He was going to do it.

Gregor said, "You reap the fruits of unheeded warnings."

The Sentry's tower dropped straight down two feet, as if it were driving into the earth. The ground rippled out from its base like the waters of a pond, and Gregor drove Connor's earth sense back in a rush.

Connor fought to hold on, but his efforts crumpled like a child trying to stop a charging torc with his bare hands.

The ground beneath Connor erupted in a spray of earth, and his tower shattered. Connor cried out as he tumbled and lost contact with the wafer of slate. His enhanced senses abruptly ceased, as if those ethereal new limbs had been amputated.

Fingers of earth shot up to catch him. They encircled him and dragged him down to the ground where they sealed him to the neck in an unbreakable prison.

Connor struggled in vain, but could not move, could barely breath. Earth coated his face. He smelled it, tasted it, breathed it. For a moment, it felt like he was drowning in it.

Did Gregor plan to kill him, to bury him in the earth where no one would ever find him? The thought chilled him to the bone. He shouted, "I thought you watched over everyone! I thought you tried to help!"

Gregor's earthen tower settled smoothly to the ground and the thick-limbed Sentry approached. His dark-tanned face looked sad. "I salute your spirit, but I am afraid you have not improved the situation."

Fingers of earth tore through the ropes still binding the guards. Gregor made a little motion with one hand, and Connor lifted up into an earthen column that began sliding along the ground toward camp.

Connor struggled mightily, but to no avail. He could not so much as move a finger and reach for his granite. With this cursed strength, he might be able to fight.

Who was he kidding? He couldn't fight Gregor. The man stood against Anton in battle. He'd mastered the powers of earth while Connor had barely touched them.

The truth beat him like a hammer. He'd failed.

CHAPTER 73

hen they reached the edge of camp, the earthen prison melted away and Gregor grabbed Connor's arm before he could try to run. Without breaking stride, the Sentry propelled Connor toward the command tent.

While they walked, Connor slipped a hand into his belt pouch and found a small piece of marble. As he ducked through the flap into the tent, he popped it into his mouth. The instant explosion of fiery spice helped clear his head and settle his nerves.

He'd burned one command tent down. He'd do it again if he had to.

General Carbrey, the captains, and Shona were all still gathered inside. "What is this?" Carbrey demanded.

"This boy attempted to free the prisoners."

Shona exclaimed, "You idiot, you didn't!"

Carbrey motioned her to silence and advanced on Connor. "After all the honors we granted you above your station, this is how you repay me?"

"With all due respect, sir, you betrayed the trust of everyone in Alasdair."

"You've been in league with Wolfram all along, haven't you?" He hefted the pouch of weakening powder he still carried. "This was all a lie, wasn't it? We'll learn this is nothing but dirt."

"Try it and find out."

Carbrey's face reddened. "You're going to talk yourself into an early grave, boy."

"You weren't complaining when I saved Shona, or when I captured Verena. I've done most of your job for you, and you won't even protect my people."

Carbrey raised a hand to strike, but Captain Rory interjected. "Sir, I think it would be wise to consider the matter a moment."

Shona added, "I agree, General. Don't do anything rash."

Carbrey rounded on Shona. "Me, rash? Listen to yourself. Your judgment is impaired, Lady Shona. Your infatuation with this commoner is twisting your vision."

Shona tossed her hair and huffed. "My judgment is clear, General."

Connor's hopes rose a little as she walked around the general and approached. She hadn't denied she cared for him. Maybe she could help.

"This boy holds a rare talent, nothing more. I wish not to waste it."

Connor's hopes shattered, as they had often of late in this tent.

Captain Rory spoke. "The lad has proven himself, sir. Yes, he acted rashly, but remember he is untrained, unused to the hard decisions of war. He is driven only by the desire to see his family safe."

Carbrey paced away. When he turned, he regarded Connor calmly once more. "What am I to do with you, boy?"

Connor shook himself loose of Gregor's grip and tried to gather his thoughts and rein in his own frustrated anger. He could not afford to waste this opportunity.

"I only want to see my family safe. It's what a Guardian is supposed to do."

"You're not a Guardian yet."

"I want to be. I want to serve, and help." Connor took a step forward. "Just show me you're a man of honor, keep the agreement I made with Wolfram, and save Alasdair. I'll swear my loyalty to you for life."

Maybe that wasn't the right way to put it.

Carbrey's eyes hardened and he advanced angrily and lifted a hand to strike. "You dare impugn my honor, you common Linn?"

Connor reacted instinctively. He tapped his basalt, leaped forward under Carbrey's swing, and grabbed the pouch of weakening powder from the general's hand as he ran past.

"Get back here," Carbrey shouted, but Connor poured on the speed. The hulking, plate-armored captain stepped into his path, thick-fingered hands grasping for him.

Connor leaned hard over and kicked off against the heavy captain. He shot back in the opposite direction and burst out of the tent. Behind him, the captains started to give chase, but none of them stood a chance at catching him.

Carbrey shouted, "Guards!"

Shona shouted, "Connor, don't!"

Connor poured on the speed, raced past the guards stationed outside the tent, and focused on the river beyond the far side of the camp. It saved him from the Grandurians. It could save him again.

Before he took ten blurring strides, the ground softened under his feet and, despite his great speed, he sank just a fraction of an inch into it.

That was enough.

The ground hardened to stone and yanked him to a stop. The sudden change whipped Connor forward to slam into the hardened ground with crushing force. He cried out from the pain and clutched at his screaming face.

He coughed and spat a mouthful of blood. He tasted smoke, and his teeth felt like the impact had loosened them in his jaw. He nearly swallowed the piece of marble he'd been sucking.

He grabbed the sandstone pendant around his neck and drank in its healing warmth. He'd fallen close to the central fire and, despite the very late hour, several soldiers had been sitting around it. They all leaped up and stared at him.

Connor forced himself to his hands and knees as Carbrey and the others boiled out of the tent.

"Give me that powder!" Carbrey roared.

"You don't deserve it."

Connor threw it in the nearby fire.

Shona screamed, "No!" and rushed to the fire. As she ran, her body hardened into the perfectly sculpted lines of granite. She thrust one hand into the flames and pulled the pouch back out. Ash coated her white skin, but she appeared unharmed. The pouch had started to smolder, but had not yet started to burn.

As Shona turned and held out the bag in triumph, Carbrey shouted, "You stupid Linn, do you realize what you almost did?"

Connor tapped marble.

Fiery agony exploded in his mouth, and he vomited fire. Flames washed over the pouch and Shona. He tried to concentrate the flames, narrow them, and after a second he figured out how.

Shona screamed and stumbled into the central campfire, with Connor's marble flames roaring over her hand.

The pouch of weakening powder disintegrated under the intense heat. Shona's silk blouse and skirt began smoking under the onslaught, and the smell of burning hair grew strong.

Connor bit off the stream of fire and extinguished the marble. Shona stumbled out of the fire. Her clothing looking like it had melted to her granite-hard, perfect body.

Connor gaped as she hopped around, shrieking, until

Captain Rory wrapped her in her heavy cloak and patted out the still-burning ends of her once-luxurious long hair. Only charred ends remained, making her look more than a little scary.

Carbrey dropped to his knees where the remnants of the pouch had fallen, vainly trying to salvage something. He rounded on Connor, "You'll die for this, boy."

Shona grabbed Connor and lifted him with one hand. She pulled him close and shouted, "Look what you did to me!"

She punched him in the face.

The blow drove him back to the ground where blackness welcomed him with open arms.

CHAPTER 74

onnor awakened to the sensation of movement. His toes scraped forward across the ground and he blinked a couple of times and managed to focus on the hard-packed earth sliding slowly past under his hanging head. His face throbbed so hard where Shona had punched him, it felt like someone was still beating him.

He groaned and raised his head to look around. The two Blades were dragging him by the arms toward a towering tree in the center of camp not far from the command tent. A large fire burned nearby, and the army stood on the far side, hundreds of soldiers standing at attention, silently watching.

As soon as he moved, the Blades paused and hauled him to his feet. His knees nearly buckled, but he caught his balance. Everyone was watching him, so he refused to let them see how much he hurt, how terrified he felt.

The heavily armored captain who Connor had pushed off against in his escape attempt, stepped up to the tree with a long rope. He tossed the knotted loop on one end over a heavy branch ten feet up.

A hangman's noose.

No. No no no no no, this couldn't be happening.

Connor glanced around, but only stone-hard stares met his gaze. His legs started to shake, and his mouth went dry. Vestiges of the spicy marble lingered under his tongue, but the burning power had dissipated.

The fire popped loudly in the silence, and General Carbrey approached, flanked by his other captains and by Shona, her head covered by the hood of her cloak. Carbrey ignored Connor, as did most of the captains. Captain Rory met his gaze for a moment and, although he maintained an expressionless mask, his eyes looked sad.

The Blades propelled Connor forward. He tried to struggle, but one of them cuffed him in the back of the head. While his vision swam and his ears rang, they pushed him forward until he stood before the noose.

The giant captain fitted the noose over Connor's head and drew it tight until it bit into his skin. Connor tried to breathe normally, but started to pant. He didn't dare exhale all the way for fear the brute would pull the rope tight and strangle him.

His mind raced, but he couldn't think. The terrible truth chilled him to the bone and made him want to howl with terror. They were going to kill him. There was nothing he could do about it.

General Carbrey spoke into the silence. "We are assembled here, at the dawn of the day of our victory, to celebrate the freedom we defend, to renew our dedication to the cause of justice. To witness the tragedy of one who succumbed to subtle Grandurian lies."

He pointed at Connor. "This boy, who showed such great promise, who played a key role in positioning us against the invaders, has fallen."

As he spoke, the stares of the gathered soldiers became angry. Connor looked to Shona, but could not see beneath the shadow of her cloak.

Carbrey continued. "This boy, who could have become a powerful Guardian, has chosen treason. Not only did he conspire with the enemy to free our prisoners, but he fought to maintain the secret of how they weakened our forces.

"His actions directly threaten the lives of everyone gathered here today."

Connor shook his head in denial and shouted, "You lie!"

One of the Blades cuffed him hard on one cheek, snapping his head around. He blinked through the tears, searching for someone who believed him.

His gaze picked out Marcus, Tomas, Cameron, and a handful of soldiers he'd healed in past days. Many of them looked sad, confused, but none of them protested or challenged Carbrey.

For the first time, he noticed Lord Gavin and his family standing off to one side. Lord Gavin looked shaken, while Lady Isobel grinned and fingered her scorched hair. Moira met his gaze briefly, wide-eyed and ashen-faced.

Hope lay cold and dead in his heart. He would join it soon.

The ground felt cold under his one foot that still lacked a boot, but he tried to dig his toe into it anyway. He wanted to feel the clean earth on his skin. He'd acted in good faith. He only wanted to protect this land, his people.

How did things get so confused?

Carbrey's voice rang through the silent clearing, "His crime is punishable by death. Sentence to be carried out immediately."

The general nodded to the hulking Boulder. The man took up the rope, but stepped closer to Connor. He extended a leather pouch and spoke in a surprisingly gentle voice.

"Granite, if you wish to prolong the inevitable."

Connor looked from the proffered bag to Carbrey. The general said, "Take it if you like. The record is three days. I don't think you'll last an hour."

Connor bit back the reply he yearned to make. He couldn't risk it, not until he felt the granite strength itching through him. He nodded, and the captain shifted the bag around to his tied hands.

Connor drove his hand inside, but paused. He'd almost forgotten to purge the last of his basalt. He closed his eyes, focused the coursing energy of the stone into the center of his chest and drove it out through the skin.

Then he opened himself to granite. Instantly the so-familiar itching sensation blossomed in his hand and skittered up his arm into his torso. He couldn't prevent a little smile at the familiar annoyance. Somehow it felt right to die with granite.

436

As soon as he drained the pouch, the captain dropped it and, without additional warning, hauled mightily on the rope.

As it yanked him off the ground, Connor tapped granite, and his entire torso burned with the itch of the Curse as it flared to life. His muscles hardened and became the perfectly sculpted lines of granite strength. His body deadened to all sensation as his skin hardened.

Connor held his breath at first, but when he felt nothing through the contact with the rope, he dared let out a little. His throat felt tight, but the air passed. He breathed a sigh of relief and then quickly gulped a full breath.

He started twisting slowly as he swung gently on the rope. His gaze swept across the army and the assembled captains. Shona pushed back her hood, and watched wide-eyed, as if shocked to see the hanging.

Maybe she'd never seen one before? It served her right. Hopefully she'd have nightmares about it all her life.

As his gaze fell on Carbrey, the general said, "You waste your powers, boy. You won't last ten minutes."

He wanted to spit on the man, but couldn't ignore the advice. He closed his eyes and tried to ignore the crowd standing around, waiting for him to die, and focused on limiting the curse just to his neck.

It was harder than he expected. All his life, he'd concentrated the curse into one hand without even realizing what he was doing. He should be able to do this.

It took a couple of minutes. The Curse kept trying to skitter down his arm and he had to force it back to his neck before the muscles there weakened and the rope tightened.

Finally he mastered it, and opened his eyes in triumph. No one had moved.

Fine. If he couldn't stop them from attacking Alasdair by freeing the prisoners, he'd stop them by forcing them to watch him die for days. The record might be three days, but he'd last a week.

His stomach rumbled and he grimaced.

What a miserable way to die.

CHAPTER 75

ervous, Hamish stood near the tall, imposing General Wolfram outside the big barn as dawn stained the eastern mountains pink. He caught himself glancing at the little shed where he'd stolen the rocks the previous night and forced his gaze away.

Idiot. They hadn't mentioned the theft yet. Don't give them any ideas.

That was the problem. They hadn't mentioned anything. He tried to mask his fear, but he couldn't imagine what they wanted.

Were they planning to hold him hostage until Connor returned? What good would that do? The entire town was hostage already.

Half a dozen soldiers pushed a large, covered … something out of the barn. Heavy canvas masked it, but it must be some kind of wagon. It rolled on four heavy wheels.

A man wearing spectacles on his pinched nose hovered around the soldiers and gave useless advice as they wheeled it toward the southern edge of the plateau. When they positioned it to his satisfaction, they locked the wheels and removed the tarp.

Hamish stared, and for a moment wonder overshadowed his fear. It wasn't a wagon. It was, well, it looked like a giant crossbow with dreams of becoming something more. Made with braided-steel cable and heavy wooden arms braced with metal, but equipped with a wire mesh sling instead of a bolt.

Still, that part made sense. It was the rest of it that had him puzzled. A framework of timbers, built right onto the wheeled carriage, jutted out in front of the giant crossbow, supporting a six-foot tube of basalt, two feet in diameter. It extended out the front at a forty-five degree angle.

Hamish drew closer as he studied the weapon that looked designed to shoot something up through the tube. That didn't make a whole lot of sense.

The soldiers setting up the weapon cranked a big flywheel that cocked the crossbow arms back until they locked into position. They then slid out of the basalt tube a smaller tube that had been resting inside, and pulled it all the way under the cocked crossbow arms to the wire basket.

Hamish drew closer still. It looked like they were going to fire the smaller tube into the bigger one, but why? The tube wouldn't make a good missile.

The spectacled man who oversaw the operation, carefully lifted a round ceramic pot out of a padded crate and lifted it toward the mesh basket.

One of the soldiers called out, "Hey, wait. We'll give you a hand."

"Don't worry, I've got … " the pot slipped out of the man's hands.

Soldiers shouted and dove away while the spectacled man fumbled to catch it.

Hamish reacted instinctively, jumped forward, and caught the pot just before it hit the ground. The spectacled man shared a terrified look with him and wiped his face.

Soldiers rushed over and carefully lifted the pot out of their hands and placed it into the cradle. They all looked shaken.

"Thank you, young man," the spectacled man said and shook Hamish's hand.

Hamish grinned. "No problem. I drop things all the time, so I've gotten pretty good at catching them."

"You're Hamish, aren't you?"

"Yes," he said slowly, suddenly nervous again.

"I am Builder Dierk. Verena told me about you."

Another Builder!

Hamish pumped Dierk's hand. "My pleasure." He glanced at Wolfram, who had not moved, and leaned closer to Dierk. "So, what's with the basalt tubes?"

Dierk's entire face lit up. He pulled Hamish over to the tubes and laid a hand on one. "This is my baby. General calls it the modified ballista, but I call it the Thump Driver."

Hamish touched the smooth basalt tube, and instantly felt throbbing energy coursing through it. They'd unlocked a lot of its power. It was a wonder the entire tube didn't jump right off the track.

He grinned with sudden understanding and scanned the entire contraption again. "So the tubes accelerate together?"

"Very good," Dierk said. "The double tubes are the key. We can achieve three hundred and eighty percent accelerated velocity of the projectile …"

General Wolfram, who Hamish had not noticed drawing closer, interrupted. "Builder Dierk, perhaps we should complete the calibration. Time is short."

Dierk bobbed a little bow in apology and added softly to Hamish, "I can talk about the thumper all day once I get started, but we don't want to leave your friend hanging that long do we?"

"What?"

Wolfram cast a warning glance at Dierk and interjected smoothly, "Come, Hamish. You can watch Dierk prime the projectile."

Dierk scurried over to the ceramic pot and unscrewed the threaded lid. Hamish caught a strong whiff of lamp oil.

"What is that?"

"Fuel. An enhanced mixture. My private recipe." Dierk pulled a leather pouch from a satchel he wore over one shoulder and carefully dumped the contents into the pot with the fuel.

"What's that?" Hamish leaned closer to examine the glittering powder as it spilled into the pot.

"Diorite."

Hamish recognized the tiny salt-and-pepper colored grains.

Where did they get ... ?

He gasped. "You broke up one of the chisels?"

Dierk nodded happily, keeping his eyes on his careful operation. "Very handy having those chisels around."

"Are you crazy?" Hamish exclaimed.

How could they destroy one of the precious chisels? It took families entire generations to pay the enormous debt incurred to obtain a single chisel, and Dierk had pounded it to dust?

Dierk finished adding the diorite and screwed the cap back onto the ceramic pot. He rubbed his long nose and regarded Hamish. "Your precious diorite tools contain more power than you comprehend, Hamish."

"What do you mean?"

Dierk removed his spectacles and cleaned them carefully. "How do you imagine those chisels of yours cut through solid granite so easily?"

Hamish shrugged. "The Cutters ... " he paused as realization struck.

Dierk nodded, his eyes intent. "Yes, somehow they interact with a tiny fraction of the latent diorite power. This is a gift we have not yet studied."

Hamish struggled to comprehend the magnitude of what that meant. "So, when a Builder unlocks diorite, what can it do?"

"Watch."

Dierk stepped back from the Thump Driver, and the soldiers slid the lower tube down over the pot. Dierk consulted a small piece of parchment filled with scribbled notes, then walked around the entire weapon, checking placement of wheels and markings of several elevation cranks.

"We are aimed and ready, general," he declared.

"Release," Wolfram commanded.

A soldier pulled the lever releasing the steel cable.

The crossbow arms snapped forward with a loud *whump*, hurling the ceramic pot and the lower tube into the upper tube. The lower tube slammed to a stop, and the ceramic pot hurled impossibly high into the air. Hamish watched with open-mouthed amazement as it arced across the valley and tumbled down into the trees at least two miles downriver.

A moment later, a column of fire erupted out of the trees and reared over a hundred feet into the air.

Dierk clapped Hamish on the back.

"It blows up. Big."

Hamish glanced over at the little shed where he'd taken the rocks the previous night, and got an idea.

CHAPTER 76

ou dead yet?"

Connor opened his eyes and looked down at flame-haired Captain Aonghus, who stood with fire flickering out of his mouth like the flaming tongue of a snake.

"Is it time for breakfast?" he managed to whisper.

He hadn't tried talking much. It was too hard to hold the granite curse around his throat and still move his vocal cords. The first time he tried speaking, he'd lost focus and the granite faded, allowing the rope to tighten a little. He didn't want to risk it happening again, but could not let Aonghus taunt him without responding. It gave him a tiny outlet to stave off the growing panic.

Captain Aonghus laughed, flames licking along his teeth. Holding the fire inside like that hurt a lot. He wondered if Aonghus even felt it any more, or if he'd burned away all feeling?

"You think it funny to watch a man die?" Shona demanded angrily. Connor had caught her looking at him several times, but she never met his gaze. She tried to maintain an impassive expression, but Connor could tell she was deeply uncomfortable.

Or maybe it was just the blackened ends of her now-short hair, and the missing eyebrows.

She advanced on Aonghus and her deep blue cloak billowed behind her. Underneath, she wore her black battle leathers.

When did she find time to change? Wasn't everyone supposed to stand around doing nothing until he finally choked to death? Her lack of respect for the dying was so inappropriate. He'd have to last an extra day just to spite her.

Most of the rest of the army still stood in formation, but their attention was wavering already too. In the first moments of the hanging, many had bet loudly how long it would take for him to succumb, and they'd seemed eager to get it over with quickly. Captain Rory had finally silenced the loud betting with an angry word.

In the past half hour, their interest had faded to boredom.

Captain Aonghus started making a rambling excuse to Shona, but a glint of light drew Connor's gaze up into the early morning sky.

There.

A second glint helped him locate the object hurtling down toward the camp at impossible speed.

Uh oh.

Despite the need to nurse his remaining granite powder carefully, Connor increased his tap rate and directed it all through his body. His muscles hardened into sculpted perfection.

"Connor, what are you doing?" Shona demanded.

He winked at her. "Boom."

The missile struck the large fire burning nearby.

It exploded. Big. A firestorm blasted through the clearing. The wind caught Connor and threw him back against the rope. If he hadn't already been tapping granite, his neck would have snapped for sure.

For half a second, the rope held, and he swung back, like a fish on a line in a strong current. Then the rope snapped, and Connor tumbled through the air, crashed hard to the ground, and continued rolling all the way to the edge of the camp.

With a little effort, Connor managed to draw his bound arms around his feet and stand. The shackles proved too strong to burst, even with granite-hard muscles.

After the initial blast, the flames were already dissipating, but the super-heated air seared his lungs and tasted like ash.

The clearing lay in shambles, with soldiers tumbled into twisted piles where the explosion had tossed them like grout tailings. Many of them struggled to extricate themselves. Some did not. Tents, equipment and supplies were scattered everywhere, broken and burning.

A deep silence hung over the clearing, although Connor couldn't understand how. He could see men screaming as they beat flames out, or cradling blackened wounds, but he heard nothing. It felt like a nightmare.

He clutched for the sandstone pendant on its chain around his neck, but found nothing.

Tallan take them! They'd stripped everything.

The huge, plate-armored captain staggered to his feet and looked around wildly. Connor's first instinct was to flee into the trees near the river, but without his equipment, he wouldn't last long. Unfortunately, he wasn't sure where to look for it.

A gentle hand touched his shoulder. He turned to find Moira standing close behind him. She smiled, and her soot-streaked face never looked so welcome.

In her hands, she held his belongings, including the sandstone pendant.

Connor wrapped her hands and the pendant with his and drew upon its power. Healing warmth flooded through him and washed away the aches and pains. Something popped in his ears, and sound crashed in on his mind.

He ignored the roaring of flames, the screaming of men, and shouted orders from leaders, and listened only to the welcome sound of Moira's familiar voice.

She gasped as healing warmth flowed through her hands also, and straightened a little. "What did you do?"

"A gift for a gift," he smiled. "Where did you find all this?"

As he slung his satchel over one shoulder and shoved his foot into his boot, Moira said, "While everyone was busy watching you ... die," her voice cracked on the word before she continued in a rush. "I snuck into the command tent to find a keepsake of you. When everything exploded, I thought you might need this."

"You're amazing." He cupped her face in one hand. "Whatever happens, you are always my dear friend."

She gave him a weak smile and sighed, "I suppose that's the best we ever could have hoped for."

She pushed him toward the trees, "You'd better run."

He risked one last glance around the clearing, and caught sight of Shona as she climbed to her feet. The blast has burned off the last of her hair, and her face was singed.

Served her right.

Not far from Shona, Lord Gavin, his clothes charred and face burned, was trying to lift Lady Isobel. Her clothes were badly burned and her face blackened. Her wails drowned out all the other screams in the clearing.

Carbrey noticed him, and shouted, "Striders, bring me that traitor!"

So he ran for the forest, and the river beyond, and tried to tap basalt until he remembered he'd purged it all. Granite had just saved his life, but it didn't help now. It strengthened his legs, driving him in long strides, but his legs moved more ponderously, making him run like a torc with heavy steps that shook the forest.

He paused when he reached River Road, and glanced back. Two of the Striders raced in his direction, closing fast. He'd never make it to the river in time.

Connor thrust a hand into his belt pouch, and his fingers closed not on the pouch of powder he sought, but on a small rock. He drew it forth as the Striders moved in for the kill, nets raised to snare him.

He dropped the rock, a piece of smooth slate, the Wallstone gifted to him that first night from Verena, a night that felt years past.

A wall of earth erupted from the ground along the road between him and the Striders, and he distinctly heard two loud thumps from the other side. He winced.

As he ran for the river, he thanked Verena for that precious gift. The water beckoned him on. Carbrey lacked a Water Moccasin like Kilian, and Gregor couldn't sense through water.

That sparked an idea. Connor dove deep and swam hard downriver as he considered his options. He'd failed the last time, but did he dare try again?

What did he have to lose?

After all, they'd already executed him once.

CHAPTER 77

regor stood atop his earthen tower near the narrow ravine leading up to the prison cave and searched the surrounding lands for signs of an enemy assault. He also searched along the river for Connor.

He found and removed the Wallstone the boy triggered. The Striders would survive, but wouldn't be running anywhere soon. He could not sense the boy anywhere. Either he fled into the river where Gregor's senses could not follow, or he fled on the wings of basalt.

As Gregor prepared to extend his senses further afield, the brush across the clearing started to shake. He frowned. He sensed nothing moving in that area.

Then he gasped as a wildly spinning sphere of water eight feet in diameter churned the brush under and careened into the clearing, moving at speed. Visible like a shadowed wraith in the center of the racing sphere stood Connor.

Gregor smiled and reached for fingers of earth.

Clever boy.

Connor whooped with excitement as the water sphere ripped through the underbrush and churned across the clearing toward the startled Gregor. Connor stood with hands and legs spread-eagled, each point touching the inner edge of the wildly spinning sphere.

Everything looked distorted through the water, but he could see enough to guide the sphere. More or less.

He spit water from his mouth, but it did little to help. The middle of the sphere was only a little drier than the middle of the river, and it felt like he breathed in as much water as air with each coughing breath.

He wasn't entirely sure how he made the sphere move, and he made sure not to think about it too much. It was like running Fracked. Too much thought would make him stumble, and he couldn't afford it.

The sphere hurtled across the clearing on a crash course with Gregor's tower. The Sentry could not sense through water, and Connor's gamble appeared to have paid off. He would not fail a second time. Fingers of earth shot out of the ground and grasped for the sphere, but Connor drove right through them, and the spinning water tore the grasping fingers to shreds.

Sometimes in the quarry they used water funneled through ever-shrinking pipes to blast away dirt. Water could not be compressed, so as the same volume was forced through smaller and smaller pipes, the pressure built fast. Pressurized water could scour even granite. The relatively soft fingers of earth stood no chance.

Unhindered by Gregor's initial attack, Connor rode the sphere across the clearing until barely forty feet separated the two of them. He roared a wordless challenge and battle rage howled through him.

Nothing could stop him!

A wall of earth erupted from the ground right in front of him, too close to dodge. The sphere collided with the wall so hard, Connor almost lost control of the water and tumbled right out.

He fought to regain control and resume the spinning before he lost momentum, but a second wall shuddered up out of the ground right behind him. Two more rose between the first two, creating a box to hem him in on all sides.

Connor fumed. Gregor was proving as resourceful as he'd feared. With a loud rumbling, the walls began shrinking, closing in around Connor's sphere.

Connor max-tapped the soapstone powder in his stomach and drew the sphere in tighter, spinning it faster. The water blurred around him, sounding like roaring rapids. His hands began to burn from the friction, but he could not spare the concentration to tap his granite strength.

The earthen walls seemed to melt under the watery onslaught, but more earth flowed up to shore up the barrier.

He needed something stronger to break out.

Connor curled his fingers into claws and focused the churning water. Spikes like shards of ice rippled outward along the outer edge of the sphere.

Those spikes dug into the earthen walls and the sphere shot *up the wall.*

He whooped as the sphere churned up and over the wall and sailed the last thirty feet to Gregor's tower. The Sentry gaped in amazement, wasting a precious second before trying to shift his tower out of the way.

Connor's sphere crashed into the tower, and sheared through. He and Gregor fell together to the muddy ground as the tower and sphere collapsed together.

Connor landed hard, but tapped his granite and powered through the thick mud even as it continued to rain down around him. Gregor staggered to his feet nearby and spun to meet him.

Connor Curse-punched him in the jaw.

Gregor's head whipped back, his dark eyes rolled up into his head, and the powerful Guardian toppled to the ground. Connor laughed at the impossibility of it, and shook out his hand. Feeling returned, along with the maddening itch, but Connor relished it this time.

He threw back his head and roared his victory.

"That's a sight I never expected to see."

Connor spun to find Captain Rory standing a dozen paces away. The burly captain advanced slowly, and Connor's hopes fell with every step. He couldn't beat Rory, not with granite.

He gestured at Gregor. "I hope I didn't hurt him too much."

Rory grunted. "You could hit him with a tree and it wouldn't damage him for long."

Connor stepped closer to the ravine. "Don't try to stop me, Captain."

"You know I have orders, lad."

Rory whistled sharply. An answering whistle echoed down from the ledge above. Connor faced Rory, nerves so tight he could barely breathe, and dared not move. He couldn't make himself attack the powerful Fast Roller, and waited to see what Rory would do.

He did nothing. While they faced each other from ten paces, Connor considered the few stones remaining in his satchel. He needed them if he was to have any chance at escape.

A rattle of stones in the ravine drew his gaze. Tomas and Cameron descended the ravine and blocked Connor's path. He wanted to scream with frustration.

Why these men? Of all the soldiers under Carbrey's' command, he felt most connected to Rory and these Fast Rollers. They'd taken him in, treated him like one of their own. He didn't want to fight them.

Tomas surprised him by grinning. "You took down Gregor! Fantastic! Couldn't have asked for a better view of it either."

Cameron snorted. "Not as funny as the time you fell off the wall in Merkland."

"Stones take it, man. This is serious business."

"Enough." Rory moved to stand with the other two. "Although it was well played, Connor."

"Captain, you have to let me pass."

Rory frowned. "I have orders."

"Forget your orders! If I don't free them, everyone I know will die."

"Tough lot, that," Tomas said with a shrug. He spat to one side. "Glad I don't have to make that choice."

"You're Guardians," Connor exclaimed. "Supposed to protect the weak, help those who can't help themselves."

"Supposed to," Cameron said. He tugged on his long,

crooked nose, "Reckon I'd better check on Gregor." He circled around Connor and moved to the fallen Sentry's side.

Rory rubbed his chin. "Never sat right with me, kidnapping children."

Tomas said, "Now that firecracker lady friend of yours up there, I don't reckon she's helpless. But the boy. That aint right."

Then he smiled. "You'd better have a plan, lad, cause there's no way the general'll let you walk back up that plateau."

"I have a plan."

"Good. Tallan take the whole business." He moved off toward Gregor and started complaining to Cameron that he was killing the unconscious Sentry the way he was trying to tend to him.

Connor wasn't sure what was happening, but two of the Fast Rollers were out of the way. "Please, Captain. Let me pass."

Rory said, "Like I said, I have orders. We are to apprehend you if we see you."

"Ain't seen nothing, Captain," Tomas called. "'Cept old Gregor falling off his tower."

"Never thought him a clumsy one," Cameron laughed.

Rory grinned. "Guess we're still looking." He snapped a sharp salute, "Connor, it's been an honor. You have the heart of a true Guardian. Good luck."

"Thank you, sir." Connor ran for the ravine.

Rory called after him. "Tell Anika …" He grinned, and for a moment looked like a much younger man. "Well, tell her I hope we get to wrestle again soon."

Tomas' voice echoed up the ravine. "She'll spank you next time, Captain, if you get all soft."

Cameron added, "I get the next round."

The two continued arguing, but Connor stopped listening. He returned Rory's grin. "I'll tell her, Captain."

Then he ran for the cave holding Verena and Nicklaus.

Now for the hard part.

CHAPTER 78

he cave mouth was blocked by a heavy oak door. Connor ripped it off the hinges and tossed it off the ledge.

"Hey, watch it," Tomas called up from below.

"Sorry."

Inside the cave a single, flickering torch filled the small chamber with shifting shadows. A couple of blankets lay against the far wall, near remnants of a simple meal. The air smelled musky from rotting wood, the decaying remnants of the treasures Connor and Hamish used to collect.

Verena stood just inside the cave entrance with the boy Nicklaus standing behind her. Despite disheveled hair and rumpled clothes, Verena's big blue eyes lit up when she saw him.

"Connor!" She rushed to him, and threw her arms around him. He sighed with relief and released his granite strength. She wasn't still mad at him.

She pulled back, gave him a warm smile, and punched him in the stomach.

Connor doubled over and coughed up phlegm. His eyes watered, and he tapped granite just a little in case she planned to hit him again. He didn't want her to break her hand, but he didn't want her to break anything on him either.

He held up a hand to forestall any more violence. "Wait. I'm here to help."

"I know," she said gently and helped him stand. "But you deserved that."

"Will you stop? We don't have much time."

"We have a little, though." She gave him a mischievous little smile, stepped close, and kissed him tenderly on the lips.

Nicklaus approached. "Do I get to hit him too?"

Verena ruffled his hair. "No, silly. I took care of it."

Nicklaus looked a little disappointed, but Connor said, "Come one. We have to get out of here fast."

He led the way out to the ledge, but stopped and groaned. Carbrey, Shona, and half a hundred soldiers were already approaching from across the clearing. Rory and his Fast Rollers now lay on the ground near Gregor, covered in mud, looking like they'd fallen in battle.

Carbrey caught sight of Connor and shouted, "You're a dead man!"

Connor grunted. "Been there."

"What?" Verena asked.

"Tell you later."

Carbrey broke into a run, "I'll torture that vixen a year before she dies."

"What did you do to make him so mad?"

"I kind of busted his army and I burned up that weakening powder he wanted."

"You've been busy." She kissed him lightly again. "Now please tell me you have a plan."

Connor pulled from his satchel the pair of quartzite blocks Hamish stole from the shed of Verena's treasures.

Verena took them with a grin. "You're a quick study, aren't you?"

"Can you make us fly like you did the wagon?"

She frowned and chewed on her lip. Connor glanced at the rapidly approaching army. He didn't see any slingers yet, but that wouldn't matter in half a minute.

"We don't really have much time."

She shook her head slowly. "I don't think it'll work for you. I've had practice, but even for me it took a while to learn control."

"I'm not as clueless as you think. Besides, do you have a better idea?"

"Fine. I hope you learn fast. Keep your legs in and bent, crouch over the stone. Small movements."

That sounded right. He'd learned that much trying to fly the Heatstone oven. Of course, that hadn't turned out so well.

"I saw you fly into the manor house that first night. You sure you can do it?" he asked.

"Not fair. You shot my block."

Carbrey reached the bottom of the ravine and led a dozen soldiers, including Shona, in a fast scramble. They'd reach the ledge in seconds.

Verena concentrated over the blocks, and then handed one to Connor. He held the block against his stomach and motioned Nicklaus over.

"Better try it first," Verena said.

"Good idea. Do it."

Verena said, "Lean forward against the wind. It should hold you up." She touched the block.

Air exploded out of it in a shrieking whirlwind and drove the block up against Connor's stomach. He'd set himself, but the sheer force of the wind still caught him by surprise. Instead of lodging against his lower ribs, it slammed into his sternum and drove him up and backward off the ledge.

Connor flailed wildly to maintain his balance and sent himself corkscrewing through the air.

"Control the flow!" Verena shouted from the ledge. The roaring of the wind drowned out the rest of her words as Connor fought to adjust the angle of the block against his chest to keep from arcing down into the field and crashing.

For just a second he had it and started gaining altitude, then he crashed through the tops of a couple of trees and lost all control. He swooped back across the field, ten feet above the army. Since he was flying backward, he got a great view of their startled expressions as they turned to stare after him.

He tapped granite and twisted the stone to avoid hitting the cliff face. It almost worked. Granite skittered all through his body and hardened his muscles just before he struck and scraped across the rough face of the cliff. His shirt shredded under the onslaught, loose stones rained down over him, and he spit out a mouthful of dirt.

He shot past the ravine, shouting with the thrill and terror of flight. Near the top of the ravine, Carbrey paused and raised an angry fist as Connor shot past.

"After him!"

Connor twisted and kicked off from the wall. He plummeted, twisted the block again and leveled out barely six feet above the ground.

The rest of the army stood directly in his backward flying path. Slingers moved to the front ranks, and stones started bouncing off Connor's hardened back.

He chose not to change course and plowed through the ranks of soldiers like a battering ram. After leaving the scattered, cursing army behind, he twisted the block again and tried to apply Verena's warning to use small movements.

He arced up out of the clearing, barely missed a towering oak, and soared in a broad arc back toward the cave. Verena had found a piece of slate in his satchel and dropped it at the head of the ravine, blocking access from below. He tried to angle the block to rise up along the mountain, but misjudged the angle and slammed into cliff just below the ledge where Verena stood.

He groaned and pushed against the stone that was trying to drive him through the cliff face, but even with granite, the shock of impact rattled him. He hung in the air, pinned to the rock by the roaring quartzite block.

Above him, Verena lay on the ledge and reached down to help. Her fingers grasped the air just inches above his head. "Hurry, Connor! Carbrey's coming."

He tried to shout, "Save yourself, grout-for-brains," but with the stone crushing out all breath, the mumbled words came out more like, "Sava sava goo beans."

"What was that?"

Connor increased the tap rate and gave the maddening block a fierce yank. It twisted and shot him up the ledge.

Verena yelped with surprise as he slammed into her and the block whisked them both across the ledge and back into the cave.

Verena's hand slipped around Connor's chest and touched the stone. The air cut off. The two of them hit the ground and tumbled over each other in a wild somersault across the small cave. Connor pulled Verena against his chest, wrapping his hardened arms around her to absorb most of the shock.

They landed on her bedroll in the corner and lay still for a couple of seconds, just breathing. Verena, who ended up lying atop him, pushed hair out of her face and started to laugh. Connor released his granite strength and managed a weak grin. Thank the spirits she hadn't been hurt.

She took his face in both hands and said, "Thank you, Connor."

She kissed the tip of his nose, rose, and pulled him to his feet. "We have to get out of here."

Connor scooped up the quartzite block. Nicklaus waited for them on the ledge, and he pointed toward the ravine. "They're coming."

"Think you got the hang of it?" Verena asked.

"I think I have a better idea." He closed his eyes and purged granite. He hated to let the cursed power go, but he needed basalt.

He absorbed the last of his basalt powder, and its coursing energy filled him with the need to run.

"Hurry. That wall won't hold them for long."

"You should have made it higher."

"Can't. Not enough earth. Too much stone."

"Not good."

Connor grabbed up Nicklaus and had the boy hold on tight against his chest. He positioned the quartzite block awkwardly against the small of his own back.

Verena frowned. "That might not be such a good idea."

"It'll work. Just don't open it up so far."

"It won't carry you like that."

"I don't need it to carry, just to push."

"You're not making sense."

Pounding began on the far side of the wall, and Carbrey's voice echoed up from below. "Connor, you're a dead man."

"He gets repetitive, doesn't he?" Verena said.

"That precious town of yours is doomed," Carbrey shouted. "I will not spare them. Not now. They'll die in the fighting, and anyone left will be enslaved to pay for your crimes."

Connor staggered and shared a horrified look with Verena.

She hugged him, "Focus, Connor. We have to get out of here."

For a couple of seconds, Connor stood frozen in place, unable to decided what to do. If he surrendered, Verena could still escape and maybe his family would be spared.

As if reading his thoughts, Verena said, "Connor, you can't help anyone if you're dead."

The wall blocking Carbrey's way began to crack.

Connor made his choice.

"Do it," he said to Verena.

"I hope this works." She touched the stone.

Air blasted out of it, although not quite as fierce as last time. It drove Connor toward the face of the cliff. He tapped basalt and ran straight for the cliff face. When he reached the side of the mountain, he leaped, and propelled by air, raced up the near-vertical slope.

Nicklaus clutched Connor tight, "Don't fall."

As Connor sped up the slope, Verena prepared to activate her quartzite block. He was really a special man, and she had to convince him. Only, she wasn't sure how to make everything work out with the threat against his town.

The wall at the far end of the ledge exploded and Carbrey lurched through and lunged for her. Verena leaped off the ledge and activated her stone. She sank halfway to the ground before the blasting air caught her and drove her back up. She adjusted the flow, slowed and hovered off the ledge, just out of reach.

"I'd say it's been a pleasure, general, but you're too good a liar to not see through that one."

Shona snarled, "You filthy wretch!" And leaped off the ledge

Verena increased the air power and shot up, just past Shona's outstretched hand. Shona shouted all the way down to the ground where she hit hard not far from where Gregor lay.

Connor focused on running, and raced up the side of the mountain. Another thousand feet or so, and they'd reach a high ridge with a trail back to Alasdair.

Verena caught them quickly. Either she used more of the quartzite power, or her lighter weight made it easier to fly.

She slowed to match their pace. "That looks like a lot of work."

"Better than flying out of control."

"But not nearly as good as flying in control," Verena laughed. She managed the stone like she'd flown all her life. Her hair whipped around her cute face, and she grinned.

"What happens if your basalt runs out?" she asked a moment later.

Connor just glared.

Nicklaus laughed like a normal six year-old and shouted, "Faster!"

They reached the high ridge a moment later, and Connor carefully adjusted the angle of the stone. Wide crevasses cut through the rough slope, but he just jumped them, sailing fifty or sixty feet at a time. He landed with legs already blurring with basalt speed to handle the impact.

After descending to a long, low valley that Connor recognized, he had Verena cut the flow of air and they slowed.

After allowing him to regain his breath, Verena asked, "What now?"

"Get you back to Wolfram."

"What about your town?"

Connor scrubbed his face with rough hands and scraped fingers through his dirty hair. "I don't know, but we have to get your army out of here. Once the battle starts, I don't think I can stop it."

"Then we'd better hurry."

CHAPTER 79

hall I order the withdrawal?" Captain Ilse asked.

Wolfram stood at the southern end of the plateau overlooking the long slope down to the distant forest where Carbrey's forces gathered. He did not answer immediately, but weighed the latest intelligence that both confirmed his greatest hopes and reinforced his worst fears.

"No, Captain. The strategic situation has changed. Deploy the troops to defend the plateau. All weapons at the ready."

Beside him, Kilian said, "I agree. It must be done."

Ilse hesitated. "Sir, Connor did it. We can pick up Verena and Nicklaus on the way out."

"We could, but we cannot withdraw now."

"May I ask why?"

Kilian spoke. "The boy, Connor."

"I don't understand."

Of course she didn't understand. How could she?

Wolfram barely grasped the shadows of the full ramifications of the situation. He glanced at Kilian, but the Water Moccasin said nothing.

So be it. He'd earned the right to keep his secrets.

"There is far more at stake now than even the safety of Nicklaus, Captain. Connor represents a fundamental shift in the entire escalating conflict."

"How is that possible?"

"You've seen the reports," Kilian said. "By Tallan's living memory, you've seen what he can do."

"Of course. We counted on that very talent to free Nicklaus."

Wolfram nodded. "Indeed. However, that was only part of what we sought to learn." He gave her a long, thoughtful look. "If we retreat now and that boy falls into Carbrey's hands again, do you honestly think he'd squander such a talent?"

"Unlikely."

Kilian grunted. "More than unlikely. Even if Carbrey cannot see the truth, High Lord Dougal understands."

"Understands what?"

"History has come full circle, Captain. Builders are rediscovered for the first time since the purge, and now this boy." He leaned close, his eyes blazing with intensity. "We have waited and searched for generations for this moment. The entire disgusting Obrion breeding program seeks only for this very manifestation."

Wolfram said, "If we leave now, leave Carbrey's primary forces intact, leave that boy in their hands, Dougal will have all the pieces he needs."

Kilian rubbed a hand across his face and for the first time Wolfram had ever seen, he looked afraid. "The thresholds he could drive that boy through, the monstrosity he could force that honorable boy to become, would fill your veins with ice, Captain. It cannot be allowed."

Wolfram placed a calming hand on his old mentor's shoulder. "If Verena's mission proves successful, with this final push we can return home with him in our company."

"Pray she succeeds," Kilian said. His face became resolute, his eyes hard as ice. "That boy must be freed, or he must be destroyed."

Captain Ilse looked shaken, but maintained her discipline. "Very well, sir. I will prepare to defend the plateau."

"No, Captain. Prepare to destroy Carbrey's forces completely."

She saluted and turned to leave.

He called after her, "Send the two villagers to me."

CHAPTER 80

amish approached General Wolfram and Kilian with mixed feelings as he walked in the shadow of the powerful Petralist, Erich. He still didn't entirely understand what he witnessed barely an hour ago other than the fact that the Grandurians possessed terrifying weapons.

Well, that and the fact that being a Builder meant so much more than tasting rocks. The glimpses he'd seen into what Verena and Dierk knew had opened his eyes and whetted his appetite. He yearned to know more. So, despite his nerves, he approached the dangerous men with guarded excitement.

Unfortunately, Jean walked on the far side of Erich. She wore the simple blue dress that enhanced the color of her eyes.

He used to love that dress.

She walked beside Erich, eyes straight ahead, chin up as if proud of her traitorous actions. A long canvas bag hung from one shoulder. She'd shifted it once and something inside made a metallic clang. Probably held more shackles for when she next betrayed someone.

Hamish tried unsuccessfully to bury the seething fury triggered by the sight of her.

General Wolfram turned to them, serious. Behind him, along the southern edge of the plateau, the Grandurian forces were assembling for battle. Hopefully whatever he wanted to show them wouldn't take long. Hamish wanted to be long gone before the fighting started. He'd seen more than enough already.

"Hamish," General Wolfram greeted him with a nod. "And young Jean." She made a graceful curtsy.

"I summoned you here to receive orders for the citizens of Alasdair."

Hamish glared at Jean. How dare she stand for the people of Alasdair? She had the decency to look away, and her cheeks flushed just a little.

Wolfram continued. "Today, this conflict will be settled." He swept a hand out toward the gathering soldiers. "Your General Carbrey has cast aside restraint and chosen the path of destruction. I will oblige him."

He paused, with a fleeting look of sorrow. Hamish wasn't sure how to react to that. Grandurians were the enemy, they'd caused all the death and destruction, and shattered Alasdair, no matter what happened next.

And yet, he did not hate Wolfram.

What was wrong with him?

"Hamish, you will escort the Cutters to the quarry."

"Really?"

"There, they will cut into the lower eastern wall with all haste."

"I don't understand, sir."

Kilian spoke. "There's an underground spring that runs right through the mountain there. Same one that flooded the old quarries."

Hamish gasped as realization struck. "You can't be serious."

"On the contrary, I am deadly serious," Wolfram said. "As per the terms of our negotiation, the quarry must be flooded."

As Hamish struggled to find words to argue, Wolfram turned to Jean. "And you, young lady. You will return to the town with the prisoner, Lilias, and organize every soul there to gather and package all foodstuffs. They are to line the main street in preparation for our withdrawal."

"Why would you take all our food?"

"If you prove diligent, we will spare your lives, although some few of you may need to join us in our retreat."

"You're going to kidnap us?"

"Call it strategic planning."

"I call it monstrous!"

Wolfram raised a single eyebrow at her outburst. "I promised Carbrey to kill everyone in Alasdair. Would you prefer I hold to that commitment instead?"

"No." Jean clutched at her dress, her eyes downcast.

"Know this," Wolfram said in a quiet, deadly voice. "Should the Cutters fail in their efforts in any way, their families will be executed, starting with those of the Ashlar and the foreman."

Hamish gaped. He disliked the foreman almost as much as his wicked shrew wife, Cinaed, but he didn't want the man dead. And the Ashlar, Connor's father, was a pillar of the community.

"And should the villagers attempt any further insurrection, the Cutters will be tied and left in the quarry as it floods. Do I make myself clear?"

"Yes," Hamish and Jean said together softly.

"Then go. Time is short, and I will hold you both responsible for any lives lost."

Hamish turned away, trembling with rage and horror. He barely noticed Jean walking beside him as he moved toward the northern edge of the plateau. In the distance, all the prisoners stood gathered in preparation for their assignment to destroy their very livelihood.

The Grandurians' pretended courtesy had all been a lie. They were worse than monsters.

What could he possibly do?

CHAPTER 81

"Why do you torment them so?"

Wolfram turned to Kilian and said heavily, "I trust you in all matters of cryptic powers and ancient evils, but you must trust me in this."

"It is a dangerous game you play. Are you prepared for the consequences if they don't act?"

"It is the only way to prove they are worthy."

"I hope for your sake that they are."

Wolfram blew out his long mustaches. "So do I."

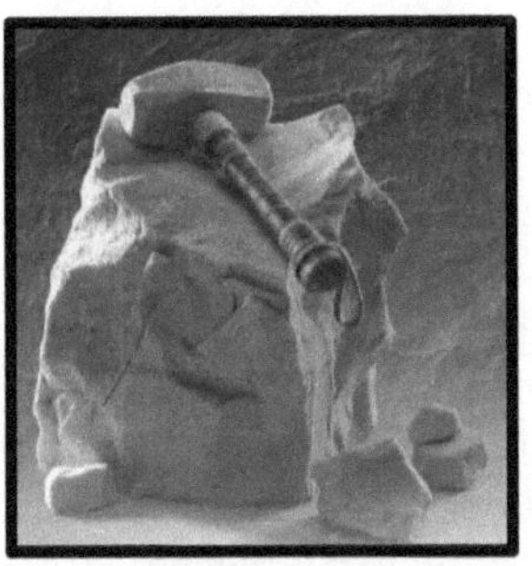

CHAPTER 82

s Hamish reached the stables on the east side of the manor's burned-out husk, Jean suddenly grabbed his arm and pulled him to the side. He stumbled after her as she dragged him around the corner of the stable.

Hamish regained his footing and yanked his arm out of her grasp. Did she plan to kill him? What else was left?

Jean threw her arms around his neck and hugged him close.

"Oh, Hamish. I'm so sorry!"

He pushed her away. "Back off."

Jean's lovely eyes filled with tears, and her full lips quivered. "Hamish, please listen to me."

He hated himself that even then he couldn't entirely deny her when she looked at him that way. "Why should I? You betrayed everything!"

"Don't you see? It was the only way to save you."

Hamish opened his mouth to shout an angry retort, but her words sank in and he stood there, open-mouthed.

Jean smiled. "You look like a fish."

"What did you say?"

"Oh, Hamish. I'd hoped you'd figure it out."

"Figure what out? You betrayed us. You took my sword."

Jean unslung the long canvas bag from her shoulder and extracted his sword belt, complete with sheathed sword and dagger. Hamish reverently accepted it.

"I took it to keep Cinaed from getting it. I doubt we'd have seen it again if she got her claws on it and ..." She looked down and added softly, "I don't want you to lose it."

She met his gaze, her eyes wide and vulnerable. "It means too much."

Hamish gripped the sword tight and tried to breathe as conflicting emotions battled through him.

Did he dare trust her after what she'd done?

"You turned on Lilias. You helped Cinaed." He spit out the vile woman's name like a piece of rotten apple.

Jean put her hands on her hips and gave him that look she'd perfected through their childhoods when she thought him particularly thick-headed. "Lilias was already in chains. Cinaed betrayed us. We'd already lost. I acted to preserve your sword, to save your life, and to gain her trust."

"You thought of all that?"

"I had to learn her plans and figure out how to get around them. I had to stay close to her, get into her confidence so I could undermine her insanity."

"Oh." He'd wanted nothing more than to stay as far from Cinaed as possible. "You figured all that out right there in the square?"

"Didn't have much time, did we?"

Hamish regarded her with fresh eyes, and she'd never looked so beautiful. "Jean, you're amazing."

She blushed. "We don't have much time. Wolfram gave us this one chance to save everyone."

"What? He threatened to kill us all."

"Weren't you listening?" Jean was starting to look impatient, which helped Hamish feel even better. It was good to see her acting natural again.

"We can't escape," Hamish said. "If either group tries anything, the others will be killed."

"That's the key, isn't it?" Jean said triumphantly. "We have to act at the same time."

For the second time in as many minutes, Hamish stared at her, mouth open, no words forthcoming.

Jean giggled. "You still look like a fish. You should work on that. Fish aren't very attractive."

"You should've seen that river sturgeon I almost landed last summer."

She only shook her head. "Listen, here's what we have to do."

CHAPTER 83

onnor paused on the steep, wooded trail they followed toward Quarry Road. Moss and scrub grass covered the rocky ground in patches, and underbrush grew thick along both sides of the trail.

Verena staggered to a stop and wiped her face. "Are we there yet?"

"Another hour or so." Hiking the long way around added so much distance. Connor chafed at the slow pace, but Verena couldn't run with basalt legs.

Verena groaned and dropped onto a patch of moss, panting. Nicklaus scampered into view from up the trail where he'd run ahead chasing a squirrel.

Verena, her eyes closed, said, "Connor, when we get back, what are you going to do?"

"I'm still working on that."

She rolled up onto one elbow. "Carbrey wants you dead. He's not going to stop, not going to spare your town until he's convinced you are."

"I know." Connor dropped to the ground beside her and dug his fingers into the soft moss. "I'm not sure what to do."

Verena took his chin and pulled his face around until he looked into her big eyes. "It's simple, isn't it?"

"What?"

"You have to die."

Connor barked a laugh. "Are you so anxious to get rid of me?"

She spoke softly, her eyes intent. "No, Connor. I want to take you back with me."

For a second, he wasn't sure how to respond. The simple sincerity in her voice tugged at his heart. She'd never looked so pretty as she did then, propped up on the moss, disheveled, sweaty, and dirty.

Then again, was he totally missing the point?

"As your prisoner?"

She punched him in the shoulder and gave him a withering look. "I'm serious."

She touched his face, and her anger faded. "You know me better than that, Connor."

He tried swallowing, but his mouth felt dry. Her fingers felt hot against his skin, and he yearned to kiss her again. A light breeze ruffled her hair and brought the scent of moss and earth.

She did not look away, and he grew uncomfortably warm under her stare.

He leaned back, "So, you're going to kill me, show my body to Carbrey, and take it back to Granadure for burial?"

"Oh, Connor, that's not what I mean at all."

"Then how is it possible?"

She frowned, "I'm not sure yet, but there's got to be a way."

Connor rose to his feet and helped her stand. "Well, if you figure out how to do it without actually killing me, then I'll come."

"You'll love it."

Unlikely. If it hadn't been for the Grandurian invaders, he'd have gained Patronage in Merkland and started a new life there. His family would be safe and life would be good. Then again, if not for the kidnapping of Nicklaus, the Grandurians wouldn't have invaded.

Connor rubbed his temples where a dull ache had started, "Verena, it might not be safe for you. I don't have Patronage. My Curse will turn me into a monster."

"I doubt that."

"How can you? Everyone knows it."

"Not in Granadure." Verena stepped close and placed her hands on his chest. "Connor, do you really think our powers, generated by the same stones, work any differently because we've drawn a line on a map and call ourselves by a different name?"

"How else could you explain it?"

"I don't know, Connor. All I know is that in Granadure we don't have Cursed, we don't need Patronage. Anyone found with the gift of stone affinities is called Petralist."

"Not just the nobles?"

"Of course not. I can't answer all your questions, but I know Kilian could."

Connor grimaced. "Kilian's not very happy with me right now."

"He'll forgive you, especially when you return Nicklaus to him."

Connor looked around. "Where is Nicklaus?"

"He probably ran off again, but he won't wander far."

They headed up the trail, calling for Nicklaus. While they listened for a reply, Verena said, "Connor, the powers themselves don't define you. It's only a curse if you let it be."

"It's not that simple."

Before she could reply, a breathless Nicklaus pushed through some brush. "Connor, come look. The soldiers are getting ready to fight."

Connor and Verena followed him up a short, steep slope. At the top, they found an unobstructed view over the valley. South of where they crouched, and three thousand feet below, Carbrey's army was massing along the edge of the forest at the base of the long slope up to the plateau. Companies were already assembled, their armor flashing in the early morning sun.

Atop the plateau, Wolfram's army stood assembled, ready for battle. His much smaller force marshaled at the lip of the plateau, several ranks deep. Without quartzite, Connor could not see many details.

He groaned. "This can't be happening. Not yet."

Verena frowned. "Wolfram should've withdrawn by now. What's he waiting for?"

472

Connor scooped up Nicklaus, "He doesn't know you're free. Come on, we have to hurry." He barreled down the thickly covered slope, crashing headlong through the brush to reach the trail. Verena followed more slowly. She looked worried, and chewed her lip.

"Hurry, Verena!"

"Connor, there's something I think you should know."

"Not now. We have to get back or Wolfram will kill my family. And if he doesn't, Carbrey will."

"But, Connor."

"Later. Can you fly for a while?"

"What?" She seemed dazed. The climb must have exhausted her.

"Use the block. Can you do it until we get back to the trail above Quarry Road?"

"Yes, there's enough power left. But Connor, listen."

"I don't have time to waste! My family's going to die!" He tapped basalt and sprinted up the trail with Nicklaus. As he ran, he couldn't shake a growing dread. No matter how deep he drew from the basalt, he wouldn't be able to outrun the fate that hung over Alasdair.

CHAPTER 84

endry, who sat resting on a block of recently-cut granite in the quarry, hefted a precious diorite chisel and gestured with it. "Hamish, do you really understand what they did to these?"

"Sort of." He shifted the canvas sack holding his sword over one shoulder, took the proffered chisel and concentrated over it.

He'd never been allowed to hold one of the precious chisels before, and barely suppressed a grin as a thrill of excitement coursed through him. He'd never expected to touch a diorite chisel, and the Ashlar himself was asking *him* about them.

He instantly recognized the thrumming power concealed in the chisel. He slid his fingers across the smooth, two-foot shaft and barely resisted the urge to lick it. He'd never tasted diorite, but Hendry would probably never let him hold it again if he did.

After a moment's study, he detected the almost imperceptible crack in the stone where Dierk had pried open just a tiny fraction of its power. He glanced at the twenty-foot deep square tunnel they'd bored into the mountain in just two hours with the enhanced chisels, and shivered with the possibilities.

With its power completely sealed, the diorite chisels in the hand of experienced Cutters sliced through living granite a hundred times faster than steel, in much the same way the Ashlar's hammer pounded stones to dust. The miniscule amount of power released by Dierk magnified the chisels' effectiveness a thousand times. Every blow drove the chisel half its length into the stone amidst an explosion of granite chips.

What would happen if he opened the crack all the way?

The memory of the small handful of diorite poured into the projectile the Grandurians had launched down the valley flashed into his mind. The explosion had reared a hundred feet.

He handed the chisel back to Hendry.

"What can you feel?" Hendry asked.

For the first time in his life, someone spoke to Hamish with respect, and he couldn't help grinning.

"There's power in the stone."

Stuart barked a laugh. "Didn't even need to lick it to figure that one out, did you?"

"Eat rocks, block-head."

Stuart glared, but did not dare do more with Hendry and the other Cutters looking on. Hamish ignored him.

"Dierk, the Builder who touched your chisels, unlocked a little of that power. That's why it cuts so fast now."

"Do you know how it's done?"

"I'm learning."

"So you could make it even more powerful?" Stuart asked. His eyes glowed with excitement, his previous belligerence gone. "Show me."

"I'm not sure that's such a good idea."

"Oh, come on. I won't tease you anymore."

"Well, if I release too much, you might blow yourself up."

"Really?" Stuart looked even more excited.

"And, the more power I release, the sooner it will run out and crumble to dust."

Stuart gasped and pulled his chisel close.

Keith, the foreman, emerged from the six-foot square tunnel they'd carved into the eastern wall of the quarry. "We've got seepage."

"So soon?" Hendry asked.

"That last blow did it. Any more, and we'll breach the wall and let the river in."

Hamish never would have imagined the water could lie so close to the wall. All they ever had to do was dig twenty feet to the east, and the quarry would've flooded too. Given the situation, it looked like nothing could stop that from happening.

Keith dropped onto a block nearby and blew out a tired breath as he shed his helmet and protective goggles. One of the other Cutters brought him some water. The rest of them sat on surrounding blocks, forced to wait for a turn with one of the only three chisels returned to them for the work.

Hendry's Ashlar hammer had also been returned, although so far he'd declined to pound any of the blocks they'd cut out of the mountain to dust. He didn't want to provide any new power for the Grandurian Petralists.

Anika descended the steep road from the cut in the ridge that led to Quarry Road. "Why stop?"

Hendry said, "The stone is starting to seep. It's about to flood."

"Is good," Anika said. "Wait I give command."

"We'll wait," Hendry said. After Anika turned and headed back up the slope he added, "We can't do anything else."

"Actually, we can," Hamish said.

"What are you talking about?" Keith growled from where he crouched in the mouth of the square tunnel, eyeing Anika's back.

Hamish almost teased him about hiding, but since Keith could squash him like a bug, he decided against it. Keith was ornery enough since Anika picked him up like a little boy when he'd mouthed off to her earlier.

She'd held him up with one hand and said, "Cut, or I spank."

Just thinking about the giant foreman so unmanned by the gorgeous woman made Hamish grin.

"What are you smiling at, dolt?" Keith said. "Can't answer a simple question?"

"Sorry, just enjoying a memory."

Keith scowled.

Hamish said quickly, "Listen, we need to make a run for it now, while Anika's not looking."

476

"Are you daft?" Keith shouted. "You're the one that told us they'll kill our families if we make a move."

Hamish made a shushing gesture and glanced up the steep road. Anika did not come to investigate the shouting. "Jean figured it out. If we run, they'll kill our families--"

"Like I just said," Keith interrupted.

"Let the boy finish," Hendry said.

Keith glared but held his tongue.

"And if our families run, they'll tie us up and leave us here to drown."

"Tallan-loving pedra spawn," Stuart said and spat.

"The key is we all have to act at the same time."

"Impossible," Keith snorted. "You've sucked on too many rocks."

Stuart chuckled, "Probably sucked on some nuall dung by mistake."

Hendry said, "Jean's a bright lass. What's the signal?"

"We light a torch and wave it on the edge by the crane. They see it and start running. We do the same."

Hendry nodded. "It's simple enough, it might work."

"You've gone cracked, Hendry. You really want to put our families at risk?" Keith said.

"They're already at risk. If the fighting goes bad, you think they'll just let us go?"

Keith muttered, "They might."

"No, they won't," Hendry said fiercely. "We're the ones that need to take responsibility for our families. We have to act, or we'll all die."

"And what if they catch us?" Keith protested. "We got no weapons against Petralists."

Hamish said, "Actually, I can help."

"How?"

He extended a hand toward Stuart. "Let me see your chisel."

"No way." Stuart edged away.

"Don't be a coward, son. Give him the blasted chisel."

"Don't break it," Stuart warned as he hesitantly handed it over.

Hamish took it and concentrated over it. Just like Hendry's chisel, Dierk had opened this one a crack. He probed the crack and, as he concentrated on the stone, he couldn't help but lick the handle.

An explosion of taste shot through his tongue and rippled out to the rest of his body. His face flushed with sudden heat, and he gasped with the intensity of it. He'd never tasted anything so alive, so dangerous in his entire life. It tasted fierce, like a pedra's blood-lust scream bottled up and heated to boiling.

"Aw, that's disgusting," Stuart complained and snatched for the chisel.

Hamish pulled it away. "It's how I work. You don't want it to crumble to dust, do you?"

"No!" Stuart hovered, hands clenching, but did not advance.

Hamish forced down a smile. He'd never cowered Stuart like that before.

Although he wasn't sure he should have tasted the stone with its power cracked. He hesitated to unlock any more of the raw power sheathed in the innocent looking chisel.

He didn't have a choice.

Hamish closed his eyes, breathing slow and steady, as he gently pried at the inner crack holding the power in check. It shifted a hair, and he gasped at the rush of lightning-like power that rippled through his arms.

"What?" Stuart demanded. "What happened?"

Hamish handed the chisel over and pointed at a granite block a couple dozen feet away. "Try it out. Wear your protection."

Stuart donned one of the steel helmets and special goggles, set the chisel and struck a solid blow with his hammer.

The granite block exploded.

A thunderclap rocked the quarry and white powder blasted in every direction, covering them all in its billowing cloud. Tiny pellets of granite stung Hamish's face. The dust clung to his mouth like old bread, and smelled like charred stone.

When the dust cleared, Stuart stood in a thigh-deep pile of granite rubble, covered head to toe with a thick layer of white powder. He looked from the chisel to the destruction he'd wreaked and laughed.

Hamish scooped up a double-handful of precious granite powder from the pile and slid it into his belt pouch. He wished he could take more, but lacked anything to carry it in.

"What you do?" Anika called as she came running.

"It's all right," Hamish said, and moved to intercept her. "Just a … tradition we Cutters have before our quarry is destroyed."

She frowned suspiciously at him and glanced around. "Weird men."

"You're not exactly normal yourself," Hamish said.

Anika flashed a smile. "Maybe we wrestle later, red."

He flushed, and that only made her grin wider.

"You stay," she added, once again serious. "I go loch."

"Why?"

"Orders."

"All right. Good luck."

Hamish watched as she disappeared up through the cut again, and then shared an incredulous look with Hendry.

"Did she really just leave us alone?"

"Sounds like it."

Keith frowned. "Has to be a trap."

"Can we not take that chance?" Hendry asked.

CHAPTER 85

ilias stood shackled to a broken beam at the edge of the pile of rubble that had been Lord Gavin's pavilion. Townsfolk packed the square, but none ventured within ten feet of her. Most of them pretended she did not exist, and the few who cast furtive glances in her direction looked away without meeting her gaze.

Lilias stood tall and forced a look of calm serenity as she surveyed the mass of fearful, beaten people she was responsible to protect. She could not blame them for not daring to draw close. After all, it was she who had failed them.

She caught a brief glimpse of Jean as the girl ushered in the last of the villagers.

Good. Everyone had gathered before the conflict started.

Wagons and carts, piled high with crates, barrels, boxes, and bags full of all the provisions that could be gathered in the past couple of hours lined Market Street. Everyone had worked hard to follow the Grandurians' orders as dictated by Cinaed.

No one wanted to risk upsetting the usurper or her Grandurian masters. The recent fighting took a heavy toll. The number of dead had been mercifully small, but it seemed half of them had suffered some kind of injury. The weight of grief, added to the burden of fear, broke wills that had stood undaunted against the mountain for generations.

"Who ordered this assembly?"

Cinaed climbed the pile of rubble that had been Neasa's bakery and surveyed the gathering. The blocky, red-haired woman glared at the crowd. "I didn't tell you to come here."

"I did," Lilias spoke into the silence.

Cinaed snarled and scrambled down from her perch and advanced across the square. People melted out of her path, and the looks of universal fear sparked a wave of anger that bolstered Lilias' courage.

That woman had done so much to harm the town, it was good that Lilias' hands were shackled.

Cinaed stopped several paces away, flanked by her crony, pretty young Ellaran. Jean appeared out of the crowd and flanked Cinaed on the far side. She kept her face impassive and her eyes downcast.

"How dare you give any more orders?" Cinaed growled. "I'll have you muzzled, Lilias."

"You can't help but abuse the power you think you've taken, can you?"

"I am in charge here," Cinaed shouted. "Everyone will disperse."

As the crowd began shuffling away, Lilias raised her voice, "Wait! I called everyone here because we have this one chance to escape."

Cinaed advanced and shouted, "We can't escape! Weren't you listening? They'll kill our husbands if we try."

"Not if they run the same time we do." A rippling murmur ran through the crowd as the idea spread.

Cinaed slapped Lilias across the face. The blow rang through the square and many gasped. "You would see everyone named Daor too?"

Lilias ignored the stinging pain and spoke through the blood in her mouth. "Look past your petty hatred, Cinaed. We can save our people."

"We can't! They'll kill the Cutters and enslave us all. You may not care about that, but I do."

"Look to the cliff," Lilias said loudly. "When you see a torch waving by the crane, it's the signal. The men will flee the quarry and we can escape across the Wick."

More murmurs rippled through the crowd, and Cinaed looked unsure. Someone called for runners to head for the wall gate.

Cinaed shouted, "No one goes anywhere!" She drew a long dagger from the folds of her skirt and lay the blade against Lilias' throat.

"If you murder me, you'll have the blood of the entire town on your hands," Lilias said. Her frustration at Cinaed's blind idiocy helped hold back the fear. She had to stay strong, or everyone would die.

"You poison everyone with your lies," Cinaed said. "Say another word, and I'll slit your throat."

Lilias drew in a deep breath, and Cinaed pressed the dagger forward, pricking her skin and releasing a trickle of blood. Lilias fought the need to speak out again. The rubble smelled of wet ash, and the crowd smelled of rank fear.

Jean said, "Cinaed, don't let her goad you into violence."

Cinaed glared at Lilias for another heartbeat, clearly fighting the urge to drive the blade home. In that moment, Lilias understood the truth. Cinaed would never relinquish power. She'd see everyone dead first.

That simplified things.

Cinaed removed the dagger and said softly, "Jean, gag her."

As Jean prepared to tie a cloth over her mouth, Lilias whispered, "The time is now, my dear."

Jean made no reply, and tied the gag tight.

Across the square, someone shouted, "A torch! I see a torch on the cliff."

Townsfolk started talking excitedly, and arguments broke out. Cinaed pushed through the crowd and climbed atop the rubble of the bakery again.

"Quiet!"

As an expectant hush fell over the square, the same voice as before cried, "The torch. It's gone out!"

Cinaed raised her dagger high. Ellaran, who had climbed to stand beside her, raised her own dagger.

"You see? It was all one of Lilias' lies. Anyone found trying to leave this town will be executed." She pointed across the square at Lilias. "But she'll be the first to die."

Jean climbed the rubble, carrying a pair of earthen mugs. She handed them to the two ladies.

Cinaed smiled. "Bless you, my dear. You make me proud."

She and Ellaran both drank deep.

CHAPTER 86

eneral Carbrey raised one hand and said simply, "Begin."

Far to the rear, Grahame the Pathfinder, who had been listening with enhanced ears, signaled to the towering captain of the recently arrived reinforcements. The man waved to the crews manning three giant catapults that had been assembled in a small clearing just south of the slope, where the forest masked them from the Grandurians.

"Commence the Stone Rain," the captain said.

As one, the three catapults fired. The heavy arms shot up and forward with an ominous creaking of timber and a whoosh of air. They fired three spheres of steel mesh, five feet in diameter and packed with goose down.

The earth under Grahame surged upward as Gregor lifted him high onto a pillar of earth so he could watch the battle and relay progress to Striders stationed below.

A horn blared, and the entire army roared their battle cries and broke into a charge. The spheres soared up the slope and struck just behind the front lines of Wolfram's army. The impacts blasted waves of earth, and the spheres bounced across the plateau.

Those were good shots.

One crashed through the southern wall of the big barn. The second landed in the burned-out remains of the manor house. The third bounced off a tree and ricocheted across the plateau before finally coming to a stop on the northern edge near the road to Alasdair.

Already the catapult teams worked feverishly to crank the mighty weapons back to fire again. Two more steel spheres waited their turns behind each one, with hulking Boulders standing beside them.

Up on the plateau, as soon as the spheres came to rest, they burst asunder and the Boulders who had ridden in their padded hearts leaped out and charged the Grandurian lines.

General Wolfram stood near the big barn, barely fifty feet from where one of the spheres crashed into the building. The Boulder who had ridden inside caught sight of Wolfram, bellowed a battle cry, and charged with heavy hammers raised high.

Erich met him head-on. He dodged a mighty blow that would have cracked even his rock-hard head, and plowed into the bigger warrior. The Boulder shrugged off the blow and knocked Erich aside with a blow to the chest with his other hammer.

Erich rolled back to his feet and grinned. "Got you."

Wolfram noted the timing with satisfaction as Anton struck the distracted Boulder.

Fingers of earth reached up out of the ground and encircled the surprised Boulder's legs. Even as he beat at the restraining ground, two Wingrunners zipped past and cracked his knees with meteor hammers.

Not even granite strength could protect the vulnerable knees from well-placed meteor hammers.

The Boulder howled and clutched at his wounded legs. Soldiers tossed heavy nets over the man, and within seconds he lay bound so securely even his granite power could not free him.

The other two Boulders suffered similar fates. One fell victim to Kilian's icy powers, while the other was met by four Rumblers who beat him down and tied him up.

That's when the second wave of Stone Rain fell.

As his forces moved to nullify the falling Boulders, Wolfram turned his gaze to the lower slope. Had Carbrey's Stone Rain been a surprise, as Carbrey expected it to be, it would have proven extremely effective.

Instead, the general was walking into a fatal trap.

Carbrey's forces were closing fast and, as they approached, a wall of moving earth reared up to shield them.

"Where's the Sentry?"

"Got him," called a nearby Longseer. "Base of the slope."

She moved to the Thump Driver and relayed the coordinates. The team manning the weapon adjusted the position and angle of elevation, and Dierk loaded a single stone.

The *whump* of the weapon as it fired the ceramic pot was drowned out by the crashing of the third wave of Stone Rain. The missile struck right at the base of the distant Sentry's tower. It did not blow up. Instead, after three long seconds, a thick column of water erupted and flooded the tower. It started to shift to the side, but the disintegrating tower sent the distant Sentry plummeting to the muddy ground.

The shield wall that had been leading Carbrey's army collapsed and shook the plateau with the impact. Carbrey's army, barely one hundred yards downslope, stood exposed.

Good. The Sentry would waste precious seconds relocating himself and reestablishing contact with the earth.

Wolfram signaled Ilse. Slingers started launching spiked granite balls at the advancing army while a dozen strong soldiers moved to the front of the lines. They carried odd-looking weapons so new, Wolfram had only ever seen them test-fired once.

Once was enough. He pitied the men of Carbrey's army.

The weapons were as ugly as they were deadly. Little more than basalt drums, twelve inches in diameter, set in steel frames lined with more basalt. A two-foot basalt acceleration tube extended out the fronts. The heavy assemblies hung from the weapon bearers' shoulders on sturdy harnesses.

Four Builders paused at each weapon, triggering the various basalt components to increase speed. After they touched them all, soldiers stationed next to each weapon bearer yanked the ends of ropes coiled around the drums, setting them spinning.

As soon as the drums reached maximum, enhanced speed, Ilse raised one clenched fist. The signal to fire.

The weapon bearers pulled back levers opening connecting ports on the front ends of the fast-spinning drums, allowing the hardened granite projectiles spinning inside to release down the acceleration tubes.

Streams of small projectiles shot out of the tubes in deadly, blurring streams. The little projectiles made an ominous buzzing sound as they ripped through the air. The rain of tiny missiles cut through the front ranks of Carbrey's army like a blizzard of daggers. The hardened granite drilled through armor and flesh alike. Soldiers collapsed by the dozen under the withering barrage, and their screams echoed across the battlefield.

Carbrey wanted this, curse his eyes, and his men paid the penalty for his pride. Wolfram forced himself to watch the carnage with calm composure. The Stone Rain was so far contained, and Carbrey's initial advance already faltered.

Soon, the real battle would begin.

CHAPTER 87

This is a bad idea," Keith said as Hendry lit the torch.

"We cannot ignore this one chance," Hendry said. He moved to stand beside the tall wooden crane and started waving the torch in the air.

Just then, one of the Cutters stationed on Quarry Road to spy on Anika, rushed into the quarry. His voice echoed from the stone walls.

"The fighting is starting."

Keith swore and tackled Hendry. The torch fell as the two men struggled on the outer edge, above the five hundred foot drop down to the Powder House.

Hamish ran forward to help, but Stuart moved faster. The brawny young Cutter pushed Hamish tumbling, and then stomped out the torch.

"No!" Hendry heaved the bigger man off and surged to his feet. "Stop, you fool. Don't you see we need to act?"

Keith rolled to his feet, "Finally, we both agree." He snatched the chisel from his son's hands and ran for the cut in the eastern wall.

Hamish shared an incredulous look with Hendry, and they gave chase. For a giant of a man, Keith ran like a gazelle.

"Don't!" Hamish shouted. "You'll die in there!"

Keith didn't enter the cut. He threw the chisel.

An explosion of granite, followed by a solid wall of water, blasted out of the cut and swept Keith off his feet. The ground shook, and thunder rumbled through the quarry.

The water gushed into the quarry and quickly spread to cover the area. Stuart ran to help his father rise. Keith shook his head violently and, after staggering a couple of steps, seemed to regain his balance.

He returned to the group near the gushing flood and smiled in victory. "Now we're safe. We've done what they ordered, so they'll leave us alone."

Hendry shouted, "Tallan-loving pedra-spawn!" and launched himself at Keith.

With the rushing water already filling the floor of the doomed quarry to their ankles, and with the level rising quickly, the two powerful Cutters pummeled each other with fists hardened from battling the mountain all their lives.

Hamish looked on in despair. Did Jean see the signal? Were the villagers even now escaping?

Hopefully. Hamish wished them on with all his heart. Someone needed to escape this insanity.

CHAPTER 88

onnor paused at Lookout Rock above Quarry Road and sucked in deep breaths of air. Nicklaus crouched beside him, watching. The long run back to this point had taxed even his basalt-enhanced legs. Verena touched down nearby, her face worried.

As soon as she cut the power of her quartzite block, she said, "Connor, you need to know why Wolfram should've left already."

"It doesn't matter. Look." Down in the valley, three huge spheres were arcing up out of the forest at the base of the slope. They crashed onto the plateau, and hulking Boulders erupted from them. The broken remains of other spheres already littered the plateau.

Carbrey's army was moving up the slope, but just then the long wall that shielded them collapsed. A few seconds later, men started crumpling under some unknown assault from Wolfram's army. Connor was too far to see the source, but he dropped to one knee and groaned.

"Why couldn't they wait just a little longer?"

Distant screams echoed from the valley and shattered the last shreds of hope he'd clung to on the long run. Now that the armies were openly fighting, how could he ever break them apart? Men were dying, and Carbrey would blame him for all of it.

On the switchback road that led down to the plateau, Anika ran for the battle. No other Grandurians appeared anywhere nearby.

Verena placed a gentle hand on his shoulder, "We'll think of something." But her confident tone sounded forced.

An explosion rumbled from the direction of the quarry. Connor frowned. "What's going on down there?"

"Probably nothing," Verena said too quickly.

"What do you know?"

She bit her lip, "Wolfram promised to flood the quarry if fighting started."

Horrified, Connor leaped down the slope to Quarry Road and ran for the quarry with Verena and Nicklaus trailing. He should take them back to Wolfram, should try to stop the fighting, but he had to know.

The quarry was the lifeblood of Alasdair. He'd fought so hard to protect the town, but if the quarry flooded, it would die anyway. He reached the cut in the mountain leading into the open pit of the quarry and ran through to the narrow road that led to the lowest level.

There, splashing through ankle deep water near a cut in the eastern wall that gushed water like a mortal wound, his father fought Keith. Hamish and the other Cutters stood in a half-circle, shouting the men on, but no one looked ready to intervene.

Connor skidded to a stop. Keith was a giant of a man, a legend among the Cutters, and a fierce scrapper.

Hendry seemed to have forgotten all that.

Although smaller, Hendry pummeled Keith with a fury Connor had never seen before. He shrugged off the foreman's blows and drove the bigger man back, his face a mask of rage. One particularly powerful blow staggered Keith, and he tripped into the rising water

Before Hendry could advance, Stuart tackled him from behind and drove him to into the churning water. Connor tapped and ran down the road. He'd murder the traitor for that.

Stuart hauled Hendry to his feet and Keith, still on hands and knees, spat out a mouthful of dirty water, "Kill him, son."

Even though Connor was still fifty feet away, he clearly saw Stuart's shock. The burly young Cutter released Hendry and backed away, shaking his head.

The other Cutters advanced, an angry crowd.

Keith climbed painfully to his feet and snarled, "I saved you all, ungrateful cowards."

Hendry spat, "You're the coward, Keith."

Keith's face reddened with rage and he charged.

Connor arrived first. Keith turned at the sound of his splashing advance, and hesitated at the sight.

As Connor whipped past, he grabbed Keith's thick overalls and held on tight. Secured by the bigger man, his feet left the ground and he swung wide. The unexpected attack tumbled Keith into the rising water in a geyser of spray.

"Touch my father again, and I'll kill you," Connor growled.

"Connor!" Hendry wrapped him in a powerful hug, and Hamish joined them a moment later. It felt good to find them both safe, but the icy waters, already to mid-calf, wrecked the reunion.

"What happened?"

Hamish explained, and Connor groaned. He rounded on Keith, who was advancing slowly. "You idiot!"

"Don't you talk to me like that boy. I'll thrash your hide."

Connor advanced on Keith, anger driving him beyond fear. "If you hadn't noticed, I'm Cursed."

Keith recoiled and backed away. Connor continued his advance. "I've already been burned and beaten and hung, so if you think you can do better than an army full of Petralists, stop wasting my time and give me your best shot!" He ended shouting right in Keith's face.

The big foreman raised his hands and backed away.

Hamish caught Connor's shoulder. "Connor, what are we going to do?"

"The battle's started."

"I told you," Keith said. "We had to flood it, or they'll murder everyone."

"It won't help." Connor said, suddenly exhausted. After everything he'd done, it didn't matter. "There'll be fighting in the streets soon. Anyone not killed in the battle will be enslaved by Carbrey."

As one, the assembled Cutters gasped. Keith shook his head. "Wolfram said we'd be spared."

"Wolfram's only one problem, and not the biggest one." Connor waved toward Verena and Nicklaus who stood at the base of the entrance road, just above the rising water. "They were Carbrey's prisoners, the reason Wolfram's here. Once I return them, he'll leave."

Keith glanced at the gushing waters, and for a moment looked horrified by what he'd done. Then his face hardened, "No, we have to hold them hostage until after the battle. We can use them to force Wolfram to leave."

"He'll leave anyway."

"We have the hostages. I say we use them."

"No."

Hendry said, "Connor's right." Hamish nodded his agreement. Even Stuart said, "Dad, listen to Connor."

Keith shouted, "You're no son of mine!"

He lunged at Connor.

Connor grabbed up a chunk of granite from the ground and tapped basalt. Instead of fueling his legs, it rippled up into his arm as he launched the stone.

The missile struck the big man in the knee just as he took a heavy stride. It buckled under the blow and he fell sprawling into the rising water.

He screamed and clutched at his broken leg. Stuart moved to help him, but he shoved his son aside and pulled himself onto a half-submerged granite block.

Hendry said, "Connor, I haven't met your friends."

"I'd like to introduce Verena, a brilliant Builder and one of the bravest people I've ever met."

She made a little curtsy to Hendry. "Pleased to meet you, sir."

She waved to Hamish, who grinned in reply.

Connor turned back to Keith, and decided on a plan. "Take him to the crane."

Assisted by two other Cutters, Keith limped painfully up the ramp to the western edge of the quarry where the heavy crane lowered huge blocks to the blocking yard. "So, you're going to kill me, then?"

"Whether you live or die is up to you."

One of the Cutters re-lit the torch and Connor passed it to Keith, who reluctantly took it. Then Connor turned to Verena.

"How much power is left in your block?"

"Not much. Maybe a couple minutes."

"It's enough." He took the quartzite block and handed it to Keith. "Hold this."

"What is it?"

"Legs together. Knee bent. Crouch over the stone. Small movements"

"You've gone mad," Keith spat.

"And you're going for a ride. Enjoy flying."

Verena touched the block.

A rush of air blasted Keith off the edge. He screamed and flailed his arms and legs as the stone propelled him out over the five-hundred foot drop.

"What did you do?" Stuart cried.

"He deserved to die," Connor said coldly. "I gave him a chance to live. His choice."

They watched as Keith started turning back and forth through the air and plummeting fast toward the distant ground.

"He's panicking," Verena said.

"Of course he's panicking," Stuart clenched his fists and whispered, "Come on, dad. You can do it."

Despite his anger, Connor found himself wishing right along with Stuart. He didn't really want to kill anyone.

They all watched as Keith descended in a wild spiral, the torch leaving a wake of fire behind him, until he splashed down hard into Loch Wick. Stuart laughed and raised a fist in triumph.

Hendry said, "Son, can you stop the water?"

Connor started to shake his head, but then a thought struck him and he stared from Hamish to Verena, for a moment overwhelmed by the idea.

"What is it?" they both asked together.

"I know how to do it."
"What?"
"All of it. Come on!"
He ran for Quarry Road.

CHAPTER 89

inaed dropped her cup and collapsed to her hands and knees, retching. Ellaran fell a second later in a dead faint. As Cinaed moaned and vomited a second time, Jean snatched the dagger from her loose grip and pulled a large, iron key from her belt. Then she relieved the unconscious Ellaran of her weapon.

"Why?" Cinaed gasped.

"Because you do not rule," Jean said. "You're an evil, petty woman, and I will not let you destroy this town."

"You wicked, double-cross ..." Cinaed fell forward vomiting again.

Jean turned to the mass of townsfolk who watched silently.

"Some of you come tie up these criminals."

Only old Mhairi stepped out of the crowd. Her grandmother, who had raised her since her parents died so many years ago, squeezed her shoulder in a gesture that communicated volumes.

Then she turned to the crowd and said, "My Jean can't be the only intelligent person left in Alasdair."

Hamish's parents stepped out of the crowd, followed by several of their children. Neasa, along with Lilias' children, came with them. They grabbed the protesting Cinaed and bound her hands behind her back. That seemed to snap the spell of hesitation, and a crowd of angry villagers surged onto the rubble to help.

"No!" Cinaed shrieked. "You must obey mmmmmmm --" Her rant cut off as Hamish's mother shoved a piece of cloth into her open mouth and tied it in place.

Jean left them to the work and rushed back to Lilias. She unlocked the chains, and Lilias embraced her. Jean allowed herself a couple of seconds to enjoy one of the plump woman's legendary hugs.

"Well done, my dear." Lilias touched her head in blessing and then spoke loudly over the hundred voices filling the square.

"Listen up! We have to get out of here, immediately."

She marched for the wall gate, surrounded by her excited children. Jean flanked her with Mhairi and a limping Neasa. They couldn't force people to choose wisely. All they could do was show them the way.

As they left the square, people started following, led by Hamish's parents and the bound prisoners.

Just as they reached the wall gate, a flicker of light caught Jean's eye.

"Look!"

A torch burned atop the quarry cliff near the block crane.

Then it started to fly. Dozens of people cried out and pointed the marvel out to others. As the torch sailed over the village, Jean realized it was carried by a person.

"That's Keith," Hamish's father shouted.

Cinaed, hands bound and gag still in her mouth, rushed forward to see. Her eyes bugged wide.

He swooped back past the amazed villagers, much lower this time. He seemed to be flying backward, arms and legs flailing out behind him, the torch held in one hand.

Jean followed Lilias down toward Loch Wick as they watched Keith's flying descent become wilder. He turned and twisted crazily in the air.

He was going to crash. Jean watched in growing horror as Keith's descent accelerated. He'd kill himself if he hit the ground like that.

Luckily, he landed in Loch Wick. He struck at an angle and bounced several times like a really big skipping stone. As Lilias led the group toward the Upper Wick, Cinaed pushed her way through the crowd and blocked her path. She gestured toward the loch several times.

"Very well," Lilias said. "We'll set you free to see to Keith. But if you interfere with us again, I will not spare you."

As soon as Cinaed could speak, she shrieked, "Tallan take you all!"

Then she ran to the long stone dock that jutted into the loch. Keith was swimming slowly in that direction, grimacing in pain. Their three youngest children trailed along behind their mother.

"Come on," Lilias said, and led the way across the Upper Wick. Jean followed, as did the rest of the people of Alasdair.

Behind them, Keith and Cinaed took their children and moved back toward the wall gate and the abandoned town. Beyond the town, atop the plateau, light flashed and huge missiles sailed through the air where the battle raged.

Jean glanced up the high cliff toward the quarry and wished Hamish all speed.

CHAPTER 90

nika approached Wolfram where he stood near the half-destroyed barn overseeing the escalating battle. She gave her brief report in Grandurian.

"Very good. It is now in their hands."

Dierk the Builder approached, "General, we have word. Verena and Nicklaus are up at the quarry."

Wolfram surveyed the battlefield. The Stone Rain had stopped, and the Boulders had all been subdued, although the last volley had come before the previous group had been entirely controlled. The fighting had been fierce and casualties were mounting. Worse, one of the Boulders had smashed the ballista.

Anton fought the distant Sentry, Gregor for control of the earth. Kilian had moved to intercept the Firetongue, and the two fought with elemental fury on the eastern edge of the battlefield. Everyone gave them wide berth.

The initial charge faltered under the barrage of the basalt rapid-slings, but Carbrey was massing for a second attack with his remaining Boulders in the front lines carrying massive shields. Even the rapid-slings would probably prove ineffective against them.

Hand-to-hand fighting would come next, and the Obrioners held the advantage in a full-on bash-fight.

As Wolfram considered the various redeployment options, he turned to Anika. "Take a squad and go fetch Verena and Nicklaus. I want them here. If anyone remains in the quarry, flood it."

"Send three squads down to the village. Apprehend anyone who still remains there and prepare to defend the town."

By the Tallan's blessed name, he hoped the foolish villagers had chosen the path of wisdom and fled. Be it upon their own heads the consequences if they chose not to.

Half a hundred of Carbrey's men moved north along the river road toward Alasdair. Three squads should be able to hold the town, as long as no Petralists lurked in the group.

Wolfram turned back to his captains and began issuing orders to respond to the next assault. Hopefully Anton would overwhelm Gregor soon. On that single duel hung the fate of the entire battle.

CHAPTER 91

onnor slowed to a stop at the edge of the ridge, at the very top of the steep switchback road that descended to the plateau. To his right, the calm waters of Loch Sholto reflected the bright morning light.

Down in the valley, battle raged. Dead and wounded littered the slope to the plateau, and Carbrey's army was just beginning a new advance, led by hulking Boulders carrying massive shields.

"Connor, wait!"

He turned as his father, Hamish, Verena and Nicklaus caught up. Stuart lagged farther behind, burdened by the heavy weight of a large granite block. The group stood at the edge of the ridge and watched the battle for a moment in silence.

Verena gripped his arm, "Connor, I have to get down there."

"It won't help." Connor pointed to the right, toward Alasdair. "Carbrey and Wolfram both promised to destroy the town. Looks like they plan on keeping their word."

On the plateau, a group of Grandurian soldiers was heading toward the road to Alasdair, while a larger force moved up River Road from the south. It looked like the two forces would reach the town at roughly the same time. Alasdair would soon become a battleground. Any villagers still there would die this time.

Hamish gripped his shoulder. "From this angle, I can't see if they've left."

Hendry pointed to the base of the switchback road leading up to their position, and a smaller group of soldiers heading for the road. "Someone's coming this way too."

"I have to stop it."

"It's not possible," Verena said. "You'll die if you try."

"Didn't you say that was the only way?" He tried to keep his voice light, but she wasn't fooled.

Stuart reached them finally and dropped the heavy granite block. He leaned on it and gasped for breath.

Connor clapped him on the shoulder. "Thanks, Stuart. This will be key."

Stuart looked out over the edge of the ridge, "Not a bad idea to throw rocks down on them, but we should've brought more."

"Throwing rocks won't be enough. Come on."

Connor headed out along the narrow shore of Loch Sholto where the solid stone shelf, barely ten feet wide, held back the waters of the loch. The ancient quarry had been dug right into this outer edge of the ridge before it flooded generations ago.

"What's your plan, son?" Hendry asked.

Hamish muttered, "I don't see how rope and a block of stone are going to stop anything."

Connor didn't speak until he reached the midpoint of the loch. Several hundred feet directly below where he stood, the brush-choked cave clung to the steep slope. Lower still, the stream that bubbled from the cave cut across the switchback road.

Connor turned to the others, "I'm going to flood the valley."

Hendry shook his head slowly. "I don't think it's possible, son.

"I have to try."

Stuart frowned. "I don't get it."

"Do you know what that cave down there really is?"

Hamish spit out a rock he'd been sucking, "It's supposed to be some kind of chute that cuts back up into the mountain.

They used to slide cut stones down it from the quarry before it flooded."

"So?" Stuart asked.

"It's blocked off," Connor said. "There's a solid iron gate on the inside."

"That's right," Hamish nodded. "You found it that time you climbed up in there."

Connor nodded. "I think it must be starting to rust. That's why there's a stream. Some of the water from the loch is leaking through."

"So?" Stuart asked again.

"I'm going to move the gate."

"You can't," Verena protested, her face pale as she looked down the long cliff face to the cave mouth.

"Of course," Hamish said. "If the gate's moved, that little stream will turn into a flood and wash out the road."

"I'm hoping it'll do more than that." Connor leaned close and whispered, "That chute's close to three hundred feet down. There's a lot of pressure down there. The water should come out pretty fast."

"Why are you whispering?" Hamish asked.

"Wolfram has Longseers. I don't want them to hear."

"I don't get it," Stuart said in a whisper, frowning. "How can you climb through that chute when we're stuck up here. We can't get down there fast enough."

"I can't move it from the outside." Connor turned toward the cold, still waters of Loch Sholto.

Stuart stared from him to the loch and back again. His eyes widened with comprehension and he gaped. "You can't be serious."

"It's the only way."

"You'll never swim down that far."

Connor pointed at the heavy rock Stuart had carried for him. "I won't have to swim."

"You can't," Verena whispered again. "Please."

"I'm the only one who can."

"You'll die."

Connor cupped her face in one hand. "With your help, maybe not."

He reached into his nearly empty satchel and pulled out the quartzite block he'd used to run up the mountain and handed it to his father. "Dad, can you break off a long, thin chunk of this for me?"

"Of course." He took the block over to Stuart's big granite stone, and pulled his diorite hammer from his belt.

While his father broke the quartzite block, Connor absorbed the granite powder Hamish had collected from the block Stuart had blown up. The familiar itch of the Curse skittered up his arm and filled him with strength.

Verena dipped a hand into the loch and pulled it back immediately. "Connor, this water's freezing."

He grimaced. "I know. Wish I had some marble."

Hamish said, "Wait, I have a piece." He extracted a small stone from his belt pouch. "I've been practicing with marble ever since you shattered the Heatstone oven."

Connor took the stone, "Have you been sucking on this? No, wait. Never mind. I really don't want to know."

"Be careful, Connor," Verena said.

She kissed him hard and clung to him. Connor kissed her back, held her close and tried to memorize the moment. Her warmth, her minty lips, the salty tears on her face, even her sweaty scent. He held the memory in his mind as a shield against the fear that threatened to break his will.

This had to work. He'd studied the way water worked under pressure. With so much weight driving it, the water should cut the plateau and block access to Alasdair until the villagers could escape. If the loch emptied, it should flood the entire valley, making the ground all but impassable for Carbrey's army. Hopefully that would provide the excuse Wolfram needed to withdraw. Maybe then Carbrey's wrath could be sated.

Hendry returned with a thin piece of quartzite about six inches long. Connor handed it to Verena.

"Touch this, please. Just a gentle stream, enough to breathe."

She nodded in understanding, pressed the quartzite to her lips and closed her eyes in concentration.

Stuart said, "Somehow I don't mind when she does that." He punched Hamish lightly on the shoulder. "Not like when you lick things."

Hendry caught Connor in a fierce hug, and he returned it as hard as he could. Voice thick with emotion, he said, "Tell mom I love her."

"You tell her when you return."

Connor popped the marble into his mouth and wiggled it under his tongue, careful not to think about where it might have been in the past, and sucked deep. The spicy burn of fire radiated through his mouth, and he drove it down through the rest of his body where it poured warmth into his muscles.

Then he tapped granite, and the itch of the Curse intensified, skittering all through him, just under the skin. His muscles hardened and his skin deadened under granite's power.

Stuart gasped as he swelled, and even Hendry looked amazed. Hamish just grinned, and Verena kissed him again.

Nicklaus, who had stood silently watching the entire preparation, said, "Good luck, Connor. I like you. Don't die."

Stuart tied the rope to him with the same knots they used to haul heavy blocks of granite. Then Connor easily hefted the large stone Stuart had carried from the quarry, and faced the loch.

"When you see the water pouring out of the cave, pull me up."

Hendry and the others took up the end of the long rope. "Don't worry, son. We've got you."

Verena pressed the quartzite stone to his lips, and he clenched it in his teeth and took an experimental breath. The steady stream of air provided enough, although he had to breathe slowly.

Time to jump.

CHAPTER 92

he shock of the icy waters made him gasp involuntarily as he plunged through the surface into the eternal blue of the loch. The quartzite air tasted minty, like a lingering kiss from Verena, and the thought comforted him as he sank like a stone.

He shot down, quickly passing into colder layers of water until their freezing embrace felt like he was sliding down a column of ice. The outer cold fought to seep through the protection of his granite-hard skin, so he released a wave of marble heat through his body to hold it at bay.

Despite the bright morning sunshine above, he quickly passed into pitch darkness in the depths of the loch. He'd thought the Lower Wick had been dark when he'd hidden under the surface with Shona, but this darkness pressed upon him, magnifying the fast-increasing pressure. It shrouded even the quarry wall sliding past barely an arms-length away.

He wouldn't hit anything until he reached the bottom. He'd stared down into the pure, clean waters of the loch with the sun directly overhead many times. Some days, he could see all the way to the bottom. The wall of the loch descended nearly three hundred feet in a straight vertical cliff, marred only by chisel marks from their ancestors.

The pressure grew steadily against his ears. That was his biggest concern. He'd swum many times in the loch with Stuart, Hamish and Jean over the years and many times they dove deep into the waters. Connor was a good diver and had managed to reach almost thirty feet once. He'd almost run out of breath, but it was the terrible pressure that finally forced him to turn back. As he plunged through the darkness, dragged ever-downward by the weight of the boulder, he'd be plummeting ten times as deep.

What would the pressure do to him? Was even granite strength enough to protect against it?

Connor focused on breathing. The pressure mounted in his ears until it became painful. He'd never make it, not like this.

Then he swallowed a mouthful of saliva triggered by the marble in his mouth, and something in his head popped, and the pressure eased.

Connor tried again, and again the popping deep in his ears helped relieve the rapidly building pressure. He wasn't sure why, but as he sank fast in the stygian waters, he focused on swallowing between every breath, and it held the pain at bay.

It didn't help with the cold, though, that fought to breach the shield of his granite-hard skin and douse the marble fire coursing through his limbs.

Despite sucking more marble heat and driving it through his limbs, his hands succumbed first, falling numb in addition to feeling granite-dead, which was a uniquely disturbing feeling. If he lost his grip on the rock, he'd never make it to the bottom.

He couldn't vomit fire with the quartzite in his mouth, but as he sucked harder on the marble and increased the tap rate to force more of the burning power through his fast-chilling limbs, the fire seemed to burn inside him. He grimaced against the pain and willed it out toward his hardened skin.

Blistering waves of heat burned through his muscles. It felt like he was cooking from the inside out. He gritted his teeth against it, but did not relent. It hurt, but was better than the numbing cold.

He was not prepared to see living fire seep through his skin that burned as if he'd placed his hand on the cook stove. Flames flickered to life all along his torso, only to succumb to the icy waters.

In that second, the flames illuminated the grim, gray walls of the quarry slipping past. The sight unnerved him, but when the waters extinguished the flames and darkness again ruled, Connor desperately yearned to see that wall again.

Frowning with concentration, he willed the fire out through his skin a second time. Flames burst into life around his torso, ringing him in living fire. Again it illuminated the wall that he dropped past with startling speed.

Before the implacable waters of the loch could extinguish the flames anew, he replenished them, providing enough fuel to keep the flames alive underwater.

He had no idea how long he could keep it up before the marble extinguished. He only needed a few minutes.

Connor breathed slowly, deeply, but even though the stream of air continued unchanged, it seemed inadequate to fill his lungs.

How much air did this little piece of stone contain?

He decided not to think about that.

After sinking for almost a minute, Connor looked down, vainly trying to penetrate the blackness beneath his feet. The flames licking along his body illuminated little. He had to be close.

He had to know.

Doubling the tap rate, Connor willed the rush of piercing heat out his feet. His skin burned and he had to fight to keep from jerking his legs up in response. Flames blasted down below him in twin streams that bored a dozen feet down before succumbing to the icy embrace of the waters.

It was enough. The flames illuminated a wide area and Connor caught a reflected gleam from something below, something on the bottom. He clutched the rock tighter, grateful that he'd risked the precious fire. Within seconds, the wall before him changed to heavy iron bars framing a huge iron gate.

Before impact, he released the rock to slow his descent, and landed softly on a wide stone shelf that protruded eight feet from the wall at the foot of the gate. His boots sank about an inch in the muddy silt that lay on the shelf. He'd expected it to be deeper, although he shouldn't be surprised at the lack of mud in the pure waters.

Connor wanted to shout for joy, but all he could do was grin with lips clenched tight around the life-giving quartzite.

He'd reached the bottom.

In Alasdair, Keith hobbled into town leaning heavily on Cinaed. Sharp pain stabbed through his leg at each step from where the cursed boy struck him. His limbs ached, and he still shook from the remembered terror of his out-of-control flight into the loch.

They stopped in the deserted town center and gathered their three youngest children around them. Stuart may have betrayed them, but the boy was old enough to suffer the consequences of his stupidity.

Cinaed had related her brave attempts to save the village. Keith hugged her close, and pride for her helped wash away some of the aches.

He shouted into the silence, "We're still here! I flooded the quarry and my wife defended the town. We alone are worthy!"

Unbroken silence was all that answered.

CHAPTER 93

onnor inspected the gate. The monstrous thing, bigger than he'd expected, clung to the smooth wall, held in place by a heavy frame. The square, reinforced gate spanned ten feet, with grooved, iron runners extending up the sides of the frame. In times past the door could be slid up those runners to open the chute and allow large blocks of cut granite to slide through.

Thick rust coated every surface, but the gate still appeared sound. Only the bottom right corner looked frayed. That was probably where the water was slipping through.

Breathing felt more difficult, as if he'd been underwater for hours, or as if the quartzite was running out. He pushed the flash of panic aside. It wouldn't take that long. He should have plenty of time to finish.

"I can still see the fire," Hamish said. The red-headed young man knelt at the edge of the loch beside Verena, peering into the darkness. "He's doing something."

Stuart, who stood near the edge of the cliff, shook his head and frowned. "I still don't get how he can have fire underwater."

"He's using the marble somehow," Hamish said.

Verena added, "He seems to be moving around."

Stuart glanced over the cliff edge again, checking the stream for the expected burst of water. "He'd better hurry. The Grandurians are about to start up the road."

They peered again into the depths where the eerie flickering fire still glowed, while Hendry stood nearby, both hands holding the end of the lifeline they'd use to pull Connor back up.

"Hurry, Connor," Hamish whispered as a growing fear chilled his heart.

Connor dug his hands into the silt at the base of the gate, feeling for hand holds. It was no use, the gate fit tight against the stone, as if sunk into a groove. So Connor stood and grasped a heavy crossbar at waist level. Bracing his legs, he heaved.

The gate did not budge. Connor banged a fist against it and felt, more than heard, the dull boom. He had expected to be able to lift the gate, hadn't considered the possibility he couldn't move it.

He inspected the rails that the gate would slide up if he could move it. That was the problem. Even strengthened by granite, he'd never overwhelm the resistance of all the rust built up there. He didn't have time to chip it free. He'd run out of air, or the Grandurians would pass the stream, or he'd run out of marble and freeze to death.

Marble! That was it.

He grasped the left rail with both hands and increased his tap rate. A firestorm blasted through him, shaking him with its intensity, a searing heat on the verge of melting his innards. No wonder Captain Aonghus seemed more than a little crazy. Only a madman would use marble often.

Connor focused all that burning energy through his hands. White-hot power burned along his arms and blasted out his palms in twin streams that enveloped the iron rail and blazed so bright he had to look away. He held the rail for ten long seconds, rubbing free the rust as waves of fire left the iron gleaming, clean and red-hot. Water boiled around him, easing the constant chill of the loch as it encircled him in a rapidly cooling cocoon of warmth.

He reluctantly left the warmer water and swam to the other rail and repeated the process.

Inside his mouth, the marble melted away, leaving his mouth tasting of ash. He'd run out of fire in seconds without more power to replenish the heat already burning through him.

Connor planted his feet, and grasped the reinforced crossbar again. The flames licking along his body and holding the icy cold of the deep waters at bay now burned noticeably dimmer.

He refused to think about what would happen if this gamble failed. Instead, he braced his legs, tapped the granite power of his Curse, and threw it all into one convulsive heave.

Nothing happened.

"What's he waiting for?" Stuart asked, eyes locked on the long drop. The Grandurian soldiers, led by Anika, had just reached the small stream where it crossed the road.

"I don't know," Hamish said, his voice tight with concern.

Verena clenched the rope that connected them with Connor so tight her fingers shone white against it.

Hendry whispered, "Come on, son. Do it, so we can get you out of there."

Connor heaved, his body shaking with the strain and his lungs burning with the need for more air than the quartzite could supply. Spots danced in front of his eyes and he feared he might pass out.

Then with a terrifying groan, the gate lurched upward a foot. Connor lost his hold, his feet slipped in the thin layer of silt, and for a second he floated free next to the gate. Then a terrific force yanked him down onto the shelf so hard the quartzite popped out of his mouth and disappeared in the gloom. Water tore against him in a mighty current, roaring so loud it drowned out thought, and slammed him against the gate so hard it would have broken bones if not for the protection of granite strength.

Only then did he understand. Pressed against the gate, with his legs sticking under and through the gap he'd made, and water rushing past on either side, he finally grasped the terrible flaw in his plan.

With the gate open, the pressure of three hundred feet of water had a release. The fierce current was like an angry beast dragging at his limbs, trying to push him through the gate, down the chute, and out over the long drop to the plateau floor.

His legs were jammed in tight beneath the gate. The awful truth chilled him more than the icy waters of the loch.

He could not escape.

He was going to die.

CHAPTER 94

heavy rumbling rolled across the valley like distant thunder. Verena glanced over the cliff at Anika and the soldiers of her company, who paused to look around.

A solid wave of water burst from the small cave on the steep slope. It ripped bushes free by the roots and flung them out into space before arcing out from the cliff face in a majestic waterfall that splashed down onto the center of the road right at Anika's feet.

Mud and earth blasted in every direction, driven by the thundering waterfall, and the torrent tumbled her to the next switchback fifty feet below. She landed on her back and lay unmoving, while the rest of the company retreated from the sudden deluge.

Verena cringed at the sight. She really liked Anika, and didn't want to see the woman hurt, but her concern was swallowed up with a thrill of excitement.

"He did it!"

Beside her, Stuart pumped a fist in victory as the others joined them. As they all stared at the continuous torrent of water gushing out of the face of the mountain, Verena marveled at Connor's tenacity.

The water struck with such force that it had already gouged through the hard-packed surface of the road and was attacking the decomposed granite beneath. No one could cross that deluge, and soon the road would be washed out and impassable.

Hendry returned to the loch. "Let's pull him up."

All of them, even Nicklaus, grabbed up the slack and tugged, but the rope did not move. They shared a look and, adjusting their holds, hauled on the rope. Still nothing.

"He's stuck," Nicklaus said.

"Oh no," Verena groaned and peered into the depths of the loch, where the flames flickered, far dimmer than before. Fear for Connor's safety threatened to break forth into panic, and she couldn't think of what to do.

She knew why he risked his life. He'd never leave Alasdair without doing everything in his power to help his people. That tenacity, that integrity, attracted her deeply.

He was so special, in ways he didn't comprehend yet. She understood only a shadow of the truth, and that was enough.

"By the Tallan's grace," she whispered, "let him survive this."

Hendry dropped the rope and yanked the precious diorite hammer from his belt. He thrust it into Hamish's hands.

"Unleash its power, all of it."

Hamish paled. "I don't …"

"Do it! It's the only tool I can send him."

Understanding filled Verena with a glimmer of hope and she reached for the hammer, but Hamish took it. "I'll do it."

She barely restrained the urge to touch it, to make sure he did it right as Hamish concentrated over the hammer.

After a few seconds, his entire body shook, and his eyes bulged. Verena snatched the hammer from his hands as his knees buckled and he plopped to the ground.

"What is it?" Hendry asked.

Hamish stammered and pointed a shaking hand at the hammer. "We should turn that off."

Verena concentrated on the hammer, and lightning-like energy rippled through her from it, shaking her to the core. She'd touched diorite before, but never felt its power so strong. This hammer contained a concentrated supply of explosive power far greater than its mass suggested it should.

Hendry took the hammer from her, and she said, "I think maybe Hamish is right."

She wanted to help Connor, not kill him.

Hendry hefted the hammer and slid one hand across the unbroken end.

Then he sighed, and tossed it into the loch.

Stuart shouted, "What did you do that for?"

"It's the fastest way to send him help."

Verena scurried over to the edge and peered into the deep blue waters.

Did Hendry just help Connor, or seal his fate?

Connor tried to think through rising panic. With the quartzite gone, he'd soon run out of breath and drown, pinned against the huge gate.

He struggled to pull his legs out, but the current drove him too hard, overwhelming his nearly-spent granite strength. In desperation, he even tried to push the gate higher, but with so little granite remaining, he lacked the power or the leverage, and the gate remained stuck fast.

At that moment, his marble power ran out and the flames flickering along his body disappeared. Immediately the numbing cold of the deep loch attacked his limbs. It was so cold it burned, as if mocking him.

He wanted to scream. He hadn't come so far to drown like a trapped rat. He doggedly struggled against the gate despite lacking the strength to move it. His hands became clumsy and his movements sluggish.

The rope tied around his torso went taut as his father and friends tried to haul him to safety, but their efforts were laughable against the tremendous current.

Connor leaned his head against the cold iron of the gate and considered his meager options, but only triggered a fresh wave of panic. He didn't have any options.

He beat against the unyielding gate in desperation, but he might as well try to take down the mountain with his fists. He felt for the sandstone pendant pressed against his chest and gentle healing warmth flowed into him. It didn't help much. The healing power reminded him of his mother's embrace. If only he could see her again, hug her, and tell her he was sorry. The cold water was making thought difficult and he had to fight to stay focused.

Something banged into Connor's hip. He felt around in the darkness and found the heavy boulder he'd used to drag him to his death had slid across the stone platform and was now wedged against his hip as the water strove to drive it under the gate.

Connor's lungs shuddered and he barely suppressed the urge to take an involuntary breath. He couldn't hold out much longer.

If only he could apologize to his father for never being the son his parents wanted, for never being able to take up the diorite hammer after his father and become the next Ashlar.

Something struck Connor in the hip hard enough to draw his attention. He felt around in the darkness and found something jammed between his hip and the boulder. At first he thought it was just a rock that had been swept toward the opening by the current. Then his hand slipped further around it and he felt a jagged edge, and then a handle.

Connor clutched the diorite hammer to him, stunned by the magnitude of his father's gift. He glanced up toward the distant surface, filled with heartfelt gratitude and a spark of renewed hope.

The icy cold water slipped into his nose, nearly choking him, and he had to fight not to cough out the last remnants of air. His body tensed against the need to breath, to cough, and started to shake with the numbing cold.

He was nearly out of time.

At the edge of the loch, the group paused in their vain struggle to haul up the rope. Verena stepped to the edge of the cliff to check on Anika, and to relieve some of the overwhelming tension knotting her innards. Anika, apparently healthy, led her group back toward the plateau.

The torrent of water still ripped out of the cave and thundered onto the road. It had already cut several feet into the hard-packed earth, and a gap spanning a dozen feet yawned in the road. The waters cascaded down the cliff in a mighty waterfall that flowed across the road connecting the plateau with Alasdair before plunging off the western edge of the plateau above River Road.

The soldiers that had been moving toward town paused at the new river. Far to the south, Carbrey's forces were advancing again. Despite Connor's heroic efforts, the armies would still clash, Carbrey's forces would still reach Alasdair.

How could he die in vain?

Hamish shouted, "Connor is going to die down there!" He continued yanking despairingly against the rope.

Hendry placed a steady hand on his shoulder. "He'll make it. Pray he gets the hammer."

Verena did, with all her heart.

CHAPTER 95

onnor focused, and his numbed fingers closed around the handle of the hammer with agonizing slowness. Despite his awkward position against the gate, he raised it over his head and leaned as far away from the gate as he could against the powerful current.

He focused every ounce of remaining granite power into his hands, and the itch of the Curse intensified until he nearly screamed from the madness of it. His hands and arms deadened completely under its power, and swelled further with deadly strength.

With every ounce of it, Connor slammed the diorite hammer against the gate.

The rope whipped down, right through Hamish and Stuart and Verena's hands. All three cried out as it burned their hands.

Hendry did not let go. The rope yanked him off his feet and into the loch. As they dropped to their knees to help, he surfaced, spitting water, and grabbed handholds on the bank.

The water of the loch boiled around him and dropped twenty feet in an instant, leaving him dangling from his precarious handholds, his legs scrambling to find purchase against the slick granite walls.

Hamish grabbed one of his wrists while Stuart grabbed the other, and Verena pulled against his shirt. By the time he rolled up over the edge, the ground beneath them had begun to shake.

Only then did Verena become aware of the loud rumbling from the far edge of the cliff.

The cliff above the plateau exploded outward in an avalanche of water and stone. A giant wave thundered down toward Wolfram's army.

Wolfram blinked, the only outward sign of his surprise at the unexpected catastrophe. Even as his soldiers gaped in amazement, he grasped the full implications of their situation and reacted with instincts honed through decades of cat-and-mouse conflicts along the border.

"Move!" Wolfram shouted, his words echoed a second later by Captain Ilse. Many of his forces had been looking at the cliff and the unexpected torrent already raining down its face when the mountain exploded. The terrifying sight of that wall of water barreling down upon them sped them on faster than Wolfram had ever seen them run.

Wolfram ran with his army along the edge of the plateau, across the path of the onrushing wave, toward higher ground. The terrifying sight of millions of gallons of water thundering toward him shattered any other thought but flight.

Rumblers tossed weapons aside and struggled to sprint, their superhuman strength meaningless against the raw power of nature unleashed. The Wingrunners caught up stragglers and used their amazing speed to haul them to safety.

Despite their incredible efforts, they weren't going to make it. Fully a third of Wolfram's forces would be cut off and swept away by the flood.

Kilian alone turned back toward the onrushing tide, a tiny, solitary figure facing the flood. He planted his feet and raised his hands in a pitiful gesture of defiance against the churning waters.

Barely thirty strides from Kilian, the frothing wall of water seemed to howl with anticipation as it plunged toward him. Kilian threw open his hands, and the front face of the wave glanced upward as if rebounding off an invisible barrier.

The spray-filled air at the leading edge of the flood billowed around him, obscuring him from view. Half a heartbeat later, the rough outline of a giant man rose out of the spray where Kilian had stood.

The giant solidified and braced his back against the flood, lifted arms wide, as if the raging waters were one immense load on its back.

The flood rolled back upon itself like an inverted cresting wave, rising higher and higher into the air until the black waters boiled half a hundred feet high, held at bay by the watery giant.

The stragglers of Wolfram's army pounded across the water's path and out of harm's way. Some called questions, asking if anyone still saw Kilian standing at the feet of the giant.

Wolfram watched silently, awed by the spectacle of a threshold not crossed since the Tallan Wars. He doubted more than a couple other people in the valley understood what the ancient Kilian did there.

Then rippling fire flickered up through the giant's body, and it shuddered. Kilian appeared between its feet, retreating slowly, his salt-and-pepper hair plastered to his skull from the water-laden air, arms shaking from the strain.

Wolfram mouthed his encouragement, thunderstruck by the display of control. He had not imagined such a transition possible. Soldiers flanking him began to cheer and chant Kilian's name. The sound reverberated back from the wall of water that continued to grow until it towered far above the puny human and his giant who strove to check its path.

Kilian continued his retreat, although each step appeared to tax him more. The watery giant began to shake, its arms to give way under the strain.

Kilian retreated past the manor house, and then took a single step to the right, toward the safety of higher ground.

Then he collapsed.

The watery giant imploded. The waters of the flood burst free of the invisible restraints and thundered onto the burned out shell of the manor house in an explosion of foam that catapulted stones and charred timbers hundreds of feet out over the long slope. The leading edge tore through the outbuildings around the manor and boiled down toward Kilian's prone form.

Wolfram took a step toward Kilian, driven forward by the sight of the helpless hero about to be swept away, even though he knew there was nothing he could do to help.

A Wingrunner blurred past him, hips Fracked and legs pumping in a max-tapped sprint. He moved so fast he reached Kilian before Wolfram registered his passing.

As the enormous wave bore down upon them, the Wingrunner hoisted Kilian onto his shoulder and sprinted back toward safety, his movements slowed dramatically by the unconscious man's weight. The water boiled behind him and a surge twenty feet deep rolled over the struggling man. For a terrible heartbeat, he was lost from view within the churning foam.

Then he reappeared, his blurring feet throwing a long stream of spray behind as he literally ran up and over the wave. Wolfram cheered, his voice drowned out by the thunderous crashing of the waters and the equally thunderous chorus of cheering from his army.

The Wingrunner, still carrying Kilian, flashed across the leading edge of the flood, but his momentum slowed and he started to sink. Even his amazing speed was unable to defy gravity for long. He kept running as the water carried him toward the lip of the plateau in a race to reach the edge of the flood before being thrown over the edge.

He wasn't going to make it.

"General, get down!"

Wolfram dropped to the ground at Ilse's shouted call and twisted to see what new danger she warned of. He turned just in time to see Erich and three other Rumblers throw her.

Tied securely around the waist by a long rope, Ilse flew over the flood toward the struggling Wingrunner, arms spread wide as if she were a great bird. She reached the end of the rope, anchored by Erich, and fell into the torrent directly on top of the Wingrunner and Kilian.

The roiling waters hurled the three of them over the lip of the plateau as Erich and the other Rumblers hauled mightily on the line. As the waters rumbled down the slope toward Carbrey's advancing forces, Ilse and the Wingrunner surfaced, clinging to each other, with Kilian held between.

Three Wingrunners risked the unsteady footing and leaped into the edge of the flood to pull them to safety.

The group joined Wolfram and the rest of the army as they moved to higher ground. When Ilse dropped to the earth next to him, Wolfram crouched beside her and took her cold, dripping hand.

"Well done, Captain."

She was too tired to do more than smile.

On the slope below, Carbrey paused in his advance at the sound of the first thunderous explosion. He held up a hand and his well-trained soldiers stopped in a single stride, all eyes scanning the slope for sign of Wolfram's next attack.

Carbrey frowned and flexed his fingers on the hilt of his sword. What else could the old devil throw at them? They'd already advanced to within a hundred yards of the plateau, and he was eager to unleash his Boulders in a bash-fight that would squash the Grandurians for good.

Instead of attacking, Wolfram's army scurried toward the mountains like rabbits before a fox.

"Prepare," Carbrey shouted. He could not imagine what devilry Wolfram had concocted, but it looked like it might have back-fired on the old wolf.

Carbrey began to smile.

Then a torrent of water thirty feet high and three times as wide plunged over the lip of the plateau, directly toward his army.

"How?" Shona whispered nearby.

Carbrey forced his own shock aside. He could ask questions later. Refusing to acknowledge the primal fear that threatened to sap his strength, he shouted, "Run!" and turned to the right and sprinted across the path of the onrushing tide for the steep slopes and the salvation they offered.

The smartest of his soldiers followed immediately. The others were only a heartbeat behind. Carbrey sprinted for the slopes as the avalanche of water thundered down toward him, and for the first time in his life he wished he were a Strider instead of a Boulder.

The rushing waters caught the stragglers of his army and swept away scores of soldiers who could not outrun the flood, tumbling them down the slope and back into the trees. The first ranks of trees in the forest shattered, torn from their roots and swept along by the torrent.

Spray rained over Carbrey as he ran, and water lapped against his boots. He and the remainder of his army reached the slopes and clambered upward as the floodwaters covered the slope and poured into the Lower Wick.

Disbelief warred against frustrated anger as Carbrey stared at the devastation. His army was scattered, many lost, weapons and equipment destroyed. It would be hours before the waters subsided enough for him to attempt to slog up the muddy slope to confront Wolfram, but his position was fatally weakened by the unexpected disaster.

How could this have happened? How could the old wolf have done this to him?

Keith and Cinaed stood in the center of the main street and stared at the catastrophe consuming the plateau. They shared a look of shocked disbelief.

A frothing wall of water roared down the road from the plateau straight for the upper gate.

Cinaed screamed and Keith shouted, "Go!"

They started running, but after two steps, his leg buckled. Cinaed helped him up, but he'd never outrun the flood. The rows of heavily-packed wagons lining the street hemmed them in like walls.

Keith grabbed up each of his children and tossed them over the barricade and shouted for them to run.

His last view of them, through the spokes of a wagon, was of their tiny legs running wildly toward the shelter of buildings against the cliff.

"This can't be happening," Cinaed screamed. "We did everything right!"

Keith clutched Cinaed tight just as the raging flood blasted through the upper gate and swept them away.

Atop the edge of the cliff, Hendry and the others scrambled on hands and knees to the edge to see what had happened. They gawked at the flood erupting from the huge breach in the cliff.

"Oh, son, I am so sorry," Hendry whispered. He'd only wanted to help, but in trying to save his son, he'd destroyed him.

The thundering of water and rending of stone made thinking difficult, and as Loch Sholto poured through the breach, more of the mountainside tore free, shaking the ground where they lay.

Hendry surged to his feet as he realized the terrifying truth. "Run!"

He hauled Hamish to his feet and all but threw him toward the safety of Quarry Road. Then he grabbed up Nicklaus as Stuart pushed Verena in that direction, and they all sprinted along the narrow ledge that ran along the banks of Loch Sholto while the waters swiftly drained.

The ground shook harder and Hamish staggered, nearly falling.

Stuart caught his arm, steadying him and shouted, "If you fall, you die! Run!"

Behind them, the lip of the plateau began to collapse with a terrifying grinding of stones. They raced past the edge of the loch and kept running until they were far back from the edge of the cliff before turning back to look. With a final shudder of ground, the entire outer shore of the loch collapsed, releasing a final avalanche of granite and water.

It was as if the very elements mourned Connor's death. Hendry clutched Nicklaus tight while tears streamed down his face.

Not far away, Verena threw her arms around Hamish and sobbed into his chest.

"Connor."

Hamish awkwardly patted her hair. "He did it."

"He's gone."

Those two words pierced Hendry's heart deeper than any knife every could. He sank to his knees, and the boy Nicklaus awkwardly patted his shoulder.

CHAPTER 96

hen Connor struck the iron gate with the diorite hammer, lightning-like power erupted from the hammer, blasting through every pore of his skin in a white-hot sheet of living fire. It eclipsed the cold of the waters as it consumed the hammer, the iron gate, and the wall of the cliff.

For a moment, it felt like it consumed him too.

In that second, Connor united with the earth-shattering power, and it filled him with unquenchable power, as if he could shatter the roots of the mountain. Then the flash blinded all sight from his eyes while the booming shockwave ripped something deep in his ears. The searing agony rippling along his skin overwhelmed his ability to comprehend it.

Everything went dark, and silent, and numb as the blows to his senses smashed him to the brink of oblivion.

As if in a dream, he felt the cliff explode. Millions of gallons of water erupted from the mountainside, dragging Connor along with them.

The only sensation that penetrated the numb deadness enveloping him was the screaming of his lungs for air. He focused on his eyes, desperate to determine his location, or even if he still lived.

Images blurred past. He blinked again and tried to rub at his face, but only managed to club himself in the side of the head. He barely felt the blow.

Then he realized what he was seeing. Stone. Ground. It appeared blurry because he was hurtling over it at tremendous speed, bare inches above the ground, propelled forward by the relentless flood.

The vision changed. The ground fell away, and the waters dragged Connor vertical. For a second he looked out through the smooth front edge of the flood as he whisked upward, over the back of a giant.

Connor blinked, but the image did not disappear as he rose up along the legs and then the torso of the translucent titan. Then the waters tossed Connor out into open air. As he tumbled along the inverted crest of the wave, understanding no longer mattered. He breathed.

Connor sucked in two life-giving lungs full before splashing down into the churning waters. He plunged deep, tumbled wildly before being dragged to the surface again.

Connor managed a gasp, and nearly choked before falling below the surface again. He still heard nothing and the silence gave everything a surreal quality, like a nightmare. He felt nothing, his sense of touch as dead as if his mind inhabited the body of a man already entombed.

As he whirled in the torrent like a leaf caught in the raging Upper Wick, he caught glimpses of the world outside the still-growing wall of water. The watery giant bent under the strain but still somehow holding the flood at bay. The Grandurian soldiers scrambled out of the water's path. Even the figures that ran along the edge of the cliff high above.

He tried to fight the current, to swim to the surface, but lacked the strength to make any headway.

Rippling flames shot through the giant's form as the waters drove Connor along its torso again. Kilian appeared between the giant's feet, ringed with flames, as if flowing out of the titan's watery form. He coalesced in a single heartbeat, and the giant shuddered.

Then the waters tossed Connor high again, and broke his view. A few seconds later, the watery giant collapsed and the floodwaters thundered down upon the shell of the manor house.

The wild tumbling subsided. With an outlet available, the waters dragged Connor along, floating near the top of the torrent. He fought to the surface and, as the flood raced for the southern edge of the plateau, Connor swam hard across the current, hoping to reach the outer edge and escape.

He didn't make it. The flood thundered off the edge of the plateau, dragging him with it. The current tumbled him around several times and he saw very little of Carbrey's army as it scrambled for safety.

Then he reached the forest. Giant forms of trees appeared out of the murky waters, some with long branches grasping at him like demons of the underworld. Others, torn from their roots, tumbled in the churning flood, threatening to smash the life out of him.

Then the wild tumble through the trees ended. The long rope, still secured around his torso, snagged on something and snapped him to a halt against the current. He hung there, tethered and unable to break free. He pawed for his belt knife, but he'd lost it.

His world faded to black as he hung helpless in the flood. It was insulting to think he'd survived so much only to drown because he couldn't untie one blasted knot.

He flailed around in blind desperation, and his hand closed on the branch of a tree. He pulled himself to it and tried to climb toward the surface, but the tangled rope prevented him from rising more than a foot.

The surge of water shifted, dragging him down against the branch, and a spark of renewed hope flickered to life like the dawn of a new world.

The flood was receding.

CHAPTER 97

n hour after the flood, the solid wooden lift descended like a wraith through a heavy fog that had suddenly rolled in off the river. Hamish stood in its center with Verena and Nicklaus both clinging to him. He regarded the fog suspiciously. He'd never seen fog appear so thick or so fast.

Then again, after the events they had just witnessed, nothing would surprise him. The lift touched down in the blocking yard, and Verena led Nicklaus off.

Hamish, his unruly red hair dirty and his face streaked with tears, squared his shoulders and followed. Wolfram stood nearby, flanked by half a dozen soldiers. Several carried torches that did little to illuminate the fog. Dierk, the Builder, pulled Verena into a bear hug.

Nicklaus launched himself across the blocking yard and threw himself into the arms of a very tired-looking Kilian.

"Uncle Kilian!"

The Water Moccasin held the little boy close and whispered soothing words.

As the lift began to rise behind Hamish, Wolfram stepped forward and extended a hand. Hamish stared at it for a moment but kept his own hands by his side.

"Connor?" Wolfram asked.

Verena started to cry again, and Hamish shook his head, fresh tears glinting in his eyes. "Connor is dead."

"I am truly sorry."

"Are you really?" Hamish asked, not bothering to hide the bitterness in his voice. "You were going to kill us all. He died to protect us from you. It's your fault he's dead."

Wolfram sighed, looking older. "Regardless, I am sorry."

"Then keep your word. Leave everyone alone. Leave and never return."

"That is exactly what I plan to do."

Verena moved to Hamish's side and gently took his hand. "Come."

Hamish shifted his sword belt and followed along as she led him up the road to Alasdair and through the wall gate into town. Dierk clapped him on the shoulder and fell in beside them.

He was already missing his family, but there could be no other choice for him. He faced a sentence of death in Obrion for being a Builder, and he could not hide his powers now that he'd unlocked them. Besides, he needed to learn the secrets only Verena and Dierk could share with him. He blamed Wolfram and Carbrey equally for Connor's death, but he needed Verena, needed to learn all he could.

He would never again be a victim.

Verena had assured him she could teach him to use his new sword just as she would teach him the skills of the Builders. He chose to trust her. What choice did he have, really?

The fog thinned to mist beyond the wall gate, although it formed a solid low cloud just above the few intact rooftops.

Hamish paused to stare at the destruction. Every building in the center of town was simply gone, the stone of the streets stripped. Only a few houses, particularly those along Cliff Street, had escaped the devastation.

Alasdair would have to be rebuilt.

In the center of town, where the village square should have stood, Ilse reported to Wolfram, "The troops are ready."

"Then it is time to go."

The Grandurian army stood clustered around half a dozen strange looking wagons. They were long and wide and filled with rows of benches. Instead of wheels, they were equipped with skids like sleighs, but there were no harnesses in the front for horses or oxen.

Verena led Hamish to the first wagon and climbed up to the high front seat while the army found their places in the backs. Wolfram sat on the other side of Hamish.

Ilse called, "General, all troops present or accounted for."

"Very well. Can we thicken the camouflage?"

"No, sir. Kilian barely managed this much."

Wolfram blew out his mustaches. "It will do." To Verena he said, "Take us home."

Hamish realized the wagons must be like the flying wagon Connor told him about, and a thrill of excitement flared for a second before fading under the blanket of grief.

Verena sighed and leaned forward over a series of long, stone levers. She grasped two of them, closed her eyes in concentration, then pulled them back.

The wagon gave a lurch and rose smoothly into the air. Hamish grabbed for a handhold, and Wolfram placed a hand on his shoulder.

"Easy, son."

The wagon rose until it hovered just under the ceiling of fog. Nearby, the other wagons followed until they all hovered in a tight formation.

Hamish gaped in unabashed astonishment. "Amazing."

Verena smiled, although her eyes glittered as if with unshed tears. "We call them Windriders."

"How is it possible?"

Verena patted the rail, "They're so new, we barely invented them in time for this excursion. Now that Builder powers are re-discovered, there's so much we're learning, but there's still so much we don't know yet."

"What else have you built?"

Verena tugged on another lever and the wagon banked to the right and floated down the street, over the wall gate, and out over Loch Wick. She adjusted their course and they began following the Upper Wick around the mountain to the north. The other wagons followed, shadowy figures only dimly visible in the concealing fog.

Verena squeezed his hand and, after a final look back, said, "This is just the beginning."

Hendry stepped off the lift platform with half a dozen men armed with picks and long-handled hammers. Stuart met them at the bottom.

"What did you find?" Hendry asked as the lift began the ascent for the last load of Cutters.

"Grandurians are all gone. I found sign of our families on the far side of the Wick."

Hendry breathed a sigh of relief. "They escaped."

"It appears so."

Stuart gestured toward the wall gate. "Sir, the village is smashed to pieces."

"Our families are safe. We can rebuild." Hendry fought down a wave of grief. They were safe because of Connor, because he'd been willing to do what no one else could.

He said, "Any idea where the Grandurians went?"

"No, sir. They're gone, with Hamish."

"They won't be returning."

"How do you know?"

"There is no need."

"What do we do now?"

"Post guards at both gates and up on the plateau, and let's see what can be salvaged. Our families will want dinner tonight. I expect Carbrey's army will arrive soon."

Stuart relayed the orders and moved off on his assigned duties. Hendry watched him for a moment before sighing and moving toward the shattered village.

He had to be strong for Lilias, for their family, and for the village. Hard times loomed ahead, but they'd see it through.

They had no choice.

CHAPTER 98

ome," High Lord Dougal called. He sat in a comfortable padded chair in the simple sitting room in the Ashlar's home. The solid man had insisted on offering his home for Dougal's use almost as soon as he arrived in Alasdair with his army that afternoon.

Although battered by recent events, the house still stood, one of the few buildings not swept away or destroyed. Despite the Ashlar's obvious grief at the recent loss of a son, he seemed a remarkably capable man.

It was a shame so many townsfolk died or suffered injuries, although reports credited the Ashlar and his wife with saving the bulk of the town. Their efforts, from everything he'd learned so far, were nothing short of heroic.

Then there was the young man, Connor. Dougal knew little about him beyond his name and accounts of his powers. It was enough. The lad was the right age, and from what Dougal had learned so far, he'd possessed the rare gift Dougal had been searching for these long years.

Carbrey and Shona entered the room, and Dougal kept his face impassive, despite a flash of anger. He would learn all the facts before judging, but initial reports suggested they both failed spectacularly.

Carbrey still wore his muddy uniform although he'd washed his face. Shona had changed out of her battle leathers and wore a green linen skirt and blue silk blouse. She'd washed, and wore a wide-brimmed silk hat to cover her shaved head.

"Any sign of Wolfram?" High Lord Dougal asked without preamble.

"None," Carbrey reported with a salute. He still looked angry, as if Wolfram's escape was a personal insult.

He should look ashamed.

"How did he do it?"

"I don't know," Carbrey said. He paced back and forth across the room. "I should have had him this time."

"But you didn't."

Carbrey turned, "No, my lord. I did not."

"You've bungled a singular opportunity here, Carbrey."

"My lord," Carbrey said, coming to attention. "With all due respect, there was no way I could have foreseen the new weapons he used against us, and no one could have foreseen that wave. I still can't fathom how Wolfram brought down the mountain."

"Perhaps not," Dougal said.

"I don't know how he escaped," Carbrey continued, "but I cannot believe the fog carried them off like these superstitious villagers suggested."

"It does seem unlikely," Dougal said, "But we have no better idea, have we?"

"No, sir."

"And you have found no further information on how he weakened our Boulders?"

"No, sir."

"I must know this secret. We cannot meet them in battle with this threat unresolved. We are vulnerable, general."

"We know it is a stone," Shona offered.

"And how do you know that?" Dougal asked, turning to her. "Only through that boy, Connor."

"That boy," Carbrey growled, his fists clenching at his sides.

"At least the quarry is safe," Shona offered weakly.

"But we don't know why."

"Of course we do," Shona said. "Wolfram flooded the valley to have time to get away."

"Perhaps."

"He threatened to flood the quarry."

"The quarry is not flooded."

Carbrey interjected, "Wolfram blew the mountain. There can be no other explanation. Just like the other tricks he played on us. I can't explain any of them."

"Neither can I," Dougal said. "That worries me." He rose and paced across the room. "If only I could get my hands on that boy."

"I've been wishing the same thing all day," Carbrey growled. Beside him, Shona sighed and touched her burned scalp.

"Not to execute him, you fool."

"You'd try to use his gift, even now?" Carbrey asked.

"Of course," Shona snapped before Dougal could respond. "That's what we should have done."

"He burned the secret, burned you, Lady Shona."

"It doesn't matter. Don't you see we made the wrong choice?"

"Yes, you did," Dougal said. "You had the Blood of the Tallan in your hands, and you threw it away."

"If only he hadn't made me so angry," Shona said, and her eyes glinted with the hint of tears.

"Only now you see what I've been trying to teach you all your life," Dougal said. "When you're angry you need to exercise double caution. You had the chance, my daughter, to stand among the great ones of history, but instead you proved unworthy."

Shona opened her mouth to protest, but he added, "You must learn to think like a leader, and not like a little girl, if you hope to take your place at my side. Leave me."

The two slipped from the room and he dropped into the chair, sighed, and clenched his fists, "so close."

Another knock at the door drew his angry glare and he snapped, "Report."

A soldier entered, "Lord Gavin's servant, my lord."

Dougal sighed. So much to do. "Show him in."

A big man with a square face, short-cropped brown hair, and bright blue eyes stepped inside and bowed. At Dougal's gesture, the soldier left and closed the door behind him.

Dougal leaned back in his chair, "Tell me what really happened here, Bruce."

"I've never seen such a screwed-up operation in my life, sir, and that's a fact."

"And yet you failed to identify the boy Connor's potential, despite the years you knew him."

Bruce shrugged. "He hid the curse surprisingly well. I orchestrated his escape from Isobel, knowing he'd run downriver, but then the Tallan's fury broke loose here."

"Tell me what you know."

As Bruce talked, Dougal's frustration grew. For that gift to have been within his grasp, only to slip away again made him want to howl. So many years of work wasted.

When Bruce finished, Dougal said, "And you're sure about the other one?"

"Aye, m'lord. He was a Builder, sure as living."

He hadn't thought the news could be worse. Such assets could not be wasted! The board was set, all the other pieces positioned.

With those boys, everything would have been ready.

He hid his frustration from the spy, "You've done well. Return to your lord."

Bruce bowed and retreated, leaving Dougal alone with his thoughts as he considered his options.

CHAPTER 99

s night covered Alasdair with its concealing blanket, Connor slipped through the kitchen door of Jean's house. It stood virtually undamaged by the flood, one of the few, although Cliff Street had fared the best. The flood had removed the center of town, and much of Wall Street, leaving most of the rest of town heavily damaged.

It was a wonder anything survived. On the long trek upriver, Connor had been staggered by the utter devastation. Entire acres of trees were just gone, while the plateau and much of the long southern slope that had seen so much blood in recent days lay stripped to bare rock.

Torches lined the soldiers' barracks and the bare place that had been the town center. In the darkness, he could almost imagine the town still existed. Most of the villagers were already gathering in the center of town for the feast in honor of High Lord Dougal, although the fare would be simple.

Jean sat at the round kitchen table, slumped over her folded arms. At the sound of the opening door, she looked up and stared at him for a moment in uncomprehending wonder. Her cheeks were streaked with tears and her eyes puffy from crying.

He probably didn't look much better. He'd barely survived the flood, and he'd drained much of the remaining healing power from his pendant before feeling nearly human again. His clothes were ragged and torn, he'd lost one boot somewhere again, and he was caked in mud.

He smiled. "Miss me?"

Jean leaped across the room into his arms. They held each other for long moments, and Connor drank in the feel of her. She smelled of mud and river and Mhairi's tonic, but he didn't care.

After a long time, she pulled away. "How is it possible?"

"It's kind of a long story. Can you fetch my parents and Hamish? I'd like to tell everyone."

"Hamish is gone. He left with the Grandurians."

Connor sighed. He was not surprised, but wished he'd gotten to say good-bye. If he'd managed to return sooner, he probably would have joined them. He didn't dare show his face to anyone but Jean and his parents. Even so, he was taking a huge risk.

If Carbrey caught him … well, the next time he was executed, they'd probably do the job right.

Jean brought him some bread, dried beef and some tea which he devoured while she fetched his parents.

Hendry and Lilias buried him in an avalanche of hugs and kisses and questions. He explained what he could about what happened, and they in turn shared their own experiences.

Finally Lilias said, "Oh, Connor. It's so good to have you home."

Hendry said softly, "You mean it's good he came to say good-bye."

"What do you mean?" Jean asked, and the radiant joy that had been shining in her face faded.

"I can't stay," Connor said.

"Of course you can," Jean protested. She came and took his hands. "Just hide until the soldiers leave."

"Lady Isobel is still here."

"Where will you go?" Hendry asked.

Lilias said, "South. Go to Raineach, to my sister, Ailsa. You'll be safe with her."

"Aunt Ailsa?" Connor had always wanted to meet his aunt, but she lived on the far side of the kingdom, completely outside of High Lord Dougal's realm. He thought back to Carbrey's map, where he'd seen Raineach.

"If I know you're with my sister, I won't worry as much." Lilias hugged him again. "Please be safe. Send us word."

"I promise."

Hendry said, "Don't leave yet. We'll fetch you some clothes and supplies."

After another round of hugs and kisses, his parents left and Jean threw herself into his arms and held him for a long time.

"Oh, Connor. How can I lose you and Hamish both in the same day?"

He brushed her hair back from her beautiful face, "I'll miss you, too."

Jean kissed him softly. She tasted of tears.

They held each other for another minute before she whispered, "Be safe."

They separated, and tears ran unashamedly down her cheeks. He hated to see her sorrow, but could think of no alternative.

"I will see you again."

With his new pack weighing down his shoulders, he slipped toward the wall gate. As he ghosted through the shattered town, a cheer rang out from the center of town.

He'd never felt so lonely.

He pulled from his tattered belt pouch the small quartzite stone Verena had gifted to him in the manor house. It felt like years ago instead of just a couple of days.

He studied the white stone and slid his fingers across its smooth surface, and suddenly he understood. That's what Verena was trying to tell him after he freed her. That's where her voice came from the night she led him from camp just prior to the fiery attack.

That's how Wolfram knew so much.

He should have known nothing could be simple with Verena. He should be angry by the betrayal, but all his rage had died in the flood. Instead, he focused on how the thought of her helped ease some of the lonely ache.

Despite the many reasons he shouldn't do it, he brought the small stone to his lips.

"Verena, if you're there. Know that I am well."

After slipping through the wall gate and crossing the Wick, he considered the little stone again for a long moment before throwing it far out into the loch. Then he turned south and started the long trek toward Raineach.

CHAPTER 100

igh Lord Dougal ate lightly. The simple feast was impressive, given the circumstances. These folk cooked what they had with skill. They were very enthusiastic in their gratitude for the presence of his army, and he smiled with renewed optimism.

The recent conflict was a disaster in many ways, but these simple folk had the right attitude. Despite the dead and wounded among them, despite the devastation of their town and the horror they'd experienced, they chose to focus on gratitude for the many who still lived. The Ashlar and his wife were the bedrock upon which the heart of this town was built. Despite their own tragedy, they led their people with love and enthusiasm. He would celebrate these small victories with them.

Dougal sat on a raised platform assembled from rubble. Shona sat at his right hand with Carbrey to her right. To his left sat Lord Gavin and his family. Lady Isobel frowned at her food, and their lovely daughter, Moira ate quietly. If only her father followed her example.

Lord Gavin talked incessantly, trying to impress Dougal with his wit and knowledge of current events.

What an idiot.

It amazed Dougal that the town prospered with Gavin in control. Again, most of the credit was probably due the Ashlar and his wife. Dougal considered the man, who had not shown up for the feast yet. Perhaps he would lure him to Merkland. It seemed a waste of talent to leave him here.

As he thought of them, the Ashlar and his wife slipped through the crowd and joined their family at one of the tables in the center. Dougal watched them with growing interest. They no longer looked mournful. Earlier in the day, they'd worn their grief openly, without shame, and led their fellow townsfolk despite it.

Now, despite a valiant attempt to mask the change, they no longer grieved as they had.

They were hiding something, and doing an admirable job, but to Dougal they might as well have stood up and shouted the fact. What would they have to conceal from him?

Dougal ate for a moment, considering possibilities. He tapped his obsidian and his thoughts expanded tenfold. One possibility struck him with such force that he nearly choked on his food.

He turned to Lord Gavin, who had been speaking the entire time, and interrupted. "Gavin, tell me about the boy, Connor."

Gavin opened his mouth, but for the first time seemed at a loss.

Dougal spoke into the silence. "Who were his parents?"

"The Ashlar, of course. Hendry and Lilias."

Dougal glanced back at the Ashlar. He and his wife were sitting close as they ate. They sat straight, their faces clear. They no longer looked like parents grieving the loss of a child.

The truth blazed bright in his mind and Dougal smiled. If only he had skill with quartzite to quest into the darkness with his senses.

Connor had to be close.

Lord Gavin recovered from his surprised silence and began prattling on about Connor and his family. Dougal half listened, filtering the running monologue for useful information. He needed information, every scrap he could gather.

One scrap caught his attention.

"Who is this girl, Jean?"

Gavin pointed with his fork at a beautiful young woman sitting near the Ashlar and his wife. She too looked sad, and yet not overwhelmed by deep mourning as many villagers.

"Is something wrong, father?" Shona asked.

Dougal lowered the fork he'd held halfway to his mouth and smiled. "No, my dear. In fact, things are brightening as we speak."

"What do you mean?"

Dougal ate for a moment and explored myriad possibilities.

"My dear, I see an opportunity for you to redeem yourself from this fiasco. Are you up for a journey?"

"Of course. Where?"

Dougal took another bite and chewed slowly. "I'll know soon." Still smiling, Dougal turned back to Lord Gavin, "Tell me more about the Ashlar."

As Gavin eagerly complied, Dougal considered what he knew of the boy, Connor.

The final piece.

PETRALIST STONES

Igneous

Basalt
Speed, agility
Tapped: Powder through the skin
Obrion: Strider
Granadure: Wingrunner

Granite
Strength, summoning
Tapped: Powder through the skin
Obrion: Boulder or Fast Roller
Granadure: Rumbler

Obsidian
Magnifies innate abilities
Tapped: Powder through the skin
Obrion: Blade
Granadure: Allcarver

Sedimentary

Limestone
Light
Tapped: Held or worn
Obrion: Solas
Granadure: Solas

Sandstone
Healing
Tapped: Held or worn
Obrion: Healer
Granadure: Healer

Metamorphic

Marble
Fire
Tapped: Under the tongue
Obrion: Firetongue
Granadure: Flameweaver

Quartzite
Air, senses
Tapped: Placed in Mouth
Obrion: Pathfinder
Granadure: Longseer

Slate
Earth
Tapped: Soles of feet
Obrion: Sentry
Granadure: Sapper

Soapstone
Water
Tapped: Powder swallowed
with water
Obrion: Spitter
Granadure: Water Moccasin

Find all books here!

www.frankmorin.org

Amazon

AUTHOR'S NOTE

Set in Stone started as an oral story. In our home, we have a long tradition of making up stories, but the kids got more and more challenging with their demands. Often one of them would say as we jumped in the car, "Okay dad, we've got half an hour. Let's have a story with a wizard, a necromancer, a warrior and a bunch of orcs. Go!"

It was tons of fun, but honestly I started feeling exhausted. It was hard to keep up. So I told Kate and Kyle, my demanding, story-loving older children that they had to help me come up with a cool magic system and then we'd develop some fun stories using it. I figured I'd get a breather, and we'd see what they could come up with.

They came up with Petralists.

I thought it was a cool idea, so I sent them off to research different types of stones, and then we brainstormed what we could do with the story. The original idea didn't resemble Set in Stone very much, but it was a good start. We called our main protagonist George and launched a series of crazy adventures with him that spanned Obrion and Granadure and helped develop the core concepts of the story.

It became one of our family's all-time most popular stories, so I decided to write it down. It has matured and evolved into what it is today, but its publication is a special milestone for us.

I hope you enjoyed this story. Check my website www.frankmorin.org for updates on future novels. Until then, look deep, see clear, and keep sweetbreads out of your pockets!

ABOUT THE AUTHOR

Frank grew up in Maine with a voracious appetite for reading. He consumed great stories in every form, from novels to movies to campfire tales. It was only natural that he start writing his own stories as a teen, but he got sidetracked into a computer programming career. Eventually the writing bug bit him again and he jumped back into writing with a passion.

Frank writes all types of fantasy, from urban fantasy thrillers, to YA fantasy, to alternate history fantasy, to classic epic fantasy. He is publishing eight novels in 2015 to launch three separate series. Check his website for the latest updates: www.frankmorin.org.

Frank lives in Oregon with his family. In their home, storytelling is a cherished family tradition that keeps magic alive.

He is also part of the Fictorians, a group blog by writers for writers and fans of great writing. Check out their web site at:
www.fictorians.com.